TEMPLE OF THE SERPENT

'GO-FETCH MAN-THINGS!' THANQUOL snarled at his minions. 'I want all-all man-things! Bring them to me, live-live! If you kill-kill, I'll cut out your brains and feed them to you!'

His minions didn't stop to question the impossibility of Thanquol's threat, but turned back and raced into the jungle, eager to obey his command. Thanquol watched them go, his tail lashing behind him impatiently. Now that the plan had formed in his mind, he wanted to try it out. If he was right, very soon they would be inside the Temple of the Serpent.

If he was wrong… Thanquol shuddered and started thinking about what he would do if he was wrong.

By the same author

• THANQUOL & BONERIPPER •

Book 1– GREY SEER
Book 2– TEMPLE OF THE SERPENT

PALACE OF THE PLAGUE LORD
BLOOD FOR THE BLOOD GOD

MATHIAS THULMANN: WITCH HUNTER
(Contains books the novels *Witch Hunter, Witch Finder* & *Witch Killer*)

BRUNNER THE BOUNTY HUNTER
(Contains books the novels *Blood & Steel, Blood Money* & *Blood of the Dragon*)

RUNEFANG

Also available

• GOTREK & FELIX •

GOTREK & FELIX: THE FIRST OMNIBUS
by William King
(Contains books 1-3: *Trollslayer, Skavenslayer* & *Daemonslayer*)

GOTREK & FELIX: THE SECOND OMNIBUS
by William King
(Contains books 4-6: *Dragonslayer, Beastslayer* & *Vampireslayer*)

GOTREK & FELIX: THE THIRD OMNIBUS
by William King and Nathan Long
(Contains books 7-9: *Giantslayer, Orcslayer* & *Manslayer*)

Book 10 – ELFSLAYER
by Nathan Long

Book 11 – SHAMANSLAYER
by Nathan Long

Book 12 – ZOMBIESLAYER
by Nathan Long

A WARHAMMER NOVEL

Thanquol & Boneripper

TEMPLE OF THE SERPENT

C. L. Werner

BLACK LIBRARY

For Emily - who will appreciate the lizards, snakes and dinosaurs if not the rats.

A BLACK LIBRARY PUBLICATION

First published in Great Britain in 2010 by
BL Publishing,
Games Workshop Ltd.,
Willow Road, Nottingham,
NG7 2WS, UK

10 9 8 7 6 5 4 3 2 1

Cover illustration by Ralph Horsley
Maps by Nuala Kinrade

A CIP record for this book is available from the British Library.

ISBN 13: 978 1 84416 873 6

Distributed in the US by Simon & Schuster
1230 Avenue of the Americas, New York, NY 10020.

Printed and bound in the US.

THIS IS A DARK age, a bloody age, an age of daemons and of sorcery. It is an age of battle and death, and of the world's ending. Amidst all of the fire, flame and fury it is a time, too, of mighty heroes, of bold deeds and great courage.

AT THE HEART of the Old World sprawls the Empire, the largest and most powerful of the human realms. Known for its engineers, sorcerers, traders and soldiers, it is a land of great mountains, mighty rivers, dark forests and vast cities. And from his throne in Altdorf reigns the Emperor Karl Franz, sacred descendant of the founder of these lands, Sigmar, and wielder of his magical warhammer.

BUT THESE ARE far from civilised times. Across the length and breadth of the Old World, from the knightly palaces of Bretonnia to ice-bound Kislev in the far north, come rumblings of war. In the towering Worlds Edge Mountains, the orc tribes are gathering for another assault. Bandits and renegades harry the wild southern lands of the Border Princes. There are rumours of rat-things, the skaven, emerging from the sewers and swamps across the land. And from the northern wildernesses there is the ever-present threat of Chaos, of daemons and beastmen corrupted by the foul powers of the Dark Gods. As the time of battle draws ever nearer, the Empire needs heroes like never before.

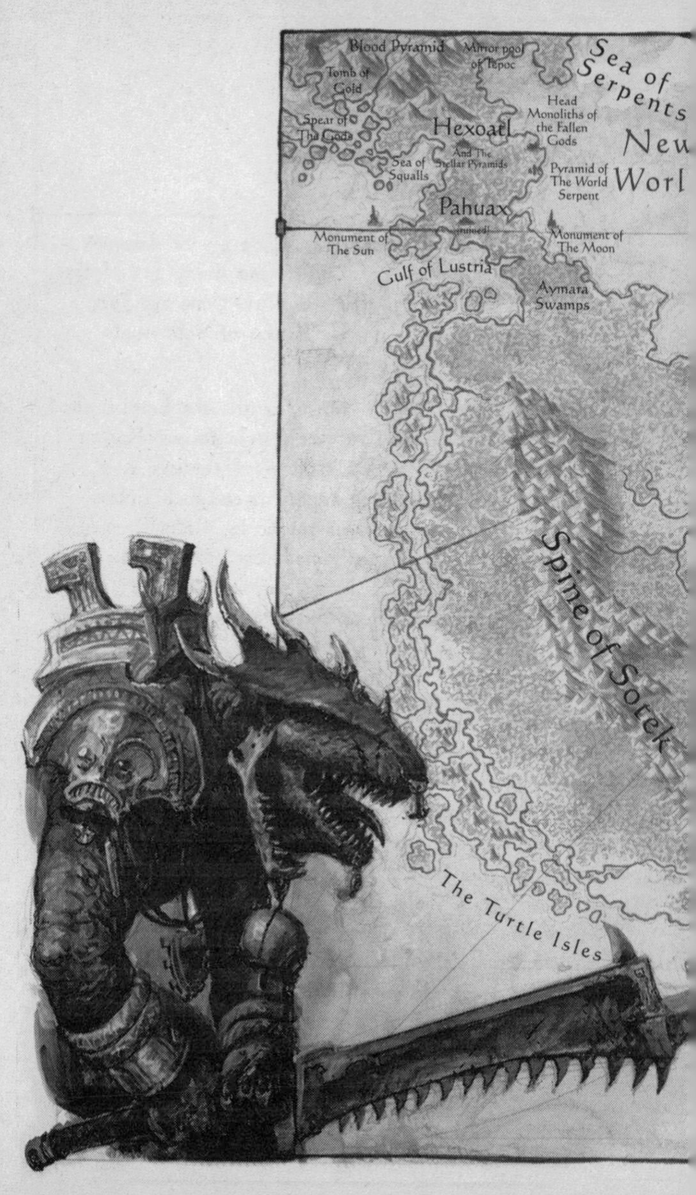

Blood Pyramid
Mirror pool of Tepoc
Tomb of Gold
Spear of
Sea of Serpents
Head Monoliths of the Fallen Gods
Hexoatl
And The Stellar Pyramids
Sea of Squalls
Pyramid of The World Serpent
Pahuax
Monument of The Sun
Monument of The Moon
Gulf of Lustria
Aymara Swamps
Spine of Sotek
The Turtle Isles

The Great Ocean
Scorpion Coast
lanxla
(ruined)
Xahutec
(ruined)
Tarantula Coast
Tlaxtlan
Tlax
River Qurveza
Chaqua
(ruined)
Huatl
(ruined)
The Vampire Coast
Xlanhuapec
Quetza
(ruined)
River Amaxon
Axlotl
(ruined)
River Lambada
Volcanic Islands
Itza
Oyxl
(ruined)
Mangrove Coast
Lustria
Xhotel
(ruined)
Chupayotl
(submerged)
300 Miles

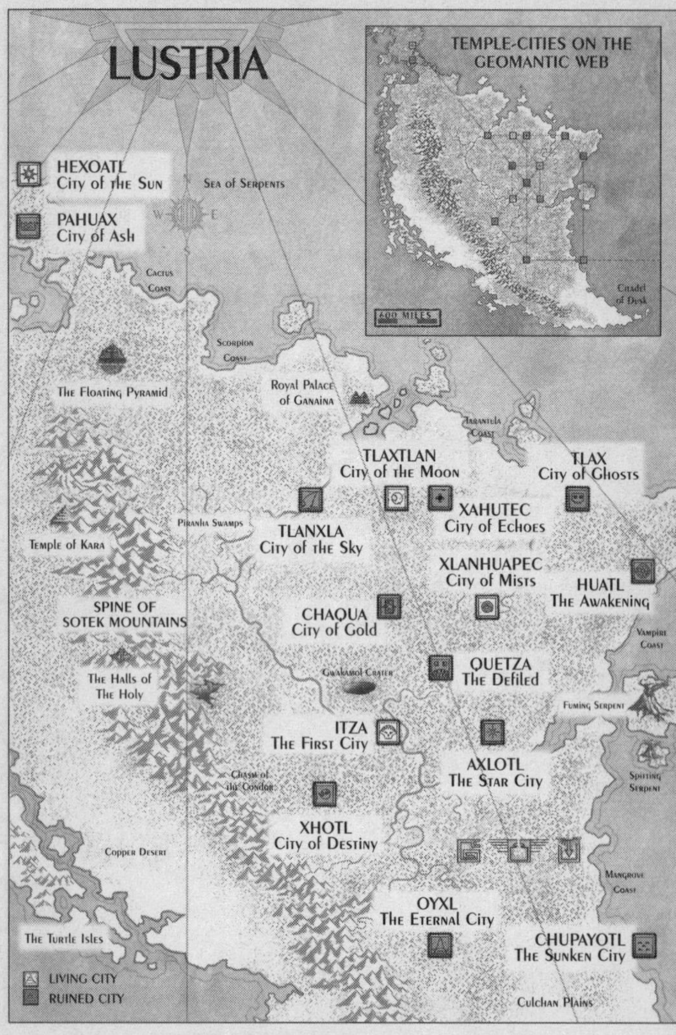
LUSTRIA
TEMPLE-CITIES ON THE GEOMANTIC WEB
Citadel of Dusk
600 MILES
HEXOATL
City of the Sun
PAHUAX
City of Ash
Sea of Serpents
W
E
Cactus Coast
Scorpion Coast
The Floating Pyramid
Royal Palace of Ganaina
Tarantula Coast
TLAXTLAN
City of the Moon
TLAX
City of Ghosts
XAHUTEC
City of Echoes
TLANXLA
City of the Sky
Piranha Swamps
Temple of Kara
XLANHUAPEC
City of Mists
HUATL
The Awakening
SPINE OF SOTEK MOUNTAINS
CHAQUA
City of Gold
Vampire Coast
QUETZA
The Defiled
Gwakamol Crater
The Halls of The Holy
Fuming Serpent
ITZA
The First City
AXLOTL
The Star City
Chasm of the Condor
Spitting Serpent
XHOTL
City of Destiny
Copper Desert
Mangrove Coast
OYXL
The Eternal City
The Turtle Isles
CHUPAYOTL
The Sunken City
LIVING CITY
RUINED CITY
Culchan Plains

PROLOGUE

UNBLINKING EYES STARED with cold, emotionless intensity at the bloated bulk that sprawled in the half-light of a subterranean chamber. The cloying stench of reptilian musk mixed with the pungent humidity of the air to create an almost tangible fug within the buried grotto. Insects buzzed about the surface of a scum-covered pool while creeping things crawled along the damp walls to bask in the few beams of daylight stabbing through the cracked tiles of the ceiling, drawing the heat of the sun to warm their cold bodies.

The eyes of the watchers ignored the small lizards basking on the walls, their bodies bobbing upwards in little displays of bravado to warn away the other reptiles. Tiny snakes, their bright bodies like ribbons of black and crimson, writhed between the carvings that covered the stone walls, sometimes pausing to taste the foetid air with their flickering tongues. In the darkness, wiry grey spiders mended their webs, shaking shimmering beads of dew from the strands so that their gossamer traps would not be betrayed.

It was something more subtle than the chores of spiders that caused the slit-like pupils of the watchers to widen with interest. From dagger-thin slivers of black, the pupils expanded to nearly overwhelm the amber puddles of their eyes. Leathery crests of scaly skin undulated upon the blunt, wedge-like heads of the watchers in silent expression of the concern that intruded upon their vigil.

The watchers surrounded a bloated, slimy mass, a thing of scummy green and festering yellow, mottled with patches of black dots and stripes. Under their gaze, the pattern of blotches was shifting, fading and changing, assuming new patterns almost faster than the minds of the watchers could follow.

The largest of the watchers straightened its body from where it had crouched upon the damp floor. The crest atop its reptilian head flapped open, a brilliant flash of scarlet that contrasted with the blue-grey scales that covered its wiry body. In response to the skink's display, several of the smaller watchers set little thimble-like contrivances over their claws. The tools gleamed in the dim light like tiny stars as they slid into place over the reptilian hands, diamonds reflecting the fiery brilliance of the sun.

Other skinks came forward and set stone tablets in the laps of the diamond-fingered watchers, who then began scratching their claws into the faces of the tablets. Everything was conducted with a deliberate, but somehow calm, haste. The skinks studied the shifting patterns of the slimy body, recording each change in stone.

The amphibian shape soaking within its hibernation pool was oblivious to the hurried labours of the skinks. The golden, bulging eyes of the creature were open, but there was neither sight nor intelligence behind the slumbering gaze. The frog-like slann was as oblivious to the skinks as they were to the lizards and insects that scurried around them. Only its dreams were real to it as it slumbered, dreams that engulfed its mind and caused its skin to shift colour and pattern.

THERE WERE MANY dimensions beyond the physical, many that no brain could ever perceive, much less imagine. Lord Tlaco'amoxtli'ueman was among the oldest of his kind, a being that had been spawned by the Old Ones to understand these dimensions, to see the vectors of the Great Math and their impact upon the higher phases. The harmonies of the equations became increasingly complex as the labours of the Old Ones brought existence further and further from the universal null towards which all things decayed.

Perhaps the Old Ones had needed things of flesh to appreciate the impact of their algebra upon the lower phases, or perhaps they had needed beings such as the slann to understand how the lower dimensions could cast fractions of themselves into the higher in an effort to escape final decay. Whatever their logic, the brains of the slann had been engineered to see the arithmetic behind all existence that they might keep the equations of the Old Ones balanced.

But things had gone wrong. In their experiments the Old Ones had created low phase creatures with the potential for devastating impact upon the higher phases of order. The essences of these beings expressed themselves in simple algorithms, but of immense numerical size, as though in defiance of their inevitable decay and negation. Too late did the slann understand the impact of these arrays upon the higher dimensions. Too late did the Old Ones understand the illogic that had infected their carefully plotted vectors.

The design of the Old Ones collapsed under the corruption of persistent fractals, fractals that were not merely echoes of life, but things that existed in multidimensional displacements. Their numerical values did not decay, but swelled by adding into themselves the algorithms of the low phase creatures. Under the madness of these persistent fractals, the equations of the Old Ones were unbalanced, broken by a perverse arithmetic.

The Old Ones had faded from the malignance of the persistent fractals, incapable of enduring within their broken vectors. Sometimes, Lord Tlaco could almost perceive the lingering shades of the shattered vectors, recast into persistent fractals themselves. It was a disharmony that even a mage-priest could not fully comprehend. Were these shards of the masters or simply new fractals cast into the semblance of the old vectors?

The slann considered one of these persistent fractals. It was a repugnance of irrational numbers and unbalanced singularities. Yet, at the very core, Lord Tlaco could almost sense a string of the ancient harmonies. It troubled the slann's thoughts. Was this simply another creation of the low phase algorithms coalescing in the higher dimensions, or was it an expression of the broken vectors trying to reassert itself? Could the equation be balanced by the addition of yet another persistent fractal? Would even the Old Ones dare to work in such a reckless manner?

There were no easy answers. The slann knew that this particular fractal had expressed itself in a way that made many of the low phase minions of the mage-priests venerate it. The fractal had manifested as a low phase being and routed the infestation of corrupted algorithms that had once threatened to return the slann and all of their minions to the universal null.

Lord Tlaco's mind focused upon the discordant memory of those corrupted algorithms. Like so many of the unbalancing influences, they were warm-quick, emotional and illogical. To contemplate them was to contemplate the square root of negation. More so than any other beings, they were the product of persistent fractals, the spawn of debased mathematics and disordered equations. Of all the pollution befouling the patterns of the Old Ones, they were the most debased.

Yet might they not serve to further the vision of the Old Ones? Might they not be used to balance the equation?

The slann shivered in his slumber and considered the dangers of inviting such terrible potentialities into the ordered math of his own domain.

CHAPTER ONE

Shadows of Skavenblight

'WE HAVE LISTENED to your report, Grey Seer Thanquol.'

The voice was like the snap of a whip lashing out from the darkness of the immense chamber. The speaker himself was lost in the cloying darkness that filled the hall, nothing more than a shadow and a whisper.

Grey Seer Thanquol stood at the centre of the cavernous chamber, bathed in a sickly green spotlight that all but blinded his sensitive eyes. He could feel the pit below the trap creak and groan beneath him, could smell the faint scent of stagnant water and reptilian musk wafting up from the pit beneath the trap door. It was muttered among the inhabitants of Skavenblight that their tyrannical masters, the Lords of Decay, used the pit to execute those who had displeased them. At a sign from one of the sinister overlords of the skaven race a lever would be thrown and the offending ratman would be dropped into the watery depths far below, there to have his flesh devoured by obscene hybrids of rat and alligator, mutant creations of Clan Moulder.

Thanquol swallowed the knot growing in his throat and controlled the urge to leap from the trap door at the centre of the room. To do so would be to invite certain death. He knew the shadows concealed any number of the Council's elite bodyguard, mute albino stormvermin chosen for their strength and relative fearlessness. Then there were the members of the Council themselves to consider, a dozen of the most vicious villains ever bred by the teeming hordes of skavendom. Challenging them on their own ground would be an act of lunacy Thanquol doubted if even the accursed crimson-furred dwarf who had interfered with so many of his past schemes would be mad enough to attempt.

The numbing scent of smouldering warpstone made it difficult for Thanquol to concentrate, to focus his senses on the raised dais at the far end of the chamber and the sinister figures hidden behind it in the dark. He knew that if the need arose, it would be all but impossible to conjure a spell with the warpstone vapours befuddling his thoughts. Ancient and evil, the despotic Council of Thirteen was taking no chances with him. Backed into a corner, even the lowest skaven would show his fangs. When that skaven could command the powerful magic of the Horned Rat, even the Lords of Decay preferred to take no chances.

'The loss of the Wormstone causes us great concern.' This voice was oily and foul, the slobbering lisp of a thawing swamp. Thanquol shuddered as he recognised the decayed tones of Arch-Plaguelord Nurglitch, supreme leader of the plague monks of Clan Pestilens. The Council had sent Thanquol as their representative to secure the Wormstone from beneath the man-thing city of Altdorf, but there had been a rival expedition dispatched to steal it from him when he had found it. Thanquol wasn't sure how many of the Council were behind the plot, but since his rivals had been plague monks led by the ghastly Lord Skrolk, there was no question that Nurglitch had been a prominent patron of the scheme.

Thanquol bruxed his fangs together, grinding his teeth in a fit of nervous anxiety. It would be like Nurglitch to be the first of the Council to express his anger over the loss of the Wormstone, even if it was the self-serving treachery of Clan Pestilens that had resulted in its loss. What lies had Nurglitch told the other Lords of Decay, and what bribes and pacts had he made to ensure they were believed? There was no love between Clan Pestilens and the grey seers, and even less between the plague monks and Thanquol himself. But did Thanquol dare to try and exploit that fissure of mutual hate and distrust? Could he depend on the support of Seerlord Kritislik and his allies on the Council if he accused Nurglitch of treachery? More importantly, if he did so would he be able to scramble off the trap door before Nurglitch had the switch thrown and sent him plummeting into an unclimbable pit of death?

The grey seer squinted into the harsh green spotlight. He couldn't see any of the Lords of Decay, not even his master Kritislik. Faintly, he could make out the outline of the huge empty seat at the centre of the dais, the one kept empty and waiting for the presence of the Horned Rat himself. Kritislik, as Seerlord, was counted the voice of the skaven god and was allowed to interpret the Horned Rat's will whenever the Council debated a subject. Thanquol doubted if even the effective double vote this gave Kritislik would be enough to sway the Council into open hostility with Clan Pestilens. The last time the other clans made war with Clan Pestilens, the entire Under-Empire had been ravaged. Worse, Clan Pestilens had nearly succeeded in overcoming the combined might of the other great clans! Only the timely re-appearance of Clan Eshin from the distant lands of Grand Cathay had prevented Clan Pestilens from overthrowing the Council of Thirteen. Even so, their power was such that they could not be denied a position on the Council and a place among the great clans.

No, Thanquol decided, Kritislik won't put his neck out by openly provoking Nurglitch, and if he does, the other great clans won't support him.

A decision reached, Thanquol stared at the spot in the darkness where he thought Nurglitch's voice had spoken. 'Great and putrescent Plaguelord,' he said, careful to keep his tone the proper mix of fawning respect and cowering fear. 'The Wormstone has indeed been lost to us. The cowardice and stupidity of the Under-Altdorf leaders made it impossible to recover the artefact from the man-things that stole it.'

Thanquol coughed and tried not to choke on the next words that hissed past his fangs. 'Even the timely assistance of Clan Pestilens and your brave champion Lord Skrolk was not enough to undo the treachery of the Under-Altdorf leaders.'

There was a grotesque rumble from the darkness, like an ogre being sucked down into a bog. It took Thanquol several breaths to realise that it was the sound of Nurglitch laughing.

'The loss of our brave kin from Clan Pestilens is to be lamented,' the thin snarl of Kritislik cut through the boiling exuberance of Nurglitch's laughter. 'But how is it that the Wormstone was placed in such jeopardy in the first place?'

Thanquol cringed as he heard the Seerlord make his accusation. Kritislik clearly wasn't happy with the way he had appealed to Nurglitch by ignoring the grab the plague monks had made for the Wormstone. His mind fought through the numbing confusion of the incense, racing to find a new scapegoat for the Seerlord's ire.

'It was Grey Seer Thratquee,' Thanquol said, mentioning the first name that occurred to him. Thratquee was the ancient, corrupt grey seer who led the council of Under-Altdorf. As he thought it over, everything had been Thratquee's fault. If he'd been more aware of what was going on in Under-Altdorf, there was no way Lord Skrolk would have been able to subvert some of its inhabitants and use them in several attempts to murder Thanquol and steal the artefact. Besides, Thanquol didn't like the old priest anyway. 'It was his idea to grind up the Wormstone and use it to poison the humans. Every moment I was in Under-Altdorf, I was under the watch-sniff of his minions. At no time could I get away from my guards and return to tell this most terrible Council of Thratquee's plans. I tried-wanted to stop him...'

'We must congratulate Grey Seer Thratquee for his most keen foresight,' the brutal snap of General Paskrit's voice growled. 'My agents tell me that a tenth of Under-Altdorf's population was killed in the flooding of their warrens, that the damage inflicted upon that upstart burrow will cripple its growth for generations. It will be a long time before they dare think themselves as mighty as Skavenblight!'

'... from executing his plan in a way that would cause the loss of the Wormstone...' Thanquol hurried to elaborate as he heard Paskrit speak.

'The Wormstone would have been most useful to us,' came the unctuous voice of Doomclaw, warlord of Clan Rictus. 'However, perhaps it is better lost where it cannot be found again and used against us.'

'... because I believed there was a better-better way to lose-hide the Wormstone.' Thanquol bruxed his fangs again as he spoke. It was unfair that the Council was prepared to give Thratquee the acclaim and reward that was rightfully his own!

'It is to be regretted that the Wormstone has been lost,' the metallic groan of Warlock Lord Morskittar's voice echoed through the Chamber of Thirteen. After centuries of unnatural life, the leader of Clan Skryre was more arcane machine than flesh and blood skaven. 'However, its very existence would have been a threat to the stability of the Under-Empire. Grey

Seer Thratquee has done this Council a great service by removing such a tempting morsel from the plate of any ambitious upstarts.'

There was an angry wheeze from the shadows where Nurglitch sat as Morskittar spoke. Hatred of Clan Skryre was probably the only common ground that Clan Pestilens and the grey seers shared.

'The humbling of Under-Altdorf at the same time shows a skaven who knows where his loyalties lie,' mused the shrill chittering voice of Packlord Verminkin, master of Clan Moulder.

Thanquol's eyes narrowed with hate. This was ridiculous! The mad old Thratquee had done nothing but sit in his decadent burrow with his breeders and rot his brain with warpdust! Thanquol had been the one who took all the risks! He had been the one who dared the corruption of touching the Wormstone by having his minions experiment with it! He had been the one who had braved the treacherous blades of assassins and the putrid magic of Lord Skrolk! It was his brilliance that had concocted the plan to poison the reservoir beneath Altdorf and doom both the human city and the upstart skaven metropolis beneath it to a lingering death! It was his bravery that had nearly won the day, defying both the treason of Clan Pestilens and the frightful magic of the human wizard-thing! If not for the cowardice of his minions, if not for the betrayal of his adored apprentice Kratch, if not for the brainless stupidity of his rat ogre bodyguard Boneripper, he would have succeeded! The Council of Thirteen would be showering him with praises and honours!

'We must take pains to ensure that Thratquee is able to exploit the reconstruction of Under-Altdorf to increase his control over the city,' Kritislik said. 'As Thanquol's report shows, we cannot trust the other members of Under-Altdorf's council... even if they are from our own clan.' The last barb was thrust at Morskittar. The council of Under-Altdorf was bloated with representatives of Clan Skryre, giving the warlock-engineers a distinct dominance in the city.

'Something to take under consideration,' Morskittar agreed, a sullen tone in his iron voice.

Thanquol lashed his tail in annoyance at what he was hearing. Were they really going to make Thratquee de facto warlord of Under-Altdorf? He found himself suddenly wishing Morskittar luck in the inevitable assassination attempts Clan Skryre would mount against Thratquee to prevent such a possibility.

'Something disturbs you, Grey Seer Thanquol?' Nurglitch's voice snarled. Even if Thanquol could not see the Lords of Decay through the shadows and the glare of the green light, they could clearly see him. His display of irritation had not failed to be noticed.

'No-no, great and monstrous Nurglitch,' Thanquol stammered, not quite managing to keep a hint of pride in his fawning contrition. 'It is just that I have come far-far and this one finds himself tired from his journey.'

'Then you are dismissed, Thanquol,' the knife-edged voice of Nightlord Sneek, leader of Clan Eshin and its murderous assassins, spoke from a patch of darkness that seemed somehow even blacker than that which cloaked the other Lords of Decay. 'We would not wish to get between yourself and your rest.'

The way Nightlord Sneek made the parting remark caused Thanquol's fur to stand on end. Even as he bowed and scraped his way from the Council of Thirteen, his pulse was racing, his mind screaming in horror. None of the other Lords of Decay called for him to remain, a fact Thanquol took as a bad sign. Whatever Sneek was planning, the others had already abandoned him to it!

It wasn't a lot, the small stash of warp-tokens Thanquol was able to take with him when he fled Altdorf, barely the surface of what he had hoped to extort from the bickering clan lords of Under-Altdorf. Certainly it would take more to pay off Nightlord Sneek and make him reconsider the interest he had suddenly shown in the grey seer. The slicing voice of Sneek kept echoing in Thanquol's mind, that whispered threat about helping him rest. Clan Eshin had helped a lot of skaven rest, the kind of rest that usually involved poisoned blades and quick stabs in the dark. Thanquol had even paid for the services of their assassins in the past. He knew only too well their hideous and lethal efficiency. Once the trained killers of Clan Eshin were on a ratman's tail it was only a matter of time...

Thanquol lashed his tail in frustration, his fingers curling tighter about the haft of his staff. He wasn't some flea-ridden clawleader from some three-bat warren! He was Grey Seer Thanquol, the supreme sorcerer-general of the Under-Empire, the most brilliant, valiant and loyal servant to ever serve the Council of Thirteen! If Sneek thought he would be easy prey, then the Nightlord would learn how wrong he was! Thanquol was the chosen of the Horned Rat himself, blessed by the god of all skaven!

Of course, the Horned Rat's blessings had been rather mixed of late. It was all the fault of his incompetent and treacherous underlings of course. That snivelling fool Skrim Gnawtail and that backstabbing cur Kratch! If not for them, the Wormstone would have been his and his alone, to use in whatever way he saw fit. That ancient idiot Thratquee and all of the decadent inhabitants of Under-Altdorf would have been scoured from the tunnels of skavendom if Thanquol's craven minions hadn't let him down!

The grey seer ground his teeth together and stared up at the night sky. Unlike the rest of the Under-Empire, much of Skavenblight was upon the surface, infesting the crumbled ruins of the ancient human city that had once dominated what would later become the Blighted Marshes. Some even whispered that the Shattered Tower, within which the Council of Thirteen held their chambers, had been built not by skaven paws but reared by human hands. Such heresy was, of course, punished by a good tongue-cutting whenever it was spoken, but as he glanced up at the crooked spire which dominated the cityscape, Thanquol had to admit it had the ugly stamp of human engineering to it, perhaps even a trace of dwarf-thing too. Naturally, even if the thought came to him, he wasn't fool enough to ever speak of it.

Thanquol turned his gaze back to the wide street around him. The avenue was packed with a scrabbling, struggling mass of ratkin, a sea of fur and fangs that bobbed and weaved, squirmed and squeezed in their efforts to navigate through the city. The air was thick with the smell of decaying timber, rancid fur, musk and excrement, the distinct tang of black corn in the skaven droppings giving the city a scent unique to itself. The snarls, whines and chittering of ratmen rang from the crumbling stone walls that flanked the street.

Much of the city was sinking into its foundations, slowly collapsing into the maze of burrows and ratruns teeming generations of skaven had dug beneath it. Everywhere, timber supports and buttresses hugged the sagging walls, trying to stave off the creeping ruin. Many structures had become so mired in mud and earth that their lower floors were lost beneath the ground. Some still sported the weathered husks of once elegant columns and promenades, a few even had the faint remnants of tiled frescos peeping out from beneath the layers of grime that coated them. Before one tilted manor, the misshapen bulk of a corroded iron statue stood upon a cracked marble pillar, a mass of rust that might once have been a sword raised high in a lump that once could have been an arm.

Home, Thanquol thought as the smells, sounds and sights of Skavenblight crawled across his senses. Wherever he went, there was nothing to compare with the press of Skavenblight's masses, feeling the presence of hundreds of thousands of ratmen all around him. Even Under-Altdorf felt deserted and empty next to Skavenblight. This was the way the world was meant to be, filled to bursting with the swarming masses of the Under-Empire. A world alive with the numberless hordes of the skaven, all looking up from the gutter, looking for the leadership only Grey Seer Thanquol could give them.

Thanquol stroked his whiskers as he thought about the happy vision of himself as unquestioned master of skavendom. One day he would dare place his paw upon the Pillar of Commandments, that obelisk of pure warpstone set down before the Shattered Tower by the Horned Rat himself. He had no doubt that he would survive the ordeal, survive to challenge Grey Seer Kritislik and take his place upon the Council. Then, then he would begin to eliminate the other Lords of Decay. That bloated pustule Nurglitch and that scrap-metal mage-rat Morskittar and that slinking throatcutter Sneek...

Thanquol nearly spurted the musk of fear as he thought of Nightlord Sneek. The black-clad murderers of Clan Eshin were a nightmare to every ratman, from the lowest clanrat to the most exalted warlord. They could be anywhere, lurking with their poisoned knives and their deadly blowguns. Thanquol's eyes narrowed with suspicion, squinting as he studied the mass of skaven filling the street around him. Suddenly, the press of so many ratmen swarming on every side wasn't so reassuring as it had been a few moments before. Almost involuntarily, he backed away from a clutch of scabby clanrats wearing the colours of a clan he didn't recognise. He watched them pass, one hand locked about the tiny chunk of warpstone he had secreted in a pocket of his robe. Were they watching him more closely than they should? Perhaps he should simply blast them with a spell and worry about whether they worked for Clan Eshin later.

Shaking his head, Thanquol decided against striking prematurely. A display of magic might annihilate his enemies, but it would also panic the skaven filling the street. Being stampeded by the crowd would make him just as dead as any assassin's blade. He continued to watch the three clanrats until they were lost in the mass of furry bodies. Most likely, they had simply recognised him and been overawed by his formidable presence. Yes, that was certainly it.

A sharp growl to the hulking brute towering behind him, and Thanquol made his way through the swarm of ratkin. It had taken most of his carefully hoarded warp-tokens to buy the behemoth, but after that sinister encounter with Nightlord Sneek, he reasoned that he had to do something to protect himself. The rat ogre had been the biggest, nastiest one he could find in the beast pens, a brown-furred giant with fists like boulders and a face filled with dagger-like fangs. He'd named the monster Boneripper after the brave, clever bodyguard that had fought so valiantly to protect him from Lord Skrolk's treachery and the profane magic of the grey mage-man.

The crowd parted before Thanquol's advance, Boneripper looming over them like the very shadow of doom. There were frightened squeaks, whines of fawning protest and frequent spurts of musk. A rat ogre, he reflected, was a marvellous instrument for reminding the lower castes who their betters were.

A flash of darkness among the throng arrested Thanquol's attention. Had that been a flash of black cloak? The sort of cloak an assassin might wear? Thanquol chided himself for such foolishness. It was ludicrous! Why would an assassin bother to wear black when he could so effortlessly blend in with the crowd without it! It wasn't as if they were required to wear a uniform, to carry a placard that announced their profession to any skaven they might meet!

Through the crowd, Thanquol saw a black-cloaked skaven creeping purposefully towards him, one paw curled beneath the folds of the creeper's cloak. Thanquol blinked in disbelief. It was still ridiculous, but that creep really was hiding a knife under his cloak! As he looked again, he saw a second cloaked ratman slinking towards him, and still a third coming from the opposite direction.

Thanquol quickly edged himself away from the approaching killers, his fingers curling around the chunk of warpstone in his pocket. He was a bit more willing to risk the stampede now that there was no question that Sneek's assassins were coming for him.

Abruptly, Boneripper's huge maw dropped open in a fierce roar. The rat ogre's huge paws slammed against his chest, pounding a drumlike tattoo that rumbled over the heads of the skaven filling the street. The monster's beady red eyes were ablaze with malice. He took a ponderous step towards the closest assassin, crushing a hapless bystander beneath his immense foot.

Thanquol gloated as he saw the look of terror crawling onto the murderer's face. They hadn't been expecting this. He had been very careful picking his bodyguard, choosing one that had been trained to hate the cloaked adepts of Clan Eshin. The rat ogre's body was still criss-crossed with the scars the pack-masters had left when they had beaten hate into the beast's tiny brain. The effectiveness of that training, however, was quite obvious as Boneripper stomped a gory path through the crowd, focused upon rending the assassin limb from limb.

'Yes-yes!' Thanquol hissed through his fangs. 'Kill them, Boneripper! Kill the faithless little maggots!'

Hearing his master's voice snapped the last composure Boneripper possessed. Uttering a deep, groaning roar, the rat ogre ploughed through the massed skaven, hurling squealing ratmen aside with each sweep of his claws, crushing those too slow or too terrified to scramble out of his way beneath his clawed feet. The black-cloaked assassin stood paralysed as he saw the immense behemoth charging towards him. The killer threw back his cloak, revealing the knife he held. Shrieking in terror, he threw his weapon at Boneripper. The poisoned edge sank into the rat ogre's shoulder with a meaty *thwack*.

Boneripper paused in his rush. He turned his head and stared at the knife sticking out of his body. The brute reached down, ripping the blade from his flesh, staring at it with confused eyes. His huge nose twitched as he sniffed the ugly green muck dripping from the knife's poisoned edge. It took a moment for the smell to register with his dull brain, but when the rat ogre remembered the lessons he had been so painfully taught by the packmasters, he came alive with fury. The knife crumpled into an unrecognisable lump of steel as Boneripper angrily closed his fist around it.

The assassin squealed in fright and turned to flee, horrified that Boneripper had survived the poison. He couldn't know the toxic provender the packmasters had reared the rat ogre on, the slowly increased doses of venom they had injected into his veins since he had been a whelp. The result had made Boneripper's body develop a pronounced resistance to a wide range of diseases and toxins.

The rat ogre reached down to the street beside him, snatching a cowering skaven from the flagstones. The wretch screamed and writhed in Boneripper's grasp, but his efforts went unnoticed by the brute. Glaring at the assassin as he started to scurry away, Boneripper flung the screaming ratman at him. The living missile wailed as he flew across the street, slashing fleeing spectators with his flailing claws. The skaven smashed into the assassin as though fired from a cannon. Both ratmen were hurled through the air, battering a path through the packed street.

In the aftermath, the panicked mass of the crowd struggled even more fiercely to flee, but their very numbers hampered any real hope of progress. Crippled, cringing ratmen, limbs shattered by the impact of Boneripper's living missile, crawled along the ground, trying desperately to avoid being crushed by the feet of other ratkin. The skaven Boneripper had thrown was a shattered mess of broken bones and bloody fur smashed against the stone wall on the other side of the street. Beneath the dripping carcass, the crumpled body of the assassin struggled. The impact had snapped the killer's spine, leaving him helpless from the waist down.

Boneripper lumbered through the shrieking mob, stalking through the packed skaven with powerful strides. Soon he towered over the crippled assassin. The rat ogre stared down at the trapped ratman, then brought his clawed foot smashing down into the assassin's skull.

Thanquol grinned in savage challenge as he watched Boneripper kill the assassin. He glanced to either side, pleased when he saw the other two killers slinking back into the crowd, clearly less than eager to have any part in attacking the grey seer after watching their comrade slain so brutally. Thanquol snarled a command to Boneripper, gesturing with his claw to one of the retreating murderers. He felt a flare of angry frustration when the brute ignored him, too intent on pounding the skull of the first assassin into paste to pay attention to his master's voice.

With an effort, Thanquol calmed himself. It was just as well that the others escaped. They would bear word of their experience back to the other skulking murderers of Clan Eshin. They would tell their fellows that to face Grey Seer Thanquol was to face their own deaths! Yes, the assassins would know that killing Grey Seer Thanquol was no easy task!

A troubling thought came to Thanquol then and his fur began to rise in anxiety. It had been easy. Much too easy. Positively bumbling on the part of the assassins to let themselves be spotted so quickly. Perhaps they were simply murderers in training, neophytes at the arts of assassination. But why would Sneek send amateurs to kill someone of his formidable powers?

On impulse, Thanquol spun about and dropped into a crouch. There was a wail of agony just behind him. The grey seer risked a glance, saw one of the skaven that had been cowering near him during Boneripper's rampage lying on the ground, his body twitching in a violent spasm. A dart as long as Thanquol's finger was buried in the stricken ratman's cheek.

The grey seer's eyes went wide with fright. The killers he had sent Boneripper after weren't the assassins! They were the diversion! Something to keep Thanquol occupied while the real assassin made his move!

Thanquol threw himself across the ground, rolling along the muck-strewn stones. He imagined he could hear something whistle past his face, but there was no imagination behind the pained shriek of the skaven behind him. The ratman was hopping on one foot, pawing at the black needle sticking out of his other foot. A moment later, the skaven fell in a twitching mass, froth bubbling from his mouth.

Above! The dart had come from above! Thanquol glared at the stone wall, gnashing his teeth as he saw his attacker. Clinging to the ancient stones like some mammoth spider, the assassin was swathed in black from the base of his tail to the tip of his muzzle, only his beady red eyes left exposed by the cloth mask wrapped around his face. A sniff told Thanquol this was indeed a true assassin, the glands that produced the distinctive personal scent having been removed in one of Clan Eshin's macabre rituals.

The assassin glared back at Thanquol and raised a long, slender blowgun to his cloth-covered lips. The grey seer ducked his head, pressing himself against the filthy ground, trying to hide his face from the coming attack. This time he distinctly heard the dart as it raced through the air. He felt something brush against him, holding his breath in horror as he waited for the poison to do its lethal work.

It took Thanquol a heartbeat to realise what had happened. The dart had missed him, glancing off his horn. Fear and rage warred for mastery of him when he realised how close he had come to dying. Fear put up a good fight, but in the end it was rage that won out.

Thanquol lifted himself from the ground, his eyes focused on the assassin clinging to the wall above him. The grey seer's hand closed about the chunk of warpstone in his pocket, breaking off a tiny fragment and popping it into his mouth. The assassin seemed paralysed with horror, as unable to move as the decoy had been when faced by Boneripper's unstoppable charge.

A sickly green light crackled within the depths of Thanquol's eyes as the magical energies of the warpstone flowed through his mind and seeped into his soul. He could feel the awesome power of the Horned Rat rippling through him, the magical winds seeping into his body. He ground his fangs together, his brain flooded with images of destruction. He would incinerate this entire street and everything in it, leave the buildings nothing but heaps of slag. He would burn the assassin's shadow into the very stone with the fury of his magic and send his soul shrieking into Kweethul's sunken hell! Then he would cast down the Shattered Tower and drag Sneek's shattered corpse from the rubble...

Shaking his head, Thanquol fought down the overwhelming influence of the warpstone. He focused on what was at hand. All he needed to do was kill the assassin, nothing more.

Suddenly, Thanquol's concentration was shattered by a deafening shriek of terror. The air was pungent with the stink of musk and the very ground shook with the violence of hundreds of ratmen stampeding. The grey seer turned and watched as the panicked crowd surged away from him, horrified by the crackling lightning dancing about the head of his staff, frightened by the malignant aura that had settled about him like a mantle as he invoked the awful magic of the Horned Rat. The mob surged away from him as quickly and as far as it could. But even the wide streets of Skavenblight could not accommodate the mass of struggling, frantic ratmen. They soon became packed and pressed together at either end of the street, unable to flee further. When that happened, the blind terror of the mob drove them back, turned them around to find escape in the other direction.

From either end of the street, a wave of squealing, snarling skaven came stampeding. Between the two panicked hordes stood Grey Seer Thanquol, suddenly feeling very small and vulnerable for all the magic burning through his veins.

The assassin chittered maliciously from his perch upon the wall. Thanquol scowled spitefully as the murderer climbed to the roof of the building and retreated from view. This had been the plan all along, he realised. The assassin wasn't trying to kill Thanquol with the darts, he was trying to provoke him into using his magic to defend himself, thereby throwing the mob into a panic. When Thanquol was crushed beneath the paws of the crowd there would be no evidence that his death had been the work of Clan Eshin.

Defiantly, Thanquol stood his ground. Mostly because there was nowhere to run. He raised his staff, sent a crackling blast of green lightning searing into the foremost ranks of the stampeding skaven. Several ratmen shrieked and fell, their bodies quickly crushed beneath the feet of the mob. In a blind panic, the skaven were oblivious even to the death-dealing sorcery of Thanquol. The grey seer turned and sent a second blast searing through the ranks of the mass of skaven rushing towards him from the other end of the street. Again, the mob refused to break.

Thanquol spurted the musk of fear. He could blast a hundred of the craven vermin into cinders and still there would be enough of them left to crush his body beneath their feet!

As he contemplated his doom, a huge shape charged at him from across the street. Thanquol spun, sending a blast of lightning crackling past Boneripper's face. The panic of the skaven mob had infected Boneripper's tiny brain! The slack-witted brute was turning on him!

Thanquol did not have time to send another blast of magic at Boneripper before the beast was upon him. Huge claws closed around the grey seer's body, pinning his arms to his sides and lifting him from the ground. Thanquol struggled and cursed, trying to wriggle free of his treacherous bodyguard's grip.

The panicked mob of skaven came crashing together, savagely attacking one another as the two sides met. The street became a sea of flashing fangs and raking claws as the frightened skaven tore at each other. The pungent stink of black skaven blood filled Thanquol's senses.

Boneripper lifted the grey seer still higher, keeping him well above the frenzied mob's reach.

Fear drained out of Thanquol and he bit back the last of he curses he had been heaping on his bodyguard's head. Such a clever servant, he considered, to see his master's distress and come rushing to his aid.

He would need to find some suitable way to reward Boneripper for such selfless service.

Perhaps he would let Boneripper eat Sneek's heart after he tore it from the Nightlord's mutilated chest.

CHAPTER TWO

Streets of Skavenblight

GREY SEER THANQUOL sat in the gloom of his rented burrow and carefully plotted his next move. Nightlord Sneek had failed in his first attempt to murder him, but he knew the master of Clan Eshin would try again. Once the assassins had a skaven's scent, they never lost it.

The warpstone-induced madness had passed. Thanquol wasn't thinking in terms of killing Sneek. The very thought set his body trembling with fear. No, the only way to save his hide was to find out why Clan Eshin wanted him dead. Then he would need to find a way to make them change their mind. The only other alternative was to try and find an ally powerful enough to protect him from Sneek. That wouldn't be an easy task. None of the warlord clans, even the mighty Mors, was strong enough to defy

Eshin. The warlock-engineers of Clan Skryre were cosy as fleas with the assassins, developing all kinds of new murder devices for them. No help there.

Clan Moulder was a possibility, if the ungrateful beastmasters didn't blame him for the slave revolt that had nearly destroyed Hell Pit! Now was not the time to remind them that the attack on their city had been the work of the rebellious mutant Lurk Snitch-tongue, not the steadfast and selfless Grey Seer Thanquol. Pestilens, the traditional adversaries of Eshin, was an even worse proposition. Thanquol had earned his fame at the expense of Pestilens by defeating the renegade Plaguelord Skratsquik. Now he'd undermined their efforts to steal the Wormstone and been an unwilling participant in the destruction of Nurglitch's favourite disciple, Lord Skrolk. The only reason the plague monks would protect him from Sneek would be so they could kill him themselves.

Thanquol picked a flea from his fur, staring in distaste at his grungy surroundings. It had been too dangerous to return to his own chambers: that would be the first place his would-be killers would look for him. The burrow his failing store of warp-tokens had allowed him to rent was little more than a hole clawed out from the muddy foundations of Skavenblight. The dirt walls dripped with moisture, ugly orange roots protruding from them at every turn. The ceiling was sagging, a few rotten beams and pillars cobbled from broken bricks the only thing keeping it from collapsing into the burrow. For accoutrements, Thanquol had a pile of insect-infested straw that smelled like it had last been changed when the Grey

Lords were in power. A dilapidated desk pilfered from some Tilean villa leaned against a corner while an iron-banded trunk slowly rotted in another. This, the services of a diseased human slave, three meals a day and all the stagnant water he could suck from a bronze pipe in the tunnel outside his chamber had cost Thanquol seventeen precious warp-tokens.

That was what angered him the most. His formidable reputation should have been enough to bully the burrow-master down to at least seven warp-tokens. It was almost as if the ratman hadn't wanted Thanquol in his tunnels. Even after Boneripper broke a few of the insolent swine's fingers, he'd stuck to his price. The filthy rat knew that Thanquol was in hiding and had used that knowledge to mercilessly extort money from him. Thanquol didn't like to think that news of his problems with Clan Eshin had percolated down even into the squalor of the Sink, but it certainly looked that way. He had hoped to lose himself among the teeming masses of Skavenblight's lesser clans while he plotted his next move. But if the wretches around him were more afraid of Clan Eshin than they were of Grey Seer Thanquol…

He ground his fangs together in aggravation. If the filthy sewer rats of the flea-clans thought they could snitch to Sneek about his being down in the Sink he'd gut every last one of the vermin! He'd burn down their hovels and collapse their burrows! He'd string their living guts from one end of Skavenblight to the other! He'd feed their nethers…

Thanquol snapped from his vengeful ruminations, his nose bristling as the stink of human blood struck his senses. He could see the dim outline of the man-thing slave at the entrance to his burrow. The dim-witted thing had probably been stumbling about in the dark again. Humans were as good as blind down in the tunnels anyway. Thanquol was sorely tempted to let Boneripper take a bite out of the idiot thing, but was less than optimistic about his chances of training the rat ogre to do domestic chores.

'I did not call you,' Thanquol snapped irritably, lashing his tail against the floor.

The slave staggered a few steps deeper into his burrow and Thanquol was able to see the wretch better. He could see the scabby, sickly skin of the slave, clinging tight to his bones. He could see the thin, scraggly hair growing in patches on the human's sore-strewn scalp. Most of all, however, he could see the wet, dripping wound that stretched across the man-thing's neck.

Someone had slit the slave's throat from ear to ear.

Alarm flared down Thanquol's spine while fear-musk spurted from his glands. The grey seer leapt towards the pile of straw, tearing through it to retrieve his sword and staff, cursing himself for using his last piece of warpstone in the street.

Clan Eshin had found him! Clan Eshin was here!

Something blacker than black oozed into the burrow from the darkness of the tunnel. For a frantic moment, Thanquol imagined that the shadow wizard had followed him from Altdorf. Then the blackness moved towards him, moved with a speed beyond even a wizard-thing. He could see a black-furred hand gripping a dripping blade.

But Grey Seer Thanquol was not the only one who saw. Bellowing his fury, Boneripper lurched up from the floor, his back cracking against the sagging ceiling of the burrow. Thumping his claws against his chest, the crouching rat ogre lumbered towards the assassin.

The killer spun away from Thanquol, springing at Boneripper in a fluid motion that carried him under the hulking monster's claws. The rat ogre snarled in pain, his jaws snapping at the murderous shadow as it sprang away from him. Boneripper took a single step in pursuit, then crashed noisily to the floor. In that brief moment of contact, the assassin had expertly severed the tendons in each of the rat ogre's legs.

Boneripper snarled and snapped from the floor, dragging himself after the assassin. Thanquol hoped killing the brute would distract his attacker long enough for him to call upon his own powers to annihilate the scum. He could feel sorcerous energies gathering about him, seeping down into his veins. He felt a pang of longing for warpstone that churned his belly into a little knot of agony. His system felt empty drawing magic into it without warpstone to support the effort. Angrily, Thanquol gnashed his fangs and redoubled his exertions. If he did not strike quickly, there wouldn't be any more warpstone, either now or later.

Impossibly, even with a raging rat ogre roaring at him, the assassin noticed Thanquol's efforts. Even as the grey seer's eyes began to glow with power, a sharpened length of steel flew through the darkness.

The knife slammed into Thanquol's staff, splintering the wood and missing the grey seer by inches. He stared in horror at the evil-smelling blade and the green venom dripping from its edge. The poison wasn't applied, it was oozing from the black metal itself. A weeping blade, a weapon carried by only the most expert of Eshin's killers!

Repulsed, horrified, Thanquol pulled the revolting thing free and threw it to the floor. His concentration broken, the grey seer's eyes no longer glowed as he cringed against the wall of his burrow.

The assassin, however, was again focused upon Boneripper. With a leap and a roll, the skaven swept beneath the rat ogre's claws, bringing the blades he carried in his hands scything through the tendons of the powerful arms. The killer ended his attack just beneath Boneripper's lashing jaws. A third blade, clutched in the coils of the assassin's tail, stabbed upwards, scraping past Boneripper's fangs to punch through the roof of his mouth and pierce the tiny brain inside his thick skull.

Boneripper shivered, gasped, and then crashed against the floor. The assassin chittered coldly and stepped away from his kill, turning towards Thanquol once more.

The death of his bodyguard had taken less than a few heartbeats, too little time for even Thanquol to find an opportunity to escape. Now, as he watched the black-cloaked murderer creep towards him, sheer desperation gripped Thanquol's mind. Drawing quickly upon the dregs of magical energy still left in his body from his still-born spell, Thanquol sent a bolt of raw aethyric energy sizzling towards the assassin. The nimble ratman easily dived out of the spell's path. It continued onwards, smashing into one of the supports. A great groaning noise sounded from overhead. Eyes wide with horror, Thanquol watched as the ceiling came crashing down.

Thanquol expected to be crushed. For an instant, he thought he had been as his body was seized and all the air smashed from his lungs. Only when he was in the tunnel outside, coughing dust from his mouth, did he realise he was still alive.

At least for the moment. Looking up from the floor of the tunnel, Thanquol found himself gazing at a sinister figure swathed in black. Black fur, black leather leggings, black silk trousers and blouse, black cloak and hood. Even the assassin's scaly tail had been dyed black and the teeth in his muzzle had been stained to match the rest of him. Only the eyes were different, red and gleaming with amused malice. The eyes, and the green poison glowing on the edge of the knife he still held in his tail.

'You owe your fur to the Nightlord,' the assassin said. His voice sent shivers down Thanquol's spine. It was a thin whispering sound, the kind of noise a dagger makes as it sharpens against a stone.

Thanquol's head swam as he heard the words. Clearly it had been no effort on his part that had saved him from the collapse. But why would the assassin save him after coming so far into the depths of the Sink to kill him?

The grey seer bared his fangs in a threatening display and made a show of brushing mud from his robes. 'Since it was you who put my life in fear-doubt, I am...'

The assassin bared his own fangs, his tail arcing to his side, its menacing blade poised to strike. 'You owe your fur to the Nightlord,' the skaven repeated, his whisper becoming a growl. 'Because all-all he sent me to do was find-bring you.'

THANQUOL WASN'T SURE exactly where in Skavenblight Clan Eshin had built Sneek's pagoda. It was somewhere deep under the city, the pressure on his ears told him that, yet there was also the stagnant smell of the Blighted Marshes in his nose that told him he was near the surface. Eshin made a habit of using dwarf slaves to build their strongholds, and the dwarf-things had many ways of tricking skaven. Perhaps they used extremely dense rock in the ceiling to increase the sense of pressure, or maybe they had some way of piping the smell of the marshes deep underground. It was a puzzle Thanquol promised himself he would look into.

Allowing, of course, that he ever left this place alive.

He stood in a dark, spacious chamber. The floor beneath his claws was piled with elaborately woven rugs, their pattern tickling the pads of his paws. The ceiling was lost somewhere in the darkness above him, the walls obscured by silken veils that swayed and trembled in the warm breeze that crawled through the room. A thick, heady scent of incense pressed in around him, filling his nose with a not unpleasant stinging feeling, like a faint echo of the warpstone snuff he enjoyed upon occasion.

Considering his favourite diversion, Thanquol dug a paw into the pocket of his robe. He stared in confusion at the slow, clumsy way his hand moved. There was a warning snarl from behind him, and a powerful claw dug painfully into his shoulder. Thanquol spun around at the contact, a spasm of fear running through him as he realised how slow his reactions were.

The incense! Far more potent than even that employed by the Lords of Decay in the Shattered Tower, it was intoxicating his nerves with its soporific stink, rendering him slow and clumsy. His thoughts were no less sharp, however, and a grim gleam crept into Thanquol's eye as he saw how slowly the Eshin guard moved to restrain him. Whatever the vapour was, the assassins were not immune to it either.

The guard bared his blackened fangs, reading the change in Thanquol's posture as a sign of the grey seer's discovery. Like lightning, his paw drew a dripping knife from beneath his blouse. Thanquol pulled away, trying to ward away the assassin with his paws. This was the same killer who had murdered Boneripper. He was under no delusion about his ability to meet the assassin's speed, even without the incense dulling his reflexes.

'Peace, Grey Seer Thanquol,' a voice like the whisper of a drawn dagger scratched at the edge of Thanquol's hearing. The Eshin guard-rat released him and he turned back around to find himself facing a raised dais upon which stood an elaborately engraved throne, a seat of musky-scented wood carved from top to foot with writhing dragons and leering devils. Impossibly, the sputtering light of the warpstone braziers smouldering to either side of the chair illuminated the crown and sides, but left the seat itself in perfect shadow. From that shadow, a pair of sinister red eyes glistened in serene malevolence. A shiver crawled down Thanquol's spine as he understood who it was sitting in the darkness.

Nightlord Sneek's black-furred paw emerged into the light to beckon him forwards. Thanquol could see the long, ghastly nails that tipped each of Sneek's fingers, grotesque things that had not been gnawed or trimmed since he'd risen to the ranks of the Council. Now each was almost as long as the Nightlord's hands. They had been painted with curious characters, the weird writing of the men of Cathay. It was a language unknown even to most of the Lords of Decay, a secret known only to the Nightlord and his closest disciples. Thanquol wondered what sinister message was written on those talons and who was meant to read them.

The guard-rat sheathed his weeping blade, shuffling back to lean against one of the Cathayan columns that lined the centre of the chamber. His eyes, however, continued to regard Thanquol with unnerving intensity.

'Come forward, Grey Seer Thanquol,' Sneek repeated. 'There is much I would speak-say with the famous-honoured Thanquol.' The Nightlord's paw vanished back into the shadow and there came the sound of hands clapping together. From behind the silken veils, a train of skavenslaves emerged, bearing platters of sweetmeats and pungent Tilean cheeses, jugs of bloodwine and pots of the pungent green liquid Clan Eshin had become addicted to during their long sojourn in Cathay.

Thanquol eyed the victuals suspiciously, even as his stomach rebelliously growled. He started to reach for a tray of sweetmeats before common sense drew his hand back. It seemed a lot of work to bring him here just to poison him, but the Lords of Decay were not known for the practicality of their often-murderous whims. Thanquol pushed the tray away from him. He knew enough about the weird rituals of Eshin to turn and bow to the Nightlord's throne as he refused his hospitality.

There was just the slightest hint of a chuckle from the shadows, then Sneek clapped his hands together a second time. The slave carrying the smelly pot of tea scurried up the steps of the dais to present the beverage to his master.

'You are curious why I call you, Thanquol,' Sneek's thin whisper cut through the darkness of his lair. 'I find myself in need of a grey seer. One with every reason to be loyal to me.'

Thanquol licked his fangs nervously. Loyalty to Clan Eshin was something of a lifetime commitment, however short that might be. 'I–I am honoured by your confidence, exalted murder-master, but my oath-service to the Horned Rat is my bond. I can serve-obey no other.'

'Kritislik and Tisqueek are even now selling your mangy pelt to curry favour with Nurglitch,' Sneek said. 'The seerlords hope to use Clan Pestilens to curb the ambitions of Clan Skryre. Giving Nurglitch your glands in a warpstone bowl will go far to impressing that diseased pustule of their sincerity.'

Thanquol felt his knees buckle beneath him and he slumped to the floor. Kritislik was betraying him to Clan Pestilens? After he had selflessly risked his life to keep the Wormstone out of Nurglitch's paws? The plague monks were heretics, worshipping some grotesque daemon-thing and pretending it was the Horned One! He knew Kritislik hated Warplord Morskittar with a passion, but to condone the blasphemous ways of Pestilens in order to restrain the warlock-engineers was utter madness! Age had finally crippled Kritislik's senses, or else the poison Tisqueek kept trying to lace the senior seerlord's food with was finally having an effect!

Again Nightlord Sneek clapped his paws. In response, the veils behind his throne parted. A pair of sinister-looking skaven emerged from the blackness beyond the veils. One was a cloaked killer, his face wrapped in strips of darkened leather, his left hand encased within a wickedly sharp steel fighting claw. The other was a lean, emaciated ratman with a sickly pelt of charcoal-coloured fur. He wore a dark robe of Cathayan silk and leaned upon a gnarled staff. Thanquol stared in alarm at the talismans dangling from thongs affixed to the staff. The stories were true, then. Clan Eshin had their own heathen sorcerers, versed in some arcane art they had learned in the mysterious east.

'This is Shiwan Stalkscent,' Sneek said, one of his grotesquely long claws indicating the cloaked skaven. The assassin gave Thanquol a mocking bow, then ran the back of his paw across his dripping nose. Sneek indicated the other skaven. 'This is Shen Tsinge,' his whispery voice rasped. The sorcerer simply bared his fangs at Thanquol. 'They have been entrusted with an honour-task of importance to me. To ensure they succeed, I am sending you with them, Grey Seer Thanquol.'

Thanquol stared at the two sinister skaven. He could see the hate in their eyes. Shiwan, like most of Eshin's assassins, had his scent glands removed so there was nothing in his smell to make Thanquol any wiser about the emotions coursing through him. Shen, however, stank of hostility, the envious fug of a whelp pushed from its brood-mother's teat by a stronger sibling. His own exploits were known far and wide throughout the Under-Empire, yet these two showed not the slightest trace of intimidation in his presence. To be so open about challenging a grey seer meant more than impiety. It suggested a hideous degree of ability and ambition as well.

'I wish-pray them much-much success on their venture,' Thanquol said, repeating his deferential bow to the Nightlord. 'Unfortunately my duty demands I stay-stay in Skavenblight.'

The chilling chuckle of Nightlord Sneek wheezed from the darkness. 'If you leave, Thanquol, it will cause me much unhappiness.' Sneek waved his open palms in a helpless gesture. 'I would need to send Deathmaster Snikch looking for you again. Only this time he would not bring you back.'

Eyes wide as saucers, Thanquol turned in horror to the guard-rat leaning against the Cathayan column.

Deathmaster Snikch grinned at him with a muzzle filled with blackened fangs. Thanquol couldn't keep a squeal of terror from rumbling up his throat.

'Perhaps you have reconsidered?' Nightlord Sneek did not even give Thanquol time to answer him. 'To offset the ambitions of Seerlord Kritislik and prevent alliance between the grey seers and Clan Pestilens, I find it necessary to treat with the plague priests in my own way.' Sneek clapped his paws together. In response, Shen Tsinge scurried forward, approaching the base of the dais.

'Many breedings ago, when Grey Lords yet ruled the Under-Empire, Clan Pestilens build-make own empire far across great waters. Long-long they stay, lost-forgot by all skaven.' Shen lifted his finger for emphasis as he made his next point. 'Plague monks fight-fight cold-things to rule-keep jungle. Many-many battles they fight-fight, but always plague monks win. Then cold-things call great magic. Bring new-new god-devil into world.'

Thanquol's heart hammered in his chest. No skaven had failed to hear of the horrible devil-god that had routed Clan Pestilens from their ancient homeland and pursued them into the swamps of the Southlands. Sotek the Snake Daemon, whose jaws could swallow an entire warren in a single bite!

'Long-time ago, we steal-take map from plaguelords,' Shiwan boasted, wiping his paw across his nose again as a string of mucus brushed his whiskers. 'Map show-tell old cold-thing place where they call snake-devil.'

'Cold-things build-make temple of serpent there,' Shen explained. 'Keep snake-devil fed with skaven hearts. Great prophet of snake-devil there, listening for snake-devil's words.'

Nightlord Sneek clapped his paws together again. Shen and Shiwan bowed to their master and were silent. Sneek pointed one of his talons at Thanquol. 'Pestilens has tried many times to kill the snake-prophet. If Eshin succeeds where the plaguelords have failed, it will make them afraid. Too afraid to oppose my power.'

Thanquol shuddered at the idea. Sneaking into the very temple of Sotek to kill the snake-devil's high priest! It was on his tongue to suggest a certain dwarf-thing and his human pet for the job when an even more disturbing thought occurred to him. Sneek wasn't worried about Pestilens making alliances against the rest of the Council; he wanted Pestilens to ally with Eshin! By murdering the arch-foe of the plaguelords, Eshin would be able to treat with them from a position of dominance and dictate the terms of their alliance. In the last civil war, only the opposition of the assassins had prevented the plague monks from overwhelming all the other clans. If the two united together there might be nothing that could stop them!

'You are quiet, Grey Seer Thanquol,' Nightlord Sneek said. 'Are you thinking of leaving us?'

An eager hiss of anticipation rasped through Deathmaster Snikch's fangs as Sneek spoke. Thanquol resisted the urge to turn and see if he was drawing one of his poisoned blades.

'No-no!' Thanquol assured the Nightlord. 'I was only worrying that there are traitors trying to stop-stop your great and glorious plan, oh murderous daimyo! Only a few days ago I was attacked in the streets...'

The Nightlord's talons stabbed accusingly at the grey seer. 'There are no traitors in Clan Eshin!' Sneek's voice was a rumbling growl now, the serene whisper cracking in the heat of his fury. 'An adept would sooner slit his own belly than defy me!'

Thanquol's fur crawled as he felt the Nightlord's rage fixed on him. However, the only way to escape that anger was to feed it.

'Grand slayer of kings, I do not doubt-question your mighty power! First among the Lords of Decay, feared even by those who sit upon the Council! Yet I speak-say no lie when I tell you an assassin of your clan tried to murder me in the street! The slinking-coward used darts from a blow-gun to goad me into using my meagre knowledge of magic to defend myself, knowing such a display of power would set the crowd into a mindless panic. He thought to hide his crime by crushing me beneath their paws!'

Nightlord Sneek's paws disappeared back into the shadow. 'I will look into this, Thanquol. If you have spoken true, I will have the traitor's spleen in my hand. If you are trying to trick me, Deathmaster Snikch will bring me your spleen instead.'

Thanquol risked a sidewise glance at the lounging master-killer. Snikch grinned back at him, his pink tongue licking his painted teeth. There was no place in the Under-Empire anyone could hide from the Deathmaster.

Clapping paws ended Thanquol's audience with the Nightlord. 'Shiwan and Shen will attend you,' Sneek said. 'They are fully versed in my plans. Follow-obey them, Thanquol. Defy their orders and I shall consider it defying my own.'

Deathmaster Snikch's bloodthirsty chuckle at the Nightlord's threat was still ringing in Thanquol's ears as Shiwan and Shen led him into one of the narrow tunnels hidden behind the veils.

CHANG FANG WAS a skaven with big problems. As he made his way through the streets of Skavenblight, he hugged the manskin cloak tight around his body. He'd dyed his fur, rubbed the disembodied glands of two clanrats into his skin, discarded all of his weapons and equipment lest their smell betray him. In every way and in every detail he tried to present the appearance of a Clan Muskrit bog hunter. From smell to posture to appearance, he tried to make himself inconspicuous.

He was realistic about his chances of fooling his kinsrats of Clan Eshin. If he lived until dawn it would be a wonder worthy of the Horned Rat.

The disguised assassin ground his fangs together and cursed for the thousandth time the scent of Grey Seer Thanquol. The maggot should have been dead, crushed beneath the stampeding paws of a hundred skaven. An ignoble death for a conniving, cowardly, self-important flea! Long overdue, far too long delayed. Thanquol needed to be shown that he could not betray his fellow skaven with impunity. There were consequences and Chang Fang intended the grey seer would suffer them!

His own ruin was Thanquol's fault. The grey seer had used Chang Squik in his crazed scheme to destroy the man-thing nest called Nuln. To cover his own incompetence, Thanquol had abandoned Chang Squik to die, then blamed his many failures on the dead assassin.

Chang Squik had been trained as part of the same triad of assassins as Chang Fang; the disgrace suffered by Chang Squik infected the reputations of the survivors of the triad. No one would hire the services of an assassin tainted with the stink of failure, even Clan Eshin. Unable to expand the fortunes of their clan through murder, Chang Fang and Chang Kritch had been expunged from the ranks of the assassins. Chang Kritch had opened his belly in shame, but Chang Fang had endured. The need for vengeance had sustained him.

He would survive! He would escape the daggers of his kin and he would find Grey Seer Thanquol again!

Chang Fang lashed his tail in annoyance, nearly tripping an overburdened skavenslave scurrying down the street beside him. It was unfair! How was he to know the Nightlord wanted the damn grey seer for one of his schemes! By the time he found out, he'd already made the attempt to kill his hated enemy. Of course, that only made things even worse. To interfere with the Nightlord was bad enough, but for an assassin, even a disgraced one, to fail to kill his target was a crime that could be redeemed only with blood. If it was not to be his own, then he must kill Thanquol. Otherwise the Horned Rat would gnaw on his soul when he died.

The assassin's face split in a vicious snarl, his claws curling into his palms. It would be Thanquol's blood, not his own! Somehow, he would find the slippery grey seer and make him pay.

A green-robed figure intruded upon Chang Fang's thoughts of vengeance. So intently had the assassin been watching for others of his kind that he had not noticed the plague monks as they oozed their way through the teeming mass of skaven that filled the narrow street. Chang Fang maintained his pose of bog-hunter and tried to squirm past the odious monk. He realised his mistake when the monk's decayed paw closed around his arm. He brought his foot smashing into the ratman's belly in a savage kick that sent him crashing through the throng around them.

Chang Fang did not wait to see how badly the kick had crippled the plague monk, instead turning to vanish into the crowd. His escape was blocked, however, by a solid mass of tattered robes and mangy fur. A rusty knife pressed against his chest.

'Greetings, murder-meat,' the knife-holding plague monk coughed. 'Our master would speak-say much-much. You come with us, yes-yes.'

The plague monks were silent as they marched their captive through the dingy alleyways of Skavenblight, down dark corridors so desolate that they barely had to push anyone out of their way. Soon, the strange procession stood before a partially collapsed stone structure, its broken blocks jutting up from the mud around it. One of the plague monks indicated a window gaping a few feet above the mud. Another of the monks pushed Chang Fang towards it.

Briefly the thought of fighting back flashed through Chang Fang's mind. Quickly it was discarded. Even if he won clear of so many foes, the skirmish was sure to be noticed. The Nightlord's spies were everywhere. Besides, if the plague monks wanted him dead, he would already be so.

Chang Fang squirmed through the window, sliding into the room beyond. The floor of the room above had been torn down to open the ceiling of the mud-choked chamber he now found himself in. The air was rank with the pestilent stench of rot and decay. Half-eaten things were piled on the floor before a bloated warpstone idol only the deranged imagination of the plaguelords would see as representing the Horned Rat. If his glands hadn't been removed, Chang Fang would have spurted the musk of fear just looking at the noxious thing.

Revolted, he turned his eyes from the idol. Now he saw that it was not the only occupant of the slimy room. Several green-robed plague monks were seated on the floor, each of them furiously polishing a small chunk of warpstone. Behind them, seated atop one of the fallen blocks of stone, was a shape almost as ghastly as the obese idol. It was a bloated ratman, his skin peeling, his hair hanging in lumpy patches, his flesh a sickly green where it was not blotched with sores and boils. The ratman's muzzle was a decayed stump, his rotten lips unable to cover his fangs. Most hideous of all were his eyes. One was an empty hole in his face, the other was a polished piece of pure warpstone. Despite the impossibility, Chang Fang knew the creature could see him with that warpstone eye.

'They work to fashion a new eye for Lord Skrolk,' the grisly thing on the stone block declared, pointing a withered finger at his empty eye socket. 'The one whose work I choose will be made a deacon. The others will be made into meat.'

Chang Fang shivered to hear the plaguelord's bubbling, decayed voice and the callous indifference he displayed towards the fate of his underlings. If he treated his own clan in such fashion, what could Chang Fang expect?

'Terrible Lord Skrolk, horror of all skavendom, if this wretched-foolish one has-has offended…'

Skrolk's rotting face pulled back in a snarl. 'Do not test-tempt my patience! I know-see you are Chang Fang!'

The assassin recoiled from the threatening voice as though it were the roar of a swamp dragon. Unconsciously, he dropped into an Eshin fighting stance. His eyes darted across the room looking for a means of escape. It would take too long to climb the walls and there were more monks waiting outside the window. Perhaps behind the idol…

Lord Skrolk made a placating gesture with his paw. 'We are friends, Chang Fang,' he croaked. 'We share a common enemy.'

Suddenly escape no longer interested Chang Fang. 'Thanquol,' he growled.

The plaguelord's wormy tail lashed angrily against the stone block. 'I've had a long-long swim thanks to him,' Skrolk hissed. 'Except for his treason, I would have presented a great-great treasure to my master. Now my tongue grows heavy with excuses.'

Chang Fang ground his teeth together. 'He is protected by the Nightlord,' he cursed. 'We can't touch Thanquol without suffering his wrath.'

'Grey Seer Thanquol will soon be leaving Skavenblight,' Lord Skrolk said. 'Sneek is sending him far away, beyond even the protection of Eshin's assassins.'

There seemed to be a vengeful gleam in Skrolk's warpstone eye as he spoke. The same gleam that shone in Chang Fang's eyes as he listened.

'Sneek is sending an expedition to Lustria, sending them to kill the Prophet of Sotek.' Lord Skrolk's loathsome laughter bubbled through the sunken room. 'He is sending Thanquol with his skaven in case they need his magic to overcome the powers of the snake-devil. You will see that Thanquol fails.'

'How can I get to him if he's in Lustria?' Chang Fang asked, fumbling over the unfamiliar name.

'My henchrats have kill-killed one of your clan and made it seem he was the one sniff-sniff for Thanquol's blood. You will take his place on the expedition. Kill-slay Thanquol when you can, then make sure none of the others come back.'

Chang Fang's fur bristled as he heard Lord Skrolk's final condition. 'Kill-slay my own clan?'

'They would kill-slay you,' Lord Skrolk pointed out. 'This expedition is a fool's errand Sneek has been tricked into, your clan will take-find no profit. When you kill-slay Thanquol, none of the others can return to squeak-speak of what happened.'

The assassin considered Skrolk's words, then bowed his head.

'Thanquol will die,' Chang Fang promised.

CHAPTER THREE

Shiprats

THE TRIM SAILING ship made good time as she cut through the cold waters of the Great Western Ocean, spray dripping from the buxom, serpentine figure-head fitted to her prow. White sails billowed high above her swaying decks, flags snapping in the wind from her three towering masts. The barque seemed almost a thing alive, so gracefully did she glide upon the sea.

The *Cobra of Khemri* was out of the Free City of Marienburg. The Freetraders of Marienburg were the most prosperous merchants in all the Old World. Through their hands passed goods from all points of the compass: spices from Araby, silks from Cathay, weird beasts from the Southlands and strange metals from the savage shores of Norsca. The barque's voy-age, however, was to still more exotic shores: the elf homelands of Ulthuan. Trade with the elves of Ulthuan was strictly regulated by their Phoenix King, limited to only a handful of guilds and trading companies. These few mercantile concerns were allowed access to the elven port of Lothern, the only place in all Ulthuan where outsiders would be tolerated. Holding a very real monopoly on elven goods being brought into the Old World, these men and their elven sponsors could command their own prices on elf crafts, making the trade unspeakably lucrative. After a single voyage to Ulthuan, a sea captain could earn enough from his own meagre share of the cargo to retire comfortably. The merchants themselves lived like princes.

The *Cobra of Khemri*, however, was not owned by one of the select few traders licensed to deal with the elves. Her hold filled with furs, fruits and timber from the Old World, she would be allowed to offload her cargo and sell it on the docks to the merchants of Ulthuan for whatever pittance the elves would give for such curiosities. But to fill her holds with elf fabrics, dyes, perfumes, ceramics and objets d'art, the part of the voyage where the promise of real wealth lay, would take a formal trade agreement with the Sealords of Lothern.

The ship's owner thought about the precarious prospect of making the long voyage for nothing. Lukas van Sommerhaus was a patroon, one of the wealthy merchants of Marienburg. Or at least he had been. Under his stewardship, the enterprise built by his great-grandfather had dwindled, collapsing in upon itself until there was almost nothing left. From a fleet of fifty ships, the Sommerhaus name now controlled only three.

Van Sommerhaus stared out at the sea, watching the dark waters crash against the prow. The backers of the Sommerhaus Trading Company blamed him for the failures that beset the business. They held him to account for the ridiculous antagonism of the dogmatic royalists of the Empire, men who refused to either understand or appreciate genius! They'd tried to destroy him for refusing to be bound by tradition, and when they couldn't do that, they had set about trying to destroy his business.

The sharkskin gloves on his hands creaked as he clenched his fists. They were fools, blind superstitious fools! And his money-grubbing partners were no better! What were they, after all, but small men with petty ideas! He was above them. He was a patroon!

'Mourning the family business?'

Van Sommerhaus turned as he heard the soft, feminine voice at his elbow. The patroon was a tall man and he towered over the short woman who had spoken to him. His heavy, dull features contorted into an outraged scowl. He pulled away from the rail of the ship, his hand whipping about, cracking against the woman's cheek. She crumpled to the deck, her fingers clutching at her face where the patroon's rings had torn her delicate skin. There was resignation, not fear, in her expression as van Sommerhaus loomed over her and drew his hand back for another blow.

The slap never struck the young woman. Van Sommerhaus found his arm unable to move, saw strong fingers closed around his arm, crumpling the velvet material of his shirt. He glared into the face of the man who held him.

'You dare touch a patroon?' van Sommerhaus snarled.

'Hit her again and you'll see how daring I am,' the broad-shouldered man who held him growled back. He was a head shorter than the tall patroon, but much more powerfully built than the lean merchant. Not the wiry muscles of the barque's sailors, but the deadly brawn of a professional soldier.

'You forget your place, Adalwolf,' van Sommerhaus said. He wrenched his arm free as Adalwolf allowed his hold to slacken. Puffing out his chest, the patroon made a point of smoothing the crumpled material of his shirt before marching off to join the barque's captain on the quarterdeck.

The mercenary watched his employer stomp off, shaking his head in disgust. He'd been employed by the Sommerhaus Trading Company for nearly ten years, but this voyage marked the longest he had been called upon to suffer the patroon's company. After a week at sea with the man, he found himself wondering if there were any goblin warlords who needed a swordsman.

'That was stupid.'

Adalwolf looked down as he heard the woman speak. He reached a hand down to help her up, but she ignored the gesture, lifting herself off the deck despite the thick folds of the dress wrapped around her legs.

The mercenary couldn't help his eyes lingering over her. Hiltrude Kaestner wasn't the best looking woman he'd ever seen. She was a little too short for his tastes, a bit too full in her figure. Her features were pretty, not beautiful, and her dark hair was curled and coiled into one of the elaborate extravagances that reminded him unpleasantly of the aristocrats. Still, however much she wasn't his type, she was certainly easier on the eyes than the scruffy sea dogs who crewed the *Cobra of Khemri*.

'You're welcome,' Adalwolf grumbled.

Hiltrude pushed against his chest with one of her slender hands. 'Mind your own business,' she hissed. 'I know what I'm doing.'

Adalwolf shrugged his shoulders. 'Fine. Next time I let him hit you all he likes.'

Sharp eyes glared into the mercenary's. 'Look, van Sommerhaus retains me to entertain him, just like he retains you to carve up pirates and mutineers. That's the arrangement.'

'Seems to me you could do better,' Adalwolf said, handing her a kerchief to daub the bruise on her cheek.

Hiltrude snatched the cloth from him, pressing it to her face. 'He pays well,' she said, as if that explained everything. Seeing the words made no impact, she sighed and elaborated. 'He's under a lot of stress. The family fortune and all that. I can tell when it's getting to him.' She cast a sidewise glance at the quarterdeck where van Sommerhaus was in a heated discussion with Captain Schachter. 'I deliberately provoked him, gave him someone to lash out at. He'd feel better, I'd get knocked around a bit. No big deal. When we get back to Marienburg, he spends some of what's left of the family fortune on me.'

'He's no one to blame but himself,' Adalwolf told her. 'The trouble with the Empire is his own fault, not yours. If he hadn't decided he was a playwright…'

Despite herself, Hiltrude couldn't repress a chuckle. *'The Victorious Life of Van Hal the Vampire Hunter,'* she laughed.

'One performance before it closed,' Adalwolf grinned.

'Oh, it didn't close,' Hiltrude corrected him. 'It was closed. By order of the Lord Protector. Seems the witch hunters didn't like one of their heroes being represented as a shape-changing Child of Ulric. It was the University of Altdorf that condemned it for historical inaccuracy.'

'Van Hal hunting down Vlad von Carstein, wasn't it?' Adalwolf asked, trying to remember the details of the play.

Hiltrude laughed again and nodded her head. 'Van Hal being dead for two hundred years before the Vampire Wars wasn't the sort of detail Lukas would let get in the way of his masterpiece. I didn't see it, but Detlef Sierck did. I believe his exact words were "This moronic abomination is not theatre".'

'I don't know, it was better than his rewrite of *Prince of Nehekhara*.' The interruption came from a thin man dressed in blue-grey robes trimmed with a white wave pattern, a scrimshaw albatross pectoral strung about his neck. The levity left the man's leathery, sea-bitten face as he noted the ugly bruise on

Hiltrude's face. He removed a clam-shell flask from his belt, then reached for the kerchief the woman held. After a moment of resistance, Hiltrude let him have it. The woman's eyes were frightened as she watched him drip the contents of the flask onto the cloth before handing it back to her.

'Brother Diethelm means no harm,' Adalwolf assured her. The priest smiled at the mercenary.

'There is nothing to fear,' the priest said. 'It is just sea water. It will sting, but it will help your injury heal fast and leave no blemish.'

Hiltrude still looked suspicious, but she pressed the cloth to her cheek. She winced as the priest's prediction about it stinging proved true. 'I thought healing was the domain of Shallya, not Manann,' she quipped.

Diethelm grinned beneath his short blond beard. 'Manann has taught us a few tricks,' he said with a wink.

'Maybe he could teach a few of them to van Sommerhaus,' Adalwolf said.

'I don't think the patroon would listen,' Diethelm answered. 'He's an obstinate sort of fellow.'

That remark brought nods from both Adalwolf and Hiltrude.

'He's convinced that elf is going to help him rebuild his fortune,' Adalwolf said. All eyes turned to the forecastle where the subject of his remark was standing, one boot set upon the prow, his eyes locked upon the horizon. Ethril Feyfarer would stand there for hours watching the sea. There was no question he was eager to return to Ulthuan. It was his reason for going back that Adalwolf was dubious about. He'd never met a poor elf. He was fairly certain that still held true.

'I hope he's being honest with Lukas,' Hiltrude said, worry in her voice. She pressed the cloth a little closer to her cheek.

'Elves are very careful with their promises,' Diethelm told them. 'Anything this one has promised van Sommerhaus he will honour. But he will keep the letter of the bargain, not the spirit. A man must be careful making agreements with elves.' The priest turned away from the prow. His face grew dour.

'However, I don't think Ethril holds the future of van Sommerhaus in his hands,' the priest said, his voice heavy.

Adalwolf and Hiltrude followed the priest's staring eyes. At first, they could see nothing, then they saw what Diethelm's eerie gaze had seen before them. Black clouds rolling against the sternward horizon, sky and sea seeming to boil with the fury of their coming. It was a storm, a storm such as even Adalwolf had never seen. A storm that was bearing down on them with horrific speed.

'The future of van Sommerhaus, and everyone on this ship, is in the hands of Lord Manann,' the priest said, his words little more than an awed whisper.

THE SWELTERING TILEAN sun beat down upon the swarming harbour of Sartosa as though an angry god glowered down upon the pirate stronghold with displeasure.

A less divine figure, Captain Vittorio Borghese glowered from the quarterdeck as his crew took on the last of their supplies. Half the scum were still bleary-eyed from two weeks of drinking and wenching, and the other half were grumbling about rigged dice. The pirate captain rolled his eyes as he watched a pair of dusky Estalian buccaneers arguing about how to set the staysails between the ship's masts. He could almost smell the rot-gut rum on their breath as their rapid-fire argument grew more vitriolic. He wondered if Luka Silvaro ever had these kinds of days as his eyes roved the deck looking for his hulking first mate to crack their heads together before the argument went any further.

Instead of his mate, the pirate captain found himself watching an evil-looking Bretonnian swaggering down the dock towards his ship. Behind him, a half-dozen murderous thugs pulled a long wooden cart. Vittorio had only ever seen a similar contrivance when he'd been a boy in Miragliano and a travelling circus had come to town. The cart, with its steel bars, looked like nothing so much as a menagerie wagon. Only instead of a leering harpy or toothless manticore, the cage was filled with the groaning bodies of men.

'Clearing out the dregs of Peg Street, Levasseur?' Vittorio demanded as the strange procession approached his ship.

The cold-eyed Bretonnian doffed the tricorn hat he wore in a courtly bow. 'I heard that the *Black Mary* was in need of crew,' he said, a cruel smile on his face.

Vittorio turned a disgusted glance at the deck of his ship. 'I've no time to fetch the rest of my dogs from half the taverns on Sartosa,' he answered with a nod. He scratched at the empty socket behind his eye-patch, considering Levasseur's offer. 'What waters did you find your catch?'

Levasseur's grin broadened. 'The Hole Inn By The Hill,' he answered. 'Only the best for the *Black Mary*.'

The pirate captain nodded again. The Hole Inn By The Hill was the most notorious of Sartosa's many taverns, a place frequented by only pirates and their ilk. No weak-kneed pearl-divers or gutless fishermen there. 'Somehow I doubt they're the best,' Vittorio told Levasseur, digging through the pockets of his brocaded vest, 'but they'll have to do.' He tossed a small pouch to the grinning Bretonnian, the contents of the bag clanking together as Levasseur deftly caught it.

'Always a pleasure, *mon capitain*,' Levasseur said with another flourish of his feathered hat. He snapped quick orders and the press gang began unloading their drunken charges from the cart and carrying them onto the ship.

'Let them sleep it off in the hold,' Vittorio directed the press gang. When the indentured crew awoke, the *Black Mary* would be far at sea and well away from where the men could cause any problems.

Dismissing his new crew from his mind, Vittorio returned his attention to his old crew, barking orders at them as they made the two-hundred ton brigantine ready to sail. He did not notice the unusual number of men Levasseur's thugs brought onboard, nor the way many of them were covered in ragged cloaks and wrapped in frayed blankets.

Vittorio certainly did not see the wicked gleam in Levasseur's eye as the *Black Mary* pulled out from the Deadman's Docks.

'Bon chance, mon capitain,' Levasseur laughed as he watched the ship sail out from the pirate city of Sartosa for the last time. He fingered the small bag of silver Vittorio had paid him, tucking it beneath his tunic beside the larger bag of coins his special friends had given him earlier that night.

The *Black Mary* was going to need all the luck she could get.

A SLIGHT EXERTION of will, so insignificant only the smallest portion of its mind was focused upon the task, and the heavy golden dais beneath Tlaco'amoxtli'ueman rose from the ground. Gravity was a question of value; the slann had simply unbalanced the equation. It was something that had long ago ceased to even stir the mage-priest's thoughts. Levitation and telekinesis were among the first adjustments the Old Ones had taught their minions.

Skink attendants loped after the slann's dais as it glided slowly through the stone halls of the pyramid-temple. Beyond the golden doors that guarded the sacred well of contemplation at the heart of the pyramid, the dais rotated, facing an angular corridor with a squared ceiling. Only senses attuned to the Great Math could detect the menace behind the many glyphs carved into the walls, each possessing the power to disperse the sum of any creature daring to pass between them. Such wards had withstood the hunger of the nether-things in the Age of Strife. Lord Tlaco did not break their power when he passed between them, instead shifting it so that it curved about the dais and the skinks following after the slann.

Through the long corridor and its protecting glyphs, the dais entered a grand hall. Monstrous warriors waited here, lizardmen of more formidable shape than the slight skinks. The warriors stood twice the height of the slann's attendants, the bodies beneath their thick blue scales swollen with muscle. Their heads sported powerful jaws, sharp fangs curling across their scaly lips. Cold, passionless eyes stared from beneath thick brows. The saurus warriors wore gilded armour of fossilised bone and bore spiked clubs of bronze in their claws. Lord Tlaco's temple guard bobbed their heads in recognition of their revered master, silently forming ranks around the mage-priest.

Now surrounded by his bodyguard, Lord Tlaco's dais began to climb a set of immense stone steps. There were more protective glyphs as the dais reached a raised platform, lesser wards to keep parasitic mites and worms from the pyramid. A short passageway opened onto the platform, and up this the slann's procession proceeded. The hot stickiness of the air was a thing beneath Lord Tlaco's notice, but skink attendants quickly leapt to their master's comfort, fanning the toad-like creature and bathing its mottled skin with water drawn from the razordon bladders many of them carried.

Sunlight broke the dark gloom of the pyramid. The dais rotated again, shifting so that it could face the sun as the slann emerged from the cave-like opening set into the side of the great temple. His guards still surrounding him, skinks still bathing his hide and fanning his skin, Lord Tlaco pondered the fractals that had disturbed his meditations.

Xa'cota were at the source of the slann's unease. The unnatural spawn of the rat-fractal had caused no end of disturbance to the Great Math. Many of the cities that had survived the Cataclysm had not survived the coming of the xa'cota. Their aberrant plagues, far more virile and deadly than anything engineered as a part of the natural equation, had devastated the lizardmen. Entire spawnings of skinks had been wiped out before even setting eye upon their enemy.

The war with the rat had turned at the temple-city of Quetza and the dominance of the xa'cota had been broken, many of them driven back into the sea. Many skinks claimed the victory had been brought about by a mammoth serpent they called Sotek and which they worshipped in warm-thing fashion as a god. More than the breaking of the xa'cota, the rise of Sotek troubled Lord Tlaco's meditations. Among the names of the Old Ones, that of Sotek was not to be found. Upon the plaques of prophecy, the advent of the serpent was not foretold.

The city of Quetza was saved from destruction, but the plagues of the xa'cota festered within the very stones. It had become Quetza the Defiled and was abandoned by the lizardmen. At least for a time. Now inhabitants once again stirred within its walls, the followers of Xiuhcoatl, one of the Prophets of Sotek. Under Xiuhcoatl's leadership, the skinks erected a new pyramid in Quetza, a temple to their serpent god. Spawning pools had been dug from the foundations of the temple, holy serpents brought from the jungle. Here, where the skinks claimed Sotek had manifested before them, Xiuhcoatl did obeisance to his god.

Was this a part of the Great Math? Was it the will of the Old Ones? Lord Tlaco was uncertain. Even the slann's brain could not follow the calculations to their end. The plaques of prophecy were again silent. Had the jungles of Lustria been delivered from the unbalance of the xa'cota only to fall to a more insidious corruption?

Lord Tlaco closed his eyes as the warmth of the rising sun flowed into its damp body. Many times had the slann pondered the problem of Xiuhcoatl and Quetza the Defiled. For the skinks to survive, there needed to be something preserving them. But was it a part of the Great Plan?

The xa'cota were coming back. That fact had ended Lord Tlaco's meditative slumber. In their coming, it saw a menace to Quetza. There were other possibilities that arose, other sums that could be introduced into the algorithm. In casting its mind through the lattice of creation, Lord Tlaco became aware of a small cluster of xho'za'khanx, the untamed warm-things that infested so much of the world. The mage-priest calculated their potentiality. The spots on its skin shifted, setting skink scribes into a frenzy of activity.

Lord Tlaco concentrated on the humans and made a minor adjustment to the geomantic web...

THE STORM'S FURY descended upon the *Cobra of Khemri* like the hammer of a titan. The ship rolled violently between each undulation of the angry waves. Punishing rain pelted the decks, stinging the bodies of the crew desperately trying to secure the rigging and bring some semblance of control back to their vessel. A shrieking wind tore through the sails, setting them cracking and snapping before the masts, bulging with the malign power of the storm.

Even the most experienced of the mariners was ashen-faced; sun-baked skin turned pale by the malevolent power of the storm. Men who had spent decades upon the Great Ocean whimpered and wailed like whipped dogs, those with less experience simply clung to the rails and wept.

Adalwolf tried to help a pair of sailors secure the wheel, unaware if the effort was even worth it. The violence with which the wheel spun threatened to snap the tiller. He grimaced at the thought. Without the tiller there would be no way to steer the ship's rudder. They would be utterly at the mercy of the capricious sea.

A shriek from aloft and a body came hurtling down from the rigging. Ropes broke beneath the plunging weight. The fallen sailor struck with such violence that he bounced from the aftdeck before being thrown into the sea.

The cry of the lookout was echoed all across the main deck as the foremast began to crack. Men scrambled to fit lines to the mast, trying to strengthen it against the wind by sheer brawn. The mast continued to groan and sway, drawing more sailors to the desperate effort.

Adalwolf shook his head in disgust. It was a brave effort, but utterly doomed from the start. Splinters as long as his arm were already jutting from the surface of the mast. The men should be trying to cut it free, not hold it in place, but blind panic sometimes overwhelms even the most experienced. The mercenary ground his teeth together, waiting to hear the sickening finale of the farce.

It came with a low wooden growl that shook the ship more fiercely than the storm. Like a towering Drakwald giant, the foremast came smashing down, crashing through the railing and chewing a great gouge in the ship's hull before slipping over the side and plummeting into the depths. Several sailors were crushed beneath the impact, a half-dozen more were pulled screaming into the sea, unable to loosen the ropes with which they had struggled to save the mast.

Adalwolf felt his stomach churn at the hideous vision, violently turning his head away from the scene. At once his eyes found a sight just as ghastly.

A cluster of sailors were gathered around Brother Diethelm, boathooks and belaying pins clutched in their fists. The mercenary could see van Sommerhaus and Captain Schachter standing some small distance away, as silent as Arabyan sphinxes. Only Hiltrude's drenched figure stood between the raging sailors and their intended victim.

'You don't dare do this thing!' Hiltrude shouted at the men. 'Think what you are doing!'

A burly, scarred ruffian, his leather vest plastered to his dripping body, glared at the woman. 'Some priest!' the villain scoffed. 'What good are his prayers?' He gestured with the long dirk he held, sweeping it as though any of them could forget the storm raging around them. His outburst brought murderous oaths from the sailors around him.

Hiltrude turned desperate eyes towards van Sommerhaus and Schachter. 'Stop them!' she pleaded.

Van Sommerhaus turned his face, unwilling to meet her gaze. Captain Schachter simply spat on the deck. 'Even if I could, I don't think I would,' he muttered.

'Enough of your lip, wench!' a dusky, monkey-like sailor growled. 'Get out of our way or you go over the side with 'im!' He leered wickedly at the courtesan. 'Maybe you go over just the same. Maybe Stromfels is hungry for more than just the priest.'

The deck monkey shrieked as a fist smashed into his face, knocking yellowed teeth from his mouth. He staggered back, blood gushing from between his fingers as he clutched at his jaw. Adalwolf let the heavy chain uncoil from around his hand, the sailor's blood dripping from the iron links.

'If the Shark God is hungry, maybe we start by feeding him you,' Adalwolf threatened. In his other hand he gripped a fat-bladed short sword. He waved the weapon menacingly at the sullen crewmen.

The scar-faced sailor glared at the mercenary. 'If we don't appease the Storm God, then we'll all drown!'

He didn't wait for Adalwolf to respond, but drove his leg upwards, smashing his boot into the warrior's groin. Adalwolf doubled over. Before he could recover, sailors were swarming over him, ripping the sword from his fingers.

'First the bitch, then the friar!' the sailor roared, lunging for Hiltrude. The courtesan tried to squirm away, but the greater strength of the seaman prevailed, pulling her close and crushing her against him. Diethelm rushed to help her, but the priest was quickly beaten down by two of the other sailors.

'Damn you, Marjus, leave her alone!' Adalwolf raged, straining to free himself of the men who held him.

Marjus sneered at the mercenary, then moved towards the rail, dragging Hiltrude with him. 'You better hope this calms Stromfels,' the sailor warned. 'Or I know who else gets dropped into the drink.'

The sailor's ugly chuckle faded as he saw a shape appear between himself and the rail. While Marjus and the other sailors struggled to keep their feet on the wildly pitching deck, the apparition before him moved with eerie precision and grace. A tall, lean figure, his fine garments barely moist despite the fury of the storm, Ethril stared down the sailors. There was no rage or warning in that look, indeed, it was the chilling lack of emotion that struck the men, like the disapproving gaze of a weary teacher.

'Do you really think calling out to daemons is going to help?' Ethril's solemn voice was barely a whisper yet it carried with a quality that the wailing storm could not silence.

The elf's words made the sailors cast uncertain looks among themselves. Marjus glanced back at them for support. When he looked back, he found Ethril had drawn a curved dagger and that its point was now pressing against his throat.

'Let the girl go,' the elf told him. Reluctantly, Marjus released Hiltrude. The courtesan backed away from both sailor and elf, uncertain which to regard with more horror. Unlike the man, she had seen Ethril's hand. The elf had not drawn the dagger from some hidden sheath. It had *appeared* there, evoked from nothingness.

Marjus snarled at the cowed crew, yelling at them to help secure the deck and clear away the debris from the foremast. Even in the midst of the storm, there was no hiding the haste with which they fled the elf.

Adalwolf nodded his gratitude as Diethelm helped him off the deck. The priest's robes were torn, his face matted with blood where a belaying pin had struck him. He smiled sadly to the mercenary, then repeated the gesture when Hiltrude joined them.

'I thank you for your faith, or if not that then at least your assistance,' he said. Diethelm sighed as another great wave crashed against the deck, showering them all in spray. 'But I think perhaps it would have been best not to have interfered.'

'It would have served no purpose,' Ethril told them, stalking across the rolling deck. 'There is magic behind this storm, and it is not the work of your Stromfels. This storm blows us far off course, defying every effort, physical and magical, to oppose it.'

The elf shook his head, then turned to withdraw into the cabins within the sterncastle.

'It is almost as though the storm has a mind and a purpose behind it.'

SCREAMS AND CRIES of horror echoed across the decks of the *Black Mary*. Captain Vittorio Borghese stood with a small knot of his crew upon the quarterdeck. From the sounds, it seemed they were the last of the pirates still fighting.

The ship's attackers had boiled up from the hold like the rats they so loathsomely resembled. Vittorio did not know how many of them there were. It seemed like hundreds, certainly dozens. They were wiry, agile creatures, their furry bodies wrapped in dark cloaks. He'd grown up on stories of these creatures, of how they would snatch bad children and take them into their burrows never to return. He'd seen the ugly, man-like bodies paraded through the streets by the rat-catchers after one of their excursions into the sewers. They were a nightmare he had grown up with and one he had never forgotten.

Vittorio did not know how the monsters had gotten aboard his ship, but as the *Black Mary* was just leaving the Pirate's Bay, they had struck. There was no warning. One moment, all was calm, the next the deck was crawling with beasts of Chaos. His crew had managed to down a few of their inhuman attackers, but not enough to stem the verminous tide. The rusty blades of the skaven stabbed and slashed with cruel abandon, their chittering laughter scratching at his ears as they cut down his men.

The *Black Mary's* quartermaster stood beside the swivel gun mounted on the quarter deck. He'd refrained from firing while the crew was still fighting. Now he hesitated because the skaven had prisoners. The ratmen seemed intent on taking captives. It was a thought that evoked all of Vittorio's oldest childhood fears. He drew one of the pistols fastened to his belt and aimed it at his quartermaster.

'Blast 'em down, or I blast you!' Vittorio snarled.

The quartermaster paled beneath his dusky Tilean complexion, but swung the gun about and took aim. No sooner was the cannon pointed towards a cluster of skaven than a slim throwing knife crunched into the pirate's forehead. The quartermaster was already dead when he smashed against the rail and toppled into the sea.

Skaven were converging on the quarterdeck now. Vittorio shifted the aim of his pistol and exploded the face of a brown-furred monster scurrying up the side of the sterncastle. He drew another pistol and shot a second ratman creeping along the rigging above him. The pirates around him tried to hold back the hissing mob of ratkin trying to rush up the stairs from the main deck.

Vittorio cast about for any avenue of escape. What he saw sent raw panic pulsing through his heart. The *Black Mary* was sailing past the mid-point of Pirate's Bay. A single rock jutted up from the depths upon which had been carved an immense statue of Jack o' the Sea, the patron of all pirates. No one was certain just who had carved the strange statue, but pirates were careful to leave small offerings to it each time they sailed into Sartosa.

It wasn't Jack o' the Sea who captured Vittorio's attention, however. The waters around the statue were almost black with ships, a ramshackle fleet of dinghies, barges and flotsam, every inch of them crawling with more skaven. As soon as the *Black Mary* drew near, the ghastly fleet debarked from their moorings around the rock and began rowing towards the brigantine.

'Every man for himself, lads,' Vittorio snarled, hurling his spent pistols into the bay. The pirates watched in alarm as their captain climbed onto the rail and followed his weapons into the sea.

GREY SEER THANQUOL stood tall in the bow of his boat, his staff clenched tight in his fist, his robes whipping about him in the crisp ocean breeze. He enjoyed the smell of the sea, it excited his senses with its suggestion of far-off places. Of course, the vastness of it was profoundly disturbing. Sometimes he felt his head spinning with the sheer immensity of it. No skaven liked open spaces, they preferred the comforting feeling of close walls, firm floor and a thick ceiling overhead. Thanquol wasn't immune to the psychology of his kind. Indeed, he was finding this first phase of Nightlord Sneek's plan unsettling.

The Eshin flotilla had waited for hours sheltering beside the lonely rock and its ugly human statue, their boats swaying sickeningly beneath their paws. Some of Shiwan Stalkscent's warriors had passed the time poking through the jumbled heap of trash the man-things had piled at the base of the statue. Thanquol took a detached interest in their investigation. He'd seen enough evidence that humans were all insane, he didn't really need more. Why they would row out into the middle of so much water to throw something away he couldn't understand, even less when he saw little metal disks among the rubbish. Man-things would kill each other for little circles of gold and silver, yet here they had gone and left a pile of them on this abandoned rock. Perhaps they were trying to hide it from their clan leaders? It was the only conclusion that made any sort of sense to him, though he would have thought even a human could hide something a little better.

Thanquol shook his horned head and stared once again at the ship his minions had decided to steal. He wasn't any kind of sailor, but even he could appreciate the sleek lines of the brigantine, the intimidating black hull of the ship with her yawning gun ports. He knew enough about seafaring to understand the importance of the huge white sails billowing from her two masts. He even liked the little black flag flying from her bow, the one with a grinning human skull set between two leg bones. It was a ship worthy of Grey Seer Thanquol and his brilliance.

'Sit-sit or have knife stuck in back,' Shiwan Stalkscent growled from the stern of their little boat. Thanquol stared back over the heads of the cloaked skaven sitting at the oars, his lip curled back in a challenging snarl. The assassin snarled back, a dripping knife in his paw.

Thanquol decided to cover his own fangs and sit down. It wasn't the right time to challenge the upstart assassin, not when that old mage-rat Shen Tsinge was sitting right beside him. Thanquol lashed his tail in annoyance as he thought about the sorcerer. Clearly Shen had little confidence in his supposed abilities, otherwise he wouldn't be hiding behind the bulk of a rat ogre. He couldn't imagine what kind of magic such a coward would be good for! A real mage-rat, one with real power, didn't need the mindless brawn of a rat ogre to keep him safe! A real mage-rat was able to bend the aethyr to his will, command its forces to protect him, petition the Horned One for his divine might! A real mage-rat didn't need a stupid rat ogre stumbling after him, getting in the way and making his boat ride dangerously low in the water!

Bruxing his fangs in annoyance at all so-called sorcerers who felt the need to compensate for their inadequacies with a rat ogre bodyguard, Thanquol turned his eyes again to the *Black Mary*. His fur bristled as he studied the ship. It was little more than a scow, probably so worm-eaten that it would sink before it left the bay. If he was in charge of things, he would have Tsang Kweek and his gutter runners skinned for their temerity in stealing such a dilapidated vessel and endangering the lives of their betters. Certainly they could have stolen one that could actually be seen at night and that didn't have such a worrying over-abundance of sail. There was such a thing as going too fast, after all. And that ugly little flag with its smiling skull; what kind of morbid sadist thought that was appropriate?

Yes, Thanquol would have much to say to Shiwan about this reckless display of incompetence from his skaven. He'd wait until he could discuss the matter in private, when Shen Tsinge and his rat ogre weren't around to eavesdrop. There was no sense embarrassing Shiwan before his subordinates, after all.

Taking another glance behind him, Thanquol decided he'd also wait until the assassin put away his knife before talking to him.

CHAPTER FOUR

Green Hell

ADALWOLF COULD NOT take his eyes off the endless green wall before the prow of the *Cobra of Khemri*. It was like watching a hungry wolf slowly licking its chops.

He could feel the hot, stinking damp of the jungle pawing at him, driving back the clean ocean breeze like a lion snapping at jackals. There was a putrid, rotten smell in the air, a charnel reek of death. The coastline was thick with towering palms, their thin trunks mottled with parasitic growths, their fronds dripping with clinging vines. Bulky, nasty-looking bushes squatted beneath the trees, their thorny branches sometimes sporting oversized flowers of brilliant crimson and vibrant orange. Stalk-like plants for which Adalwolf could think of no name, but which looked like an oversized sort of grass peppered the few dozen yards of beach between sea and jungle, hordes of flies buzzing about them.

Raucous croaks, insane cackles, piercing cries, all told of the animal life lurking beyond the face of the jungle. The incessant drone of unseen insects pounded upon his ears, punishing them with a remorseless intensity that made Adalwolf long for the deafening boom of a broadside or the angry howl of a storm.

The storm. It had raged against them for two full days. Adalwolf was not a firm believer in the beneficence of his gods – he felt they had better things to do than bother about men – but he was convinced only a miracle sent by Manann could have kept the barque in one piece throughout the long ordeal. As if to illustrate the limit of Manann's indulgence, the keel of the ship had snapped as it grounded itself on the twisted grey rocks that jutted from the shore.

'By Khaine's fiery hell, where are we?'

The outburst came from Lukas van Sommerhaus. Like the rest, he had clustered at the rail to stare at the forbidding jungle. The *Cobra of Khemri* had come aground in the middle of the night, forcing them to wait until dawn to discover what new land had received them.

Ethril turned a withering look upon the patroon, making even the arrogant burgher wilt. 'Do not swear by the gods of my people, human,' the elf snapped.

'It looks like the Southlands beyond Araby,' Captain Schachter said after contemplating the jungle for a moment. There was uncertainty in his voice as he trawled the depths of memory for every sailor's tale he'd every heard about those mysterious lands beyond the desert. He moved stiffly, favouring his left leg. Trying to keep the ship afloat had taxed the stamina of all her crew and her passengers. Only the patroon had had the nerve to hide in his cabin through such an ordeal.

'That would be impossible,' Diethelm corrected the captain. The priest's tone was dolorous, his expression drawn and haggard. 'The storm blew us southwest. Araby would have been to our east.'

'Maybe… maybe this is… Ulthuan?' Hiltrude at least presented a better appearance than Diethelm, even if her voice was more uncertain. Van Sommerhaus had provided her with a considerable wardrobe for the voyage. The last thing he wanted was a consort unequipped to hang off his arm at any social engagements they might encounter.

The patroon was the only one who looked to Ethril with any real hope that the elf would confirm the woman's feeble suggestion. Ethril shook his head with a humourless smile on his lips.

'We don't have jungles in Ulthuan,' the elf said. 'This… this is the place you call Lustria.'

A babble of excited conversation swept through the crew, seizing even the captain in its grip. No seaman, certainly no sailor out of Marienburg, had failed to hear stories of fabled Lustria, a land where there were entire cities built of gold, a place where untold treasures waited to be found. The men who had braved the Great Ocean and entered the jungles of Lustria returned richer than kings.

'Lustria?' van Sommerhaus mused, rolling the word over on his tongue. 'Yes, wasn't that the place where Lord Melchin made his fortune?'

'More than just Lord Melchin!' scar-faced Marjus Pfaff exclaimed. 'Pirazzo came back so wealthy that Prince Borgio of Miragliano tried to seize his riches and assassinate him.'

'Marco Columbo came back rich enough to make himself Prince of Trantio!' quipped one of the other sailors.

'Aye!' agreed a third seaman. 'They call Lustria the Land of Gold, the Jewelled Jungle, the...'

'The only thing I've heard it called is Green Hell,' Adalwolf's grim voice drowned out the avaricious exuberance of the crew. Sullen faces turned towards the mercenary. The warrior ignored their annoyance. 'You talk about the men who came back rich. What about all the others? The ones who never came back.'

The sailors grumbled and cursed among themselves, none of them willing to concede Adalwolf's point, but none of them able to deny the ugly truth behind his words.

Van Sommerhaus, as usual, was oblivious to the changing mood. 'This is a fantastic opportunity!' he exclaimed. 'I think you are overcautious, Graetz,' he told the mercenary. 'Chance and the gods have favoured me with an opportunity greater even than establishing trade with Lothern! Why, I can return to Marienburg with a hold bursting with treasure, enough to make even the blinkered fools in the Empire forget their petty prejudices.'

'What'll you use for a ship?' Adalwolf growled back. He stamped his foot on the deck, setting it shaking. 'Or have you forgotten our keel is broken?'

The patroon waved his hand in annoyance at the mercenary. 'Small details. We can just carve a new one,' the remark had some of the sailors rolling their eyes in disbelief. 'The important thing is we find the gold.'

'I suggest you leave mindless greed to the dwarfs,' Ethril's melodious tones punctured the patroon's posturing. 'The swordman is quite right when he speaks of how dangerous this place is. My people have learned to leave it alone. You would be wise to do the same.'

Van Sommerhaus stared hard at the elf, then grinned. 'Are you warning me away because there is treasure?'

'Oh, there is certainly treasure,' Ethril replied. 'But don't think it is unguarded. There are things in the jungle, powers even we have learned to respect. They are best not disturbed.'

The patroon laughed at Ethril's warning. 'If they are so powerful, why do they hide themselves in a stinking jungle? No, my friend, you are just trying to keep me from making a fortune here instead of in Ulthuan.'

Ethril spread his hands in a hopeless gesture. 'Do as you like. Lustria never tires of finding new ways to kill fools.'

THICK COILS OF vine dangled from the palms, choking the jungle like some mammoth cobweb. Filthy black mould carpeted the earth, boiling up from the decaying plant matter caked into the ground. Saw-edged grass sprouted wherever the mould had not found purchase, each blade of grass as sharp as the edge of a dagger. Dried husks crashed downwards from the towering palms, smashing through the tangled canopy with enough force to crush a man's skull. Dead trees, their innards devoured by parasite growths and hungry insects, leaned sickly against their neighbours, only the clinging vines preventing them from hurtling to the jungle floor.

Droning insects, chattering monkeys, growling jaguars and the thousand insane cries of unseen birds filled the air with a deafening din. Hot and foetid, the atmosphere of the jungle seeped through the trees like wet wool, stifling those who tried to draw breath from it.

Adalwolf drove the meat cleaver into his hundredth vine, snapping the ropey growth in a spurt of rancid sap. The other men in the scouting party turned their faces upward, their ears perked to catch the first groan of a falling tree. Twice they had been surprised by dead trunks crashing down on them from the overgrown canopy above their heads. It had been simple luck that had prevented them from suffering casualties from either incident. Now they were better prepared, ready to scatter the instant they heard any kind of sound above them.

The mercenary hesitated, listening just as hard as the others. He waited a moment, then gritted his teeth. If nothing had moved, then nothing was apt to. He hefted the meat cleaver again, shaking his head at its already notched blade. Chopping through the vines was harder than cutting through bone, it was like trying to hack through iron wrapped in wet leather. Much further and he'd have to use the cook's cleaver as a saw. As slow as their progress was already proving, he was certain it wouldn't improve when that time came. He would be damned, however, if he was going to take van Sommerhaus's advice and ruin the edge of his sword on the cursed vines.

'Can't you go faster?' the question came from van Sommerhaus for what had to be the hundredth time. The patroon's face was drenched in sweat, his fine clothes scratched and torn, the ostrich-plume fan in his gloved hand wilting in the humidity. Discomfort did not bring out the best in the man.

Adalwolf paused in mid-stroke, the cleaver gleaming in his hand. 'Maybe you should go back to the beach with the others,' he suggested.

'Maybe you should remember who is directing this expedition,' van Sommerhaus growled back. He waved the dripping fan at Adalwolf. 'While you're indulging in the novelty of thinking, consider who's paying you while you're at it.'

The cleaver crunched noisily into the vine, not quite chopping through it. Adalwolf clenched his fist around the handle of the hatchet, his breath an angry hiss scraping through his teeth. Need strangled pride even as it started to find purchase on his tongue. He had family back in Marienburg. There was a wife he hadn't seen in four years, three children who barely knew his face. They were his obligation, even if the woman he had married wouldn't let him share her life. She'd never agreed to his taking up the sword, but the gold his blade earned kept their children with a roof over their heads and clothes on their backs. They needed him, and because they did, Adalwolf held his tongue and took the patroon's abuse.

'I'm sorry, patroon,' Adalwolf said. 'I forgot my place in my eagerness to find fresh water.'

'Forgiven,' van Sommerhaus smiled in his most magnanimous fashion. 'However, water is the least of our concerns. Brother Diethelm has an entire ocean he can mumble prayers over and make clean for us to drink.'

The dismissive way the patroon discussed the miracle the priest had performed early that morning shocked Adalwolf and the sailors. Even the men who had been ready to sacrifice Diethelm to Stromfels felt horror at van Sommerhaus's words. Commoners would accept a lot of abuse from their social betters, but they expected even emperors to respect the gods and their powers.

'I think you have your priest confused with a wizard,' Ethril told van Sommerhaus. 'Graetz is right. You should be looking for fresh water. In case Diethelm's god decides to stop listening to his prayers.'

Van Sommerhaus screwed his face into a sour expression, dropping the damp fan. 'I'm not such a fool as that,' he said. 'I was just trying to reassure the men there was nothing to worry about if we don't find water.'

The elf favoured van Sommerhaus with a slight bow. 'Then I apologise, patroon.' Ethril's eyes were cold as Kislevite snow as he spoke. 'I forgot my place.'

The moment of tension was broken by the crack and roar of a falling tree. Adalwolf dived for cover, sheltering behind a scaly dwarf palm. The sailors scrambled in every direction, van Sommerhaus among them. Ethril simply glanced upward. As casually as a man navigating his own parlour, the elf took two steps. An instant later, the dead tree slammed into the ground beside him.

'If you are done scampering through the forest,' Ethril's withering voice snapped at the scattered men, 'I suggest we get back to work. At some point the sun will set and we don't want to be in the jungle when it does. Before then, it would be nice if we found game, water and some sort of hill I can see the coast from.'

Adalwolf extracted himself from behind his refuge, brushing muck from his tunic. 'You still hope to recognise the coastline?'

The elf nodded his head. 'There is an asur settlement at the tip of Lustria. If we can find a point high enough for me to see a good part of the coast, I should be able to determine how far from it we are.'

'What about these treasure cities?' a black-bearded sailor named Joost asked eagerly. 'You know where any of them are?'

'I doubt I could find one for you before nightfall,' the elf told him, his tone dripping with scorn. Suddenly he pointed one of his long, slender fingers at the tree Adalwolf had taken shelter beneath. His finger indicated a clump of withered husks dangling from the palm fronds.

'You see that,' Ethril said. 'It might look like rotten fruit, but it isn't. Those are blood-bats. They sleep now, but when the sun sets, they will take wing. They aren't greedy though. They'll just take a small bite, you won't even feel it. Then they start lapping up the blood that fills the wound. Once their little bellies are filled, they fly off. If only a few land on you and you don't get sick from their bites, you should live. If a whole flock decides to feed…'

Ethril left the threat to the imagination of the sailor. He turned back to Adalwolf, motioning for the mercenary to continue hacking a path through the undergrowth.

Adalwolf's eyes went wide with shock as he turned. The cleaver fell from his numbed fingers. He took a staggering pace back, staring in disbelief. 'That wasn't there a minute ago,' he muttered. 'That wasn't there a minute ago!' he repeated, almost as though to assure himself of the fact.

The green wall of the jungle was parted a small distance from where the mercenary stood, opened apart in a path as wide as an Altdorf boulevard, as regular as though bored through the jungle with a giant corkscrew. No beast, however colossal, had torn such a regular path through the jungle.

Ethril stared in amazement at the pathway. The elf's eyes were filled with an almost reverential awe, the sort of look an amateur carpenter might have when walking into a cathedral built by a master architect. Quickly the look passed and the elf's cold demeanour returned. He backed away from the mysterious path with something akin to repugnance.

'We need to go back now,' the elf said.

'Why?' van Sommerhaus demanded. 'The jungle is open ahead. We can make good time now.'

Ethril stepped in front of van Sommerhaus, blocking him from the strange pathway. 'Even you must sense something wrong here.'

Van Sommerhaus laughed in the elf's face. 'The only thing wrong here is that we aren't supposed to make use of a good thing when we find it.'

'I rather think your "good thing" found us,' Ethril said. 'We didn't find it. This whole thing feels of magic.' The elf turned his head, casting frightened eyes over the weird tunnel through the jungle.

Marjus Pfaff pushed past Ethril. 'An elf afraid of sorcery!' he scoffed, spitting into the underbrush.

'Whatever did this has enough power that only a complete fool would not fear it,' Ethril warned. 'There is a saying in Caledor. "Let sleeping dragons lie." I advise you use the same wisdom.'

'The long-eared fey is trying to keep us from finding the treasure!' exclaimed Joost. The sailor brandished a fat-bladed cutlass in his hand. 'Somebody cut that road through this mess, and I'll bet my bottom teeth it goes someplace. Someplace with lots of gold and jewels just waiting to be scooped up!'

Ethril shook his head, then stepped aside with a sigh. 'If you are so eager for death, I will not stand in your way.'

Joost stared suspiciously at the elf as he passed him. An avaricious gleam was in the sailor's eyes as he stepped onto the strange pathway. The other sailors watched him proceed a few steps down the trail. Adalwolf turned his attention instead to Ethril. It was hard to read the expression on the elf's mask-like face, but what he saw there suggested a deep-set fear, fear far greater than would be occasioned simply by the prospect of losing a trade contract with van Sommerhaus.

'Joost!' Adalwolf called out, hurrying after the man. 'Wait! Don't go! Let's think this through first!'

Coming near the sailor, Adalwolf was forced back by a desultory sweep of Joost's cutlass. 'I've waited all my life for a chance like this!' Joost snarled. 'Keep out of my way, because you aren't stopping me!'

Adalwolf's hand dropped to the sword at his side. Sadly, he shook his head. There weren't many of Schachter's crew he was friendly with. It was fate's sick humour that Joost was one of them. Grimly, he let his fingers slip away from the sword and tightened his hold on the cleaver in his other hand.

'Joost, there's something wrong here!' Adalwolf pleaded. He gestured back at Marjus and the other sailors. None of them had made the first move to enter the pathway. They were watching and waiting. 'They can feel it,' Adalwolf said, pointing back to their comrades. 'Something's wrong here.'

The sailor glared at the mercenary. He swept his cutlass through the empty air between them, warning Adalwolf back. 'Let me be! I don't want to hurt you!'

'Nor I you,' Adalwolf said. With a swift lunge, he dived beneath the sweep of the sailor's cutlass. His fist cracked against Joost's jaw, staggering the seaman. The flat of the cleaver cracked against Joost's shoulder, numbing the arm that held the cutlass.

'Let me be, damn you!' Joost shouted. The sailor drove his knee into Adalwolf's gut, knocking the wind out of him. Joost lifted the cutlass with his numbed hand, making a sloppy strike at the mercenary's ribs.

Adalwolf brought the flat of the cleaver cracking against Joost's hand, knocking the cutlass from his grip. Furious, the sailor charged at him, his face twisted with rage. The mercenary kicked Joost in the leg, knocking him off balance. The sailor hurtled past Adalwolf, crashing into the ferns at the edge of the path.

Adalwolf turned to help the sailor back to his feet, but a piercing scream froze him in his steps. He watched in horror as Joost leaped from the green tangle of vegetation, blood streaming from his face. A pair of ghastly creatures clung to his beard, lean grey things with splotches of black along their scaly backs. They were lizards of some breed Adalwolf had never seen, reptiles as long as a man's forefinger and only slightly broader.

More hideous than their appearance, however, was what the lizards were doing to the screaming sailor. From where they clung to his beard, the blunt-faced reptiles darted their heads at Joost's face, sinking their fangs into his flesh, ripping little slivers of meat away with writhing jerks of their bodies. Joost shrieked again, trying to tear the lizards from his beard. Adalwolf started to rush to his aid when the frenzied shaking of the ferns behind the sailor froze him in his steps.

The entire cluster of plants was shaking and trembling. From every branch, a scrawny grey shape crawled, an entire swarm of the ghastly lizards. Purple tongues licked scaly lips as the reptiles converged upon the screaming man, leaping at his body, scrambling up his legs. At first they were drawn to his face, but soon they gathered wherever a bit of skin was exposed by the sailor's tattered garments.

In less time than it took for Adalwolf to draw a breath, Joost had vanished beneath a living mantle of snapping, biting death. When his agonised body crashed to the ground, the lizards scattered from it, retreating in all directions. The gory spectacle that reached blindly towards Adalwolf was barely recognisable as human. Quickly, the lizards returned and Joost was lost once more beneath a carpet of hungry grey scales.

Horrified, the men could only watch in mute fascination as the reptiles made short work of the mariner.

'Cannibal lizards,' Ethril's sombre voice told Adalwolf. 'Once they set upon prey, nothing can be done. They will gorge themselves until only bones are left.' He turned and faced the other sailors. 'Maybe you still want to follow the path?'

Van Sommerhaus, his eyes locked on the hideous sight, tried to answer Ethril, but instead doubled over and was noisily sick.

'We're going back,' Adalwolf said, marching away from the gruesome spectacle. 'We'll try again tomorrow,' he decided. 'Only next time we do everything Ethril says we do.'

'A wise course,' Ethril agreed.

Adalwolf looked over his shoulder at the feeding cannibal lizards. 'Nothing wise about it, just fear. I don't want to end up like Joost. You're the only one with any practical knowledge of this place. That means we follow you and leave the treasure hunts to the dead.'

LIDLESS EYES WATCHED as the warm-bloods chopped their way back through the jungle. As the men vanished into the jungle, five shapes detached themselves from where they had hidden alongside the strange path. As they moved through the jungle, the scales that covered them shifted colour to match the fronds and grass they moved through.

As they emerged onto the path, the reptiles savoured the warm sunlight trickling down through the trees. For a moment, instinct overwhelmed the purpose that had brought them so very far through the jungle. The chameleon skinks basked in the warmth, feeling the heat invigorating their cold bodies. The chromatophores in their bodies relaxed, the camouflage colouring of their scales brightening into a dull yellow hue.

One of the skinks emerged from its torpor, stalking towards the lizard-covered carcass of Joost. The chameleon moved with an odd, swaying motion, each step of its tong-like feet deliberate and precise. It removed a long, hollow tube of bamboo from a sling wound about its scaly chest. Carefully, the skink prodded and poked at the grey cannibal lizards sitting on the corpse. There was small threat of danger from the lizards now that they had eaten their fill. Far from the ferocious swarm that had engulfed Joost, now they were slothful and ungainly.

The other skinks now joined the first, gathering around the gory corpse. With a darting motion, one of the chameleons seized a cannibal lizard in its splayed hand, popping the struggling lizard in its crushing jaws. The other cannibal lizards scurried away, but only for the few paces it took their tiny brains to forget what had frightened them.

The first chameleon extended his tongue, absorbing the scent of the dead man with the organ's sensitive receptors. It was, as the skink expected, the scent he had been told to seek out. It was puzzled at first over the way the warm-bloods had failed to behave as expected. The answer, it realised, must lie with the one who smelled different and who had tried to dominate the others.

The skink bobbed his head from side to side, communicating the idea to the others. The warm-bloods were meant to follow the path. If the strange-smell was keeping them from doing what they were expected to do, then the strange-smell would be eliminated.

Soundlessly, the chameleon skinks withdrew from the body, vanishing back into the jungle, their scales again camouflaging their every motion.

THE ENCAMPMENT ON the beach was a rough cluster of tents fashioned from sailcloth and a somewhat more robust lean-to built from lumber scavenged from the ship. Captain Schachter had supervised the construction of the camp while the scouting party had penetrated into the jungle. Such supplies as could be easily removed from the *Cobra of Khemri* were brought ashore. The manner in which the ship was caught upon the rocks made it unlikely that it would sink, but Schachter was a man who didn't believe in taking undue chances. A storm the likes of which had brought them to Lustria was unlikely too.

As the scouting party returned from the jungle, they were greeted by the unexpected smell of cooking meat. They could see a plume of smoke rising from a pit dug some small distance from the tents. Across the beach there was a great swathe of blood-drenched sand. Some distance from the scene of violence, the men could see a number of squat, sheep-sized creatures lounging in the fading sunlight, soaking up the last rays of warmth before the humid tropical night settled in.

Hiltrude and a few sailors hurried from the camp to greet the men as they returned. Van Sommerhaus gave his consort a lingering kiss as they met, his hands crumpling the velvet of her dress. The sailors leered lewdly at the display. Adalwolf turned and looked away. There was little in the way of passion in the patroon. Hiltrude was just another possession to him, something to lord over the rest of them. Like the lizards basking on the beach, van Sommerhaus basked in the envy of those under him. Adalwolf hoped he enjoyed himself while he could. Once the reality of their situation set in, once even men like Marjus Pfaff understood how unlikely their return to Marienburg was, all of the patroon's promises of wealth and privilege when they returned to civilization would be as worthless as the man's titles and airs.

'Schachter's crew collected some bird eggs and a few shellfish. They killed some big lizards while you were gone,' Hiltrude told van Sommerhaus, shifting her gaze to include the others. Her eyes lingered for a moment on Adalwolf. 'They came out of the jungle and just sat down and went to sleep on the beach. A few of the sailors went over and clubbed them over the head. They didn't even put up any kind of fight. Almost like they'd never seen people before.'

'They probably haven't,' Adalwolf said.

Van Sommerhaus let Hiltrude slip from his grasp. 'More important, what do they taste like?'

'A bit like iguana,' one of the sailors said, his head-scarf carefully held before him against his chest. 'I sailed on an Estalian galleon for a few years, all up and down the Araby coast. Ate all sorts of strange things: monkey, bat, seal.'

Van Sommerhaus gave the man a patronising smile. 'And what does iguana taste like?' he demanded.

The sailor laughed, then caught himself and forced solemnity back into his voice. 'Well, it don't really taste like nothin'. That is, you can chew it and all, but it's like water really, where it don't have a taste of its own. Not bad mind, and decent fare if you have the spices to liven it up a bit.'

The patroon rolled his eyes. 'I will stick to the dry rations. You can have your water-flavoured reptile.'

Adalwolf caught van Sommerhaus's arm. 'We should save the dry food for an emergency.'

'My palate is too sensitive to be subjected to charred lizard,' van Sommerhaus said, brushing off the mercenary's hand. 'This threat against my stomach is an emergency to me.' The patroon did not linger to argue with Adalwolf. With one arm circling Hiltrude's waist, he strolled down the beach towards the lean-to Schachter had erected for his employer.

'That man is bucking for a fall,' Adalwolf growled under his breath.

'No more than the rest of you,' Ethril cautioned. The elf pointed at the bloody sand along the beach. 'Your men would do better not to slaughter anything so close to their camp. There are any number of things that could be drawn by the smell of blood. Not the least of which are ground leeches.' The elf smiled grimly as he saw Adalwolf's ignorance of the creatures. 'Each of them is longer than your arm and they move in a slithering army through the jungle. They can sense a drop of blood from a mile away. Once they latch onto flesh, they can't be pulled or cut off. They have to be burned away and while they are being burned, they try to chew their way deeper into their victim. I've listened to swordmasters beg for death rather than endure such pain.'

Adalwolf licked his lips nervously and cast an anxious gaze at the jungle. 'Marjus!' he called out. 'Get a few of your lads together and help me cover up all this blood!'

ETHRIL SAT UPON one of the coastal rocks and watched the little encampment below. Certainly the humans had posted their own sentries, but Ethril knew full well how feeble the vision of men was compared to that of his own people. With everything else already stacked against them, the elf knew they needed every advantage they could get.

Watching the stars sparkling on the sea, Ethril could almost imagine himself back in Ulthuan. It had been centuries since he had last set foot in his father's house. He had left with the bold words of youth, the pride of an elf determined to wrest his own glory from the world, to reclaim some of the lost wonders of the asur's fading empire. Many lands had passed beneath his boots, years had fallen away like leaves from a dying tree. All they had done was to crush the boldness of youth, replacing it with the jaded wisdom of experience. It was a sorry thing to outlive one's dreams. Perhaps, Ethril considered, that was why the civilization of the elves continued to diminish and pass into history.

Four centuries of wandering and all he was left with was the homesick longing of the traveller for the places of his youth. He would see his father, see the ivory halls of their palace in Lothern. He would like to feel the crisp wind of Ulthuan against his cheeks again, to watch starlight sparkling from the waters of his own shores.

Ethril had decided he would not return to Lothern as a vagabond, dependent upon the charity of other elves to return him to his home. He had settled upon a plan that would bring him back to Ulthuan by another route. In Marienburg there were many men who traded with the elves, and many more who hoped to break into the lucrative market. It had been easy to find van Sommerhaus and play upon his hopes. Ethril was careful to make no direct promises to the man, leaving most of the details of their arrangement entirely to the patroon's imagination. Returning to Lothern aboard a human ship was hardly triumphant, but it was better than returning as a beggar on an elf vessel.

A bitter smile formed on Ethril's face. The storm had dashed that dream. He was lost more completely than before. The jungles of Lustria were a place he had hoped never to see again. He had watched them devour armies. He did not rate the chances of his ill-equipped human comrades very highly, even if they could clear their heads of idiot notions about treasure and fortune.

He had considered leaving them. Alone there was a chance, a small one, that he could follow the coastline southward until he reached the Tower of Dusk, the great port fortress the asur had built on the southern tip of Lustria. With the humans along, he was more dubious of their chances. Unless they were further south than he imagined them to be, well past the swamps of the Vampire Coast, there was small chance the humans could survive the journey.

It was strange, the elf considered, how he felt responsible for the humans. They were so short-lived, fragile as flowers in their way. It should have been easy to abandon them to their own foolishness, to wash his hands of them. Yet he knew he couldn't. He was their only hope for survival. His intrigues had led them here, now it was his obligation to lead them safely out again. The lives of men were short, but the guilt he would feel for them would pain him far longer.

There was something more at work than simply the natural dangers of the jungle, however. Ethril had sensed some manner of terrible magic behind the storm, magic on such a scale that even the mightiest archmages would baulk at evoking such power. He had seen further evidence of such powerful sorcery in the jungle when they had suddenly come upon the pathway. None of the humans had been quick enough to see the pathway form, their attention gripped by the falling tree. Ethril had, watching as leaves and branches contorted and reformed into new shapes, as an invisible fist punched a trail through the steaming growth.

Something was stirring in the jungle, something with an interest in the *Cobra of Khemri* and her crew. Ethril could not decide if the force was malignant or callously indifferent. From what he knew of the amphibian masters of Lustria, the bloated mage-priests, he knew that whatever interest was being shown would not be benevolent. The cold-blooded slann were incapable of benevolence. Everything was simply a cog in the great mechanism of their minds. They would spend the lives of their own minions by the thousands simply to settle some question that perplexed them. If they displayed such indifference to the lizardmen, they would have no compassion for foreign creatures who stumbled into their experiments.

It was a slight sound, but it had Ethril whipping about, his sword in his hand. The elf's eyes focused on the beach around him, on the rocks and the pounding waves. He opened his senses, trying to discern the influence of magic in the aethyr. There was nothing, only the crawling sense along the back of his neck that something was wrong.

Another sound. Now Ethril could identify it as a soft splash. He stared hard at the waves crashing about the rocks. Perhaps nothing more than a crab knocked loose by the waves, but somehow he doubted it.

Finally his keen vision spotted the incongruous spot on the beach, the place where the waves broke strangely. It was as though there was a delay in this one spot as the foam rushed up the sand. Eyes less sharp than those of an elf would not have been able to pick it out, to see the outline of a thin, humanoid body with a crested head and a long curled tail. The chameleon blended almost perfectly with the shore, but the chromatophores in his scaly hide weren't able to keep pace with the rolling waves.

Ethril watched the skink slowly creeping towards him. He opened his mouth to shout a warning to the camp, then felt a sting against his neck. At once the muscles in his throat went numb, his breath becoming like burning frost as he drew it down into his lungs.

A second sting and Ethril's sword fell through his cold fingers and clattered across the rock before slipping into the sea. The elf slumped to his knees, staring through cloudy eyes at the feathered dart sticking out of his hand.

The third dart struck him in the back. Ethril groped for it a moment before his numb body slammed face-first against the rock. Before he could slide off to join his sword beneath the waves, scaly, tong-like hands closed about him, lifting him off the rocks and carrying him to shore.

Ethril's eyes had been sharper than those of any human. He had spotted one of the chameleon skinks lurking on the beach.

It was no slight upon his wariness that he had failed to see the other four.

Silently, the skinks bore their unmoving burden across the starlit beach. One chameleon lingered behind, a blowgun clutched in its scaly paws, its unblinking eyes fixed on the camp of the humans. When his comrades reached the shadows of the jungle without any stir from the camp, the chameleon replaced its weapon in the sling he carried and quickly joined them in the darkness.

CHAPTER FIVE

Return of the Skaven

THE BLACK MARY swayed ever so slightly as her anchor plunged into the crystal blue waters of the little bay. Beyond the ship, the white sands of the beach glistened in the sun, shimmering like a field of diamonds. Past the beach, the trees of the jungle swayed and sighed in the cool sea breeze. A parrot, its plumage a bright crimson, squawked its annoyance as it flew above the beach, unsettled by the appearance of the big black ship.

The parrot quickly retreated into the trees when longboats were lowered from the sides of the brigantine. The deck of the *Black Mary* swarmed with foul life, verminous shapes cloaked in black, staring up at the sun with hateful eyes. They clambered over the rails, swinging down on frayed ropes before dropping into the lowered boats. On and on the ratmen came, crawling and scurrying until the boats sagged beneath their weight and water began to swamp them. Angrily, the bigger skaven threw their smaller kin into the bay until the boats rode the waves more easily. Clumsily, they fumbled at the oars, gradually pulling away from the *Black Mary*. As the skaven rowed towards shore, their displaced kin paddled after them, whining their displeasure to an uncaring audience.

Grey Seer Thanquol swam with the rest, his eyes glaring daggers at the last longboat and its cargo of skaven. All the leaders of the expedition had taken seats in the boat, by rights his place was there among them. Instead, he'd been knocked over the side by Shen Tsinge's ungainly rat ogre. Oh, no doubt the sorcerer would claim it was an accident! He'd twist his tongue to some clever lie about how no insult had been meant! He'd pretend to be utterly innocent of any slight upon Thanquol's authority and position as a priest of the Horned Rat and an invaluable servant of the Council!

Thanquol knew better. When he reached shore, there would be a reckoning! He'd show these Eshin gutter-lickers who was the master and who the slave! He'd teach them a thing or thirteen about respect! They'd go slinking back to Cathay with their tails tucked up their nethers when he was through with them!

Chisel-like fangs sank into ancient wood. Thanquol forced his anger to abate when he heard the staff clenched in his jaws start to splinter. The Staff of the Horned One was his most treasured possession, beside the warpstone amulet that went with it. He'd worked hard and long to earn the right to carry the magical talismans, to bind their magic so that it complemented his own incredible command of the aethyr. His old mentor had been reluctant to give them up, and had taken an unreasonable amount of time to die when Thanquol did present his claim on the artefacts to him. Some grey seers simply weren't gracious enough to step aside in their dotage and open the way for the young and vibrant.

Something brushed against Thanquol's leg, something big and cold. The grey seer gritted his teeth – though being careful not to splinter the wood of his staff again – and began paddling a bit more quickly towards the shore. He pushed a struggling young night runner beneath the waves as he found his path choked with the swimming figures of Clan Eshin runts. The night runner pawed frantically as his head was pushed under, but Thanquol had already dismissed the whelp from his thoughts. He reached out and seized the tail of the next runt, pulling savagely on it and dragging the paddling ratman out of his path.

A sharp squeal of mortal agony snapped across the waves. The tang of skaven blood struck Thanquol's senses and he twisted about. The night runner he'd pushed underwater was back on the surface – flailing about in the jaws of a monstrous fish. Thanquol's eyes fairly bulged from his head as he saw the immense creature. It was all grey on top with a white belly and eyes as black as crushed warpstone. Its teeth were gigantic saw-edged things that filled its entire face. When it tightened its hold on the screaming skaven, its jaws actually shot forwards from its face before recoiling back into the leathery white mouth.

There was a mad scramble of skaven as the shock of seeing the great fish wore off. Knife-like fins were already slicing through the waves, drawn by the night runner's blood. The ratmen had no idea what a shark was, but they could appreciate what they had seen the first one do. Snapping, biting, and clawing, the skaven flung themselves towards shore. One knot of cloaked ratkin swarmed a longboat, pitching its occupants into the sea. A cluster of them quickly surfaced, scurrying onto the overturned boat. A cloud of blood and a submerging fin showed at least one of their number whose scramble for the shore was over.

Warplock pistols cracked, swimming skaven shrieked as the occupants of the other boats ensured their vessels would not suffer the same fate. Carefully, Thanquol edged away from the longboat he had been paddling towards. He saw a huge dorsal fin glide past him, watched as an armoured ratman desperately trying to tread water was jerked under, vanishing into a watery ring of blood.

A cloaked assassin rose from the bottom of the longboat, a blowgun clutched in his paws. Thanquol could not see the ratman's face beneath the shadow cast by his hood, but he could see the skaven swing around to face him. With a quick motion, the assassin brought the blowgun to his lips. Thanquol's fur crawled at the sight, remembering how near such a weapon had come to killing him in Skavenblight.

Despite the sharks in the water around him, he clenched his eyes tight and dived beneath the surface.

Desperately Thanquol clawed his way through the bloody sea. He could smell the sharks frenziedly tearing at their prey all around him. It was a reek that sent stark terror pulsing down his spine. He felt his lungs burning for want of air as he blindly swam through the water. Something brushed against his arm. Frantically he lashed out at it with his claws. When he discovered his target was covered in fur, he grabbed it, holding it in a terrified embrace. Thanquol tried to climb the body of the skaven he gripped, then opened his eyes in horror as he found there was nothing attached to the leg he held.

The last of Thanquol's breath escaped in a terrified burst of bubbles. Frantic, he followed them to the surface, gasping for air as his head bobbed above the blackened waves. Almost as soon as he broke the surface, a whistling sound whizzed through his ears. A dart shot over his head, so near to his skin that Thanquol could feel his fur ripple in its wake.

Behind him, Thanquol felt the sea undulate with violence. He turned himself about to watch as an immense shark thrashed in the water. After a few moments, the monstrous fish rolled onto its back, its eyes rolled into the back of its head, a poisoned dart protruding from its snout.

Thanquol glanced back at the longboat. It was being swarmed by terrified skaven, desperate to escape the sharks. He could make out the shape of the cloaked assassin whose shot had saved him from the shark. The wretch didn't seem happy about it, breaking his blowgun across his knee before turning with a long dagger to help fend off the ratmen trying to swarm into the boat.

There was no personal scent to the assassin, like most of his kind the identifying glands had been surgically extracted. Thanquol tried to fix the killer's appearance in his mind. It was no easy task – the skaven of Clan Eshin all looked alike to him. When a ratman treading water nearby cried out before a shark dragged him under, Thanquol decided he'd studied the assassin long enough.

Ensuring he had a firm hold on his staff, Thanquol paddled towards the sandy shore.

'DUNG-CHEWING FLEA! You read-say map wrong-wrong!' Shiwan Stalkscent snatched the mouldy map from the paws of Shen Tsinge. The sorcerer bared his fangs at the master assassin, but waved a placating hand at his rat ogre when the brute began to move towards Shiwan.

Thanquol reclined beneath a palm tree, quietly eating the weird yellow fruit he'd confiscated from a pair of gutter runners. He was rather enjoying watching the Eshin big shots fall out among themselves. There was something deeply satisfying about watching his enemies tear into each other. He only hoped their argument would come to blows sooner than later. Given the Eshin penchant for poison, the expedition would quickly have a few less leaders if that happened.

It had been a long, taxing voyage to Lustria from Sartosa. They'd kept the human crew alive for most of the voyage, using them to crew the ship. The voyage, however, had been a bit farther than they had planned on. It had taken only a few weeks for the skaven to exhaust the provisions in the hold. Then they had started using the humans to supplement their diet. Only a few days and the skaven had exhausted that food source. Fortunately, Tsang Kweek, head of the gutter runners, had the cunning to have his ratmen watch the pirates. They had managed a reasonable enough job of sailing the ship when the last pirate was butchered. Even so, it had taken a further two weeks to sight land. By then, the skaven were just finishing off their emergency-emergency food supply, the skavenslaves Shiwan had brought from Skavenblight.

Thanquol took a bite of his confiscated fruit, wondering if perhaps it might not taste better with the fleshy yellow shell peeled away. He wrinkled his nose at the strange idea. Then again, it wasn't the first strange idea he'd had. There was his conviction that one of the assassins had tried to kill him while the sharks were eating the slow, lazy skaven. Nor had that been the only incident. A falling spar had nearly split his skull only a day out from Sartosa. Then there had been the time he'd been on deck at night and been knocked over the rail by someone he didn't see or smell. Only by the grace of the Horned Rat had he managed to grip the hull of the ship and climb his way back onboard.

They'd blamed that accident on an uppity pirate, but their efforts to explain away how he had been nearly smothered while he slept and thrown into the hold with the humans had been a good deal harder. If he hadn't awakened in time, and if he hadn't hidden a few nuggets of warpstone in his cheek pouches, the vengeful pirates would have killed him with their bare hands. As it was, it had taken every ounce of his cunning and his sorcery to keep them off him before he was finally discovered three days later.

Someone, it appeared, wasn't too happy about the Nightlord's decision to send him on this expedition!

Thanquol bruxed his fangs together, glaring at the little group of ratmen arguing over the rat-hide map. Any one of them might be the one! Or why did it need to be only one? Yes! It could be a conspiracy, a subterfuge being plotted by two of them! Maybe more! Maybe they were all in on it!

The grey seer worked his tongue to extract the last, miniscule portion of warpstone from his cheek pouch. He could swallow it, draw on its innate power and fuel a spell of such magnitude that all of the Eshin leaders would become nothing but a bloody smear on the sand!

He blinked his eyes and shook his head, moving the bit of warpstone back into the corner of his mouth. Yes, he could blast all of his enemies at one go, and then what would he do. He'd still be a thousand food-stops from home, surrounded by impenetrable jungle, shark-infested water and a few hundred Clan Eshin warriors that might not take too kindly to his extermination of their leaders – however justified. Reluctantly, Thanquol let the murderous vision fade and cocked his ears forwards to listen to the argument unfold.

'Maybe it wrong map!' Shen Tsinge hissed, shaking his staff at the cloaked assassin. He spun and pointed a slender claw at Tsang Kweek. 'Maybe you steal map to wrong place!'

The leader of the gutter runners bared his fangs, his fur bristling at the insult. 'We take-snatch map from plague priest!' Tsang protested. The brown-furred ratman was a wiry, emaciated creature beneath his cloak, taking pains to keep himself trim enough to crawl up a drain-pipe or wriggle through a chimney. 'Him say is for Pestilens come-take Lustria from snake-devil! Him say-squeak much-much,' he added with a low snarl, his thumb working along the back of a serrated dagger.

'Pirate-man maybe lie?' offered the hulking Kong Krakback. The black skaven was in charge of Eshin's clanrat warriors, a brutish monster who wore segmented armour in preference to the cloaks and robes of his assassin masters. The huge skaven leaned on his fang-edged glaive, its edge pitted with little copper rings and other protective talismans.

'Man-thing no lie-lie!' snapped Shiwan. 'I say-tell he not die-die he land ship right place!'

'Maybe man-thing know you lie-lie,' Shen observed. 'Maybe he think-know we eat anyway.'

Sullenly, Shiwan swept his cloak tight around himself, his tail lashing angrily against the sand. Immediately, the assassin's whiskers started to twitch. Forgetting the bickering of his ratkin, he bent down and scratched at the sand. There was a sinister gleam in his eye as he rose, his claws curled around a rusty piece of iron.

'Man-thing metal!' Shiwan hissed in triumph. He tossed the decayed bit of iron into the sand, nearly hitting Shen Tsinge's feet. The sorcerer scowled and picked up the rotten piece of rust. He sniffed at it, then, with a suspicious glance at Shiwan, gave it an experimental lick.

'Man-thing metal,' the sorcerer agreed. His eyes narrowed and his tail lashed behind him as he stared at Shiwan. 'What you sniff-scent?'

The master assassin wiped a drip of ooze from his nose and grinned threateningly at the others. Proudly he held up the ratskin map. His claw tapped a mark upon the inked surface. 'Map show man-thing place. Find man-thing place, find-find where on map we are!'

Shiwan's declaration excited the other skaven leaders. They all knew how rare humans were in Lustria. There were a thousand things in the jungle that would kill a human faster than a Clan Eshin blade. A human settlement of any size was an incredible rarity in the jungle. A landmark they could use to get their bearings and sniff their way to the lost city of Quetza.

Tsang Kweek snapped quick commands to his gutter runners. Lean and thin, the gutter runners had formed the bulk of the swimmers at the beachhead and had suffered the heaviest casualties from the sharks. They were eager to prove their worth and forestall worse treatment from the assassins and Kong's warriors. It was not a question of loyalty or duty, but simply a question of survival.

The gutter runners fanned out along the beach, sniffing at the sand. Sometimes one would start digging at the earth, scrabbling at some buried scrap of metal. Each discovery formed a pattern and soon the skaven had a definite idea from where in the jungle the trail of rusted junk had started.

Shiwan snarled the order for the expedition to follow Tsang's scouts into the jungle. Whining their feeble protests, the warriors and assassins got to their feet and scurried into the trees.

Thanquol leaned in the cool shade of his palm and watched them go. For a fleeting instant, he hoped they had forgotten him. Then he turned his eyes back to the shore, watching badly chewed bits of skaven roll in with the tide. He listened to the raucous calls of jungle birds, sniffed the evil smell of reptiles in the air. Anxiously, the grey seer licked his fangs.

Of course he could not desert the brave Clan Eshin in their time of need! Why their leaders couldn't even read a simple map! If there was to be any chance of success on this mission, they would need his impartial and selfless guidance. That would be the only way to spare them from the Nightlord's wrath. It would be a dangerous undertaking, but Thanquol was not one to shun his obligations merely because they might prove hazardous.

Tucking his staff under his arm, Grey Seer Thanquol dashed after the last of the warriors.

He tried not to look too undignified as he raced to catch up.

* * *

THANQUOL'S FUR WAS plastered to his skin, his robes clinging to his body like the wet rags used by ratwives to smother malformed whelps. The grey seer swatted irritably at the nasty blue fly trying to bite his neck. All considered, he must have lost a quart of blood to the abominable insects. It had been sorely tempting to draw upon his power to ward off the biting bugs, but he decided such a display of magical prowess might be unseemly. Besides, that slinking mage-rat Shen Tsinge was conserving his powers, and that made Thanquol doubly keen to husband his own.

His fur bristled as he watched the scabby little sorcerer. No trudging through the muck and mud of the jungle for him! Oh no, not when he had a big strong rat ogre to lug his mangy skin around for him! The sorcerer was cradled in the brute's arms like a favoured whelp nuzzled against a breeder. Thanquol could swear the villain was dozing. Dozing while the rest of them suffered and sweated and fought off all the filthy vermin the jungle could throw at them. Leeches! Mosquitos! Poisonous spiders! Blinding clouds of gnats! Snakes!

Thanquol's fur crawled as he thought of the snakes. The loathsome things were everywhere, watching them with their unblinking eyes, sniffing at them with their forked tongues. He'd lost count of all the hideous snakes they'd seen. Little ones the colour of man-thing blood that could kill a skaven with a single flash of their fangs. Big ones that dropped down from the branches to coil around a ratman and crush his bones in their coils. Flat ones that flew through the trees like great scaly ribbons. Most horrible of all had been the giant one with a head on each end. Fortunately that monster had been content to eat two gutter runners and then slither back into the scummy stream it had been hiding in.

He returned his angry gaze to Shen Tsinge. Of course the sorcerer didn't have to worry about snakes, not up there in the arms of his rat ogre! Thanquol studied the monstrous brute. From head to foot the beast was as black as an assassin's cloak and the immense claws on both its hands and its feet were covered in steel. The monster wore a necklace of skulls around its neck: skulls of dwarf-things and man-things and green-things, but mostly the long, narrow skulls of skaven. The threat was obvious.

Goji, the sorcerer had named his bodyguard in typical excessive fashion. Clan Eshin must have trained the beast for some time: it moved with a speed and agility that belied its bulk, and when it moved it did so without a whisper of sound to betray it. Even Tsang's gutter runners seemed clumsy beside Goji as they scurried through the jungle.

Thanquol bristled and snorted his amusement at all the wasted time and expense Shen Tsinge had squandered to train his rat ogre. What good was a quiet bodyguard? What use was it to have a hulking engine of destruction that could daintily pick its way through the jungle? A rat ogre was something to be used to scare underlings and terrify enemies! Shen Tsinge obviously had not the slightest clue about rat ogres!

The grey seer quickly moved behind a pair of clanrat warriors as the scouts ahead came scampering back. He could smell the excitement in their scent. His keen ears soon picked out their hasty report. They had found something ahead!

Carefully, the column followed the scouts back along the trail they had carved through the jungle. For some time, the ground had been growing less solid. Now it fell away into a full-fledged swamp. Gnarled mangroves thrust themselves from the scum-coated water, clouds of insects buzzing above the filth. Sandbars protruded through the muck, forming a twisty, broken bridge across the morass. Immense green crocodiles lounged upon the sand bars, basking in the sunlight dribbling down through the trees.

All of this Thanquol saw and smelled in an instant, then his attention was drawn like all of the other skaven to the ugly stone tower rising from a small island. The structure leaned crazily out over the swamp, many of its stones having collapsed and fallen into the mud banks around it. The rusted mouth of a cannon protruded from the single window that could be seen. Above the broken wooden gate that fronted the tower, a set of human bones had been fixed above the archway with mortar. Thanquol recognised the shape they formed. It was the same as the *Black Mary* had flown, a skull above two leg bones. The grey seer wondered if it was possible if the men who had built the tower and the pirates whose ship they had taken could have belonged to the same clan.

Some of Tsang Kweek's gutter runners started towards the tower, a suggestion of greed in their scent. The smell was picked up by Kong Krakback's warriors and the bigger skaven started scurrying after the small scouts.

Grey Seer Thanquol started to move forwards as well, determined to mediate any dispute over treasure for the good of the expedition – and a nominal percentage. His nose twitched as a new smell struck it. A cold shiver crept through his spine and it was an effort to control his glands. This was no scent even the keenest assassin would know. It was a smell only those attuned to the world of magic could know. Thanquol had last smelled such a foul taint when he had fought the necromancer Vorghun of Praag. It was the stench of the darkest of sorcery, the sickening reek of the undead.

Thanquol pondered his options, then carefully made his way back towards the jungle. Let the Eshin upstarts walk into trouble! It would serve them right for all the indignities they had forced upon him! Besides, someone among that murderous rabble was trying to kill him. Maybe he'd get lucky and whatever evil was hanging about the tower would take care of his unknown enemy for him.

Shen Tsinge's eyes were not quite as closed as Thanquol had supposed them to be. Far from dozing, the sorcerer had been watching all of his comrades, and most particularly the grey seer. When he saw the crafty gleam creep into Thanquol's eyes, the sorcerer dropped down from the arms of Goji. Shen sniffed at the air. His fur bristled at what he smelled. He stared accusingly at Thanquol, then scrambled forwards to warn his clan of their danger.

* * *

It was too late. The foremost of the skaven had already reached the tower. As the first ratman leapt from the sand bar to the crumbling face of the island, a shadowy figure shambled out of the darkness inside the tower. It looked something like a human, but its clothes were nothing but shreds of cloth hanging from starved bones. The skin was green with rot, blistered and split by the jungle heat. Spots of bone protruded from the decaying flesh and maggots crawled in what little meat remained. Beneath the tattered remains of a captain's hat, a desiccated skull glared at the ratmen.

One of the gutter runners squeaked in terror as he saw the apparition, scrabbling backwards in such haste that he stumbled into the scummy water. The other gutter runner bared his fangs and hurled a pair of knives into the approaching human. The blades sank deep into the man's chest, transfixing his heart. The man didn't even seem to feel their impact, but took another shambling step towards the gutter runner.

Now terrified like his comrade, the ratkin turned to flee. But as he did so, a rotten fist exploded from the ground beneath him and seized his foot in a cruel grip. The gutter runner writhed in agony, hacking desperately at the imprisoning hand. Though fingers snapped beneath his blade, the hand refused to release him. The skaven wailed, pleading with his kin for help. Too late he saw the rotten shadow of the captain fall across him. The mouldering zombie raised the rusty cutlass it carried and brought it slashing down.

Screams echoed throughout the swamp. Other zombies were now pulling themselves free from the muck, groping in mute malevolence for any skaven near them. The skaven recoiled from the frightful things, horrified at their inability to kill creatures that were already dead. Several gutter runners fell beneath the groping claws of the zombies, their shrieks rising to deafening squeals as they were slowly ripped apart. One assassin, his black cloak billowing about him, tried to fight his way back to the tower, thinking to slay the captain. Every thrust of his poisoned knives struck home, yet none of his victims fell. The zombies soon surrounded the lone assassin. In a fit of horror, the cloaked killer sliced his dagger across his own neck rather than fall to the claws of the undead.

A black whirlwind crackled into the rotten ranks of the undead, exploding a dozen of the zombies into putrid fragments. Shen Tsinge and Goji came rushing to the sand bar where Shiwan and most of his warriors were trapped. The sorcerer gestured with his staff again, howling magic exploding from it to strike down another mob of the creatures.

'Flee-flee! Quick-quick!' Shen hissed at the master assassin.

Shiwan's eyes darted longingly to the jungle, but he lashed his tail and stared instead at the map in his hand. 'Use magic!' he snarled at the sorcerer. 'Keep dead-things back-back!'

Something like terror filled Shen's glands, but when he saw the cruel intensity in Shiwan's eyes, he knew any argument would be fatal. Drawing a warpstone charm from the tip of his staff, the sorcerer nibbled a sliver from it. He felt the invigorating rush of power swell through his veins. He shut his eyes. When he opened them again, they were black pits of power. Snarling, he swept his hand through the air before him. Black wisps of energy shot from his fingers to shatter the decayed heads of a half-dozen zombies. The sorcerer snarled and tightened his hold on the staff. A second burst of dark power and more zombies were broken, their fragments sinking beneath the slime of the swamp.

Shiwan Stalkscent wiped his snout and eagerly pointed with his claw to the north. Bullying and threatening, Kong brought his warriors into a semblance of formation. With the threat of their leader's glaive at their back, the clanrats were herded towards the mob of zombies blocking them from the jungle. Frenziedly, the masses of skaven hacked their way through the eerily silent undead. Slowly, but deliberately, they began to carve their way through the horde.

Exhausted by his exertions and the noxious influence of the warpstone he had so hastily consumed, Shen Tsinge slumped into the arms of his bodyguard. Cradling his master in the crook of one arm, the hulking Goji loped after the retreating expedition, his huge claws shearing through the few zombies standing between him and Shiwan's rearguard.

Grey Seer Thanquol blinked in disbelief as he saw Shiwan's ratmen fleeing the swamp. It was not so much that they had been driven off by the zombies – he'd expected that much. It was the fact that they were making their escape on the wrong side of the swamp that incensed him. He'd expected them to come back, not press forward!

The jungle seemed to press in all around Thanquol as the scent of his fellow skaven began to grow more faint. The swamp was still alive with zombies, the vile things surrounding and slaughtering the stragglers Shiwan had abandoned. It was a hideous sight, made even more gruesome by the way the crocodiles slid into the water to snatch up the floating bits of meat the zombies left behind. Thanquol considered himself a valiant skaven, afraid of very little, but to end up in the belly of some scaly monstrosity was one of his pet horrors.

Thanquol lashed his tail and ground his fangs. The smell of Shiwan's retreating column was just a feeble hint in the air. If he didn't want to lose them, he had to move fast. His heart was already thundering in his chest, the terror of being alone flooding through his mind. Desperate, he drew his sword and tightened his grip on his staff. Hissing a hasty, but most sincere, prayer to the Horned Rat, Thanquol rushed out into the swamp.

The sand, now slimy with skaven blood and the stagnant fluids of the zombies, proved treacherous under Thanquol's feet as he scurried along the sand bars to catch up with Shiwan's ratmen. To either side, the waters of the swamp were alive with crocodiles, the huge reptiles churning the water in their brute hunger. They were careful to keep away from the zombies, however, and it was with a sinking sensation in his stomach that Thanquol watched the walking cadavers closing upon him.

Briefly, Thanquol contemplated blasting his way through the shambling corpses. For a petty mage-rat, Shen Tsinge had exhibited an impressive amount of power. Not that Thanquol couldn't do far better, even on his worst day. Still, the effort had taxed Shen terribly, leaving him to be carried off by his rat ogre. Perhaps it would be best not to indulge in any excessive display of his own magical ability. Making a quick count of the zombies still rising from the muck and mud, Thanquol decided against drawing on his powers. The undead tended to fixate on sources of magic.

Spinning about, Thanquol sprinted across the sand bar, throwing his body forwards at the first gap. He landed in a crouch, the impact almost jarring the sword from his hand. He grimaced at the hungry crocodile staring at him from the muck he had jumped over, then scurried quickly away from the gruesome creature.

Distracted by the crocodile, Thanquol almost didn't see the zombies until he was right in the middle of them. When he turned away from the frustrated reptile, Thanquol found a rotting human face smiling at him, worms spilling from its eye socket. The grey seer shrieked and ducked the club-like swing of the zombie's arm. He brought his sword chopping around, cutting through the zombie's leg just above its ankle. His staff cracked against the undead pirate's waist, spilling it into the scummy water.

Before he could appreciate dispatching his foe, Thanquol found five more zombies staggering towards him like a wall of flesh. The grey seer backed away, cringing when the undead refused to be cowed by the threat of his sword. In a panic, he tongued the nugget of warpstone out of his cheek pouch. The temptation to draw on its power to annihilate the zombies was almost overwhelming, but the knowledge that to do so would draw the attention of every undead thing in the swamp tempered his despair.

Thanquol backed away from the advancing zombies until he felt his heels hanging over emptiness. Frantically he darted forward, lifting his tail just in time to escape the snapping jaws of the crocodile. Between the zombies and the reptile, the grey seer found himself backed into a corner.

While there is even the slightest possibility of escape, a skaven will make every effort to save his skin. It is when there is no hope of escape that a fearsome fury comes upon them, a berserk madness that roars through their brains. Thanquol felt the desperate, instinctive madness seize him. His fangs grinding together, he drove into the approaching zombies with the mindless savagery of an orc warlord. The first zombie staggered from a blow of his sword that sent its forearm flying through the air. The second he caught upon the shoulder with the head of his staff, using it to tug the creature forwards and send it tumbling into the jaws of the crocodile. After that, all became a red haze of fear-crazed frenzy. When it cleared, Thanquol stood panting twenty yards from where he had started, his path strewn with mangled, mutilated bodies.

Grey Seer Thanquol took two great gulps of air. The scent of the other skaven was quickly fading – soon it would be lost completely. There wasn't time to gloat over the havoc he had caused, or even to praise the Horned Rat for whatever slight role he might have had in Thanquol's escape. Terrified at being left behind, Thanquol braced himself for another desperate gauntlet across the sand bars.

Before he took his first step, the sand at his feet exploded upwards. At first he thought it was another zombie, and that mistake almost proved his undoing. Thanquol reared back, stabbing his sword at his attacker. With distinctly un-zombielike speed, the cloaked ambusher darted to the side and brought a dripping dagger slashing at him. The poisonous blade crunched into Thanquol's staff, missing his flesh by a matter of inches.

'Die-die, murder-meat!' the assassin chittered, struggling to free his trapped blade. Thanquol swung at him with his sword, at the same time relaxing his grip on his staff.

The staff smacked into the assassin's snout with an impact that cracked fangs and sent a spray of black blood exploding from his nose. Thanquol's sword chopped down at the stunned assassin, hacking the black-furred ear from the side of his head. Before the grey seer could exploit the reversal, the assassin's clawed foot smashed into his chest, knocking him back and almost pitching him into the swamp. Only by planting the butt of his staff in the loose sand was he able to save himself from hurtling into the scummy water.

Fangs bared, the assassin snarled back at him. The killer didn't try to use his dagger again, but instead drew a pair of throwing stars from his belt. 'Think-think of Chang Squik before you die-die!'

Thanquol grinned back at the assassin. The killer never had the chance to throw the deadly shuriken. Instead, dead claws seized his legs. The more intact pieces of Thanquol's defeated enemies had been crawling steadily after him. Now the mangled zombies closed upon the assassin. The cloaked killer squeaked in horror as the zombie began to pull itself up his body, its entrails dangling from where Thanquol had cut it in half. A second zombie followed the first, closing a wormy hand around the assassin's shoulder.

Twisting and shrieking, the assassin tried to escape the relentless grip of his attackers, only to find his feet slipping on the sand. A dreadful wail rose from the assassin as both he and the zombies gripping him pitched headlong over the edge of the sand bar and splashed into the swamp. Immediately several crocodiles converged on the commotion.

Thanquol wished the reptiles a full supper.

CHAPTER SIX

A Lost World

'KHAINE'S BLACK HELLS!'

Captain Schachter's shout awakened everyone in the small camp on the beach. Men stumbled from sailcloth tents, cutlasses and bludgeons clenched in their fists. Adalwolf wiped sleep from his eyes and shrugged into his armoured vest. The chainmail felt uncomfortable against his bare skin, but the mercenary could think of many things that would feel even worse.

Schachter stood a few paces from the smoking remains of the great bonfire at the centre of the camp. For once, the sea captain's face was devoid of the ruddy glow of alcohol. His ashen features were twisted in horror, his hand trembling as he pointed at something jutting up from the pile of ashes.

Adalwolf felt his blood run cold as he looked at the thing that had so terrified the captain. He heard sailors grow sick behind him.

'Handrich's Purse!' snarled the imperious voice of van Sommerhaus. The patroon was fumbling at the buckles of his coat as he stormed out from his lean-to. Wrapped in a coarse ship's blanket, Hiltrude demurely followed after the furious merchant. 'What's all this about, Schachter? Don't you know better than to disturb my morning libations?'

The patroon stifled a gasp and pressed a gloved hand to his mouth as he saw the grisly thing that had captured the attention of the entire camp. Hiltrude gave voice to a shriek, then collapsed against the sand in a faint.

The thing rising from the ashes was a crude wooden pole, roughly the height of a man. A clutch of bright parrot feathers was bound to the thing's top, swaying in the tepid morning breeze like the fronds of a palm. Nestled among the feathers were three grotesque things that reminded Adalwolf of the sleeping bats they had seen in the jungle. Like rotten fruit, the fist-sized things drooped from the pole, but these were fruit with ghastly, shrivelled faces!

Marjus Pfaff was the first man to work up the nerve to close upon the ghastly pole. He squinted as he stared at the tortured, wrinkly faces. They were bound to the pole by their hair, which had been pulled back in a long knot to leave the horrible faces exposed. Each was darkened to the colour of old leather, lips and eyes sewn shut. Yet there was an uncomfortable sense of familiarity about the things, for all their diminutive size.

Marjus jostled one of the grisly things with the tip of his cutlass. The shrunken head rolled with the motion, displaying for all the long, pointed ear clinging to the side of the shrivelled skull. It was no human ear, but that of an elf.

'Ethril!' Adalwolf shuddered. Now that the connection was made, he could see the semblance of the asur wanderer on the withered husk.

'The others will be the sentries you posted last night,' Marjus said, spitting into the sand and making the sign of Manann. A quick call of the sailors on the beach confirmed the mate's suspicions.

'Who could have done this?' wondered van Sommerhaus when he'd finally managed to compose himself and assume some small measure of his arrogance.

Captain Schachter scratched at the stubble of beard growing on his chin. 'I've heard tales of cannibal halflings that live in the jungle, and stories of Amazons that would as soon skin a man as bed him.'

Adalwolf shook his head. 'It doesn't matter who did this,' he told Schachter. 'What does matter is the message they're sending. It wasn't enough for them to just kill Ethril and the guards. They made a point of telling us what they did. They crept into the very centre of camp and put this... this... horror right here with us all sleeping around it!'

'They're saying they can come back and do the same any time they like,' Schachter hissed in a frightened whisper. The eyes of every man on the beach turned towards the jungle, wondering what might be staring back at them.

'We're someplace somebody doesn't want us,' Adalwolf said. He gestured at the hideous totem again. 'This is their way of telling us we should be moving on.'

THE SURVIVORS OF the *Cobra of Khemri* debated for an hour over what to do. It was clear that they could not stay with the wreck of the ship. They had no way of knowing how numerous their unseen enemy was. Just because they hadn't wiped the entire camp out the night before, Diethelm argued, did not mean they weren't able to do so. The priest thought their best course of action was to build a raft from the wreck and set back out upon the open water, trusting in the grace of Manann to spirit them away from this unholy shore.

Adalwolf and Schachter supported a more sensible course. From Ethril's words, they knew there was an elf settlement somewhere on the southern tip of Lustria. How far south was any man's guess, but at least it was something to strive for. Whether the elves would receive them now that they had lost Ethril was a disturbing question neither of them could answer.

It was van Sommerhaus who proposed a third option. There was the trail they had found in the jungle. Clearly it led somewhere, somewhere big. Sailors' stories of lost cities of gold hidden in the jungle were tempered by the practical observation that any city would have the resources close at hand to support it. Even if they found nothing but a deserted ruin, there would be fresh water and feral crops to be had. They could fortify themselves, use the ruins for shelter and plan their next move at leisure without the threat of headhunters and starvation hanging over them. If they indulged in a little treasure hunting while they were at it – well, that could hardly be countenanced an ill thing.

The crew might have rejected the patroon's arguments had Marjus Pfaff not intervened. The mate had taken it upon himself to knock down the totem and bury the sad remains bound to it. He had been quite cagey at the time, uncharacteristically refusing all offers to help him in the morbid labour. Now he reluctantly showed everyone the reason behind his craft. The feathers and shrunken heads had been bound to the pole with loops of wire – golden wire!

Gold! Even in the midst of their fear, the men could feel its allure. Coils of finely wrought gold far beyond the skills of headhunting savages. Treasure that the savages could only have bartered or stolen from the city beyond the jungle. The city that must lie at the end of the trail they had found!

Despair and fear had been the only emotions the crew had shown since the discovery of the shrunken heads. Now a cruel sort of hope flared up within their hearts: the blind, unreasoning hope that is born of greed.

The vote was taken again. This time, even Captain Schachter backed van Sommerhaus. Only Adalwolf and Diethelm tried to argue against such a reckless course. The priest tried to invoke the power of his god, warning that the further they strayed from the sea, the farther they were from Manann's protection. Adalwolf tried a more practical course, trying to make the men see reason. If they were worried about a cold reception from the elves far to the south, how much more foolish was it to think they would be welcomed by whatever strange denizens had built the city they hoped to find? He reminded them of stories of lizards that walked like men and who delighted in sacrificing the beating hearts of their enemies to their strange devil-gods. He told them of the many dangers the jungle held, and all the other dangers they would be ignorant of now that Ethril was gone.

'We've small chance enough', Captain Schachter decided. 'Whichever way we turn, we're likely to die in this damn place. All things being equal, I'd rather take my chances where there might just be a pot of gold waiting for me at the end of the journey.'

The captain's sentiment quelled the last misgivings of the crew. Adalwolf looked for any of them to stand by him, but even Hiltrude voted to take the jungle trail. He stared hard at her when she cast her vote, essentially parroting van Sommerhaus. The courtesan looked away, a guilty flush tingeing her cheeks.

'If this is your decision,' Adalwolf said, casting his eyes across the crew, letting his gaze linger on the smirking face of van Sommerhaus, 'then I'll help you try to see it through. Not because I think it's right, but because I don't want to die alone in this place.' The mercenary stared at the imposing edge of the jungle.

'I'll die much easier with an audience,' he said grimly.

* * *

COLD, UNBLINKING EYES watched as the ragged survivors of the *Cobra of Khemri* gathered what supplies they could carry and began to march into the jungle. None of the warm-things so much as glanced in the direction of the chameleon skinks, little guessing that the killers of Ethril and the sentries were so near at hand.

The shifting hues of their scales allowed the skinks to creep right up to the edge of the camp. They listened to the curious chirps and squawks the warm-things uttered, cocking their scaly heads in curiosity as they watched the robed magic-thing mutter sounds over several barrels of sea water. If the skinks had been like men they might have laughed as the smell of brine left the water. It was not the paltry display of magic that interested the skinks, but rather the grave solemnity with which the warm-thing worked his spell. They had seen their own priests accomplish similar feats, but with far more practicality.

The sentinels watched as the warm-things made a strange little platform of flat wood and fitted a long length of rope to one end. Upon this they set the barrels and before it, they placed the two biggest members of their tribe. When they set out, the big ones dragged the little platform behind them. The skinks watched the operation in fascination, wondering why the warm-things expended so much effort. Did they not know they could just lick water from the leaves each morning when the rains came?

If the skinks had been like men, they might have questioned the reasons they had been dispatched by mighty Lord Tlaco to herd these strange creatures into the jungle and see that they followed the trail the slann had made for them. But the skinks were not men and the thought of questioning a mage-priest was as alien to them as their jungle world was to the humans.

So they sat and watched and waited, enjoying the sun that warmed their scaly bodies. The skinks kept their blowguns ready in their strange mitten-like hands. If the warm-things came back, they would make another totem to encourage them to follow Lord Tlaco's path.

THEY FOUND THE path much easier than on their first excursion into the jungle. Van Sommerhaus said it was because they had already chopped a path through the tangle of bushes and hanging vines. Even the jungles of Lustria, the patroon argued, were not so fecund as to efface a trail over the course of a single night.

Adalwolf was not so sure. There was something wrong. Nothing he could put into words, just a cold feeling at the back of his neck. He wondered what Ethril, with his elven wisdom, might have sensed. The jungle didn't feel right, not like a natural place. It was almost like sneaking through someone's house while they were away.

No, that wasn't quite right. Something knew they were here. He could feel it watching them, watching them with a calculating regard that was chilling in its indifference. Even the bloodlust of headhunters would have been preferable to that cold emotionless scrutiny. At least that would have been something Adalwolf could understand.

It was much as before, the path through the jungle, like a great tunnel bored through the trees. Not a vine, not a bush or blade of grass disturbed the path. Upon the ground was only the barren earth, overhead the trees and vines formed an archway fifty feet above their heads, not so much as a leaf dangling beneath that point. To even think for a moment that any natural artifice could have created such a path was absurd. Considering the enormity of the magic that must have been involved made Adalwolf think not in terms of wizards, but of gods.

'We made excellent time,' van Sommerhaus declared, breaking the awed silence that had fallen over them all. He puffed himself up, nodding as he studied the terrain. 'I told you we would have no problem finding it again.'

Adalwolf repressed a shudder. 'We didn't find it,' he corrected the patroon. 'It found us.'

'Not that mystic mumbo-jumbo of the elf again,' scoffed van Sommerhaus. He gestured impatiently at the broad path before them. 'The path is here. It's as real as I am. This is no phantom of a feverish imagination! We made good time, that's why you think it's closer than before.'

The sailors looked uncertain, their superstitious dread rising to the fore again. Marjus tried to bring the men back in line, striking those who dared speak their fears.

Adalwolf pointed at the path ahead and made an observation that sent pure terror flooding through the crew. 'If this is the same path, where are Joost's bones?'

Van Sommerhaus bristled at the question. He stared at the ground for a moment, then shrugged. 'Maybe those lizards ate him right down to the marrow,' he suggested. 'Or maybe a jaguar came along and carried off whatever the lizards left. Yes, that sounds possible enough.'

'And afterwards the cat came back with an Imperial steam tank and dragged away the tree,' Adalwolf's voice was as thin as a knife. He saw the confusion on the patroon's face. To emphasise his point, he swept his hand across the trail they had cut the previous day. 'Where's the tree? You remember, that last tree that came crashing down and nearly killed Ethril?'

The patroon tried to sputter some sort of answer, but even his inventive mind could not think of anything to explain away the undeniable fact that the tree was gone.

This last proof of sorcery was too much for the crew. Even the threats of Schachter and Marjus couldn't hold them now. They turned, intent on retreating back to the beach. In the face of this evidence that the jungle's magic wasn't ancient and placid but active and aware, the promise of gold lost its lure. They were afraid of the headhunters, but they were terrified of the jungle.

Quickly, they had new reason to fear.

The foremost of the retreating sailors had not gone far when he made a sinister discovery. The trail they had cut the previous day was overgrown again, overgrown with great bloated green plants with fleshy yellow flowers. They were ghastly looking things and the impossibility of their existence sent every man's skin crawling. Yet such was their determination to escape the jungle that the sailors soon overcame their trepidation. Boldly they stalked towards the growth, intent upon cutting it down with their axes and swords.

As the first sailor raised his arm to strike one of the plants, ropy vines shot out from the fleshy stalk, coiling about him like the arms of a kraken. The man shrieked as the tendrils pulled him towards the main body of the plant. Now the true nature of the yellow flowers was revealed. They folded inwards upon themselves, each petal as hard and unyielding as a fang. The flower snapped open and closed, like a hungry dog licking its chops.

Adalwolf rushed forwards to help the men trying to free the trapped sailor. Other tendrils shot towards them, wrapping around arms and legs, trying to drag the men back towards the plants further back along the trail. Adalwolf had known a Tilean who had kept a pet python – the strength of the tendrils put that powerful serpent to shame. He could swear he felt his very bones being rubbed raw as the vine about his leg tightened and tried to pull him off his feet. Desperately he brought the edge of his sword chopping down into the tendril. It bit halfway through the ropey plant fibre but no farther, forcing him to saw his sword free by working the blade back and forth.

When his leg was free again, Adalwolf limped over to help a sailor with vines coiled about both of his arms. Those seamen who had not been caught by the plants rushed to help their trapped crewmen. Captain Schachter tried to fend off the tendrils with a marlin pike, the only long weapon they had among them, while Marjus used his great strength to drag freed sailors from where the plants could reach them. Even Hiltrude and Diethelm lent their aid to the cause, chopping sailors free with the knives they carried. Adalwolf glanced once to where van Sommerhaus stood upon the path, frozen with horror.

New screams told the fate of the sailor who had first fallen into the clutches of the plants. Unable to get near enough to free him, they could only watch as he was pulled remorselessly towards the snapping flowers. One closed upon his outstretched arm and an agonised wail erupted from the seaman. Bubbling foam oozed from the folds of the flower. The man struggled furiously for several minutes, then managed to pull away from the flower. His shrieks became even more frantic when he stared at his arm. There was nothing left beyond the elbow; it had been dissolved in the maw of the plant. No simple weeds, these, but carnivorous monsters of the jungle!

Freed from the first flower by his efforts, the tendrils wrapped about the man began to pull at him again, dragging him to a second snapping maw.

Tears were in Captain Schachter's eyes as he pulled one of the pistols he carried and aimed it at his man. When the hammer fell, however, no shot came. The damp of the jungle had fouled the powder. Marjus Pfaff rounded on van Sommerhaus, ripping one of the engraved duelling pistols he carried from his belt.

The patroon started to protest, more from reflex than thought. The mate's fist smashed into his face and spilled van Sommerhaus on the ground.

Grimly, Marjus took aim and fired. Preserved by the jewelled holster of the patroon, the pistol discharged with a burst of smoke and flame. The screaming man in the coils of the carnivorous plant fell silent just before a flower snapped closed about his hip.

Like whipped dogs, the rest of the crew retreated from the deadly plants. Brother Diethelm commended the soul of the dead sailor to the keeping of Manann and Morr while the rest of them watched the flowers take their grisly share of the man's flesh.

'Make torches,' Schachter growled vengefully. 'We'll burn that filth into ash!'

Hiltrude caught at the captain's arm. 'We can't do that!' she said, her eyes wide with a different kind of fear. 'If you set fire to them, what's to keep the flames from coming back and getting us!'

The woman's fears had a sobering effect on the captain. 'Belay that order!' he snapped. A string of vivid curses shot from his mouth as he glared at the plants.

'It wouldn't do any good,' Diethelm told him as he finished his prayers. 'There is some infernal power in those things, something even fire might not be able to purify.'

While he spoke, the priest indicated one of the ghastly flowers. An ugly blue seed the size of a man's thumb dropped from the flower. Upon striking the ground, it instantly took root, as though some invisible hand were pushing it into the earth. In a matter of moments, a green shoot sprouted. A few minutes, and the plant was already half the size of its sire.

'We can't fight that,' Adalwolf growled.

'Then what are we supposed to do?' demanded Schachter.

Adalwolf didn't answer the captain, instead staring at the trail ahead. Schachter cursed lividly. The trail ahead was likewise alive with the hideous plants.

The mercenary turned and pointed at the eerie pathway through the jungle. 'Something wants us to go this way,' he told Schachter. 'And it won't take no for an answer.'

Schachter fingered the grip of his useless pistol. 'Where do you think it goes?' he whispered.

'Maybe to van Sommerhaus's city of gold,' Adalwolf answered, glancing at the patroon as Hiltrude helped him off the ground. He quickly looked away.

'Somehow I doubt it,' Schachter said.

THE FOETID ATMOSPHERE of the jungle was a damp heat that oppressed the lungs of the small band of intruders. Whatever power had set them upon the strange path had cleared the way for them but seemed oblivious to the inhospitable nature of the heat and humidity. Perhaps these were things beyond its power, or perhaps it was in such an atmosphere that these unseen powers thrived.

Adalwolf could not be certain, he only knew that the strange tunnel through the trees had been laid out for a purpose. What that purpose was, he could not begin to guess.

Animals seemed to shun the strange path for the most part. At first this was counted as a blessing, the memory of the cannibal lizards and Joost's terrible death still fresh in their minds. However, it quickly became obvious they would need to supplement the stores they had salvaged from the ship with fresh meat and whatever fruit they could find. To do so meant leaving the path and each of these excursions into the jungle bordering it was fraught with peril. Quicksand nearly sucked down an entire hunting party while a second came back short two men after encountering something they could only describe as a beaked bat-snake. The most hideous event of all happened to a grizzled sailor named Dirck who investigated a curious wailing sound emanating from beside the path. He discovered a little group of tiny red frogs with mottled markings. Thinking their legs would make good eating, he caught one. As soon as the frog was in his hand, however, it gave voice to another terrified wailing sound. Its slimy body began to excrete a vile brown mucus that sizzled as it touched the sailor's skin. By the time he threw the frog away, the acidic mucus had eaten clean through his hand, finger bones standing exposed in the corroded flesh. Infection, sickness and delirium had been his fate after that. When he did finally die, it seemed almost a blessing to his comrades.

Lustria. Well had those who dared its jungles named it the Green Hell.

Adalwolf scowled at a scaly, monkey-like thing perched in one of the fern-like trees. The lizard simply stared back at him, sometimes closing one eye, then the other, as though to make sure both were seeing the same thing.

The column came to a halt. Men with flagons in their hands came jogging back to the water barrels, filling their mugs. Most of the men slumped to the earth beside the sledge, greedily drinking their fill. A few jogged back to the head of the column, where they handed their cups to van Sommerhaus, who in turn pressed a few coins into their outstretched palms. Even in their current circumstances, the fading wealth of the patroon commanded respect.

Adalwolf was surprised when he saw Hiltrude turn away from the water barrels and walk in his direction instead of returning to the patroon's side. She smiled at him and offered him the silver cup she was carrying. The mercenary studied the delicately engraved cup for a moment, then handed it back to the woman.

'I'm afraid taking a drink from that would leave a bad taste in my mouth,' he told her.

Hiltrude shrugged and took a sip of water. She glanced around, then smoothed her tattered dress before sitting down on a big grey rock at the edge of the path. She smiled sadly as she felt the ragged, torn shambles of her once fine clothes.

'Don't worry, he'll buy you a new one,' Adalwolf assured her.

Fire flashed in Hiltrude's eyes. 'He didn't buy it. I bought it, if you must know.'

'I'll bet he still paid for it,' the mercenary grumbled.

'And who paid for your armour and your sword?' Hiltrude snarled back. 'If you think I'm a whore for taking his money, what does that make you?'

'It's different for me,' Adalwolf said, uncomfortable with the turn the conversation had taken.

Hiltrude cocked an eyebrow at him. 'Why? Because you're a man? Because it's right for a man to take money from someone he despises, but when a woman does, it makes her cheap and wanton?'

'I'm not selling my body to him!'

The courtesan snorted with bitter amusement. 'Aren't you? He pays you to fight his enemies and protect his ships. He expects you to get in the way of swords and axes – and ill-tempered plants! You're right, that's not selling your body. That's selling your life!' She shook her head, an arrogant expression on her face. 'Even I haven't sunk that low.'

Adalwolf shifted uncomfortably. He hadn't expected Hiltrude to defend her relationship with van Sommerhaus by challenging his own. 'I have a family depending on me back in Marienburg. That's why I do it,' he said in a quiet voice.

'I don't have even that,' Hiltrude said. 'My family died when I was almost too young to remember them. There was a pox in the neighbourhood and the plague doctors tried to burn down the infected houses. The fire got away from them. Three streets ended up burning to the ground.' She stared sadly at nothing, her cheeks trembling as she remembered the distant tragedy. 'Ever since then, I've had to make my own way as best I can.'

Adalwolf stepped towards her. 'Hiltrude…' he said in a soft voice. Then the mercenary's eyes became hard again. 'Hiltrude… don't move,' he ordered.

It was on the courtesan's lips to object to being ordered around by the mercenary, but the intensity of his expression and tone made her do as she was told. Carefully, she turned her head to follow the direction of the warrior's gaze. A short gasp escaped through her lips as she saw the thing that had slithered onto the rock beside her, warming itself in the light. It was like a thin belt of scaly leather, banded from tip to end in alternating rings of crimson, yellow and black. A blue tongue darted from its little snub of a head, tasting the air with little trembles of its forked tip.

'Don't move,' Adalwolf whispered again as Hiltrude leaned away from the jungle snake. He could see her shivering, every muscle in her body quivering with horror at the thing sitting beside her. Slowly, Adalwolf drew his sword.

The blade had not cleared its scabbard before a strong grip restrained his hand. Adalwolf found Brother Diethelm standing beside him, the priest's hand closed around his own. 'Not that way,' Diethelm advised. 'Fast as you might be, the snake might be even faster. There is another way.'

Perplexed, Adalwolf watched as the priest knelt down before the snake. The reptile fixed its black eyes on him, watching his every move. Diethelm began to murmur softly into his beard, his body swaying slightly from side to side. The ophidian head followed his motion, slowly swinging from one side to another. Gradually, the priest began to crawl towards the snake, still swaying back and forth as he did so. The snake's eyes never left Diethelm.

'Hiltrude,' the priest said softly. 'Move away from our little friend. It is quite safe, so long as you do not touch him.'

The woman quickly leapt away from the stone, clinging to Adalwolf's side. Together they watched as the priest closed the last few feet between himself and the snake. Casually, almost without apparent thought, Diethelm lifted his hand and tapped the snake's head. 'Go away,' he told it. To their amazement, instead of biting him, the serpent turned and slithered back into the jungle.

'How did you do that?' Adalwolf asked. 'I thought your powers relied upon the sea?'

Diethelm brushed dirt and leaves from his robes and nodded. 'Indeed, my connection to mighty Manann is feeble here, so far from the ocean. I can only faintly feel his presence in this place, for it is a land removed from the gods we know. To call upon Manann's strength here would be a fruitless effort.'

'Then how were you able to tame the serpent?' Hiltrude wondered.

The priest smiled. 'Do not think I have journeyed upon the seas for most of my life without learning a few tricks of my own. There are mystics in Araby who specialise in mesmerising snakes. They use them to clear rats from their homes in that arid land, you know. Once, when I was aboard an Estalian galleon, we made port in Copher. It was there I learned the skill.' Diethelm flushed with embarrassment. 'I admit, I only learned it because I thought it would allow me to charm eels. Try as I might, however, I've never been able to get a snake-fish to stare me in the eye long enough to get it to work.'

SEVEN DAYS OF marching along the path and the travellers came upon a strange sight. Previously, the jungle had bordered the strange pathway like a great wall of green. Indeed, they had been forced to cut and chop their way through to hunt and gather fruit.

Now they came upon an enormous gash in the wall, a giant hole where something huge had torn its way through the jungle. The bare earth of the path was scarred and pitted where mammoth claws had gouged the ground. There was a coppery tang in the air and with it the heavy musk of reptiles.

The men eyed the torn ground with fright, horrified by the size of the clawed footprints they saw. A fearful murmur passed among the crew, some of the men starting to edge back down the path.

'What do we do?' Schachter asked van Sommerhaus. After the incident with the carnivorous plants, the patroon had been forced to become quite liberal with his money to return to the good graces of the captain and his crew. Few of the sailors did not hold a scrip to be drawn from the van Sommerhaus coffers upon their return to Marienburg.

Van Sommerhaus considered the torn ground, then cast a nervous eye on the hole gouged through the trees. He stroked the soggy ruffles of his shirt as he considered the question. 'This might have happened any time,' he decided. 'Whatever did this could be leagues away by now. I say we stick to the path.'

'And what if you're wrong?' challenged Marjus. 'What if this thing is still lurking around here someplace?'

'More reason to stay on the path,' Adalwolf interjected. 'Our only other course is to take to the jungle. I don't know about you, but I'd prefer to face this thing out in the open where I can at least see it coming.'

It was hardly a reassuring sentiment, but it did quiet the grumblings of Marjus and the others. The tired men set out again, trudging across the broken ground, avoiding the shattered trees that had been cast down by the giant's passage. Everyone helped lift the sledge and the remaining barrels of water over the worst of the debris. It was hot, back-breaking work for the weakened crew and demanded all of their attention.

Perhaps that was why no one could say when the ghastly crunching noises began. They seemed to manifest out of nowhere as the sailors set down the last of the barrels. The sounds were gruesome, slobbering noises, like a dog nuzzling its nose in a pile of offal. Everyone stopped and listened for a time, trying to fix the sounds in their mind. But though they grew louder, the deceit of the jungle and its echoes made it impossible to say from which direction they came.

'I'm not sticking around here to find out what's making that!' exclaimed one of the sailors. The man dashed off, racing around the bend in the path ahead. Others quickly followed his example, van Sommerhaus among them as the infectious fear claimed him. Schachter called his men back, but they were beyond listening to him. Reluctantly, those who had stayed behind took up the chase, knowing that their only hope of survival lay in keeping together.

The fleeing sailors did not go far. They froze as they rounded the bend in the path, colour draining from their faces, their hearts hammering against their chests. Fleeing from the ghastly noises, the men had instead discovered their source.

Gigantic, bigger than a burgher's town house, the creature stood in the path, its scaly back glistening in the sun. In shape it was something like a plucked hawk, though with little clawed arms instead of wings. By contrast its legs were immense, thicker around than a ship's mainmast and powerfully muscled. The claws that tipped the thing's feet were huge, bigger than halberds. A thick tail, easily as long as the *Cobra of Khemri*'s hull, slashed through the air behind the creature, balancing its giant body. The head was monstrous, heavy like the skull of a bulldog and supported by a short, broad neck. The thing's face was squashed like that of a toad, and its mouth was a great gash beneath the tiny slits of its nostrils and the amber pits of its eyes. Enormous fangs, each more like a sword than a tooth, filled the monster's maw. In colour, it was a dull green striped with brown and possessing a distinct diamond pattern of orange scales running along its back. About its jaws, the scaly skin was painted red and from its fangs long ribbons of gore dangled.

Beneath the titanic reptile sprawled a behemoth even larger than itself. It was built not unlike an

Arabyan elephant, but far more massive and covered in scaly hide rather than leathery skin. The head attached to the giant's long neck seemed too small in proportion to its immense body and the teeth that filled its jaws were dull and flat, not unlike those of a cow. A great wound gaped in the beast's neck, and here its throat had been crushed almost flat by the pressure of powerful jaws.

The great predator-lizard pressed its snout into the yawning hole it had chewed into the belly of the behemoth. Noisily, it worked its jaws to rip bloody slivers of flesh from the carcass.

Suddenly, the towering lizard-monster turned, its eyes narrowed, its fat pale tongue licking at the air. The men stood transfixed as the immense creature stared at them. No man moved, each desperately hoping the monster's attention would fix on one of his comrades.

Van Sommerhaus croaked in horror as he felt the carnosaur's eyes studying him. The sudden sound aroused the monster and the giant lizard-beast reared back. Men screamed and turned to run, casting aside their weapons in their horror.

Instead of attacking, the huge reptile sank its jaws into the neck of the dead thunder lizard and dragged the carcass a dozen yards down the path. Soon it was again tearing strips of meat from the carcass.

'I think he's afraid you're going to steal his dinner,' Adalwolf laughed, clapping van Sommerhaus on the back. The patroon bristled at his humour and pulled away, glaring daggers at the mercenary.

The humour, however, had the desired effect on the other men. Gradually the sailors came back, retrieving their weapons from the ground. They pointed at the feeding monster and joked nervously among themselves at both their fear and the beast's timidity. The sound of their laughter disturbed the carnosaur. Sinking its fangs into the carcass, the huge reptile dragged its kill closer to the jungle.

Abruptly the huge predator moved again, this time dragging its prey away from the edge of the jungle. It glared at the trees, ignoring completely the puzzled men watching it.

The reason for the carnosaur's actions quickly showed themselves. A half-dozen lean, scaly creatures hopped out from among the trees. In shape they were not unlike the carnosaur, though their arms were not quite as scrawny and their legs were far less muscled. The creatures were deep blue in colour with mottled black markings running along their sides. The reptiles circled the carnosaur and its kill. Whenever the big beast focused on one of them, others would dart in and try to rip shreds of meat from the carcass. Always the bigger monster was too quick for the smaller ones and they leapt away as the carnosaur's huge jaws snapped at them.

'Like jackals annoying a lion,' Adalwolf observed.

Hiltrude shuddered at his observation. 'Even those jackals are bigger than we are,' she warned him. Adalwolf nodded grimly and turned to advise Schachter that they should be moving on.

Even as the group began to carefully make their way around the quarrelling reptiles, disaster came upon them. The sledge carrying the water became caught against the projecting root of a mangrove. In trying to force the sledge forward, the men pulling it upset one of the barrels, which toppled and crashed to the ground.

The sound upset the reptiles. The jackal-lizards and the carnosaur swung their heads around, staring at the retreating humans. The big predator-lizard again sank his jaws into the behemoth's neck and began to drag its kill away. The smaller scavengers, however, became tense, their fleshy tongues licking the air.

When the cold ones came, they came at once in a hissing, snarling pack. The men with the sledge made a last futile effort to free it, then threw down the ropes and started to run. They were too slow. Leaping at them, pouncing on them like leopards upon sheep, two of the cold ones smashed them against the ground. Piteous screams rose from the sailors as the reptiles began to rip them apart with their clawed feet and fanged jaws.

There was no thought given to helping the lost men. The other survivors were already racing down the path as the rest of the reptiles pursued them. Their attention drawn away from the carnosaur's kill, the scavenger lizards had decided the humans would make easier prey and now hunted them down the path, snapping at their very heels. One man rebelled against the instinctive terror that sent them fleeing before the hungry reptiles. He turned to chop at the cold one chasing him. His axe sank into its shoulder, syrupy blood spurting from the wound. The lizard took no notice of its wound, but instead closed its jaws about the man's head and crushed his skull. It would be several minutes before the sensation of pain registered in the cold one's tiny brain, and by then its victim would be little more than bones.

The success of the other reptiles goaded the rest of the pack to greater effort. Several of them sprang at the fleeing men, leaping clear over their prey to land in snapping coils of scales and fangs. Another seaman was crushed beneath a pouncing cold one, smashed into a lifeless mush beneath its weight. The reptile sniffed at him, jostling his broken neck with its muzzle before uttering a huff of annoyance and springing back to its feet in search of livelier prey.

For those being driven before the pack, the chase assumed the dimensions of a nightmare. The shrieks and hisses of the cold ones were a deafening clamour in their ears, broken only by the agonised screams of those who fell beneath their claws. The air was a smothering miasma, making the very act of forcing air into their panting chests an ordeal. There seemed no escape, their only hope being that the cold ones would abandon the hunt once they had eaten their fill.

A thunderous crack sounded from the trees looming over the path. Men risked their lives to glance up at the natural archway above them. One look was enough to spur them onwards. The trees were falling, crashing down like the talons of an angry god. They slammed into the ground with such impact that the men could feel tremors beneath their feet. Again and again trees came smashing down and it took every effort for the tired, desperate men to stay clear of them. Sometimes a shrill, bestial shriek would sound from somewhere behind them, but no one took the chance of being crushed to look back and see what had made the noise.

Soon the exhausted survivors could run no further, even if it meant falling to the claws and fangs of the reptiles or being crushed beneath the falling trees. Their breath was now nothing short of utter agony, their clothes clung to them in dripping tatters. Adalwolf and a few of the others made feeble displays of drawing their weapons, though each doubted he had the strength to use them.

'Look!' Hiltrude shouted between gasps. She pointed at the trees. The men followed her gesture. The trees had fallen still again, as still as the pillars of a cathedral.

Adalwolf turned and stared at the path behind them. There was no sign of the pursuing lizards now, only a great jumble of fallen trees. He remembered the bestial shrieks they had heard and could only imagine the predators to be crushed somewhere beneath the log.

'Something,' Diethelm said, 'seems interested in keeping us alive.'

Despite the heat of the jungle, the priest's dour words sent a chill rushing up each man's spine.

CHAPTER SEVEN

The Lost City

GREY SEER THANQUOL gnashed his teeth together as he stubbed his foot against the gnarled root of a mangrove tree. Spitefully he swatted the root with the butt of his staff. It was a sore temptation to draw upon his sorcery to wither the offensive plant, but reason quelled the vengeful instinct. He had to be very careful about over-exerting himself. There was no telling when he would need his powers. He certainly couldn't rely upon his supposed allies for any help.

After the fight with the zombies, the skaven had regrouped. Thanquol had been fortunate to catch up to them, but as soon as he made his appearance, Shen Tsinge started weaving all kinds of lies about how Thanquol had allowed them to walk into a trap and telling Shiwan Stalkscent that the grey seer was not to be trusted. Thanquol wanted to rip out the lying mage-rat's tongue for spewing such falsehoods, but the way Goji glared at him made the grey seer keep quiet.

It was an example of how gullible Shiwan was that he accepted Shen's story. With the master assassin's knife at his throat, Thanquol was forced to stand still while Shen searched him for any warpstone. The cursed sorcerer was most thorough, ripping open the secret pockets sewn into Thanquol's robes. He even put his paws in Thanquol's mouth to fish out the little pebble of warpstone hidden in his cheek pouch.

Thanquol endured the humiliating treatment, holding himself proud and superior even as the Eshin leaders threatened and bullied him. For the good of the mission, he agreed to take the point and lead the way. It would prove to their unreasonable, paranoid brains that he was completely innocent of Shen's outrageous claims against him. After all, from up front, if he led them into any kind of trouble, then he would be the first to suffer its effects.

He strode boldly through the jungle, preceded only by the scrawny gutter runners who cleared the worst of the vines and branches. Often he would pause to stare contemptuously at the Eshin leaders cringing at the back of the column, sheltering behind the spears of Kong's fighter-rats. Such craven display was repulsive coming from skaven of such standing as Shiwan Stalkscent and Shen Tsinge! These were the mighty leaders of the expedition! Thanquol lashed his tail in frustration that such snivelling curs could begin to think they were fit to give *him* orders!

'Thanquol, see-scent city yet?' Shiwan's grating voice called out to him in a demanding shout.

The grey seer turned and genuflected in the master assassin's direction as he had seen the Eshin clanrats do when addressing their leader. 'Nothing yet-yet, bold and mighty slitter of throats!' Thanquol said. He glanced down at the map Shiwan had given him. Assuring the master assassin he could read the illegible scrawl of the plague priests was one of the things that had kept Shiwan from killing him after the incident with the zombies. Thanquol dearly hoped he wasn't looking at it upside down.

'Thanquol-meat try trick-fool Eshin!' snapped Tsang Kweek, leader of the gutter runners. Tsang was a malicious, sadistic rodent, a slinking thug who enjoyed nothing more than inflicting as much pain as possible upon anything he thought weaker than himself. Right now, the gutter runner considered Thanquol to fall into that category. Thanquol wondered if perhaps it had been one of Tsang's scouts and not one of Shiwan's assassins that had lingered behind to ambush him in the swamp.

'Does honourable Backstabber Kweek speak-squeak true-true?' Shiwan growled. The skaven around him bared their fangs as the master assassin spoke.

'No-no!' Thanquol assured Shiwan, trying to keep panic out of his voice. Discreetly he turned the map around and stared at it, making an elaborate show of studying it. The skaven around him just glared at him suspiciously. 'Soon-soon we find-find scaly-meat city!'

Shiwan drew a long dagger from the folds of his cloak. Shen Tsinge chittered with amusement as he saw Thanquol flinch at the assassin's approach. 'Find Quetza!' Shiwan growled again. 'Find or I feed-feed Goji your spleen!'

Thanquol's glands clenched as the assassin snarled his threat. He shivered as he heard the rat ogre's belly grumble when he heard Shiwan speak his name.

'Soon-soon!' Thanquol reassured Shiwan. Quickly he turned back around and scurried to the front of the trail, snapping quick commands to the gutter runners chopping through the brush.

The other skaven snickered at his predicament, but none more-so than the cloaked assassin with the missing ear. Chang Fang had been fortunate to escape the swamp, he could still feel the filth of the mire in his fur. More than before, he was determined to settle things with Thanquol. He only hoped he would get his chance before Shiwan's patience ran out.

For his part, Thanquol was unaware his enemy from the swamp had returned. The Eshin practice of removing the scent glands from their assassins made it difficult for other skaven to recognise them. He already had enough enemies at his back, however, that even Chang Fang's presence could not have increased his fright. He knew that he was quickly running out of time to squirm his way back into the good graces of Shiwan Stalkscent.

If only he could make sense of the accursed map! Why couldn't the diseased minds of Clan Pestilens write like normal skaven? How was he supposed to make sense of a bunch of scratches and spit-stains? Nurglitch sneezes on a scrap of rat-hide and the plague monks call it a map!

It was unfair that his life should depend upon such a ridiculous, idiotic thing! The slinking murderers of Clan Eshin were clearly as mad as the plague monks to put any trust in such a mess of scribbles! Was that green slash supposed to be a hill or a river? And what by the Horned Rat's tyrannical tail was this thing that looked like a ball of snot!

Thanquol closed his eyes, bruxing his fangs in frustration. Every inch of jungle the gutter runners cleared away brought him one step closer to destruction. He couldn't expect a half-wit like Shiwan to give him anything like a reasonable amount of time to find the lost city!

Quietly, Thanquol muttered a prayer to the Horned Rat. If his god would only help him out of this predicament, he would abase himself before all his altars. He would never again be proud and boastful, but would devote himself to becoming the most humble and obedient servant of the Horned One.

Excited squeals suddenly erupted among the gutter runners. Thanquol half turned to scurry back to the main body of the expedition, but quickly realised the squeaks were happy ones, not sounds of fear. He turned his spin into a forwards dash, kicking aside the scrawny scouts.

Before him, the jungle diminished into a vast clearing. The earth was paved with immense stone blocks. These in turn supported huge structures of piled stone. The smallest of these had collapsed into jumbles of broken rock, but the largest loomed over the plaza like crouching giants. They were something like the pyramids the dead-things of Nehekhara built, but with steps carved into their faces and flattened tops. In the distance, beyond the strange pyramids, Thanquol could see great mountains jutting up from the jungle, plumes of smoke curling from their volcanic peaks.

Thanquol grinned in savage triumph. He had found the city! Here was what they had been looking for! His brilliant mind had deciphered the scrawl of the plague monks and brought them to their goal!

'Great Shiwan Stalkscent,' Thanquol said, turning to beckon the assassin forward. His eyes narrowed with suspicion, Shiwan and three of his guards crept up to join the smug grey seer.

Thanquol extended his claw, like a merchant displaying his wares. 'Behold! The lost city of Quetza!' He couldn't quite keep the pride from his tone.

Shiwan stared at the ruins, then back at Thanquol. 'Sure-certain this Quetza?' he growled.

Thanquol glanced back at the ruins. He could feel his glands starting to clench again.

THANQUOL'S FEARS THAT Shiwan's map had led them to the wrong city were quelled when the skaven descended into the wide, plaza-like expanse. Creepers and stunted little trees poked up from between the great stone blocks, vines clung to the walls of the neglected pyramids. Everywhere there was evidence of decay and abandonment. It looked like a dead city, annihilated by the ancient plagues of Clan Pestilens.

But it didn't *smell* like a dead city. The musk of reptiles was thick in the air, a pungent scent so noxious no skaven could mistake it. Thanquol remembered that according to the plague monks, Quetza had been deserted by the lizardmen, only the priests and servants of the snake-devil Sotek remaining behind. They were supposed to dwell exclusively within the Temple of the Serpent. It made sense they would take little interest in keeping up the other parts of the city.

A sharp hiss from the gutter runners sent a thrill of excitement racing through all the ratmen. The scouts had spotted some of the hated scaly-meat! The scent in the air didn't lie, the city wasn't completely deserted!

Thanquol crept forwards with the rest and stared at the weird creatures sprawled along the sunward side of a crumbling pyramid. They were shorter than the ratmen, and far thinner. Bright blue scales covered their bodies and they bore long, whip-like tails. Fan-like crests rose from the tops of their blunt, reptilian heads. They wore only scant loinclouts about their middles and jewelled armbands of gold and turquoise. The lizardmen were completely oblivious to the presence of the skaven, lounging in a kind of torpor as the sun warmed their cold bodies. Most didn't even have their eyes open.

It was too great an opportunity for the murderous assassins of Clan Eshin to pass up. Stealthily they climbed the face of the pyramid that was still in shadow. Relentlessly, the killers made their way up the shallow stone steps until they were level with their victims. Shiwan Stalkscent was the first to leap down upon his oblivious prey, slashing the skink's neck so thoroughly its head went rolling down the side of the pyramid.

The other skaven rushed to the attack now that their leader had made the first kill. Assassins fell on the sleeping skinks with ruthless abandon, their knives and swords licking out with lethal precision. Soon the side of the pyramid was dripping with the clammy blood of lizardmen. Kong's warriors scurried to intercept the few skinks who lived long enough to scramble down the stone walls, butchering them before they could even set foot on the plaza.

It was not a fight, it was a slaughter, the sort of one-sided conflict every skaven dreamed about. Thanquol even lent his own small contribution to the massacre, sending a bolt of black lightning crackling from his staff to incinerate a tiny skink trying to escape the attack by climbing over the top of the pyramid. The little creature was nothing more than a blackened husk when its smoking body came rolling down the face of the pyramid.

Thanquol exulted in his casual abuse of magic. He gave Shen Tsinge a smug look, but became a bit more conciliatory when Goji growled at him. It would be just like the slinking sorcerer to have his rat ogre take a bite out of the grey seer and then claim it had been an accident.

THE SKAVEN RUSHED from the slaughter, their blood up, eager to continue the havoc they had started.

Thanquol thought at first Shiwan had made a mistake allowing his troops to indulge their bloodlust so recklessly, but now he grudgingly appreciated the master assassin's craft. Excited as they were, his troops weren't hesitating at every turn and crossroad, trying to sniff out any lurking danger. No, instead they were sprinting straight towards their goal – the immense pyramid that loomed at the centre of Quetza.

There seemed little danger it could be the wrong place to go. Even the most dull-witted of the skaven could sense the power emanating from within those stones. The steps of the pyramid were laid out to resemble a giant snake crawling down from its flattened roof and its stairs were inlaid with polished gold that glimmered in the sunlight. No neglect or decay had been allowed to affect this place. Every ratman in the expedition knew the colossal structure was what they had been looking for: the Temple of the Serpent.

The Prophet of Sotek would be somewhere inside, waiting for the daggers of Clan Eshin to end his wretched existence. They would bring his skin back to the Nightlord and Sneek would reward them all once his alliance with Nurglitch became a reality.

Of course, Thanquol rather hoped to secure a greater amount of the credit and the reward for himself. Towards that end, he hung back as the Eshin warriors made their rush towards the pyramid. He had seen Shiwan do the same and understood the callous way the skaven leader was using his followers. It would only take one knife to end the life of Xiuhcoatl, the serpent-priest. He was using the charge of his followers to lure out any guards the lizardmen might have protecting the pyramid. While they were busy fighting his troops, Shiwan would be free to sneak inside the temple and kill Xiuhcoatl. It was a cunning plan, but Thanquol didn't appreciate being lumped in among Shiwan's disposable assets. He made a conscious effort to stay close to the master assassin in whatever was coming.

Strangely, no scaly troops emerged from the ruins to block their path as they rushed towards the temple. Thanquol braced himself for the whistle of arrows and the cough of blowguns as they raced past the tumbled heaps of collapsed buildings, but nothing answered his fear. Could the rest of the temple's guardians truly be as witless as the ones they had already killed? Or, perhaps, the ones the assassins had slaughtered were the sum total of all the temple's minions? Maybe Xiuhcoatl was already dead, perhaps he was even the tiny skink Thanquol had blasted with his magic!

The dark, cave-like opening at the base of the pyramid yawned before them now. A different smell was in the air, a stronger scent than the lizard-stink of the city. It was the loathsome scent of serpents, a smell that had even Shen Tsinge spurting the musk of fear. There was no smell more terrifying to the skaven, a scent that was imprinted upon their psyche from a time when they were still more rat than ratkin. The stench killed the bloodthirsty enthusiasm Shiwan had so craftily exploited. Now the skaven stared fearfully at every shadow and cringed against each other in little huddles of shivering fur.

Shiwan snarled, showing his fangs to his underlings. The master assassin lashed his tail, frustrated by their mindless terror. He took a bold step towards the opening, then reconsidered. Angrily, he snapped a command to Tsang Kweek. The backstabber laid into a pair of his gutter runners, cuffing the scouts about the ears and snapping his fangs at their necks until they reluctantly scampered towards the darkened opening.

As soon as the two scouts entered the passage, they squealed in alarm. It was a quick sound, it had to be because an instant later arcs of scintillating light engulfed the two ratmen. An instant of blinding white and the skaven were gone, leaving behind only little piles of smouldering ash.

Shiwan stared in horror at the sight. To appease his leader, Tsang sent another set of scouts forward, but these were annihilated in the same way as their comrades.

Shiwan rounded on Thanquol and the grey seer cringed when he saw the fury in the master assassin's eyes. Perhaps staying close to him hadn't been such a good idea after all.

'Lizard-magic!' Shiwan snapped, pointing a trembling claw at the four piles of smoking ash. 'Fix-fix, quick-quick!'

Thanquol thought about protesting the assassin's orders, but something about the way his hand was clenching his knife made the grey seer decide that might be a bad idea too. Timidly, Thanquol started to shuffle towards the cave-like opening. His slowness began to vex Shiwan. A snarled command and the grey seer found himself surrounded by some of Kong's warriors, each of the burly skaven pushing him forwards when he hesitated. Shen Tsinge and Goji followed behind them. The sorcerer was keeping just close enough to Thanquol to claim any credit for anything the grey seer managed to do, but far enough back to avoid any danger to himself.

Thanquol was really coming to hate that craven mage-rat and his brainless rat ogre.

The aura of power was heavy around the door. Thanquol could actually smell the magic rippling through the very stones of the temple. It was a malignant, hostile sort of magic, magic that was somehow aware in its own right. He'd never encountered anything quite like it, except perhaps when he'd helped Clan Moulder exterminate the army of the Chaos Lord Alarik Lionmane.

Studying the way the lines of power were concentrated, Thanquol could find nexus points set into the walls of the corridor. They were something like the conductors the warlock-engineers of Clan Skryre used to harness warp-lightning. He could see that the glyphs on the stones set at these nexus points were different than those that adorned the blocks around them. He shivered as he saw the crude representation of a giant snake swallowing a skaven repeated over and over. But it did give him an idea exactly what the purpose of the stones were and why there were no guards trying to keep them out of the temple.

To prove his theory, Thanquol swung around and seized the cloak of the warrior-rat standing behind him. Before the clanrat could recover from his surprise, Thanquol pushed him forwards and sent him staggering into the tunnel. Like the gutter runners, the warrior shrieked once and then was reduced to a pile of ash.

'It is as I thought,' Thanquol declared in his most imperious tone. The warrior-rats snarled at him, but backed away. They still had enough respect for the grey seer's powers that they didn't want to attack him while he was looking.

'What you think-think, bone-skull?' Shen hissed. Goji licked his fangs as he heard the annoyance in his master's tone.

Thanquol strode towards the sorcerer, pleased he had irritated the mage-rat. Shen had no idea what Thanquol had learned. He wondered if the sorcerer had ever even heard of guardian wards, magical sigils that were designed to destroy anyone they recognised as intruders. For the first time in a long time, Thanquol had something the sorcerer wanted – knowledge. And he was going to make Shen pay dearly to get it.

'I know much-much,' Thanquol grinned and for once he ignored the way Goji growled at him. Shen wouldn't let his monster touch him. Not now.

'I know you flea-bitten whelp-cutters aren't getting anywhere near this place without my help,' Thanquol stated.

Shen Tsinge glared daggers at him, but Thanquol could tell from the sorcerer's posture that he was beaten. Shen knew Thanquol wouldn't be so bold in his approach unless he was certain he was right.

Abruptly, Shen Tsinge was waving his hands wildly before him, gnawing on a chunk of warpstone as he did so. Thanquol could feel the sorcerer summoning power and his own magical attunement made him aware of the protective nature of Shen's spell. Quickly, Thanquol dived behind the sorcerer, sheltering between Shen and the towering bulk of Goji.

The world around the two mage-rats exploded into a pillar of fire. Gutter runners and clanrats close to them were immolated in the blast of magical flame, their shadows burned into the side of the pyramid. When the flames faded, Thanquol's gaze was drawn up the shallow stone steps set into the wall. He blinked in disbelief at the aura of sorcerous might swirling around the creature that stood upon the structure's flattened roof.

The creature was a skink, his scales the same dark blue as the lizardmen Shiwan and the assassins had killed. The crest that rose from his head was a brilliant red, however, and he wore a more elaborate robe-like garment that was looped over one shoulder, bound about his waist by a golden belt. His arms gleamed as sunlight reflected off the golden talismans and rings he wore. In his hand, the reptile held a massive staff tipped with a great golden icon – the stylised head of a fanged serpent.

Xiuhcoatl! The Prophet of Sotek! Thanquol stared in horror at the object of their mission. He had imagined some slovenly, naked savage whose sum total knowledge of magic was to brew a few poisons to keep his enemies away. Not in his wildest fears had he imagined his enemy would be like this! He could almost see the snake-devil's coils wrapped protectively around the lizardman, guarding him against any who would dare strike him. It would take the Horned Rat himself to defeat such a mighty foe.

Unfortunately, Shen Tsinge seemed to have the same idea. The sorcerer pushed Thanquol forward. 'Call upon the Horned One to save us!' he squeaked in terror.

Suddenly the arrows Thanquol had been expecting earlier began to clatter against the stones around them. He took his eyes away from Xiuhcoatl long enough to see blue-scaled skinks swarming over the tops of the ruined buildings all around them, tiny bows clutched in their claws. More of the creatures were pouring down the streets carrying javelins and holding blowguns to their mouths.

'The Horned One helps those who run fastest!' Thanquol snarled, pushing Shen down and racing away from the temple. He could hear the sorcerer hurling curses on his head, but doubted if Shen was enraged enough to send Goji lumbering after him. The sorcerer was going to need the rat ogre to make his own escape.

Fleeing skaven were all around Thanquol now. For a brief moment, Kong had tried to muster his warriors into formation to oppose the lizardmen. Any thoughts of making a stand evaporated however when the skinks came rushing at them. They herded a pair of big ugly reptiles before them, ghastly things with red scales and huge sail-like frills running along their backs. The reptiles hesitated before charging into the massed skaven, instead opening their jaws and spitting a stream of flame full into the faces of the ratmen. The only thing that allowed any of Kong's warriors to escape was the fact that the salamanders had stopped to eat the burning flesh of the skaven they had killed and no amount of goading from their handlers could get them to move on.

Thanquol felt his heart thundering in his chest as he dashed down the broad street. The expedition was in full rout, gutter runners and assassins sprinting past him on every side. The grey seer cursed every skaven that ran ahead of him, knowing that each one meant one less body between himself and the arrows of the skinks. He earnestly hoped that if he fell in this blighted place, the Horned Rat would remember to punish the vermin for their cowardice!

PANTING WITH EXHAUSTION, Thanquol darted down one of the side streets, thinking that perhaps the lizardmen would ignore a lone skaven and instead concentrate upon the group as a whole. He ran along the deserted street, sticking close to the walls, reassured by the feel of something solid against his whiskers. Behind him he could hear the sounds of battle and knew that at least some of the expedition had been caught. Once again, he prided himself upon his wisdom and foresight.

Suddenly a pair of skinks appeared around the corner before him. The ugly monsters lifted blowguns to their scaly lips and took aim. In a panic, Thanquol pointed his staff at them and sent a bolt of warp-lightning sizzling through them. The ambushers fell, smoke rising from their charred husks. It was a satisfying result, but the pounding ache in his skull wasn't. He hadn't had time to prepare himself for such a spell and – moreover – hadn't had any warpstone to ease the effort.

Thanquol staggered away from the wall, reeling dizzily as he tried to focus his senses. As he left the protection of the wall, he heard something crash behind him. His reflexes were quick enough to see something dark leaping across the rooftop. A huge stone block had fallen into the street, a plume of dust rising from it.

Angrily, Thanquol ground his fangs together. The skinks didn't wear black cloaks! And the stone didn't fall! It had been pushed! If he hadn't moved away from the wall when he did, he would have been crushed beneath it!

Red fury banished the last of Thanquol's headache. He had thought it strange that two skinks should be waiting for him so far from the main battle. Now he understood – his would-be murderer had lured them here to ambush him. When they failed, he had tried to murder Thanquol himself.

It was a cold, crafty sort of plan. Either way, no one would be able to say he had been killed by another skaven. Thanquol remembered all the other attempts on his life since his return to Skavenblight and throughout the voyage to Lustria. He thought also of a cold, crafty skaven who had been prepared to use his entire expedition as a diversion so he could sneak into the temple.

Thanquol's claws closed tightly around his staff. Now he knew who was trying to murder him.

And the grey seer wasn't going to give Shiwan Stalkscent another chance!

THANQUOL HURRIED THROUGH the side streets of Quetza, always running parallel to the main avenue down which the skaven were fleeing. He followed the smell of the ratkin. Shiwan's lack of scent glands made finding him a bit difficult, but Thanquol was reasonably certain he could do it. He had the proper motivation now. Besides, what other skaven would be trying to stem the retreat and force the ratmen back into the fight? Shiwan didn't care if his followers died, but he did need them to distract the lizardmen long enough for him to get close to Xiuhcoatl.

The grey seer spotted Shiwan close to the back of the fleeing skaven. He wasn't sure how the master assassin had gotten back to his troops so quickly, but he knew the sneaks of Clan Eshin were capable of many seemingly impossible feats.

Behind the skaven, the lizardmen were making a steady advance, herding their flame-spitting salamanders before them. Thanquol watched the few ratmen Shiwan was able to throw back into the fight being burned alive by the caustic breath of the reptiles. He gritted his teeth as a sinister plan occurred to him.

Waiting until there were no skaven near the little corner he was crouched behind, Thanquol crept forward. Using his staff to focus his concentration, he gestured with his hand at the master assassin. No bolt of lightning for Shiwan Stalkscent, oh no! Thanquol intended to deal with him as the assassin had intended to deal with the grey seer. He would be subtle and make it look like something else was responsible.

Fixing Shiwan's image in his mind, Thanquol concentrated upon his spell. Again he felt the sharp pang of longing as he was forced to work his magic without warpstone to sustain his energies, but he knew this spell was important enough that he could endure a little suffering. Thanquol closed his hand, making a fist, slowly collecting magical energy in his palm. When he had enough, he opened his hand and sent the energy speeding into Shiwan's body.

It wasn't enough energy to kill the assassin. When it struck him, it felt like nothing worse than being accidentally slapped by an excited slave's tail. However, it struck him in the knee and even so slight a blow was enough to trip him as he ran. The master assassin squealed in fright as he crashed face-first into the paving stones. Before he could recover, the fiery breath of a salamander engulfed him. Shiwan staggered to his feet, his body burning like a living torch. He took only a few shuddering steps before he fell again. The salamander sprang at him, its massive jaws ripping away at his scorched flesh.

Thanquol watched the salamander feed for a moment before turning and fleeing back into the jungle. He hoped the dull-witted beast didn't choke on anything until after it had gobbled down every last scrap of his enemy.

CHAPTER EIGHT
New Plans, New Minions

THE JUNGLE CLEARING slowly filled with panting, gasping ratmen. Although the lizardmen hadn't pursued them beyond the borders of their city, none of the skaven was willing to take the chance that it was some kind of trick. So they hadn't stopped running until they were deep in the jungle.

Stragglers continued to creep out of the jungle, drawn by the smell of the ratkin. Even with these latecomers, Thanquol judged the expedition had lost nearly half its number in the ambush. He felt no sorrow for their losses, his only worry was that there weren't enough of them to fight off the beasts of the jungle when they made their way back to the beach.

Perched upon a fallen log, Thanquol leaned back and picked leeches from his fur while he waited for the bickering assassins to make up their minds and head back to the ship. It was, after all, the only sensible thing the slinking killers could do now.

'Shiwan would not-not leave without killing scaly-meat,' Kong Krakback was grumbling. The big black skaven sported an ugly gash across his face where a skink javelin had cut him. He was lucky the weapon hadn't been poisoned.

Tsang Kweek's fur bristled and his fangs gleamed in his face as he snarled back at the warrior. 'Shiwan is dead-dead!' the gutter runner hissed. 'Who care-think what he do-don't? I say-tell we leave! Now-now!'

'We can't leave.' Shen Tsinge's cold tones contrasted with the gutter runner's frightened squeak. 'We have to finish mission!'

Tsang spun around and scowled at the thin sorcerer. 'Temple-place protected by magic! Burn-slay any skaven walk inside!'

'Scaly-meat will be looking for us now,' one of the cloaked assassins said, supporting Tsang's move that they all head back to the ship. 'Can't sneak-surprise scaly-meat now!'

Shen shook a clawed finger in the assassin's face. 'Think-find way, fool-fur! We don't go back until Xiuhcoatl is dead!'

'We can't get into temple-place!' persisted Tsang. 'How do we kill-slay scaly-meat if we can't get inside!'

For an instant, it looked like Shen was going to pounce on Tsang. The sorcerer's fur bristled with rage, his fangs gleamed savagely. Suddenly a cunning gleam came into the sorcerer's eyes. He looked aside at the log and the horned ratman sitting on it. 'We find-find way inside!' he snapped.

Leaning on his staff, Shen Tsinge walked over to Thanquol's perch, the other Eshin leaders following behind him. The sorcerer stared up at the grey seer.

'Thanquol!' Shen snapped. 'We have decided to go back to temple-place! You must break-kill scaly-spells keeping us out!'

Thanquol didn't look at the sorcerer, instead making a study of the leech he had plucked from his leg. 'I don't think so,' he said, popping the parasite between his fingers. 'I think Backstabber Tsang has the right idea. We go back.'

'We can't go back,' Shen snarled through clenched fangs. 'Nightlord Sneek will kill-eat all of us if we fail!'

The reminder of their clanlord's inevitable vengeance for failure sent a fresh pulse of terror coursing through the ratmen. Thanquol could smell the musk dripping down their legs. He didn't have to ask to know that he would be included in Sneek's revenge. If it was any other skaven, he might have suggested sailing away and finding someplace to hide, but he knew there was no hiding from the Nightlord.

It was a desperate situation. Shen was right, they couldn't go back until Xiuhcoatl was dead. Having seen the Prophet of Sotek in action, he knew that the only way to kill a sorcerer of such awesome ability was to take him unawares. To do that, they would have to get inside the pyramid. And to get inside the pyramid, they needed Thanquol to break the wards that had been placed there to destroy their kind.

Thanquol shivered with fear at the prospect of returning to Quetza and facing Xiuhcoatl again. Then, as his eyes swept across the clearing, he noticed something strange. All the skaven were looking up at him. There was a desperate hope in their eyes. Like Shen, they knew the grey seer was their only hope of getting inside the temple and killing Xiuhcoatl.

He stared down at Shen and the other leaders, lips pulled back in a fierce grin. 'I might help-save you,' Thanquol said. 'But there has been too much bungling from you mouse-murderers!' He pointed his claw threateningly at the assembled skaven. 'You thought you knew better than Grey Seer Thanquol how to do what the Nightlord told you to do! Now you know how wrong you were! I should let you all rot-fester! Let your bones warm the bellies of snakes!'

Kong Krakback threw himself to the ground, grovelling before Thanquol's feet. 'Please, great master, do not abandon us!' Kong's pleading was soon taken up by other skaven, each trying to out-do the other in his obeisance.

'I might help-save you ungrateful tick-nibblers,' Thanquol mused, scratching his chin. 'But I have been badly treated by your leaders…'

'That was all Shiwan's idea!' insisted Tsang Kweek, wringing his paws together. 'None of us would have dared treat you with dishonour if he hadn't told-ordered it so!'

Thanquol sneered at the lie. They had all taken part in maltreating him. However, he could still use the faithless vermin.

'If I help-save you,' Thanquol pronounced, one finger lifted in warning, 'then I must-must have total control. I must-must be leader and everyone must-must do what I say!'

That announcement had more than a few of the skaven gnashing their teeth. Yet even these bit down on their pride and bobbed their heads in agreement to Thanquol's terms. Even Tsang Kweek and Kong Krakback accepted Thanquol's leadership.

Rubbing his hands together in triumph, Thanquol hopped down from his perch. He grinned at Shen Tsinge. The sorcerer and his rat ogre had been the only skaven to remain standing during the display of grovelling and pleading. Shen snarled back at the grey seer, but he couldn't hide the icy fear in the depths of his eyes. Thanquol knew then that the sorcerer was broken.

'I'll need all the warpstone,' Thanquol told Shen. The sorcerer lashed his tail in outrage at Thanquol's demand, but began removing nuggets of the black stone from his pockets just the same. 'Don't forget any little bits you might have hiding in your cheek pouches,' Thanquol spitefully reminded Shen.

Shen's eyes blazed with fury at the insult, his hand falling to the sword he wore. Behind him, Goji took a menacing step forwards. It was an effort, but Thanquol managed to keep any hint of fear from his posture as he coldly regarded the twin threats of Shen and the rat ogre.

'As leader, I'll need protection,' Thanquol told Shen. 'I want your rat ogre.'

Shen almost drew his sword, but one look at the skaven around him stayed his hand. They knew Thanquol was their only hope now. If Shen killed the grey seer they would fall on him like a pack of rabid wolf-rats and tear him to pieces. Choking on his rage, the sorcerer bowed his head and waved Goji forward.

Thanquol chittered his delight as he walked around the hulking rat ogre and inspected his new property. The monster was an impressive specimen, much more so than the weakling runts he'd owned before. The beast's claws were the biggest and sharpest he'd ever seen on a rat ogre, there was an intelligence in his eyes that was almost skaven-like in their depth and understanding. The rat ogre's fur was thick and lustrous, as black as midnight. He even found the necklace of skulls around the monster's neck a pleasing touch.

'You need a better name than Goji,' Thanquol mused as he circled the rat ogre. 'I think I shall call you...' He paused in thought, picking at his ear as he considered what he would call his new bodyguard. The rat ogre stared down at him, an almost expectant look in his beady eyes.

'Boneripper,' Thanquol decided. It was a good name for a rat ogre, the kind of name that scared enemies just to hear it.

And Boneripper was going to scare his enemies. Thanquol was going to make sure of that.

GREY SEER THANQUOL rested with his back against a palm, casually nibbling on the parrot in his paws. The bird had a curious taste, and not one that he was certain he appreciated. But meat was meat, and it would be a sign of weakness to forfeit the provisions his loyal followers had brought him. He looked up from his meal, savouring the sullen stares of the Eshin skaven. Let the rats skulk! It was no less than they deserved for all the indignities they had heaped on him!

Calmly, Thanquol handed the rest of the parrot to his bodyguard. The bird's bones crunched noisily as Boneripper crushed it in his powerful jaws. Being careful to keep the rat ogre well-fed had done wonders for shifting his loyalty from Shen Tsinge. Thanquol was impressed by his intelligence and practicality. The sorcerer had always treated his bodyguard as nothing but another lackey, something that was second best. Boneripper deserved better treatment, and Thanquol was careful to put the rat ogre's needs ahead of even his own.

Thinking about needs, Thanquol studied the fruit basket the gutter runners had brought him. He picked through the assorted nuts and berries, sniffing suspiciously at the ones he wasn't certain were edible and glancing up maliciously to see which of his minions he would choose to test the suspect berries. He selected a ripe banana. He'd developed a bit of a taste for the mushy fruit. Picking out a leather-skinned melon at the same time, Thanquol let Boneripper gorge himself on the rest of the food that looked safe.

'If you are finished eating, grim and terrible slayer-lord,' one of the bowing hunter-rats started to address Thanquol.

A flash of fright raced along Thanquol's spine. His eyes narrowed with hate and his foot kicked out, cracking against the hunter's muzzle. 'Don't call me that!' he snarled, trying to banish the momentary image of a ginger-haired dwarf-thing that had risen in his mind. 'Don't ever do that again, you paw-licking whelp-stealer!' He stood, glaring down at the trembling victim of his ill-temper. Thanquol was pretty sure he knew who would be testing the suspicious berries.

'Begging indulgence, mighty tyrant,' Shen Tsinge's ingratiating tones reached Thanquol's ears. He turned to find the thin sorcerer shuffling towards him, leaning on his staff. Thanquol was pleased when he heard Boneripper growl at his old master's approach.

'What do you want, mage-rat?' Thanquol demanded, giving another spiteful kick to the prostrate hunter.

For an instant, Shen's face pulled back in a challenging grin, but he quickly covered his fangs again. 'Thanquol…'

'Grey Seer Thanquol!' Thanquol snarled at the sorcerer.

Shen bent and bowed in contrition for the improper address. 'Grey Seer Thanquol, we have been hiding in jungle-place for many-many sun-moon.'

'Yes?' Thanquol hissed at Shen, reminding the sorcerer to be very careful with whatever he was going to say.

'Grey Seer Thanquol, we have been here long-long,' Shen said. 'We follow-obey whatever Thanquol speak-squeak. We bring-take water for Thanquol's bath while we are thirsty. We bring-take meat for Thanquol's meals while we eat ants and roots.'

'Yes?' Thanquol demanded again. The grey seer cast a wary eye at the other skaven who were listening to the exchange. He'd been forced to put down one insurrection already. If Shen was going to lead another one it might be more difficult to squash.

'When we go back and kill Xiuhcoatl!' Shen snarled, lashing his tail through the underbrush. 'We stay in jungle-place we die-die!'

Thanquol bared his fangs at the rebellious sorcerer. 'I am waiting for a sign from the Horned One!' When questioned about his decisions, Thanquol always found it wisest to invoke his god. Then if his enemy persisted in doubting him, it was the same as if he was doubting the Horned Rat. It was always easy to rouse skaven to destroy a ratman who had been branded a heretic.

Unfortunately, Shen was bold enough to persist. 'When you see-scent sign?' Shen growled. 'When all Eshin-rats are bones? When only Grey Seer Thanquol still has strength to walk-scurry from jungle-place?'

'Heretic!' Thanquol snapped, pointing a claw at the defiant sorcerer. 'Seize him!' he ordered the other skaven.

None of them lifted a paw, but instead glared at him with angry eyes. Boneripper moved beside Thanquol, but even the threat of the rat ogre didn't seem to matter to the abused and starving skaven.

'I am your only chance!' Thanquol reminded the skaven. 'Without me, you can't get into temple-place!'

'We aren't getting inside with you,' Tsang Kweek hissed, fingering one of his knives. 'All we're doing is getting weak while you get fat!'

Thanquol glared at the gutter runner. 'The Horned Rat will shrivel your nethers for speaking to me like that! I am waiting for his holy scent to show us the way!'

'Liar! Coward!' one of the assassins shouted, emboldened by his lack of scent to hide his identity from Thanquol's wrath. 'Where is this sign from the Horned One!'

Suddenly a group of scouts came scurrying back into the clearing. Despite the mutiny all around him, Thanquol managed to notice with some misgiving that the hunters had come back empty-handed. However, rather than trying to slink off and avoid the grey seer, they excitedly rushed right towards him.

'Great and might paw of the Horned One!' the hunters squeaked. 'There are man-things in jungle-place! Live man-things! We saw-scented them!'

Thanquol stroked one of his horns as he digested the excited report. The only humans they had seen since landing in this accursed place had been the walking dead-things in the swamp. He had begun to believe that there were no humans on the entire continent. It had been his experience that once man-things were established in a place, they quickly built nests everywhere. Yet they had seen no trace of any human villages. Indeed, except for the zombie tower, the only buildings they had seen were the ruins left by the lizardmen.

What would humans be doing here, so far from anyplace they had any right to be? The answer came to Thanquol as he glanced down at the excited hunters. Of course! He could have bit himself for not seeing it sooner. This was the sign he had been waiting for! As soon as that realisation came to him, a plan instantly began to form in Thanquol's crooked mind.

'Go-fetch man-things!' Thanquol snarled at his minions. 'I want all-all man-things! Bring them to me, live-live! If you kill-kill, I'll cut out your brains and feed them to you!'

His minions didn't stop to question the impossibility of Thanquol's threat, but turned back and raced into the jungle, eager to obey his command. Thanquol watched them go, his tail lashing behind him impatiently. Now that the plan had formed in his mind, he wanted to try it out. If he was right, very soon they would be inside the Temple of the Serpent.

If he was wrong... Thanquol shuddered and started thinking about what he would do if he was wrong.

THE TREK THROUGH the jungle had become torture after the escape from the cold ones. With the loss of the water, there was no relief from the hot, sweltering misery that made every breath agony. Even the fine clothes of van Sommerhaus had been reduced to strips of rotten cloth hanging in damp tatters off his starving body. There had been no more straying off the path to find food since their encounter with the giant reptiles. Before, they had imagined the worst they might stumble on in the jungle was a prowling jaguar. Now they knew better and even the grumbling in their stomachs was not enough to send the men back among the trees.

Only one hope remained to them: the promise that the strange pathway was guiding them somewhere. They had all seen too much to doubt the sorcerous nature of the trail. If magic was behind the path, then it had to have some purpose, some reason for being. At each bend, they expected to see the golden city van Sommerhaus continued to talk about. Each time they felt the bitter sting of disappointment. There seemed no end to the jungle. If some distant power was watching over them, it seemed to have greatly overestimated their endurance.

Or had it? Adalwolf wondered about the brief glimpses of the night sky he could see through the trees overhead. He had a slight enough knowledge of astronomy to know there was something wrong about those stars. Captain Schachter and Marjus, men with much greater knowledge of navigating by the night sky, were positively terrified by what they saw to such an extent that as soon as the sun went down, they stubbornly refused to even glance up.

One day as they trudged along the path, Brother Diethelm offered an explanation for what had disturbed Adalwolf and frightened the sailors. 'It isn't that the stars are strange to them,' the priest said. 'It is that they move in ways no star should from night to night.' He shook his head. 'No magic, even such magic as makes this path for us, is strong enough to shift the stars from their settings. It is we who are moved in strange ways, not the heavens. Imagine a sheet of parchment upon which you draw a line. Now take the same sheet and fold it upon itself and draw a line. You have still crossed the parchment with your line, but it is a much shorter line.'

The mercenary blinked in confusion at Diethelm's words. 'I don't understand.'

Diethelm favoured him with a patient smile. 'This road,' he said. 'We know it is a creation of sorcery. But I think we make a mistake to presume it simply passes through the jungle. I believe it also *folds* the space around it. The road, like my parchment, shortens the line in some strange fashion we cannot fathom. To our eyes, nothing seems different, because we are walking within this fold and do not know how great the distance should be. The stars, however, cannot be fooled, and when they shine upon us, they shine from where they truly sit, not where we believe they should sit.'

Adalwolf's mouth went dry at the priest's explanation. 'I've heard mad tales of such things from Norse sailors about the lands beyond the Troll Country, but I never believed them. Can any magic be so powerful as to change the land itself in such a way?'

'I fear we walk within proof that there is such magic,' Diethelm said. 'We can only pray that the mind behind such magic bears us no malice.'

From the path ahead came excited voices. Adalwolf and Diethelm hurried forwards to find the remaining sailors hacking away at the vines bordering the path. Schachter stood nearby, arms folded across his chest, supervising the labour of his crew while van

Sommerhaus gave them verbal encouragement by promising each man a gold guilder if they hurried.

'What goes on here?' Adalwolf asked Hiltrude.

The woman smiled at him, her drawn face lifting in an expression of breathless anticipation. 'One of the sailors heard water flowing through the jungle close to the path! He thinks it must be some kind of river.'

'Water!' Adalwolf exclaimed. He wondered if any word had ever sounded more beautiful. The last real water they'd had was when they'd lost the sledge. Since then, they had been drinking whatever they could wring out of their sodden clothes after the jungle's frequent rainstorms. 'Are they sure?'

'They are,' Diethelm said. 'I can smell a great quantity of water close to us.'

The axes and cutlasses of the men broke through the wall of vines. Beyond, they found that the trees were more widely spaced, the ground being too moist to support the overgrowth they had become accustomed to. In the absence of trees, fern bushes and saw grass had found room to grow, clinging close to the muddy earth. They did not obscure the welcome view that warmed the hearts of the men on the pathway: a great river slashing its way through the trees, its green waters murmuring softly as they washed over the many boulders lining its boundaries.

Hunger had not driven the survivors to brave the horrors of the jungle, but thirst was a need powerful enough to stifle even their fear. With so much water so near, the sailors rushed for the river, shouting and laughing like children. Adalwolf and Hiltrude joined the mad rush to the river and even van Sommerhaus forgot his detached dignity and threw himself headlong into the emerald waters. Only Brother Diethelm remained wary, watching every tree and bush for the first sign of danger as he carefully walked down to the river bank.

The crew greedily drank their fill of the water, then began to wash the filth from their clothes and bodies. Hiltrude tried to cleanse the stains from her ragged dress, doing her best to ignore the lascivious catcalls from the seamen as she exposed her slender legs in the process. Captain Schachter filled his hat with water then turned it over his head, letting the cool liquid wash down his face. Van Sommerhaus, after his first dive into the river, lounged upon one of the boulders, gently splashing water across his neck as though he were some noble lady daintily applying perfume. Marjus and the sailors cavorted in the middle of the shallow river, revelling in the luxury of the moment.

After taking a few long sips from the river, Adalwolf sat himself on the sandy shore and started unbuckling his armour. He was still thinking clearly enough that he didn't want his armour getting any more rusty than it was from the rain. Carefully, he set the weather-beaten vest against some rocks and started to unfasten his boots. Diethelm's hand on his shoulder caused him to stop.

'I've been watching the river,' the priest said. 'What do you think of that?'

Diethelm pointed to a patch of river a dozen yards from where the sailors were swimming. At first,

Adalwolf couldn't tell exactly what he was looking at. It looked like the water was shivering, breaking out in bumps. If there had been any rain, he might have thought it was raindrops striking the water. He truly had no idea what it was.

'Fish?' he wondered. Still, that would hardly account for the chill that crept down his back. Surely the river was too shallow to harbour anything that could threaten a man? Even so, he watched the shivering patch of water begin to move towards them, moving upstream against the flow of the river.

Adalwolf rose and quickly moved down to the river bank. Sternly, he grabbed Hiltrude's arm and pulled the protesting courtesan out of the water. When she moved to grab her shoes, Adalwolf savagely pulled her back again.

'Out of the water!' the mercenary shouted. He pointed his hand at the patch of dancing water.

The sailors saw what he was pointing at and laughed, several of them shaking their fists and cursing Adalwolf for trying to scare them. Closer to the disturbance, they could see what was causing it. No terrifying river monster, just a school of ugly little silver-coloured fish.

The jeering shouts of the sailors became bloodcurdling screams as the school of fish swam into them. The green waters around them turned cloudy and red. Frantically, the men beat at the water with their hands, trying to scare away their attackers. One man lifted his hand from the water with a fish hanging from it, the animal's sharp fangs sunk deep into his flesh. Frenziedly the fish twisted and writhed, ripping gory ribbons from the sailor's palm.

Horror-stricken, the men fled the water as quickly as they could. The piranhas converged on the slowest, ripping and tearing at their bodies as they tried to make shore. From the banks of the river, those safely on land could only watch the ghoulish display as the fish devoured their prey alive. When Marjus scrambled out of the water, he sported a hideous gash across his leg where the piranhas had savaged it clear down to the bone. He was the last to escape. Three other sailors never left the water, their bodies floating gruesomely down the river, pursued by the school of cannibal fish.

ALL EYES WERE fixed on the river and the terrible scene playing out upon it, so none of the survivors noticed the first cloaked shape emerge from the jungle. Quietly, other verminous shapes detached themselves from the trees, silently forming a cordon around the humans.

Hiltrude was the first to turn her face in disgust from the spectacle of the piranhas feeding on the dead seamen. In turning, she found herself facing a sight even more ghastly. A long, rodent-like visage stared at her with beady eyes and vicious, gleaming fangs. The creature gripped a wicked-looking dagger in its furry hand.

The courtesan let out a shriek of horror, flinging her shoe at the monster. The skaven ducked the clumsy attack and snarled at her threateningly. She retreated before the monster, stopping only when she felt water lapping against her naked heel.

At Hiltrude's cry, the others swung around. Her scream was echoed by the men around her, men who were shaken to their souls by the awful sight. Even if the cold ones had returned, or the carnosaur had decided they would make nice snacks after all, the men would not have shown such horror. The giant reptiles were things they could accept, menaces they knew were real. What faced them now was nightmare, myth made flesh. Every man among them had been raised on fairy tales about the baby-stealing underfolk, nursery stories to make bad children behave. They had laughed at Tilean sailors who insisted such monsters were real and often got them drunk simply to hear such stories so they could laugh at them again. The underfolk weren't real! They couldn't be! The world couldn't harbour such fiendish things!

Yet what stood before them, knives and swords in their hands, were undeniably the underfolk! The creatures had formed a semicircle around them, surrounding them on three sides. To their back, was the river.

Adalwolf made a dive to recover his sword from where he had left it against the rocks. One of the ratmen snarled at him, and a sharp throwing knife slashed across his knuckles as he grabbed for his blade. The mercenary recoiled in pain, glaring at the hideous monsters, trying to control the fear pulsing through his veins. His horror only increased when one of the ratmen opened its muzzle and began to push words through its fangs.

'Man-things come-come!' the ratman snapped. Its words faded into a peal of chittering laughter. 'Or go swim-die,' it hissed, pointing its claw at the river.

Before any of the terrified humans could consider the ghoulish choice the ratman had given them, its fellows rushed them in a snarling swarm, smashing them down with the flats of their blades and the rusty pommels of their swords.

THANQUOL STROKED HIS whiskers thoughtfully as Tsang Kweek brought the sorry-looking pack of humans to him. They looked half-dead and smelled little better. He was familiar enough with the different breeds of man-things to know that these belonged to the big Clan Empire. Their lands were far away, beyond even Skavenblight. It made little sense to him that these humans should be here, but very little humans did made sense to him.

Tsang Kweek had brought the humans back to the clearing in haste. The gutter runners and assassins had an easy time capturing the witless animals – but after all it had been Thanquol's plan, so the ease of their success was hardly surprising. Kong Krakback and his warriors had searched Tsang's sneaks for any captured plunder. They'd found a few things that Thanquol found interesting. A little glass bottle with some strangely scented liquid inside, a curious copper tube with glass fitted at each end that made things look smaller when he looked into it, and a pair of gaudy pistols, like shabby little cousins of the warplock weapons Clan Skryre made. Thanquol had been quick to take those. He knew how easily a bullet could go astray if left in the paws of a treacherous underling.

The humans were huddled on the ground before Thanquol's perch, forced into uncomfortable bows by the kicks and threats of his loyal minions.

The grey seer was silent a long time, enjoying the frightened way the humans were looking at him. They knew who was their master, even without being told! They had sense enough to recognise his greatness, his authority, simply by looking at him! One day all of the decadent lands of the man-things would be brought under the rule of skavendom. Then all humans would grovel before him with the same look of respect and fear. Even that scrawny man-thing pet that damn dwarf had tagging along with him!

Thanquol bruxed his fangs together and lashed his tail angrily when he realised the prisoners weren't looking at him, they were looking above him. He glanced over his shoulder and his mood became even blacker. The stupid, senseless brutes thought Boneripper was the leader!

'I am Grey Seer Thanquol!' he snarled at the dull-eyed humans, putting a full measure of venom in his tone. He waited a moment, then ground his fangs together when that announcement didn't impress any of them. 'I am leader here,' he continued. 'You will call-know me as master-king! Whatever I say-squeak, you do!'

Thanquol smiled. The more he spoke, the more upset the humans became. Good! Soon he would have them completely terrified and wrapped around his tail like a trained slug.

'If you obey-please me, I will let-allow you to live,' Thanquol said.

'Filthy monster!' one of the humans suddenly shouted. The man was on his feet and leaping for Thanquol so quickly, the grey seer didn't have time to react. The human's hands closed about his robe and Thanquol felt himself being pulled down from the log.

Suddenly the grip on him grew slack. Thanquol looked down to see the human's torso laying at his feet, the man's legs a good dozen yards across the clearing. Boneripper stood above the mess, licking blood from his massive claws. Even though he obscured Thanquol's view of the humans, he decided to let the rat ogre stay where he was.

'That is an example-warning!' Thanquol hissed at the cowering humans. 'Defy me and die-die!' He let his angry gaze sweep across the trembling humans. He squinted in surprise as he noticed one of them was female. 'Next time, I feed your breeder to Boneripper!' He felt pleased when he saw one of the humans instantly wrap a protective arm around the female. In his experience, humans were never so manageable as when there were breeders and whelps around to threaten.

Strangely, one of the humans actually stared at him without the extreme fear the others showed. The animal's temerity only increased when he spoke to Thanquol.

'Are you the one who made the path we followed?' the human asked.

Thanquol's brow wrinkled in confusion. He didn't like this human, there was a faint smell of magic about him. He was tempted to have the human killed just to be safe, but that impulse was mitigated by the fact that if he was wrong about how to get inside the pyramid, the human might know another way. What this path was the mage-thing was babbling about, Thanquol had no idea, but he decided to run with it.

'Of course, fool-thing!' Thanquol snapped. 'With my powers I sent-made a trail-path to bring you to me. Now you must serve-obey Grey Seer Thanquol for saving you!'

The humans didn't look particularly grateful, but clearly they were even more afraid of him now – and this time they weren't looking at Boneripper by mistake. That was good, the more they feared him, the quicker they would be to obey his every command.

Brusquely, Thanquol snapped orders to Kong and Shen. They were to have all of the skaven ready to march. Now that he had the humans, Thanquol was eager to put his theory to the test. If he was right, they would soon be inside the pyramid and they could surprise Xiuhcoatl.

If he was wrong… well, the more skaven the lizardmen killed when they returned to Quetza, the better it would be for Thanquol!

CHAPTER NINE

The Temple of the Serpent

THE CITY OF Quetza was eerily quiet when the skaven made their return. This time there were no sunning skinks to massacre and exploit the way the late and unlamented Shiwan Stalkscent had done. Thanquol favoured a more careful approach this time. They circled around the city, entering it from the north instead of the south, and they were cautious to keep clear of the broad main roads that led directly to the pyramid, instead scurrying through the crumbling side streets and keeping to the shadows.

It was not an easy thing, moving a hundred skaven and a pawful of human slaves silently through the rubble. If Thanquol had been less of a strategic genius, he might have despaired of accomplishing such a bold manoeuvre. Of course, it probably also helped keep his troops in top form when Boneripper bit off the head of the first clanrat to make a noise. A bit of terror did wonders to reinforce obedience among the rabble, Thanquol found.

The humans, of course, were clumsy and slow. If he didn't need them so much, Thanquol would have gutted them before they'd gone more than a hundred yards into the ruins. However, they were a vital element in his plan, so he ground his teeth, kicked a convenient underling, and just concentrated on all the things he would do to the useless creatures once they'd served their purpose.

A full moon shone over the ancient city, causing the crumbling stones to shine weirdly in the silver light. The great pyramid that was the Temple of Sotek stood like a gleaming mountain amid the decaying rubble around it. The stink of reptiles and serpents was thick in the noses of the skaven as soon as they entered the city, but as they crept closer to the temple a new smell sent a twinge of fear shuddering through them: the hot stagnant smell of ratman blood.

Closer to the pyramid now, Thanquol could see that there were lizardmen lining its steps, swaying their bodies in a hideously snakelike harmony. Between the ranks of the skinks, a few bound skaven shivered and whined, prisoners taken in the first ill-fated assault on the temple.

A low hissing chant whispered down from the flattened roof of the pyramid. A great golden altar stood upon the roof and across its surface, arms and legs held firmly by four robed reptilian priests, a struggling skaven was stretched. His pitiful crying made Thanquol glance nervously towards the jungle and wonder if perhaps they might be better returning to its shelter. Thoughts of retreat vanished from Thanquol's mind as he saw a fifth skink loom over the captive.

Even from such a distance, Thanquol could sense the awful power of the lizardman. Though all the reptiles looked the same to him, there was no mistaking that aura of brooding malignance and ancient enmity. It was Xiuhcoatl himself, the dread Prophet of Sotek, who stood behind the altar and lifted an obsidian knife above the breast of the struggling prisoner!

Xiuhcoatl lifted his scaly face heavenward, singing his praises to the moon and the watching stars. Then the prophet's hand came stabbing down. The ratman screamed as the dagger bit into his breast, thrashing wildly in the remorseless grip of the skink priests. Pitilessly, Xiuhcoatl dug the dagger's edge into the flesh of his sacrifice, relenting only when he had completed a vicious circle. Xiuhcoatl reached into the gory mess with his other claw, ripping free the ratman's beating heart.

The prophet ignored the twitching corpse splayed beneath him as he lifted his gruesome offering high above his head. Xiuhcoatl held the heart up so that the moon and all the stars might see it, then stepped forwards and displayed his trophy for the skinks standing upon the stairs. They hissed in satisfaction, the crests upon their heads snapping open to better exhibit their pleasure. Xiuhcoatl handed the heart to a skink standing upon the topmost step. Uttering a quick chirp to honour his leader, the skink tore ravenously at the lump of bloody flesh.

Xiuhcoatl stepped back behind the altar. A flick of his head sent the four priests into action. In stark contrast to the reverence with which the heart had been treated, the priests simply threw the body of the ratman down the side of the pyramid, not even waiting to see where it fell. Xiuhcoatl's head undulated in an approving nod as another skaven captive was pulled up the stairs and laid out upon the golden altar.

Thanquol quivered, smelling the musk of fear rising from his followers. It was good that they showed fear – it would mask his own frightened scent. Even the humans were terrified, their faces colourless as they watched Xiuhcoatl butcher his prisoners. Perhaps they weren't as stupid as the grey seer had thought.

'We-we not fight-slay that-that!' Shen Tsinge wailed, his tail clenched tightly in his hands.

'Run-run! Quick-quick!' added Tsang Kweek, his fangs chattering against each other.

'Go tell-say Nightlord that kill-kill scaly-meat is impossible!' insisted Kong Krakback.

Thanquol grinned at each of his underlings in turn, making each of them quail before his merciless gaze. He was careful to conceal his own fear as he upbraided his minions for theirs. 'He's out of his damn hide-hole!' Thanquol snarled, pointing a claw at the top of the pyramid. 'Now-now! We strike-kill! Lizard-meat pray to snake-devil, never see-smell us until it is too late-late!

'Kong, you take your war-rats and attack-kill from this side!' Thanquol told the hulking black skaven. 'I take-take gutter runners and assassins. We strike-kill from other end! No fear-fear! The Horned One will protect us!'

His underlings looked rather uncertain about that last part, but they did think he might have a point about taking the lizardmen by surprise. Thanquol toyed with a tiny nugget of warpstone, just enough to power a deliciously destructive spell. The implied threat removed the last reservations the skaven had about following his plan. Quickly they separated into two groups. Kong's warriors made the biggest group, nearly two-thirds of their number, and Thanquol had to resist the instinctive urge to join them. Instead, he turned to Tsang Kweek and the score of scouts and assassins with him. Impatiently, he motioned them to start hurrying around to the back of the pyramid, to the face they had approached in the first attack.

'What about man-things?' Shen Tsinge asked, flicking his tail at the humans.

'I will take them with me,' Thanquol said. 'They will make a good victory feast. Now, hurry and help Kong's war-rats!'

Shen stared at Thanquol, then at the pyramid, then at the human prisoners. 'I think I stay with you,' the sorcerer said, suspicion in his voice.

Thanquol gnashed his fangs in annoyance. Shen was too clever by far. As much as he wanted to order the sorcerer to follow Kong, he couldn't have him passing his suspicions on to the black skaven. 'Of course,' Thanquol hissed, lashing his tail. 'I was only thinking your magic would help Kong.' Grudgingly, he motioned for Shen to join the group rushing to circle the pyramid. He might be forced to keep the sorcerer with him, but he wasn't going to have him at his back.

IT TOOK THE skaven only a short time to make their way around the pyramid. They would have made it even faster, but the humans slowed them down. Tsang even pointed this out to Thanquol, but the grey seer stubbornly refused to leave his pets behind. By the time they reached the other face of the pyramid, sounds of battle were already coming from the other side.

Thanquol licked his fangs eagerly as he heard the sounds and watched skinks rushing over the top of the pyramid to join the fight raging on the steps below. Kong's war-rats should be able to keep the lizardmen distracted for a little while at least. Long enough to suit his purposes.

'They are fighting Kong!' Tsang Kweek pointed out. 'Now's our chance!' The gutter runner started to lead his troops towards the steps when Thanquol's snarl called him back.

'Fool-meat!' Thanquol snapped. He pointed a claw at the top of the pyramid where Xiuhcoatl and the four skink priests still stood. They seemed to be watching the battle raging on the other side of the pyramid, but Thanquol wasn't deceived. 'Xiuhcoatl is waiting for us to attack! It's a trap-trick, just like before!'

'Then what…'

Thanquol swatted the end of Tsang's snout with his staff. 'Dung-sucking idiot!' he snapped. He gestured with his staff to the opening, the magically protected tunnel that disintegrated any skaven who set paw within it. 'We're going in there, exactly where Xiuhcoatl won't expect us!'

Understanding started to dawn in Tsang's eyes, but Thanquol didn't wait for him to come around. Impatiently, he snarled at Boneripper to bring the humans to the tunnel. Snarling, his huge arms spread wide to prevent anyone from slipping past him, the rat ogre herded the prisoners towards the pyramid.

Thanquol scurried after the huge beast, keeping one anxious eye on the top of the pyramid. If Xiuhcoatl caught on to what he was doing, there might not be enough time to make it back to the jungle before the full force of the lizardmen came down upon them.

The grey seer glowered at the sinister passageway. The skinks had cleaned away the ashes, but Thanquol could still smell the stink of fiery death in the air. He stared hatefully at the glyphs with their depiction of a snake eating a rat.

Irritably, he turned and snarled at his slaves. They had names, but the grey seer found it annoying to try to remember them. They all smelled pretty much the same and it was difficult to match the scent to a name anyway. 'Which man-thing is leader?' Thanquol demanded.

Van Sommerhaus pointed frantically at Captain Schachter. 'Him! Him, he's the captain!'

Schachter gave the patroon an icy stare. 'Thanks, Lukas.'

At Thanquol's gesture, Boneripper shoved the man forward. Schachter straightened himself up, trying to appear unafraid as he stood before the horned ratman. His bravado quickly failed and soon he was wringing his hat between his hands and nodding his head in eager servility to everything that was said to him.

'Go-go!' Thanquol snarled. 'Take down snake-stones! Take down all snake-stones you see-find!' When he saw that his slave didn't understand, Thanquol growled at Boneripper.

Before anyone could react, Boneripper swung around and snatched a gutter runner from the ground. The ratman squirmed in his grip, but the huge beast was oblivious to his victim's clawing and biting. Grimly, Boneripper turned back towards the tunnel and with a single heave of his powerful arm he threw the gutter runner down the tunnel.

As soon as the skaven passed the invisible barrier, the glyphs burned with power. There was a scream, a flash of light, and then a little pile of ashes on the floor.

'Understand now, fool-meat?' Thanquol hissed at Schachter. 'Skaven can't go inside, but stupid man-things can!'

The captain nodded his understanding. 'You want them carvings tore down so's you can go inside!' Schachter flinched as the grey seer bared his fangs. He guessed that Thanquol was quickly losing his patience. 'I can do it! But I'll need help to do it.'

Thanquol glared suspiciously at the human, then glanced at the other slaves. 'One,' he said, lifting a claw. 'Take-take one to help.'

Schachter nodded his understanding. He looked over the other captives. For a moment, he locked eyes with Adalwolf. A hint of regret came across Schachter's features, then he pointed at Marjus Pfaff. 'Him. He's the one I want.'

Thanquol watched as the two men started timidly towards the opening, both of them looking down frequently at the smoking pile of ash. 'Quick-quick!' he snapped. 'Go fast-fast or I kill other man-things!'

The threat seemed to work. The two men stepped boldly over the pile of ash. Thanquol closed his eyes and covered his ears, expecting another explosive display of magic. When nothing happened, a malicious grin of triumph spread across his face. He was right! The wards only guarded against skaven, not humans!

Any sense of triumph he felt faded when Thanquol stared down the tunnel. The humans should have stopped and started tearing down the wards. Instead they were running down the corridor as fast as they could!

'Stop-stop! I kill-kill other man-things!' Thanquol shouted. Schachter turned and flicked his hand under his chin at the grey seer before racing off. Soon both men were lost in the gloom of the tunnel.

Thanquol gnashed his fangs in fury and drew his sword. He rounded on the last of his slaves, fully intent on carrying out his threat. Only cold pragmatism stayed his hand. If he killed the humans, he would never get inside the pyramid. He glared at the trembling captives, smelling their fear-stink. Then he remembered something else about their smell.

Savagely Thanquol grabbed Hiltrude's hair, pulling the woman away from the others. Humans were very protective of their breeders, he knew, and this knowledge was born out when Adalwolf clenched his fists and lunged at the grey seer. The mercenary didn't come close to striking Thanquol. Boneripper's enormous paw closed around him like a vice before he could take more than a few steps towards the grey seer. Only a quick command from Thanquol prevented the rat ogre from crushing him like a grape.

'Good-good,' Thanquol crowed as he returned Adalwolf's enraged gaze. 'You aren't like leader man-thing.' He paused, wondering if perhaps human leaders and skaven leaders weren't really the same when it came to the lives of their underlings. 'You don't want see-smell pretty breeder get hurt.'

'Take your filthy paws off her, you scum!' Adalwolf raged.

Thanquol chuckled darkly. He pulled Hiltrude's hair, forcing her head back and exposing her soft throat. 'No talk-speak!' Thanquol hissed. 'You do what I say, or I eat she-thing's tongue!' For emphasis, he bared his fangs, displaying the murderous incisors and snapping them together. He pointed at the tunnel with his staff. 'Go do what leader-man didn't do! Break snake-stones! Break all snake-stones or she-thing die-die!'

Seeing that Adalwolf understood that he meant his threat, Thanquol motioned for Boneripper to release the man.

'Are you all right?' Adalwolf asked Hiltrude. The woman tried to nod, but Thanquol tugged her head back.

'Stop talk-speak!' the grey seer fumed. 'Work-work!'

Glaring at the skaven, Adalwolf marched into the darkness of the tunnel. Soon he started attacking the nearest of the snake-glyphs. With no other tools to use, the man removed his boot, battering at the ward with the heavy heel.

Thanquol watched the operation with keen interest. He could sense something like a sigh in the air as the glyphs were battered into dust. It was the magical energy it had contained being released. The ward was broken! Its powers were gone!

Of course, he could have Boneripper persuade one of the gutter runners to test the corridor first just in case he was wrong…

FLATTENED DISKS OF blackness abruptly expanded into great pools as the eyes of the slann focused once more on the mundane plane of matter and spirit that surrounded the mage-priest. Skink scribes hurried around Lord Tlaco, recording every change in his mottled skin.

Lord Tlaco lounged in his gilded seat, the baser elements of his consciousness savouring the cool water skink attendants splashed across his rubbery skin. It was a crude pleasure, a weakness of the fleshy vessel Lord Tlaco's mind inhabited. The mage-priest quickly suppressed the sensation, concentrating again upon probabilities and unknown quotients. The low phase algorithms had reached Quetza and through them, the decaying fractals had broken the equations that restrained them. For the first time since the city had been retaken, the Temple of the Serpent was being invaded.

Everything was proceeding as the mage-priest had predicted, but still he could not decipher the final variables. All the elements of the equation were in place, but still he could not foresee the solution. For this reason, it was important that Lord Tlaco be there to observe the events that it had engineered.

One of the skink attendants locked eyes with Lord Tlaco as the slann set a thought-image in the lizardman's mind. As soon as the thought had taken form, the skink hurried away to prepare things. There was much to do: skinks to muster from their villages, saurus warriors to rouse from their caves, beasts to gather from their lairs. Lord Tlaco was stirring from his temple for the first time in millennia, but the slann had not forgotten the need to protect his fleshy shell. When the mage-priest began to travel through the geo-spatial folds an entire army would march with Lord Tlaco.

An army that would surround the abandoned city of Quetza and ensure that nothing escaped until Lord Tlaco's equation had been solved.

GREY SEER THANQUOL congratulated himself on his craftiness as he stalked down the gloomy stone corridors. Who but the mighty Grey Seer Thanquol could have solved the riddle of getting past the ancient wards that had been set in place to destroy any skaven that dared trespass within the pyramid? No one, of course. It was a feat of genius worthy of the Horned Rat himself!

He had to give some grudging admiration to the reptilian wizards that had created the cunning trap. There had been five layers of wards in all, five separate arrangements of the deadly glyph-stones each placed ten yards deeper into the tunnel than the last. Even if one set of wards had failed, the lizardmen had prepared others to guard the way.

The human had performed well enough, smashing each glyph-stone in turn. Thanquol had considered killing him once the last layer of wards was broken and the tunnel broke into a junction of intersecting corridors. His natural paranoia kept him from giving the order, however. There might be still other wards waiting for them inside the pyramid. If so, he would need the human to smash them. The others he would keep to ensure the slave's obedience.

Thanquol sniffed at the air. It was thick and musty with the stink of snakes, enough to set his fur crawling in fear. But there was something else, something he could smell each time he took a pinch of warpstone snuff. There was a suggestion of power in the air, a brooding arcane energy that coursed through the very stones.

Tsang Kweek and the assassins wanted to find the stairs and follow them to the roof of the pyramid so they could kill Xiuhcoatl. Angrily, Thanquol upbraided them for their stupidly suicidal plan. He pointed out to them that the prophet would be able to obliterate them all with his magic before they could even get within spitting distance of him. No, they had to find the source of Xiuhcoatl's power and destroy it if they were to have any chance of completing their mission.

In truth, Thanquol was no longer thinking in terms of Nightlord Sneek and his tyrannical whims. Smelling the power inside the pyramid had given him a much different idea. Any sorcerer as powerful as Xiuhcoatl couldn't possibly harness such energies without help. The lizardman must have many arcane artefacts hidden away within the temple, foci for his malignant spells. Thanquol was determined now to find them. With such artefacts in his control, he'd be able to laugh at Nightlord Sneek's threats! At all of the Lords of Decay for that matter! None of them would dare touch him! He would place his paw upon the Pillar of Commandments where the Horned Rat himself would decree Thanquol's right to sit upon the Council! He'd make short bloody work of that decrepit villain Kritislik and then it would be Seerlord Thanquol's brilliance that would govern the Council.

Yes! With Xiuhcoatl's treasure in his paws, Thanquol could leave this jungle hell behind and return in glory and triumph to Skavenblight!

Thanquol lashed his tail anxiously against the wall of the corridor. Besides, if they were quick enough in their stealing, they'd be able to get out of the pyramid before Xiuhcoatl noticed them. He was very keen to avoid confronting that scaly nightmare, just in case he was wrong about the lizardman's reliance on relics and artefacts to bolster his power.

Instead of upwards, Thanquol followed his nose and ordered his minions to head down, deeper inside the pyramid. The humans led the way, Tsang Kweek's knife always close to the she-slave's neck to ensure the obedience of the others. The other gutter runners clung close to their leader. After them followed the assassins and Shen Tsinge. Thanquol and Boneripper took the rear position. The grey seer didn't like being exposed to whatever enemies might be creeping up behind them, but he was even more nervous about having any of his 'allies' at his back. It was better to keep everyone where he could see them.

They had proceeded for several hundred yards when the corridor began to shudder. Great stone blocks dropped down from the ceiling, smashing flat against the floor and barring both advance and retreat. The skaven intruders were trapped in a section of corridor fifty yards long, surrounded on all sides by unyielding granite.

Panic seized the skaven, and their wails of shock and fear became a deafening clamour. Thanquol resisted the impulse to join in their terror, instead trying to focus on a way to get himself out of the trap. His mind raced with horrible images of the corridor slowly filling with sand to smother them or scummy swamp water to drown them or huge army ants to devour them. He fought down the hideous visions, staring desperately at the stone block behind him for any clue how to move it. Thanquol found his eyes watering as the air trapped with them became foul with fear musk. Perhaps that was their intention, to let the skaven simply suffocate!

It was on his tongue to order Boneripper to start killing things so the oxygen would last longer when a new sound reached Thanquol's ears. It was a dull, grinding noise that throbbed through the walls of the corridor. At first he thought it was a delusion of his fear, but soon the grey seer could not deny that the walls were moving. Inch by inch they were being pressed inwards. He thought about the manner in which slug jelly was made and new horror gripped him.

'Boneripper!' Thanquol shrieked at his bodyguard, straining to make himself heard above the terrified squeals of the other skaven and the screams of the humans. 'Open-open! Quick-quick!' The grey seer pushed against the heavy stone block choking the corridor.

To Thanquol's horror, the stupid rat ogre simply turned and trudged deeper down the hall, swatting aside the skaven that got in his way. The grey seer hurled curse after curse after the lumbering brute, threatening him with all manner of terrible deaths if he didn't come back and move the block.

Thanquol returned to his desperate attack on the stone block. He sent a bolt of black lightning crashing against it, but all the spell did was to warm the rock. He tried to focus his mind around an escape spell, but knew his concentration wasn't equal to the challenge. He kept thinking that even if he successfully slipped into the Realm of Chaos and back again, he might reappear on the roof of the pyramid with Xiuhcoatl. That would be like jumping out of the cat and into the snake!

The grey seer spun about as he felt something brush against him. His hand lashed out, and he heard a skaven cry out in pain. Then he felt a tremor in the aethyr. There was a crimson flash of light, a sound like thunder and the stink of brimstone. Thanquol quickly patted his robes and found that some of his warpstone was missing. He ground his fangs together in fury, willing to bet that flea-ridden sorcerer Shen Tsinge wasn't with them anymore. It would be just like the coward to abandon his friends and save his own fur!

Boneripper had reached the middle of the passage. The walls were so close together now that the rat ogre was forced to move sideways, and even then it was a tight squeeze for him. He moved with one ear pressed against the wall. When he got to the middle of the corridor, he stopped. Crouching low to the floor, Boneripper drove one of his mammoth fists against the wall. Stone crumbled beneath the blow. A second punch and an entire block cracked away. Boneripper reached into the hole he had made, his claws scrabbling about in the darkness.

Thanquol scrabbled desperately at the stone blocking his retreat as the walls came grinding still closer. Then, suddenly, they stopped. At first he blinked in disbelief, but it was true, the walls had stopped moving. He glanced back down the corridor and saw Boneripper pulling twisted copper rods and gears from the hole he had made. The clever, loyal rat ogre had stopped the walls just in time!

Thanquol stalked through the huddled masses of his shivering minions. It was important to show them that the ordeal hadn't frightened him in the least. After all, he'd told his bodyguard to get them out of the trap. He could have easily tried to escape by using his magic, but he had stayed behind to make certain his followers were safe too. He could see they appreciated that by the way they stared at him in reverence and awe.

'Boneripper!' Thanquol called. He pointed his staff at the block choking the far end of the passage. 'Move that thing and open the way for us.'

Obediently, Boneripper squeezed his way along the corridor and began pushing the heavy block. It took a long time to get the stone moved and Thanquol was forced to have the humans and some of the gutter runners help the rat ogre. But they did get it open at last.

A shadowy figure raced at them from the darkness as soon as they emerged from the trapped corridor. The scent of the apparition told Thanquol who it was before he saw him. Briefly, Thanquol considered blasting Shen Tsinge with a bolt of warp-lightning anyway.

'Great master, you have escaped!' Shen whimpered, throwing himself at Thanquol's feet. There was genuine terror in the sorcerer's voice. After escaping the crushing walls, Shen had found himself alone in the blackness of the pyramid. Unable to smell another skaven, his nose filled with the reek of snakes instead, Shen's instincts overwhelmed him and he'd come running back.

Thanquol drove the head of his staff into Shen's belly, knocking the wind out of him and doubling him over. While the sorcerer tried to suck breath back into his lungs, Thanquol frisked him and removed the warpstone nuggets he had stolen.

'Be thankful I might still need you,' Thanquol hissed in Shen's ear. 'Otherwise I would give you to them.' He gestured at the other Eshin ratmen who stared at Shen with murderous eyes. 'I don't think they appreciate the way you left everyone behind.'

Thanquol motioned for Tsang to lead the humans forwards again. 'You should understand, mage-rat. When you are leader, you need to look after your underlings as though they were your own whelps.'

ADALWOLF KEPT WATCHING his verminous captors, waiting for the fiends to relax their guard. Unfortunately they seemed perpetually paranoid, leaping at shadows and whining at every change in the air. Only when they had all been trapped in the corridor with the moving walls had the underfolk been inattentive enough to give Adalwolf the opportunity he wanted, but there had been no place to go.

The journey through the darkness of the pyramid was a terrifying ordeal. Only sporadically did the ratmen light a torch so he could see where he was expected to lead them. Most of the time he was forced to feel his way, the image of an open pit an omnipresent fear. The vermin were oblivious and uncaring to his blindness. They scratched, kicked and bit him every time their patience wore thin. He could hear the cries of his companions each time the ratmen became impatient and vented their frustrations. Hiltrude's sharp moans, Diethelm's weary gasps and the pained curses of the two remaining sailors were knives of guilt twisting in his belly each time he heard them. Even the whines and pleas of van Sommerhaus had ceased to provide Adalwolf with sardonic satisfaction. Whatever his many faults, at least the patroon was human.

In a horrible way, Adalwolf couldn't even blame Schachter and Marjus for abandoning them. They had seen a chance for escape and they had taken it. Under such ghastly circumstances, he wondered if he would have done the same. He liked to think he wouldn't have.

Except at those times when he was allowed light, the ratmen were nothing but chitters and stench to Adalwolf. All he could see of them were their baleful red eyes gleaming in the darkness. The underfolk appeared perfectly capable of navigating the dark, but their horned leader's fear about traps caused Adalwolf to continue to walk point. The craven things intended that he should find any more of the stones with the snake-glyph on them. Adalwolf wished that he would find others. It might offer a chance for escape.

He thought of the strange creatures who had built this place. That sight of the reptilian priest cutting out the heart of a ratman was burned into his brain. He'd never seen anything quite as horrible in all his life as that gruesome spectacle. Indeed, for all their apparent enmity towards the underfolk, Adalwolf wasn't certain which of them he was more afraid of: the ratmen or the lizardmen.

During one of the frequent rests they were allowed while the ratmen bickered among themselves, Diethelm had whispered his own observations to the others. He was attuned enough to the gods and their ways to feel the divine power radiating from the lizardman they had seen conducting the sacrifice. It wasn't the warm, wholesome aura of the gods they knew, but rather something cold, distant and uncaring. However, there was no denying the magnitude of the power he sensed within the reptile-priest. It was, Diethelm confessed with a shudder, like the presence of the High Matriarch of Manann, only even greater.

The priest also wondered if Thanquol hadn't lied to them when they were captured about creating the strange path through the jungle for them. It seemed a feat of magic that was beyond the ratmen. Diethelm wasn't sure it was beyond the strange, scaly lizardmen. But if the lizardmen had brought them, the question remained as to why they had brought them.

Adalwolf shrugged aside the lingering question. It was a problem to worry about later. For now, escaping from the ratmen was the only thing.

The chance the mercenary had been watching for came when the corridor they had been travelling suddenly opened out into a vast natural cavern. The light from the torch one of the ratmen held cast weird shimmers across the floor and the air was thick with a stagnant dampness. A few steps into the room and Adalwolf discovered why the floor reflected the light. It wasn't a floor at all, but a vast pool. The water was almost level with the ledge that surrounded it and so filmed over with scum that it was easy to mistake it for solid ground in the darkness.

There was something more, however. Adalwolf could see ugly yellow bulbs floating just beneath the surface. It took him a moment to decide that they were some manner of egg. The spawn of the lizardmen? He crouched and put his hand into the water, finding it almost hot to his touch. Quickly he was pulled away by one of the vicious ratmen. Greedily, the vermin pawed at the water, scooping out one of the yellowish bulbs.

Adalwolf's suspicion that the bulbs were eggs was quickly confirmed as the ratman broke it open and began slurping out the yolk. The monster that had been keeping a knife on Hiltrude made a jealous snarl and rushed the first ratman. Tsang Kweek tore the egg from the underling's paws and gave him a spiteful kick that knocked him into the pool. Viciously, Tsang tore apart the leathery shell and began gnawing on the half-formed reptile inside.

The mercenary turned away from the hideous sight. In doing so, he noticed something moving in the water, sliding through the scummy film towards the ratman Tsang had thrown into the pool. He quickly looked back at his captors, but they were too busy pawing at the water to grab more eggs to see the menace moving towards them.

'When I say move,' Adalwolf whispered to his companions, 'we all make a rush for those stairs.' He nodded his chin to a set of stone steps a few dozen yards further along the ledge that circled the pool. It was just visible in the flickering light of the ratman's torch.

'We can't!' protested van Sommerhaus. 'They'll catch us!'

Adalwolf winced at the patroon's craven words and more particularly the volume with which they were said. He glanced at the ratmen, but none of them seemed to have heard. He grabbed van Sommerhaus by his frilled vest. 'Stay with them then, but don't get in my way!'

'We're with you,' Hiltrude told him, glancing with disgust at her benefactor. The sailors and Diethelm gave nods of approval.

Adalwolf looked back at the pool, watching for any sign of the swimming creature he had seen. He couldn't be certain, but he had the impression of other beasts moving through the water now. 'The underfolk are going to have some problems in a little while. When they're busy, make for the stairs. I'll be right behind you after I get the torch.'

His instructions had only just been whispered when the ratman in the pool suddenly vanished. The sudden disappearance wasn't noticed by the rest of the underfolk, but when a huge scaly hand erupted from the pool and pulled one of the egg thieves under the water, the entire pack began to squeal in fright. They scurried away from the edge of the pool, but their quick retreat wasn't enough to save them.

Three enormous lizardmen leapt from the pool, landing upon the stone ledge and hissing at the underfolk. They were gigantic creatures, their bodies encased in thick dark scales, their enormous jaws sporting huge fangs. There might have been some kinship between these beasts and the small, wiry lizardmen they had seen outside, but if so it was more distant even than that between the ratmen and the giant brute their leader kept as his bodyguard.

At the first sight of the lizardmen, the underfolk cringed away in fear. The hissing reptiles soon laid into them with giant clubs and axes, weapons that shone with the fiery lustre of gold. The death shrieks of ratmen became deafening as the hulking reptiles attacked the intruders.

Adalwolf knew that the ratmen would quickly overcome their fear. Either their merciless master would goad them into fighting the troll-like lizardmen or else they would retreat. Whichever choice they made, Adalwolf had no intention of following them.

Hiltrude and the others were making their panicked race to the stairs, even van Sommerhaus running along with them. Adalwolf spun about, leaping at the ratman with the torch. The creature's attention was entirely upon the lizardmen, he had forgotten the prisoners. It was the last mistake the vermin ever made. In brutally short order, Adalwolf's arm locked around the monster's neck, breaking it with a savage twist.

Swiftly, Adalwolf retrieved the torch from where it blazed on the floor. He turned and ripped the rusty sword from the ratman's belt.

Now the battle was joined. Thanquol's shrill voice rang out, imperious and tyrannical, snarling at his minions to attack the lizardmen. A crackling sheet of lightning rose from the horned ratman's staff, engulfing one of the huge lizardmen, electrocuting both it and the two underfolk caught in the reptile's paws.

Adalwolf didn't wait to see more. He spun about and made a mad dash for the stairs. He could see his friends crossing the ledge ahead of him. He could also see a scaly back moving through the waters of the pool towards them.

The mercenary opened his mouth to shout a warning, but he was too late. Another giant lizardman burst from the pool, seizing one of the sailors in its claws. The seaman screamed piteously as the monster twisted his body apart with a horrible wrenching motion of its hands.

Adalwolf roared his most fierce war cry as he saw the beast discard its first victim and reach for another. The monster turned at his call and Adalwolf shoved his torch into its eyes. The lizardman reeled back, but in a slow and clumsy fashion. Its lethargic nervous system hadn't registered the bite of the flame until the scales of its face were blackened and charred.

As the giant reptile stumbled, Adalwolf drove his sword into its gut. For an instant, he thought the rusty underfolk blade would buckle and fail to pierce the thick scaly hide, but at last the sword sank into the lizardman's flesh. Adalwolf made one effort to pull the blade free before he was forced to duck a sweep of the monster's lashing tail. The lizardman stared at him from its burnt face and opened its jaws in a vicious hiss.

If there had been anywhere to run, Adalwolf would have fled from the monster. But the beast stood between himself and the stairs, completely blocking his way. His only hope lay in the brute's slow reactions. It still seemed half asleep, perhaps adjusting its cold body to the change from the hot pool to the clammy atmosphere of the pyramid's cellars.

Roaring at the lizardman, Adalwolf lunged at the hulking brute, throwing himself flat and diving between its clawed legs. He screamed in pain as he was battered by the beast's tail as he scrambled underneath the monster, feeling as though a dragon had bounced his skull against the floor. Vengefully, he struck the monster with the torch again. The flame failed to burn the dripping scales of the lizardman's tail, but the heat was enough to drive it back.

Adalwolf leapt to his feet, stumbling towards the stairs. He saw the huge lizardman turn to pursue him, but at that moment the beast was set upon from behind. The reptile was locked in the crushing embrace of Thanquol's rat ogre. The lizardman flailed and clawed at its attacker, but Boneripper took small notice of the whipping tail and slashing claws. The rat ogre buried his fangs in the lizardman's neck, biting deep into its throat.

The mercenary didn't wait to watch the end of that struggle, but as he climbed the stairs, he thought he could hear the lizardman's ribs cracking one by one as Boneripper crushed the life from it.

'Hurry!' he shouted at Hiltrude and the others, impressed beyond words that they had waited for him. 'It looks like the underfolk are going to win that fight and I don't want to be around when they do!'

Panicked by his words, the small band of refugees fled up the stairs, hoping that whatever horrors the darkness ahead held, they would be better than the nightmare they had left behind.

CHAPTER TEN

The Sacred Serpent of Sotek

As THE FUGITIVES fled up the stairs, the stink of reptilian musk intensified, becoming an overwhelming reek that made their skin crawl with loathing. After the horrific attack by the lizardmen in the spawning pools, the humans had new reasons to find the smell intimidating, reasons that went beyond even the natural repugnance of all mammalian life for the reptiles that had ruled before them.

Adalwolf forced his companions to press on when they would have succumbed to their fear and tried to turn back. There was nothing to return to. Either the ratmen had triumphed over the guardians of the pool, or the lizardmen had slaughtered the invaders. Whichever side had won, there was only death waiting for them back there. They could only press on and hope they would find some way out of this maze of ancient horrors.

There was one thing that the mercenary found reassuring about the thick ophidian stench. In his brief time with the ratkin, he had seen the way they relied more upon their sense of smell than their sense of sight. He knew they were even more frightened of the reptiles than he was. The greater the musky reek of snakes became, the greater the likelihood that the skaven wouldn't follow them.

The mercenary led the way, holding the sputtering torch before him, watching its flame with an uneasy eye. He whispered a soft prayer to Myrmidia to keep the flame alive, glancing at Diethelm as he did so and wondering if it was impious to invoke the goddess while the priest of another god was standing beside him.

Sweaty fingers closed around Adalwolf's arm, quivering as they gripped him. He turned to find Hiltrude's ashen face staring at him with wide eyes and trembling lips.

'We can't go on,' she gasped. 'Please, we can't go any more!' Her hand fell away from the mercenary's arm. Frantically she began rubbing the tatters of her dress, as though she were trying to wipe something unclean from her clothes. 'I can feel it crawling on me!'

'There's nothing there,' Diethelm assured her, trying to use the calmness in his voice to counter the panic in hers. 'You are safe.'

Hiltrude was unconvinced, her head making erratic jerking motions as she looked down at the stairs. There was utter terror in her eyes now. Her boots, rotten from the jungle, stomped relentlessly against the steps. Adalwolf lower his torch and felt a chill race down his spine when he failed to see anything except the courtesan's feet.

'She's out of her mind,' van Sommerhaus declared. 'Forget her and let's get out of this hell hole.'

Adalwolf glared at the patroon, his fist raised to break the merchant's aquiline nose. 'We're not leaving anybody,' he growled.

'Look at her,' van Sommerhaus persisted. 'She's gone mad! A mad woman's only going to slow us down! Ruin our own chance to escape!'

'Only a little while ago, she spoke up for you when you wanted to stay with the underfolk,' Adalwolf snarled at van Sommerhaus. The reminder visibly shamed the patroon and he looked away. The mercenary turned from him and grabbed Hiltrude by the shoulders.

'We have to go,' he told her. 'It's only a little farther,' he added, feeling guilty as he spoke the lie.

Hiltrude didn't even raise her head but kept staring at the steps, stamping her foot against every shadow. 'Snakes everywhere!' she almost shrieked. 'Don't let them touch me! Can't you feel them!'

Adalwolf had to admit there was something beyond the heavy reptilian musk filling the air. There was something else, an oily sensation, like phantoms running their wispy hands along his skin. Diethelm had said it was aethyric power the mercenary sensed, that the pyramid was saturated with magical energy and they were drawing near to its source. The thought made Adalwolf even more uneasy. If there was one thing that would goad that horned ratman into braving the snake smell, it would be the lure of power.

'There's nothing there,' Adalwolf assured her, ignoring his own doubts. He lowered the torch again, lighting the steps for her. 'No snakes, see.'

The woman shook her head, but at least some of the fear had drained out of her eyes. With a little more time, Adalwolf was sure he could make her see reason.

Unfortunately, time was one thing they didn't have. Hiltrude's panicked shouts would travel far within the stone vaults of the pyramid and Adalwolf wasn't sure what might have been listening. Already he fancied he could hear something moving far behind them on the darkened stairway.

'I need you to hold this,' Adalwolf told Diethelm. The priest looked at him with some perplexity as he placed the sputtering torch in Diethelm's hand.

Without warning, Adalwolf spun about again, his fist smacking against the side of Hiltrude's head. Her eyes fluttered and he caught her before the stunned woman could fall to the floor. Slinging the woman over his shoulder, Adalwolf motioned for the others to hurry up the stairs.

A last worried look into the blackness below and Adalwolf trudged after them.

IT WAS SOME time later before Hiltrude recovered her senses. She struggled in Adalwolf's grip, beating her fists against his back until he threatened to knock her head against the wall if she didn't stop. The courtesan was a good deal more reasonable than before and quickly relented. Adalwolf breathed a quiet sigh of relief. It meant she wasn't mad as van Sommerhaus had insisted, just afraid. Handrich knew she had every right to be.

'You can set me down,' Hiltrude told him. 'I'm all right now.'

'Happy to hear it,' Adalwolf answered, making no move to slide her off his shoulder. He trudged onward, keeping his eyes on the flickering light of Diethelm's torch.

'Really, I won't cause any more problems,' Hiltrude insisted, a trace of annoyance in her tone.

'I know you won't,' Adalwolf said, still climbing the steps.

'Look you filthy pirate-stabber!' Hiltrude snapped. 'Tell me you've never been afraid of something!' Adalwolf could feel her body shiver against his. 'It was the smell. The smell of those slithering...' She shuddered, forcing Adalwolf to steady her with his arm. 'I'd rather be back down there with the ratkin than...'

'And that's why I'm not setting you down,' Adalwolf told her. 'The smell is getting worse, not better. There's a snake nest somewhere and I fear we'll have to cross it before we get out of this place.'

Hiltrude's fist pounded against his neck. Adalwolf brought his palm cracking against the firm bottom draped over his shoulder. The woman yipped in alarm at the stinging slap.

'A guilder says your arse wears out before my neck,' Adalwolf warned her. Hiltrude relented, sagging desolately against his back. It pained the mercenary to hear her soft sobs. It was for her own good, he couldn't trust her to master her fear. The idea of her racing back down the stairs and into the clutches of Thanquol was something that sickened his very soul to think about. She had to face whatever was waiting for them above, whether she wanted to or not.

Adalwolf stopped as he saw Diethelm's torch finally go out. He heard van Sommerhaus and the sailor cry out in agony as the light died. Terror gnawed at his own mind as they were plunged into darkness and he felt his legs wobble beneath him. Only the thought of Hiltrude's dependence on him steadied his nerves. He had to stay strong or they were both lost.

Gradually, as the darkness surrounded him, Adalwolf's eyes adjusted to the gloom. With a gasp, he saw that the blackness was not absolute. There was light ahead of them, distant but distinct. He forgot his fear of verminous shapes stalking after them from below and shouted the news to his companions.

Thinking it was the light of day beckoning them, the men raced up the stairs, fatigue and horror overwhelmed by a surge of renewed hope. Van Sommerhaus and the sailor were well ahead of Adalwolf and they were the first to emerge from the darkness and into the light. Their jubilant cries drifted back down the stairs, making even Hiltrude forget her fear. Adalwolf set her down and together they climbed the last section, eager to feel the clean light of day against their faces.

The light wasn't clean and it didn't come from the sun. It came from dozens of great stone pots and the fires that flickered within them. The smoke of whatever smouldered within the pots had a thin, pasty taste to it but almost no smell to call its own. It did nothing to overcome the musky serpent reek of the place, which had now grown to the nigh unbearable. If Adalwolf had wrapped a python about his face, he couldn't imagine the smell being half as bad.

The room that sheltered the stone pots was immense, so big that the *Cobra of Khemri* and three sister ships might have been set stern to prow across the middle of the floor and still not touch the walls. Great curled columns rose from the floor like a stone forest to support the ceiling of the chamber, their spiral contours seeming to writhe and slither as the flickering light set weird shadows dancing upon them.

As far as they could see every wall was covered from floor to ceiling in strange glyphs, sometimes broken by great stone murals. Adalwolf shivered to stare at the murals for there was an air of impossible ancientness about them. They depicted the lizardmen making war with creatures that defied imagination: foul cyclopean devil-beasts, dragon-like centaurs and daemon-things of every description. There were men too, huge and horrible and hoary with evil, wearing armour made from bones and carrying stone axes as they waged war upon the reptiles. The lizardmen, however, were no easy prey and Adalwolf could see ranks of huge scaly warriors fighting alongside the smaller reptiles they had seen upon the steps of the pyramid and the giant guardians of the spawning pool. Sometimes there would be a bloated, toadlike being depicted on the murals, but always rendered in such a way as to compel the same sensation of awe and reverence as had moved the chisel of the artisan who carved it.

Many doorways gaped in the walls, dark passageways that led back into the depths of the pyramid. One glance at the simple number of these openings made it clear that this was the centre of the structure, the very heart of the temple. Adalwolf noted with a start that each archway glistened in the flickering light, for each of the gateways was edged in gold and jade.

It was not this wealth that had made van Sommerhaus and the sailor cry out in glee, however. The two men stood in the middle of the chamber, having ascended a short dais that rose from the floor. At the top of the dais was a great altar. Adalwolf shook his head in disbelief as he gazed upon it, for the altar was bigger than a ship's longboat yet it shone with the same lustre as the gilded archways. The immense altar was made of gold!

Caution vanished as every avaricious thought he'd ever had thundered through his heart. Adalwolf released Hiltrude and dashed across the chamber. He ran his hands lovingly across the sleek surface of the golden altar. It was cunningly wrought in the shape of hundreds of serpents, their coils intertwined in a complex lattice of priceless wealth. The gleaming eyes of each snake were picked out with the finest rubies he'd ever seen, their blue tongues were crafted from crushed sapphires and their shining fangs were made of pearl. The mercenary could only gawk at the display of wealth beneath his hands. A man could repay the bribe that had bought Marienburg's independence from the Empire with this altar and have enough left over to lease the entire city of Carroburg as well!

'And you thought I was crazy!' van Sommerhaus boasted, running his hand along one of the snakes. 'Here's enough gold to choke a dwarf!' The patroon laughed. 'A dwarf? Handrich's Purse, there's enough here to choke a dragon!'

The sailor began trying to pry one of the rubies from the altar, having twisted his belt buckle into a crude chisel. He cursed lividly as the stone popped out and bounced away. He groped for it for a moment in the darkness, then cursed again. Turning, the seaman raced down to one of the fire pots and tore a strip of cloth from his tattered shirt. Holding it over the fire, he soon had a serviceable torch. As he swung back around to run back up to the altar, however, he froze in place and pointed dramatically at the columns.

'They're edged in jewels!' the sailor shouted. He forgot about the lost ruby and pounced on the nearest of the columns, grinning greedily as he studied it. 'Emeralds! Sapphires! A diamond as big as my fist!'

Adalwolf shared a look of jubilation with van Sommerhaus and both men rushed down to see what the sailor had found. As they ran towards the column, Adalwolf felt something snap beneath his boot. He bent down, picking it off the floor. Colour drained from his face as he found the object he had stepped on to be an arrow, its obsidian head still wet with blood. It was a stark reminder that this place was not abandoned, a cold slap to cool his dreams of gold and glory.

'We must leave this place,' Diethelm's whisper sounded in Adalwolf's ear. There was a look of mute horror on the priest's face, an expression that was almost primal in its terror. 'I feel that we stand in the house of an alien god, one who does not look upon our kind with friendly eyes. We must leave before we arouse it.'

Adalwolf tried to shove the priest away. Diethelm's words of warning made an angry resentment swell within the mercenary. What did a simple cleric of Manann know about the worth of gold? What did he know about trying to keep an estranged family fed and sheltered? What did he know about having enough money to buy a new life for himself? With the gold he saw on display all around him, Adalwolf would be wealthy and respected! He'd be somebody, not just a pirate-stabbing sellsword! He'd be able to afford the love of a woman of quality…

He glanced about to find Hiltrude. He saw her and a sense of relief filled him. She had quite forgotten her fear and was just as enthralled as the rest of them. She raced like a schoolgirl to help van Sommerhaus and the sailor pry gems from the columns, her face bright with the rapture of wealth.

Then her face went pale and her eyes became pits of despair. She froze almost in midstep, staring in mute horror into the gloom of the temple.

Adalwolf heard a sound like sailcloth being unrolled and following it he discovered both its cause and the source of Hiltrude's terror. He fell to his knees as every muscle in his body seemed to turn to jelly. The darkness of the temple wasn't empty, but what it had sheltered was an abomination that made even the horrors depicted upon the stone murals seem tame.

Gigantic, the great serpent slithered from the shadows of the inner temple. Its sleek body glistened wetly in the firelight, armoured scales of brown and black rasping against the columns, leaving slivers of grey, lifeless skin behind. A blunt head as big as a river barge rose up from the floor, the black pools of its eyes staring across the temple, the blue lash of its forked tongue flickering and dancing before its snout as it smelled the air. The enormous snake continued to crawl from the darkness, coil upon coil of its scaly bulk undulating across the floor until Adalwolf thought even this vast chamber could not contain its titanic dimensions.

Van Sommerhaus and the sailor were late in realising the peril that crawled towards them. It was only when the seaman again lost a gem he had pried loose and started to chase it across the floor that he became aware of the giant serpent. He shrieked as he saw the monster and dived back to cower behind the column. As he ran, the great snake lunged at him, driving its enormity towards the sailor.

Narrowly it missed the sailor, but as the man tried to seek refuge behind the column, van Sommerhaus thrust him back, unwilling to jeopardise his own sanctuary by sharing it with the man. The sailor sprawled on the floor, the great serpent looming above him. Its cold eyes stared at him for an instant, then great folds of flesh snapped open on either side of its neck, making its terrible head appear three times as immense. The blunt head struck, the great jaws opened and the sailor was gone. Hideously, Adalwolf could still hear the man's muffled screams rising from the serpent's maw and he could see the horrible bulge in the snake's throat as it pushed its meal down towards its stomach.

The serpent was not content with one victim, however. Its tongue lashed out again and it began to study the column behind which van Sommerhaus shivered in terror. First from one side, then from the other, the snake studied the column. Its lash-like tongue almost brushed the patroon's cheek as the snake sniffed for more prey. Van Sommerhaus, crushing himself against the column, did not move a muscle throughout the ordeal. The snake's body trembled, angry hisses seethed through its scaly jaws, yet still it failed to find the man.

Suddenly the great serpent spun its head around. Again its tongue flickered and tasted the air. It began to slither forwards again. At first it seemed the monster was interested in the altar, then it swung back around. Adalwolf's stomach turned when he saw that it was staring at Hiltrude.

The courtesan was still frozen with terror, unable to look away from the giant snake. Even as it began to slither towards her, Hiltrude did not run.

'She'll be killed,' Diethelm shuddered.

Adalwolf clenched his fists with impotent rage, his only weapon a broken arrowhead. A desperate thought came to him. 'If she doesn't move, maybe it won't see her!' he gasped. 'It couldn't find van Sommerhaus.'

Diethelm shook his head. 'It couldn't pick him out from the column,' he said. 'It could still smell him. She doesn't have a column to hide behind and confuse it.'

Terror dripped from Adalwolf's brow as he watched the snake's steady progress towards Hiltrude. He knew it was death, but he couldn't watch such an atrocity unfold before his eyes. Gripping the arrow like a dagger, he made ready to charge the reptile. Diethelm's hand restrained him.

Before Adalwolf could shake him off, Diethelm pointed him towards Hiltrude. 'Save the girl,' the priest told him. 'I have no idea if this will work. Most likely I walk to my death, far from the face of my god. But even my death might buy you the time you need.'

Diethelm walked away, marching straight towards the monstrous serpent. He shouted and shrieked at the reptile, then began stamping his feet on the floor. The giant snake swung its head around, its flickering tongue pulling the priest's smell from the air. Slowly it turned its body and began to slither towards him.

Understanding came to Adalwolf in an instant and he marvelled at the boldness of the priest's plan. The sharp sting of shame pained him at every step as he abandoned Diethelm to the approach of the serpent, but he knew if he didn't get Hiltrude away then the priest's sacrifice was for nothing.

Adalwolf reached Hiltrude at a bound. He struck her across the face, trying to snap her mind back from its terrible fascination. The woman screamed, clutching at Adalwolf, trembling and moaning in his arms. She pointed at the great serpent and shrieked again.

The mercenary risked one look back, then hesitated. He blinked in disbelief, but it was true. Diethelm sat upon the floor, his body slowly swaying from side to side. Above him, its awful hood of scales open on either side of its blunt head, the great serpent was likewise swaying back and forth. The priest had done the impossible. He had mesmerised the great serpent, just as he had done to the jungle viper days before.

Now, more than ever, the mercenary felt the impossibility of abandoning Diethelm. The priest had made a bold gamble and won. Adalwolf knew he could never call himself a man if he left such a courageous soul behind. He stared hard into Hiltrude's eyes, trying to find any flicker of reason beneath her fear.

'Go down that hallway and stay there,' he told her, praying she would understand him. The doorways were too small for the serpent to crawl into, if he could get her into one of the corridors she'd be safe from the giant snake. But there was no sign of understanding on her ashen face. 'Please,' he pleaded. 'I have to go help Diethelm. You must go down the hallway!'

'No one is going anywhere!'

Adalwolf spun around as he heard the threatening voice. He watched as Captain Schachter and Marjus Pfaff came creeping out from one of the corridors.

The two seamen held tiny bows in their hands and strange golden swords tucked beneath their belts. They grinned evilly at the mercenary.

'My thanks for taking care of the snake,' Schachter continued, nodding his head towards Diethelm. 'I forgot the priest could do that. See, Marjus, it's a good thing you didn't sacrifice him to Stromfels.'

'Schachter!' van Sommerhaus cried out, emerging from behind his column. 'Praise Handrich you're here! I'll remember this and you'll be well rewarded when we get back to Marienburg!'

The sea captain turned and aimed his bow at the patroon. 'Lukas,' he said, his voice dripping with scorn. 'I didn't see you there. I was rather hoping the ratmen had eaten you by now. If you don't want an arrow in your belly, I suggest you stop right where you are.'

The patroon froze, disbelief on his face. He made a placating gesture with his hands. 'Please, Schachter, we're old friends. You shouldn't joke like this.'

'Let's kill him now,' Marjus snarled. 'Then we don't have to listen to his mouth.'

Captain Schachter shook his head and a wicked smile twisted his mouth. 'I don't think so. Not while he's useful. Adalwolf, I wonder if you and Lukas and the girl wouldn't be nice enough to go and collect a few of those shiny stones for us.'

'Why not get them yourself?' Adalwolf growled back.

Schachter laughed. 'To be honest, I don't like the idea of going back out there. We already had a run in with the snake. He wasn't so obliging as the lizardmen who donated their weapons to us. Five poisoned arrows in it and the thing still wanted to eat us.'

Marjus drew back his arm, the arrow nocked to his bow trembling from the tension. 'Five didn't kill the snake, but one will do for you, hero.'

Adalwolf could see murder in the mate's eyes, the unreasoning bloodlust born of greed. He took a step back, moving Hiltrude behind him. If they could just reach one of the columns before the sailor loosed his arrow...

'No need for that,' Schachter scolded Marjus. 'Adalwolf is a man of honour. That's why we can trust him. That's why I picked you to escape with me instead of him. I knew he'd never leave the others behind. With that being the way things stand, I must admit I've changed my mind. Send the girl over, we'll hang on to her as an incentive to make you work fast.'

Hiltrude shook her head, clinging to Adalwolf's shoulders. Between the serpent and the murderous human snakes now threatening them, the last thing she wanted to do was leave the mercenary's side.

Van Sommerhaus noted her hesitancy. 'The whore will give you trouble, Schachter. Take me as your hostage instead!'

The two seamen laughed grimly at the patroon's offer. 'Lukas, I wouldn't break wind to save your life,' Schachter sneered. 'I don't know many men who would. So you get your arse over there and start pulling diamonds out of the walls. It'll be a rare novelty to see you do some honest work for once!

'Send the girl over, Adalwolf,' the captain demanded, turning back to the warrior. 'I don't know how long the priest can keep that snake busy and I intend to be very rich and very far away when it loses interest in him. Now send her over or I'll stick an arrow in both your gizzards!'

Regretfully, Adalwolf pushed Hiltrude away, motioning for her to do as the sailors said. He felt a stab of guilt as he watched her stagger towards Schachter. 'If you hurt her…'

'We'll do what we damn well please!' roared Marjus, drowning out the mercenary's threat. The sailor's face was crimson with rage, all of his resentment for Adalwolf rising to the fore. 'Curse us from the sunken hells of Mermedus, you stinking bilge rat!' Marjus drew his arm back again, the poisoned arrow trembling in his hand.

Marjus never loosed his arrow. Instead he screamed. He screamed as sickly green lightning crackled and sizzled around his body, as his skin blackened and the teeth rattled from his mouth, as his hair shrivelled and his blood boiled. What finally collapsed to the temple floor was little more than a smoking husk.

Schachter turned to face the darkened mouth of the tunnel Adalwolf and the others had followed up from the spawning pools. What he saw had him flinging his bow to the floor and lifting his hands over his head in surrender.

At the head of a mob of furious ratmen, Grey Seer Thanquol glared at the fugitive. Sorcerous fire continued to burn around the head of his staff. With a chittering laugh, Thanquol pointed his staff towards Schachter.

'THANQUOL!' ADALWOLF SHOUTED, trying to draw the grey seer's attention away from Schachter. The captain deserved to burn the way Marjus had, but he was afraid that Hiltrude was too close to the treacherous seaman and would be caught by Thanquol's vengeful magic. 'Thanquol, you filthy rat's pizzle!'

The grey seer's horned head spun around, his teeth bared in a feral snarl. For an instant, Adalwolf thought Thanquol was going to blast him, but then he saw the ratman's gaze drift past him, staring in wide-eyed horror at the gigantic serpent behind him. A foul, sickly stench rose from the robed ratkin. Squeals of pure terror rose from the underfolk behind Thanquol, only the fact that his huge rat ogre blocked the way keeping them from scrambling back down the stairs.

Adalwolf could almost laugh at the scene. He wondered what lies and threats Thanquol had used to force his underlings to ignore the snake-stink in their noses to get them this far. Now, faced with the titanic source of that musky scent, Thanquol's control of them had almost completely shattered.

'I see I have your attention,' Adalwolf said. 'Now listen to me. My friend is the only thing keeping that snake from crawling over here and eating the lot of you! If he stops distracting it, you're all dead!'

Thanquol bruxed his fangs together and lashed his tail against the floor, but Adalwolf could see that his anger was nothing beside the terror dripping down his robes.

'What-what does man-thing want-take?' Thanquol snarled.

CHANG FANG LINGERED towards the back of the skaven mob, listening with contempt as Thanquol negotiated with the escaped slave. Given a chance, the grey seer would no doubt find a way to squirm out of whatever deal he was brewing with the human, but the assassin was going to see to it that he didn't get that chance.

He'd lost count of how many times Thanquol had escaped his traps. With each failure, Chang Fang's anger and frustration grew. That was why he'd made his reckless attack on Thanquol in the swamp, a failure that had cost him his ear and very nearly his life. He'd been much more careful arranging the trap in the ruins, using the skinks and their crumbling city to annihilate the grey seer. Still he had escaped! What was more, he'd taken over command of the expedition! Chang Fang began to believe Thanquol's mad boasts that the Horned Rat himself was watching over him!

Standing within the profane Temple of the Serpent, watching the gigantic snake swaying from side to side above the floor, Chang Fang's heart threatened to burst from sheer terror. But he was not so lost to his fear that he forgot his murderous purpose, the one driving goal left in his life. He would avenge the betrayal of Chang Squik and his own disgrace! Thanquol would die!

He'd tried to use the lizardmen and their city to destroy Thanquol. Now he would use their god! He would pit the protection of the Horned Rat against the sacred serpent of Sotek!

Swiftly Chang Fang pulled the blowgun from beneath his cloak and placed it to his lips. The dart sped across the temple, striking its target in the neck. Chang Fang bit his tongue to keep from laughing as he watched his victim sway and fall.

'Fine-good,' Thanquol snapped at the arrogant human. 'I let-allow you take-leave with other man-things. In return you make-make snake stay-sleep.' He had no intention of keeping his word of course, but he still found it distasteful to lie to creatures so far beneath his station. A skaven lied only to those he feared, and Thanquol most certainly didn't fear a bunch of furless man-things! Once the human let him get away, he'd send a few of the assassins back to deal with him and his herd. That would be a fair toll for the animal's brazen arrogance!

Thanquol was chuckling to himself about future treacheries when he noticed the human kneeling before the big snake suddenly fall over. Cold fear ran down Thanquol's spine as he heard the impact of the man's body against the floor. Immediately he raised his eyes, squealing in horror when he saw that the snake was no longer swaying from side to side. No, it was turning, turning in his direction. The breath caught in his throat as he saw the loathsome tongue flicker out from the snubbed face, pulling the smell of skaven from the air.

Frantically, Thanquol thrust a nugget of warpstone between his fangs. He swallowed the rock whole, almost gagging as he forced the stone down his throat. For once, he didn't revel in the intoxicating rush of magical energy that filled him, instead harnessing it at once, focusing it into the head of his staff. Green energy flickered and crackled about him. Thanquol tried to force down his terror, tried to control his panic.

Then the great serpent hissed and the sound drove all reason from Thanquol's brain. Shrieking like a whelp, the grey seer pointed his staff at the giant snake. A half-formed, ragged nimbus of energy splashed harmlessly against the armoured scales.

The serpent hissed again and reared up from the floor. Thanquol glanced about him, but his minions had treacherously deserted him, stampeding over Boneripper in their craven urge to escape. Even the upstart human was running, diving behind one of the columns. Thanquol decided that was a good idea and tried to do the same, but his legs were paralysed with fear.

The snake's hood snapped open, its mouth dropping open in a wide yawn. Thanquol threw down his staff, hoping against hope the snake wouldn't think he was the one who had tried to burn it with a spell.

If the reptile noticed, it gave no sign. The great wedge-like head came hurtling down, the mammoth jaws closing around Thanquol before he could even scream.

Lashing its head from side to side, the sacred serpent of Sotek swallowed Grey Seer Thanquol in a single gulp.

CHAPTER ELEVEN

The Serpent and the Rat

As the great serpent started to move, everything within the Temple of Sotek descended into chaos. The ratmen, so menacing only an instant before, began a madcap scramble back down the stairs. Adalwolf watched them overwhelm even the huge rat ogre in their terror-ridden flight.

Adalwolf ran for the nearest column, thinking to hide himself from the snake the way van Sommerhaus had. He shouted for Hiltrude to do the same and risked a glance in her direction, fearing that she would be frozen with horror again. He breathed easier when he saw the woman scrambling for cover. Instead it was Grey Seer Thanquol who stood transfixed before the serpent's approach. The mercenary shouted joyfully when he saw the snake slither unharmed through the villain's spells and swallow the sorcerer with a single bite.

Thinking of Thanquol's magic made Adalwolf remember Diethelm. Cursing the fear that had made him hide from the snake, he looked across the floor of the temple to the priest's prone figure. He couldn't think what had happened to Diethelm, he only knew he had to try and help the man. Honour would demand nothing less. For the moment the snake was occupied trying to swallow its latest meal. If he was fast, Adalwolf knew he would be able to pass it in safety. Steeling his heart for the effort, and with one watchful eye on the snake, the warrior made a frantic dash to the fallen priest.

When he turned Diethelm onto his back, Adalwolf knew the priest was dead. He also discovered the reason for the man's collapse. It had not been the strain of keeping the great serpent mesmerised, as the mercenary had thought. There was an inch-long dart sticking from Diethelm's neck, and the veins surrounding the ugly sliver were black with the poison that had coated it. Adalwolf clenched his fists in impotent fury at such a cowardly way of dealing death. One of the ratmen, no doubt, trying to remove the one man who could threaten them.

Adalwolf glared at the bulge in the serpent's neck. Thanquol had paid for the murderous treachery of his minions. Whatever he had thought to accomplish by killing Diethelm, the mercenary was certain that ending up as a meal for the snake had been the last thing Thanquol had planned on.

A sharp scream pierced Adalwolf's ears. He turned away from the great serpent, looking again across the floor of the temple. He could see Schachter, the gold sword clenched in his fist, pulling Hiltrude from her hiding place. The sea captain was trying to take her with him down one of the many tunnels opening into the temple. With one of his hands closed about her throat, the courtesan had little choice but to go with him.

'Sommerhaus!' Adalwolf cried out, gesturing madly to the patroon. Van Sommerhaus peered out from behind his column and Adalwolf could see that he understood the meaning of the mercenary's wild gestures. He glanced at Schachter, took a few tenuous steps in the man's direction, then retreated when the captain waved his sword at him. There wasn't even a flush of guilt on the man's face as he abandoned the rescue effort. He simply shrugged his shoulders and ran into one of the other tunnels.

There was no time to curse the patroon's retreat. Adalwolf shouted at Schachter, demanding he leave Hiltrude alone. The captain's only response was a nasty smile and a quickening of his own withdrawal from the temple.

Adalwolf forced himself to dash back across the floor of the temple. The giant snake had pushed its last meal some distance down its throat and was now beginning to move its head from side to side, its tongue flickering from between its scaly lips. The mercenary knew it was looking for more prey, but he also knew he had only moments if he wanted to reach Schachter before he escaped into the tunnels. Thinking of Hiltrude in the clutches of the desperate captain removed the last of his concerns.

The mercenary wasn't even halfway across the temple before the great serpent lunged at him. The reptile's foul breath washed over him as it narrowly missed Adalwolf, its jaws snapping against the stone floor instead. He dodged back as the serpent reared up for another strike, placing its scaly bulk between himself and his goal. Hiltrude's last desperate cry tormented him as he watched her captor drag her off into one of the dark tunnels.

Then Adalwolf had no time to think of the helpless woman. The great serpent's hood flared open, its immense jaws came hurtling at him like the sword of an angry god. He dived beneath the scaly jaw, nearly crushed beneath the snake as it lashed its head angrily, frustrated by its nimble prey and slowed by the morsel still lodged in its throat.

Hissing furiously, the great serpent reared back a third time. The hood flared open, the eye-like pattern of its marking staring down at Adalwolf. The mercenary braced himself, praying to his gods that he would again prove quick enough to defy the reptile's hideous purpose.

Suddenly Adalwolf felt himself flung through the air by a powerful blow. For an instant he thought the snake had struck him, but as he crashed against the stone floor, he saw the truth. He had been thrown, yes, but it had not been the serpent's jaws that had struck him. He'd been tossed aside by a different monster.

Where Adalwolf had stood only moments before, he now saw the furry, verminous bulk of Thanquol's immense bodyguard. The rat ogre was grappling with the huge snake, its claws sunk deep into the ophidian snout, thin reptilian blood spurting from the horrible wounds. Growling with a fury Adalwolf had seen before only in the berserkers of the Norsii, the rat ogre was trying to maul the giant serpent!

BONERIPPER RAKED HIS giant claws across the great serpent's face, slashing through its thick scales like they were paper. The reptile tried to rear back but the rat ogre held fast, his enormous muscles bulging beneath his fur as he forced the ophidian head against the cold stone floor. He set his clawed foot against the snake's neck, trying to pin it in place while he slashed again at the monster's face, tearing through its jaw.

The great serpent lashed out, whipping its tail against Boneripper, sending the rat ogre rolling across the floor. The snake's coils followed after him, lashing about in a squirming dance in their effort to catch him within their lethal embrace. For all his bulk, however, Boneripper defied the deadly efforts of the snake to trap him. Reflexes hardened by the cruel training regimens of Clan Eshin were nimble even in the huge body of a rat ogre. He dived beneath the crushing coils, dodged as the lashing tail of the snake tried to swat him before he could escape. The serpent hissed in frustration, its cowl snapping open as it opened its mangled jaw.

Again the snake's strike failed, reptilian fangs scraping against stone instead of closing around flesh. A flash of pain flared through the monster as its wound was worsened by the rough impact against the floor.

It reeled back, its tail writhing in sympathy with the pain in its face. Given a chance, the great serpent would have slithered back into its lair to lick its wounds and digest its meal.

Huge claws seized the side of the snake's head as it turned to flee. Boneripper sank his sword-like claws into the reptile's neck, shredding the loose folds of flesh that formed its hood. The rat ogre pulled himself up the reptile's body, stubbornly refusing to be knocked loose when the snake's coils slammed into him. The reptile's hissing became louder, almost panicked, as Boneripper brutally withdrew his claws only to stab them in again so that he might pull himself higher along the monster's neck.

When it felt one of Boneripper's claws stab into the base of its head, the serpent's body flared with maddened convulsions. Its enormous body rolled along the floor, crashing into columns and shattering them. Brick and stone rained down from the ceiling, the entire temple seemed to tremble in its pained throes. Predation and escape were alien thoughts to the snake's primitive mind now, only the instinct to remove the pain that assailed it remained. The giant reptile thought to crush its tormentor beneath its own tremendous weight, to smash Boneripper and grind him beneath its thrashing body.

Over and across the temple the great serpent writhed, toppling fire pots and crumpling the priceless altar into a mass of flattened gold and crushed gems. The monster's hissing became a deafening susurrus, echoing from the walls, bouncing from the floor and ceiling. Again and again the snake's coils thrashed and rolled about the temple, obliterating everything in their path.

As the snake tired and fell still once more, Boneripper leaped down upon it. The rat ogre had jumped clear of the snake the moment it had started to roll over, though its primitive brain had failed to recognise the fact. While the giant reptile raged through the temple, Boneripper had watched it from the column he had climbed. The rat ogre had nearly been knocked from his perch when the serpent's agonies had caused it to strike the pillar, but he clung fiercely to the shaking stone and when the snake had passed, he remained with the broken stone stub still hanging from the ceiling.

Now Boneripper assaulted the serpent with twice the fury as before. The weary monster did not see him until the instant before his huge claws were again slashing into the scaly flesh clothing its jaws.

Bloody froth bubbled from the corners of the snake's mouth as Boneripper dislocated its jaws. The serpent lashed and flailed in agony, trying to batter its attacker with its heavy coils, but the rat ogre held fast. Exerting his tremendous strength, he wrenched the snake's lower jaw clear of its socket. The dislocated jaw flopped obscenely beneath the serpent's head, its flickering tongue thrashing wildly.

Boneripper seized the lower jaw in both hands and began to pull savagely at it. The serpent struggled against the brutal attack, but it lacked the strength to roll its body again and crush the rat ogre beneath it. Its tail whipped at Boneripper, slashing deep cuts across his limbs and back, but even these hurts were not enough to make him relent.

Straining, every vein standing out upon his brow, Boneripper began to tear the snake's lower jaw loose, ripping it free from its mouth in a single scaly strip. The serpent's struggles became more desperate and agonised, but still it could not drive off the hulking rat ogre. He continued to pull on the jaw, using it to rip a long sliver of flesh from the underside of the snake's neck, exposing the long oesophagus beneath.

The great serpent twisted in a pool of its own blood. No longer did it consciously try to escape Boneripper, though its coils continued to writhe with a mindless agony of their own. The rat ogre continued to tear a long, scaly strip of flesh from the reptile's throat, ripping a great dripping swathe down its neck. Only when he reached the bulge in the monster's throat did Boneripper relent. As the last strip of scaly flesh was pulled back, something more than reptilian meat and bone rewarded the rat ogre's efforts. Eagerly he reached into the ghastly fissure, pulling free a slimy, dripping mass.

Grey Seer Thanquol coughed and sputtered, straining to draw air into his suffocated lungs. He found it impossible to stand, his head swimming from the violent rolling of the serpent. Dizzy, he crashed to the floor, yelping in pain as the fall hurt his tail.

Foul and slimy with the reptile's juices, his robes and fur plastered against his skin, his talismans and amulets hanging from him in wild disorder, Thanquol presented a miserable, pathetic spectacle. He blinked like a newborn whelp, trying to force the world to stop spinning whenever he looked at it. The snake filth coating him choked his nose, making it almost impossible to smell anything but the reptile's muck. His ears were still ringing from the pounding of the reptile's heart.

Hacking filth from his throat, the slimy skaven stared up at Boneripper, waiting until the three rat ogres he saw merged into a single creature. Angrily, Thanquol kicked the brute's leg.

'What-what took-take you so long-long, flea-weaning maggot-spawn!' the grey seer raged. The rat ogre looked suitably chastened, cringing before Thanquol's wrath.

The grey seer wiped filth from his snout and glared at the chamber around him. Boneripper was the only one of his craven minions to stand by him, the others had fled like lice before the giant snake. When Thanquol caught up to them, they would pay dearly for such craven treachery! He'd sew up the lot of them inside the snake's carcass and let them see how it felt!

Vengeful thoughts made Thanquol spin about when he heard the sound of boots moving across the temple floor. He could see the arrogant human who had dared to set the snake on him fleeing across the chamber, making for one of the openings in the wall. He felt the impulse to blast the man-thing with a bolt of warp-lightning or to set Boneripper after him. Only the consideration that the snake might have a mate slithering about somewhere made Thanquol fight back the impulse. If only his cowardly underlings hadn't run off at the first chance!

Sounds of skaven paws scampering up stone steps made a malevolent grin spread across Thanquol's face. So the cowards were coming back! They'd realised they couldn't survive without his brilliant leadership!

Thanquol quickly wiped away the worst of the snake-slime coating him and struck his most imperious pose. He pointed his staff at the running human and growled at the skaven he saw running up the stairs.

'Kill-kill man-thing and bring-take his spleen to me!'

Audaciously, the ratmen ignored Thanquol's order but simply ran deeper into the temple. Furious, Thanquol ordered Boneripper to intercept the mob of gutter runners and assassins. The obedient rat ogre pounced upon the foremost gutter runner, crushing him beneath his paws.

That spectacle at least stopped the skaven from running, but Thanquol felt a cold chill creep along his spine when, instead of staring fearfully at the grey seer and his bodyguard, the ratmen cast terrified looks over their shoulders at the tunnel they had just emerged from.

Thanquol followed their gaze and felt a shock of horror as he watched a swarm of blue-scaled skinks and towering kroxigor rush out of the darkness and into the temple. At their head, carrying his golden staff, was Xiuhcoatl, the terrible Prophet of Sotek.

The lizardmen stared past the skaven they had been pursuing, noting the enormous bloody bulk of their sacred serpent strewn about Thanquol's feet. The grey seer felt the urge to cower as he felt those cold eyes staring at him. He could imagine the fury surging through their reptilian hearts, the murderous outrage of religious zealots who have seen their holy of holies violated and defiled. He remembered the awful vengeance Grey Seer Gnawdoom had visited upon the man-wizard Bagrain for desecrating the Black Ark. Any instant he expected to hear Xiuhcoatl shriek in rage, to send his followers sweeping forwards in a murderous frenzy.

Instead, the lizardmen regarded their slaughtered godling with an icy, passionless detachment. There was no emotion as they silently crept into the temple, only a sinister calculating gleam in their unblinking eyes.

As Thanquol backed away from the reptiles he thought that a display of honest hate and anger might have been welcome beside the cold, utterly alien serenity of the lizardmen.

THANQUOL HAD ONLY the briefest vision of Xiuhcoatl and his warriors. A wall of inky darkness suddenly spread between the lizardmen and the skaven, cutting them off from one another. He could see Shen Tsinge gesturing madly with his staff, the sorcerer's fur standing on end as he drew upon the forces of the aethyr. He felt a twinge of fear as he watched the sorcerer wield his magic, remembering the dark magic of the shadowmancer who had nearly destroyed him beneath Altdorf not long ago. More than before, Thanquol determined to arrange an accident for the treacherous sorcerer.

A thunderous explosion shook the temple and Shen's wall of shadow vanished in a burst of blinding light. Through the light stalked the lizardmen, their golden weapons raised high, their fangs bared and a threatening hiss rasping from their throats. Xiuhcoatl strode forwards with his warriors, his staff still burning with the power he had used to banish Shen's sorcery. Once again, Thanquol was awed by the creature's ability, by the sense of arcane might that the skink exuded.

Awe turned to blind panic, for as Thanquol watched the Prophet of Sotek stalk closer in his mind's eye he could see himself lying bound at the top of the pyramid and the skink's hand tearing out his beating heart. The grey seer gnashed his fangs against the horrible image and he thrust a nugget of warpstone between his jaws. Hastily he wove the winds of magic together, using the warpstone to fuel his desperate spell. Almost he forgot to mutter a pray to the Horned Rat before he unleashed his magic, but even with Xiuhcoatl marching towards him, Thanquol could not completely forget fear of his own god.

An icy wind exploded from the grey seer's staff, a gale drawn from the chill Realm of Chaos itself. Thanquol squealed in delight as he saw the lizardmen falter before his magic, their movements turning sluggish, their weapons falling slack against their sides.

'Now-now!' Thanquol shrieked at his minions. 'Kill-kill scaly-meat!'

The skaven did not have to be told twice. Predatory instincts overcame ancient fear and the ratmen fell upon the reptiles in a furious tide of slashing swords and snapping fangs. The lizardmen, rendered all but helpless by Thanquol's frozen spell, were easy prey for the agile skaven. Huge kroxigors fell, their bellies split open, their massive mauls and axes clattering against the floor beside them. Skink archers fitted arrows to their bows but so slow had they become that the ratmen were upon them before they could fire. Dozens of the cold-blooded creatures were cut down, butchered by the blades of the skaven. In almost the blink of an eye, the floor of the temple was littered with lizardman dead.

Then a flash of light burst from Xiuhcoatl's staff. The Prophet glared at the skaven around him as they slaughtered his followers. The ratmen wheeled away from the skink priest, recoiling as another pulse of energy thundered from his golden staff. With each pulse of energy, a wave of heat washed over the lizardmen, invigorating their sluggish bodies and warming the chill blood in their veins.

Now the skaven did not have such an easy time slaying their enemies. A group of gutter runners rushed a square of skink spearmen only to fall with javelins piercing their bodies when the lizardmen suddenly threw their weapons. An assassin leapt upon the back of a kroxigor, trying to slit the huge monster's scaly throat, but the towering lizardman simply turned his head and snapped his jaws, catching one of the skaven's paws in his teeth. Before the assassin could lash out, the kroxigor threw him with a savage turn of his head, then crushed the fallen killer's chest with a stomp of his scaly foot.

Thanquol sent a bolt of warp-lightning crackling at Xiuhcoatl's head. His eyes went round with horror as he saw the spell evaporate before it could even strike the skink. His terror only increased when he felt the lizardman's eyes staring at him. 'Kill-kill Xiuhcoatl!' he shrieked, diving behind the carcass of the giant snake before the skink could target him with a spell.

Peering from behind his gory refuge, Thanquol saw Tsang Kweek and a pair of assassins rush Xiuhcoatl from every side. The grey seer rubbed his paws in anticipation. The skink might stop one or even two of the ratmen, but certainly not all three! These were the cloaked killers of Clan Eshin, the finest murderers in all the Under-Empire!

Xiuhcoatl did not seem to appreciate or notice the death rushing towards him. The skink priest continued to march across the temple floor, his eyes focused upon Thanquol's hiding place. Thanquol felt his glands clench when he realised the skink was intent upon confronting him, but he grinned savagely when he thought about the three killers closing upon his enemy.

The first assassin leapt upon Xiuhcoatl as though the skink were a piece of Marienburg cheese. With daggers clenched in fists, mouth and tail, the assassin seemed certain in his triumph. Xiuhcoatl didn't even look at the skaven, simply pointing a claw in his direction. White flames engulfed the shrieking assassin, devouring him so swiftly that when he struck the stone floor his body collapsed into a pile of ash.

The second assassin tried an old Eshin trick of rolling across the floor and ending the manoeuvre in an upward stab of his sword. Again, the skink did not deign to notice him, but simply pointed in his direction. A finger of crackling blue energy shot from the lizardman's claw searing into the assassin's face. The skaven wailed in agony, then crashed to the floor, daggers slipping from lifeless hands, his head reduced to a smoking skull.

Tsang Kweek gave a terrified cry, hurling his sword at Xiuhcoatl's back before turning tail to run. The blade melted in mid-air before ever striking the Prophet. The skink slowly turned to regard the fleeing ratman. Xiuhcoatl clenched his fist and a fiery stone shot from the fanged icon upon his staff. The tiny meteor rocketed across the temple, smashing into Tsang Kweek with the force of a cannon ball. The gutter runner stared dumbly at the gaping hole the burning stone had punched through his chest, then slumped onto his side and was still.

Grey Seer Thanquol bruxed his fangs together and cursed the incompetent underlings. Finest killers in all the Under-Empire! The filthy vermin couldn't even kill a flea without someone spelling out every step for them! The miserable maggots weren't fit to pop ticks on a brood-mother's arse!

Thanquol spun about as he felt paws fumbling at his robes. As he turned, he was rewarded by a sharp blow against his snout. Recoiling in pain, Thanquol lifted his staff to block Shen Tsinge's as the sorcerer tried to strike him a second time.

'Filthy seer-rat-scum!' Shen snarled. 'All-all lost-fail because Thanquol is fool-fool!' The sorcerer raised his other paw, displaying the warpstone he had picked from Thanquol's pockets. 'Give-give all-all warpstone, Thanquol-meat, and Shen Tsinge leave you for lizard-things!'

Thanquol bared his fangs at the sorcerer. 'Aren't you forgetting something?'

Shen Tsinge grinned back, murderous and triumphant. He nodded at the huge bulk of the rat ogre standing behind him. 'Yes-yes,' he agreed. 'Goji should be the one to crush Thanquol-meat in his claws!' He pointed at the grey seer and growled at the rat ogre. 'Goji! Kill-smash Thanquol-meat!'

'Boneripper!' Thanquol shrieked back. 'Hold-take this traitor-rat!'

The rat ogre stomped forward, his beady eyes glaring first at Thanquol, then at Shen Tsinge and finally back at Thanquol. The grey seer shrank back as he felt the rat ogre start to reach for him. Then, suddenly, Boneripper spun around, his huge hands closing about Shen Tsinge, splintering the sorcerer's staff as he crushed it against his body.

'Goji! No-no! Shen Tsinge is master!' the sorcerer screeched.

Thanquol grinned maliciously at the struggling sorcerer, then glanced over the carcass of the serpent. Xiuhcoatl had been distracted by another pair of assassins, but that diversion was certain to be short. He needed something more substantial to keep the skink occupied. A gruesome laugh chittered through Thanquol's fangs.

'You want-take my warpstone?' the grey seer asked, removing several nuggets from his robe. 'I will give them to you, Shen Tsinge, to honour your faithful service.'

Shen Tsinge struggled in Boneripper's iron grip, trying to wriggle free. Thanquol would have enjoyed watching his futile efforts, but he knew there was no time. Pinching the sorcerer's nose shut with one claw, he waited until Shen was forced to draw another breath. As soon as he opened his mouth to suck down air, Thanquol thrust the entire mass of warpstone down Shen's throat. Holding the sorcerer's mouth shut, Thanquol gave him a simple choice: choke or swallow.

At last the sorcerer could endure the ordeal no longer and he gagged down the deadly black rocks. In small amounts warpstone was the lifeblood of skavendom, fuelling their industry, their magic and their diet. In greater amounts, however, even the corrupt constitution of the ratmen was unable to assimilate the lethal qualities of warpstone. What Thanquol had fed Shen Tsinge was enough to kill a hundred ratmen. In one sense, it was a waste, but in another Thanquol knew it was wealth well spent.

Boneripper dropped Shen Tsinge as the sorcerer's body began to burn from within. Glowing green pulses of light began to sear through the sorcerer's fur and robes. His body began to twist and swell as the unrestrained, unfocused energies continued to gather. Thanquol thought of a ratskin bag being filled to bursting with dwarfblood wine. He didn't want to be around when the bag burst.

'Boneripper!' Thanquol cried, pointing at the exit he had seen Adalwolf flee towards. 'Quick-quick!'

Grey seer and rat ogre dashed from behind their refuge, racing across the blood-slick floor for the exit.

Arrows loosed from the tiny skink bows clattered around them, but the distance was too great for even the jungle hunters to deliver much accuracy. Other lizardmen broke off from capturing the few skaven that had survived the fight and set off in pursuit of Thanquol and Boneripper. The stink of their scaly bodies grew stronger and stronger in his nose and Thanquol began to despair of ever reaching the tunnel. He thought of Xiuhcoatl standing over him with his heart dripping through the skink's scaly fingers. Fear lent the grey seer a new burst of speed.

Then the entire temple shook, a howling maelstrom of energy crashing and roaring through the colossal chamber. Lizardmen were battered and torn by the unleashed energies, dashed against the walls and crushed against the pillars. Thanquol himself was thrown by the explosion, only his horns saving him from a broken skull when he slid headfirst into the wall. He shook the spots from his vision and spat a cracked fang from his mouth.

Rising to his feet, Thanquol saw the chaos that had fallen upon his enemies. When Shen Tsinge's warpstone-gorged body had burst, the unleashed power had hurled lizardmen pell-mell throughout the temple. Many were limping on broken legs or holding twisted arms to their sides. Others were unmoving wrecks, necks and backs broken by the sorcerous explosion.

Xiuhcoatl himself was busy trying to contain the furious energies Shen Tsinge's destruction had unleashed. A purple fire glowed where Thanquol had left the sorcerer and in its light the temple itself began to corrode, the ancient stones crumbling into powder like bread infested with mould. Thanquol did not know how far or fast the magical corruption would spread or if Xiuhcoatl would actually be able to purge it. He only knew he wanted to be very far away before he discovered any of those answers.

'This way!' Thanquol snarled as Boneripper came limping over to him. A last glance at Xiuhcoatl showed the skink priest waving a claw frantically in Thanquol's direction and a large number of lizardmen loping off in pursuit.

'Quick-quick!' Thanquol shrieked, half-pulling the stunned rat ogre after him into the darkness of the tunnel. Thanquol was instantly struck by the similarity it bore to the corridor the skaven had used to enter the pyramid.

The glyphs! A thrill of terror rushed through him as Thanquol thought of the wards that had protected the first tunnel. Only the thought of dying on Xiuhcoatl's altar kept the grey seer moving. A new, desperate purpose guided him. They had to follow the man-thing's scent and find him so he could clear away any wards they found! And they had to do it before the lizardmen found them first!

CHAPTER TWELVE

The Breeder's Scent

SCHACHTER WIPED THE cold sweat from his brow, dearly wishing he had a good bottle of Estalian brandy to drive away the trembling he felt in his bones. He stared into the long stretch of darkness that lay between himself and the sputtering torch further down the corridor. It seemed an impossibly long way away. He felt his stomach churn at the very thought of running through it. That primitive, primal part of the human brain that told him to fear the night, to fear the dark, was like a thunder inside his head. Stay, it seemed to say. Stay in the light where you are safe.

Hiltrude tugged at him, trying to pull free from his grip. The action made him round on her irritably. A cruel twist of the cloth tether he'd tied about her wrists brought the courtesan to her knees, whimpering in pain.

'Stupid wench!' Schachter snarled down at her, his fear turning to anger now that he had an excuse to vent. He slapped her head, the crack of his palm echoing in the stone corridor. He glanced up in alarm at the loudness of the sound, but the stone lizards and snakes carved into the walls continued to stare down at him with the same icy indifference as before.

Hiltrude tried to pull away again, but Schachter pulled her arms back at such an angle she was forced up to her feet.

'What do you think's back there?' Schachter asked. 'Whichever pack of monsters won that fight, Adalwolf's dead!'

The woman glared defiantly at Schachter, shaking her head furiously, tears streaming down her face. She wouldn't listen to his words. She wouldn't believe them. Adalwolf wasn't dead. He couldn't be.

It was strange, Hiltrude thought. It wasn't until she'd lost him that she appreciated her feelings for the hardened warrior. Gruff, crude, arrogant even, yet she felt there was more nobility about Adalwolf than all the refined burghers and aristocrats she had entertained over the years. She wondered about the wife he'd left behind in Marienburg and the children she'd borne him. Perhaps, if things had been different, that woman might have been her.

She'd never know what had become of her husband. She'd never know how he'd fallen trying to save a perfumed harlot from the clutches of gruesome monsters far from the lands of men. She'd never know that Adalwolf had not abandoned her.

If it had been me, Hiltrude told herself, I would know. At least she wanted to believe that.

'Come on,' Schachter told her. This time the captain's voice wasn't so gruff and he relaxed his hold on the tether so it didn't bite into her skin. 'We can't stay here. We have to find a way out before they find us.'

Hiltrude didn't know which 'they' Schachter meant. She supposed it didn't matter. The lizardmen had no more reason to look kindly on them than Thanquol and his brood. She wasn't sure which fate she dreaded more. She had seen the hideous sacrifices of the lizardmen and their red-clawed priest. Somehow the cold, passionless way the reptiles had butchered their captives made her more afraid than whatever horrible revenge Thanquol might think of.

Schachter pushed her ahead of him into the darkness between the sputtering torches. She could feel the sea captain trembling as he followed her. Hiltrude found some comfort in the fact. If she could stay calm, if she could keep her wits about her, she might escape her captor. While Schachter was busy jumping at shadows, she'd have her chance to get away.

What she would do then, she had no idea. The pragmatic side of her told her to stay with Schachter, that he was her best hope of getting out of the pyramid alive. Hiltrude felt sick at the thought. She'd listened to her pragmatic side far too much in her life, let it lead her to places and do things that...

No, she wouldn't be pragmatic now. She would wait for her chance and she would take it. She would go back to the temple and she would find out what had happened to Adalwolf. After that, she didn't care what became of her.

Hiltrude watched as the circle of light drew nearer, like a beacon on a distant shore. Twenty paces, perhaps thirty, and they would be out of the darkness. Schachter would relax again once he was safe on that little island of light. That would be her chance.

Schachter moaned in terror behind her. 'They've found us!' he gasped, thrusting Hiltrude ahead of him. She stumbled ahead as the captain forced her into a run. She was able to glance back only once. There was an impression of shapes rushing through the bit of illumination they had just left behind, but she couldn't tell from so quick a look whether they were rats or reptiles.

'Run! Run!' Schachter's frantic voice boomed in her ears. Hiltrude sprinted ahead of him, impelled by the captain's terror, frightened that he would trample her underfoot if she fell. Twice she felt the sword in Schachter's fist jab at her back. She wasn't sure if it was a conscious threat or an unconscious motion, but she was certain she didn't want to test the man's intentions.

They reached the little circle of light. By now there was no mistaking the pad of clawed feet on the stone floor behind them. Schachter pushed her forward, intending to rush further down the corridor, light or no light, but Hiltrude staggered back into the light.

Blue-scaled creatures strode out from the darkness ahead of them, ugly little spears clutched in their clawed hands. They regarded the two humans with huge, unblinking eyes and their sharp little fangs seemed to glisten in the flickering light. The sight was too much for Schachter. With a howl, he brought his sword chopping down into one of the lizardmen.

The skink gave voice to a single sharp bark of pain, then closed its claws around the golden blade that had split it from shoulder to sternum. Schachter tried to rip the cleaver-like edge free, but the reptile's tenacious grip was too strong. Dying, the lizardman had prevented Schachter from continuing the fight.

With Schachter's sword trapped in the body of the skink, the other lizardmen lunged forward. By now the pursuers following from behind had closed the gap. Schachter and Hiltrude were dragged to the ground beneath a mass of clawing, clinging reptiles. The thick tails of the skinks battered them mercilessly, raising ugly welts wherever they struck. Sometimes the golden butt of a spear would crack against their skulls, rattling their senses as they tried to throw off their scaly antagonists.

Already bound by Schachter, Hiltrude was the first to collapse beneath the abuse of the lizardmen. As the skinks lashed her legs and arms together with heavy ropes, she could see them beating the fight out of Schachter so they could do the same to him. During the struggle, the captain's boot kicked the corpse of the dead skink, his sword still embedded in its chest. She found it strange that the lizardmen didn't try to kill Schachter for what he had done.

Then an icy chill swept through her, a sense of terrible power. Hiltrude twisted her head against the rough floor, raising her eyes as a robed skink emerged from the darkness. Her skin crawled as she felt reptilian eyes studying her, appraising her like a fishmonger appraising a catch. Xiuhcoatl's crest flared into a brilliant comb of crimson, contrasting brilliantly with his blue scales and white robes.

Even though she knew there was death in Xiuhcoatl's voice as the Prophet hissed commands to the other skinks and the two humans were lifted from the floor, Hiltrude knew there was no malice in the lizardman's direction.

She and Schachter would die upon the altar, but their killers would take no delight from it. They were above, or perhaps beneath, such things as emotions and desires.

That part of her that she had come to hate found it all quite pragmatic.

ADALWOLF CAUTIOUSLY ROUNDED the bend in the corridor, holding his torch high to illuminate as much of the darkness as he could. He knew he risked discovery by carrying the light, but he also knew he needed to see if he was to defend himself. By now the lizardmen had finished off Thanquol's vermin, but he doubted if they would stop there. Their temple had been violated, their living god slain, their kin killed. No, they would not stop with the slaughter of Thanquol and his ratmen. They would head into the tunnels to pursue the humans who had escaped. Perhaps, he realised with a feeling of sick dread, the reptiles didn't even know the difference between man and ratman.

The thought was made all the more hideous when he remembered the awful ritual they had seen the skink priests performing atop the pyramid. Certainly they were no friends of the underfolk, but that didn't mean they harboured any kindness towards mankind.

Fear flared through Adalwolf's heart. He had to find Hiltrude before the lizardmen did. To think of her alone with that scoundrel Schachter, a host of cold-blooded monsters hunting them...

The warrior scarcely stopped to consider that his own situation was worse. Schachter at least had a weapon to defend them. Adalwolf had only the torch he'd plucked from the wall of the corridor. The same menace hunted him that hunted them, only his own flight from the temple had been much later than theirs. Whatever pursuit the skink prophet had sent to scour the tunnels, they would be much closer to him than them.

Still, Adalwolf could not get the courtesan's plight out of his mind. However sorry his own situation, he knew he had to make the effort to rescue her. He felt that more than merely his life rested on trying. He'd forsake whatever dignity years of working for creatures like van Sommerhaus had left him if he abandoned her now. His honour hung upon getting her safely from the pyramid and he was not so rotten with the mercenary creed that he did not still value honour.

Something stirred in the darkness ahead. The musky stink of reptilian flesh struck Adalwolf's nose as a short, wiry lizardman scurried into the light of his torch. It paused when it saw him, shifting its grip on the short spear it carried. Adalwolf did not give the skink a chance to decide what it was going to do. Swiftly, he brought his torch slamming down into the reptile's head, knocking it against the floor. He kicked the spear away from its grasping claws.

Hisses rasped through the shadows and Adalwolf saw more lizardmen emerging from the blackness. They were of the same wiry breed as the one he had knocked down and their claws held the same little spears as their prone comrade. The mercenary tried to read some emotion on their scaly faces and in their gaping eyes, but they might have been carved from stone for all the expression he could find.

'Stay back! I don't want to hurt you!' Adalwolf warned, waving the flaming torch before him. The skinks didn't seem especially impressed by his display of bravado, but they did hang back a bit. Adalwolf began to think he might be able to bluff his way past the timid reptiles when he saw the reason for their timidity lumber out of the shadows. His blood became ice as he saw one of the huge ogre-like lizardmen from the spawning pool march between the parted ranks of its smaller fellows.

The kroxigor carried an immense axe seemingly crafted from solid gold in its over-sized claws, the blade already clotted with bits of fur and black blood. Adalwolf could smell the carrion reek of the monster's breath as a rumbling bellow pulsed up its throat and through its giant fangs. Suddenly the torch in his hand felt even punier than it had a moment before. Dragonfire might not be weapon enough to faze such a brute!

Adalwolf retreated before the kroxigor's approach. Battle-hardened reflexes made him turn about before he had taken more than a few steps. He caught the shaft of a spear one of the skinks behind him was stabbing at his back just before it struck. He wrenched the weapon from the surprised reptile's hands then drove the burning end of his torch into the creature's face. The skink barked in pain and collapsed in a writhing mass of flailing limbs, its agonies effectively blocking the advance of its fellows.

The kroxigor bellowed again, charging for Adalwolf. The mercenary ducked beneath the sweep of its axe. Stone shards sprayed from the wall as the axe smacked into stone instead of flesh. Before the huge brute could recover, Adalwolf stabbed his stolen spear into its belly. The flimsy javelin failed to penetrate the thick scales and the knotted muscle beneath, buckling like a nail upon an anvil.

Adalwolf hurled the useless weapon into the kroxigor's face, pleased to see the lizardman blink in surprise. Before he could exploit the distraction, however, he felt scaly arms grabbing at him from behind. A sinewy arm wrapped around his throat, trying to pull him down to the floor.

The mercenary gave scant attention to the skinks grappling him. His eyes were locked on the immense lizardman in front of him. The kroxigor hefted its axe again, raising it for an overhead blow that would split Adalwolf's body like a fencepost.

Adalwolf squeezed his eyes shut to keep from seeing the death blow. After a few moments, he opened them again. His first surprise was that he was alive. His second was to see a shape fully as big as the kroxigor wrestling with the reptile, ripping at it with massive claws and smashing it against the walls at every turn. He almost laughed when he realised he knew his rescuer. It was Boneripper, the giant ratman who had been Thanquol's bodyguard.

From the darkness there was a flash of flame and a crack like thunder. One of the skinks grappling Adalwolf chirped in pain and rolled away across the floor clutching at a bleeding hip. A second flash and a second skink was quivering beside the first one, its chest a ruined mess of gore.

The mercenary was as shocked as the lizardmen when a crazed figure cloaked in grey came rushing out from the shadows. Thanquol's staff split the skull of one skink, his sword opened the belly of another. The grey seer was almost frothing at the mouth, his eyes wide with terror as he ruthlessly flung himself into the fray. Skinks crumpled at every turn, unable to match the crazed fury of the ratman.

Adalwolf threw off the last of the lizardmen holding him. He smashed the head of one into the wall, hearing its skull crack. The others seemed to lose their taste for fighting the human after that, releasing him and scurrying back into the darkness.

Or perhaps they had simply seen what Adalwolf now saw. Boneripper stood over a dripping, mangled thing that had lately been the kroxigor. The huge lizardman's neck was broken, its head spun completely around so that its lifeless eyes stared straight down the length of its spine. The rat ogre shook the dead bulk of his foe, making its head roll along its shoulders in a particularly nauseating fashion.

Grey Seer Thanquol leaned against his staff, a tangle of dead skinks scattered all around him. The ratman's teeth were chattering, his chest heaving with such a frantic effort to draw breath into his lungs that Adalwolf thought the creature's entire body was going to burst. Finally, Thanquol's shivering hand fell to one of the pouches lashed to the belt of his robe. He drew what looked like a pinch of black dirt from the bag and quickly pressed his paw against his nose. He could hear the ratman inhale deeply, then quiver as a fit of furious sneezing wracked his body.

When Thanquol was recovered from the fit, his teeth had stopped chattering and his eyes were no longer the bulging pools of pure terror they had been during the fight. Indeed, the ratman's entire figure seemed to swell, to bristle with power and when the grey seer stared at Adalwolf his eyes were almost glowing with hellish energies.

'Man-thing owe-give life-skin to Grey Seer Thanquol!' he snapped, lashing his tail against the pile of dead skinks. 'Man-thing serve-do true-true what Thanquol squeak-say!'

Grey Seer Thanquol bared his teeth, displaying his rat-like fangs. 'Or I eat-take man-thing's spleen!'

LUKAS VAN SOMMERHAUS leaned against the cold stone of the corridor and fought to stifle the wracking sob that threatened to shudder past his lips. The patroon was tempted to grind his torch against the floor to blot out the hideous sight of the crawling carvings that covered the walls. He knew to do so was madness, to abandon himself to the darkness of the tunnels. He would be as helpless as a fish thrown from the water if he did so, as vulnerable as a bird knocked from the sky.

Darkness offered no safety from the things that hunted him. He only suspected that they needed light to see. He had only to remember his ghastly ordeal as the captive of the underfolk to know that there were creatures for which sight was not the chiefest of their senses. Perhaps the scaly monsters were sniffing him out even now with their flickering tongues, stalking him even as the mammoth serpent had in that awful temple!

Van Sommerhaus fingered the golden guilder in his pocket, rubbing the edge of the coin with his thumb as he invoked the name of Handrich. The patroon had always been contemptuous of the god of merchants and trade: Handrich had seemed to take a perverse delight in refusing his prayers. But now, in his agony of terror, he beseeched Handrich for succour. Rubbing a coin was said to arouse the god's interest.

They had followed him into the tunnels, van Sommerhaus was sure of that. He'd heard them, their hissing speech echoing from the stones, their claws scratching on the floor, their scaly tails slapping against the walls. He could smell their reptilian musk fouling the air, warning him of their pursuit. His skin crawled, expecting at any instant to feel the prick of an arrow. That was a horror he could not bear, to know that even the slightest scratch would kill him, would send the poison of the lizardmen rushing through his veins. It was the ignominy of such a death that terrified him. It offended his patroon blood to die like some trapped vermin, murdered by some nameless monster!

Van Sommerhaus had thought much of his death in the long hours he had spent hiding in the stone corridors. He thought about the kind of death that suited his station. To fall nobly in battle, making an end of himself that would be sung by the minstrels for hundreds of years, that would be the most fitting capstone to his career. To be remembered as merchant, mariner, playwright and hero, that was the finish he would not run from.

The patroon caught his breath and hurried down the corridor, turning his gaze away from a carving of a bloated toad that seemed to watch him with its sapphire eyes. If he escaped this horrible place, perhaps he would return to the Empire. He could face his persecutors, challenge their small-minded bigotries. Why, he'd confront Thaddeus Gamow, the Lord Protector of Sigmar's witch hunters and dare the villain to face him across bare steel! That would be a confrontation that would truly be the epic ending worthy of Lukas van Sommerhaus!

A rasping, hissing noise from further up the corridor made van Sommerhaus freeze in his steps. He turned an anxious eye back up the corridor, but all he could see were the sapphire gleams of the stone toads watching him from the edge of the torchlight. Nervously, he continued to rub the gold coin until his thumb began to bleed.

After finding the torch he now carried set into a gilded sconce, he'd tried to avoid any tunnel that flickered with light. He reasoned that they had the most chance of being populated. By sticking to the darkness, van Sommerhaus hoped to avoid the inhabitants of the pyramid. After all, he had not escaped the hunger of the ratmen simply to end up in the cooking pots of walking lizards!

Van Sommerhaus smiled as he fancied that the hissing sounds were withdrawing back up the corridor. Again he had outwitted the primitive, reptilian brutes! He would stick to his course, keep to the shadows and eventually make his way out of the ghastly temple.

He tried to ignore the ugly observation he had earlier made. He tried to forget that the corridors he followed, the ones that were not lit by torches, were leading him downward, not upward. He tried to silence the nagging fear that he was running farther and farther from any exit from the pyramid. He tried to tell himself that he imagined the sense of pressure that made his ears ring.

He wasn't deep below the earth. He wouldn't allow himself to entertain the idea. One more turn, one more archway, and he would see the sun shining. He would feel the damp heat of the jungle and he would be free.

Van Sommerhaus turned his corner and passed through his archway. He stopped rubbing the coin in his pocket. A brilliant light shone back at him.

It wasn't the light of the sun.

It was better.

Almost the patroon wished someone was with him, someone to appreciate the magnitude of what he had found. He thought of Adalwolf and Hiltrude and even the traitorous Captain Schachter. None of them would ever know of his find. Van Sommerhaus felt sorry for them, hunted like rats in the maze. They would never know the riches that could have been theirs, the riches that fate had reserved to reforge the fortune of the House van Sommerhaus!

Trembling, van Sommerhaus stepped through the archway and into a chamber so vast that his torch-light failed to illuminate more than a fragment of its enormity. He stooped and ran his hand along the floor – the floor that was paved in gold. He stared at the ceiling above – the ceiling that was roofed in gold. The columns that supported the roof were like-wise gold. So too were the great shelves that ran along the walls and the huge square altars that sat on the floor.

Handrich had answered the patroon's prayers in a way only the god of merchants could.

It was like walking into a gilded heaven, a miser's vision of Norscan Valhal.

The only thing that ruined the effect for van Sommerhaus were the long, shrivelled, cloth-wrapped shapes that stretched along the shelves on the walls. The patroon felt a twinge of uneasiness as he thought about what the things might have looked like once, trying to imagine a serpent twice the size of the one that had tried to swallow him.

He brushed aside the foolish image and returned his attention to the wealth surrounding him on every side. Whatever the things might have been once, they were dead now.

Van Sommerhaus would be damned if he was going to be frightened by a bunch of mouldering old mummies.

Grey Seer Thanquol glared at the insolent slave-thing. How dare it refuse him! He'd saved the worthless, hairless monkey from the scaly-things! He'd risked his pelt getting him away from the abominable lizardmen and this was how the filthy thing thanked him!

He drew another pinch of warpstone snuff to calm his excited nerves. The terror of his desperate battle was still throbbing through his blood. He would never have risked himself if there had been another way, but that idiot Boneripper wasn't able to do anything more than wrestle with the kroxigor, leaving all the other lizardmen for Thanquol to take care of! Of course it would have been a simple matter if he'd been able to call upon his supreme mastery of the black arts. A single spell would have reduced the entire pack of reptiles into charred husks. Nothing could withstand the magic of Thanquol once it had provoked his wrath!

But there was Xiuhcoatl to think about. Thanquol tried to keep his glands from clenching as he did think about the Prophet of Sotek and his formidable powers. Xiuhcoatl might sense any use of magic within his pyramid. The last thing Thanquol needed was to draw Xiuhcoatl's attention.

Without magic and with Boneripper making a big squeak and dance about killing one scrawny kroxigor, Thanquol had been forced to rely upon his wits and martial prowess to carry the fight. He'd emptied both of the pistols he'd confiscated from the humans, hoping the shots would be enough to send the lizardmen running. When they weren't, he'd summoned up his courage (and a bit of warpstone snuff) and charged into battle. What happened next was one big blur to him, but the pile of dead around his paws was testimony to his valour.

If only he didn't need the human so badly, he would never have put himself at such risk. But he needed the human, as much as he needed his own skin! Xiuhcoatl would know every exit from the pyramid and would have placed wards there to guard against invasion by the skaven. It was death for any skaven to pass near the wards. Thanquol needed a lesser creature to clear the path for him. As before, that meant using the human.

Unfortunately, the human knew it! The stubborn, stupid beast was exploiting its own usefulness to bargain with him! Him, Grey Seer Thanquol, bickering with a lowly man-thing like some rat-wife shopping the skrawls of Skavenblight! And after the selfless way Thanquol had rescued the miserable creature!

'I'm not leaving without Hiltrude,' Adalwolf told Thanquol for the third time.

Thanquol gnashed his fangs together. 'I don't care-want breeder-slave!' he snarled. 'We leave-leave now-now! You lead-show way!'

'Even if I knew the way out, I'm not leaving without her,' Adalwolf said. He trembled when Boneripper growled at him, but he stood his ground.

Thanquol set a restraining paw on Boneripper's leg. 'I smell-scent way out,' he assured Adalwolf, brushing the side of his furry snout. 'You smash snake-stones, I follow, we all escape-flee!'

'A good plan,' Adalwolf told Thanquol. 'But we're not leaving without Hiltrude.'

Thanquol's teeth ground against each other, his claws clenching so tight they bit into his palms. 'Forget-leave breeder-thing!' he snapped. 'I buy-barter you much-much breeder-things! All breeder-things you want!'

The mercenary smiled at Thanquol, a gesture he had learned the ratmen took as one of challenge. 'We leave with Hiltrude or you can smash your own snake-stones!'

'Stupid fool-meat!' Thanquol growled. He snapped his claws together. Before Adalwolf was even aware the huge beast was in motion, Boneripper sprang forwards and seized the man's arm, lifting him off the ground. 'Obey-listen or suffer-suffer!' Thanquol hissed.

'Not without Hiltrude,' the mercenary insisted.

Thanquol nodded to Boneripper. With a savage twist, the rat ogre broke Adalwolf's arm and dropped him back onto the floor. The warrior landed hard, screaming in pain as he clutched his shattered arm.

'I lose-forget patience, slave-meat!' Thanquol told the moaning man. 'Obey-listen!'

'Get skinned!' Adalwolf snarled back, careful to bare all of his teeth at the fuming grey seer.

Thanquol's tail lashed furiously behind him, his fur bristling as raw rage rippled through his body. He thought about blasting the insufferable human with a burst of warp-lightning, but that would hardly get him out of the pyramid.

'Fine-good,' Thanquol hissed through clenched fangs. 'You lead-show safe path, smash-wreck all snake-stones, I take you to breeder-thing.' It took Thanquol a long time to realise that the coughing cry shuddering through Adalwolf's body was laughter.

'You think I'd trust you?' the mercenary scoffed. 'How can you find Hiltrude in this maze?'

'Same-same I find stupid slave-meat!' Thanquol raged. He tapped the side of his nose again. 'I follow-find your scent. I can follow-find breeder-thing's stink even better.'

Adalwolf seemed to consider that for a moment. Even a dull-witted man-thing had to appreciate the greater senses of the skaven. It never ceased to amaze Thanquol how dull the human ability to smell was, though it went far to explain the reek of their cities.

'How do I know you aren't trying to trick me?' Adalwolf asked.

'Because I can just have Boneripper smash-crush slave-meat's empty skull!' Thanquol spat. The rat ogre took a menacing step towards Adalwolf.

'Go ahead,' the mercenary mocked. 'You'll make a pretty pile of ash.'

Thanquol swatted Boneripper with the head of his staff, moving the hulking beast away from Adalwolf. It was becoming clear to him that threats wouldn't work with this deranged human. He'd lost all sense of self-preservation. The grey seer tried to remember everything he'd learned in his dealings with humans.

He grinned as a particular bit of nonsense that seemed to have a strange effect on humans occurred to him. 'You have my word,' he told Adalwolf.

Again, the human's body shuddered as choking laughter seized him. 'You want me to trust you, I want van Sommerhaus's pistols,' he said, pointing at Thanquol's belt.

The grey seer was tempted to let Boneripper squash the arrogant slave-thing, but his need made him relent. With every muscle twitching in rebellion to his action, Thanquol unfastened the weapons and tossed them over to the wounded man.

'You need-need me,' Thanquol reminded Adalwolf. He tapped the side of his snout. 'I can smell-find breeder-thing. Slave-meat cannot.'

Gritting his teeth against the pain of his broken arm, Adalwolf stood and awkwardly buckled the pistol belt around his waist. 'All right,' he conceded. 'I need you and you need me. But I also need the gunpowder. And the bullets.'

Snarling, Thanquol tossed the flask of gunpowder and the little leather bag of shot to the human. They'd wasted enough time negotiating. Any moment might see the lizardmen return and Thanquol wanted to be far away when they did. Besides, even if the human did have the pistols, Thanquol had Boneripper and his magic.

Though to be on the safe side, he'd keep Boneripper close enough to hide behind if the human looked like he was going to use one of the pistols.

* * *

THE PATROON SMILED as he studied the pile of gold bricks he'd been able to pry from the floor. If he could get even half of it back to Marienburg, he'd be able to fund an expedition to return for the rest. He'd be able to hire an entire army to scour the jungle of the walking reptiles, engage an entire clan of dwarf engineers to build a road back to the beach. It might take a full fleet to carry everything back, but he was sure when the guildmasters saw what he was able to bring back on his own, they'd certainly back the enterprise.

Van Sommerhaus scowled as he considered exactly how he was going to get his treasure out of the pyramid. If only that idiot Adalwolf hadn't wasted his time with the girl! His brawn would be a great boon to the patroon right now. Or if Schachter hadn't been such a greedy bastard! Even split eighty-twenty there would be enough here to put the miserable old pirate up in a style far above his station in life! Van Sommerhaus would even welcome Thanquol back into his life right now. Surely even the underfolk understood the value of gold. Thanquol's rats could drag the stuff away and then they could split the treasure at their leisure someplace far away from snakes and reptiles.

Shaking his head in frustration, van Sommerhaus stopped dreaming of an easy way out. He'd have to carry the gold on his own. He wasn't a man who enjoyed physical labour, it was an activity far below his class. But there wasn't anything difficult about it either. After all, if the unwashed, illiterate stooges who infested the docks of Marienburg could do it, certainly a man of his intelligence could.

He'd need to craft some kind of sling to drag the gold behind him. That would be the best way. He could pull far more than he could lift. Van Sommerhaus ran a hand along the tattered shreds of his elegant coat, bitterly feeling the frayed cuffs and buttonholes. No, he needed something a good bit sturdier.

His eyes came to rest on one of the giant mummies stretched out along the shelves. Van Sommerhaus studied the wrappings with keen interest. They looked to be as thick as sail-cloth and about as tough as leather. Certainly they should be up to the task.

Van Sommerhaus approached the serpentine mummy. Even over the smell of musty herbs there was still an ophidian reek about the thing. He pulled his shirt up over his nose and tried to breathe through his mouth as he contemplated the unpleasant task ahead of him.

At last overcoming his repugnance, van Sommerhaus gripped the edge of one of the wrappings and started to pull it away from the shrivelled body beneath. He didn't notice when his efforts caused the scab on his thumb to crack. Blood dripped down his finger where he had worn it raw during his prayers to Handrich.

As a long strip of cloth came free, a bead of the patroon's blood splattered against the desiccated husk of the giant serpent. He didn't notice the way the ancient corpse absorbed the liquid, or the slight shudder that passed through its sinuous bulk.

It was when van Sommerhaus turned to rip free a second strip of cloth that he discovered something was wrong. He had just set the first cloth down beside his plunder and was turning back to the mummy when he saw it move. There was nothing subtle about the motion, no chance to scoff and try to deny the evidence of his eyes. The head and neck of the mummified snake reared up off the shelf, rising into the air and staring down at him. Great emeralds shone from the skull of the snake, jewelled replacements for the eyes decay had claimed. Lifeless, yet gleaming with a hideous intelligence, the emeralds glared at the man who cowered below.

Van Sommerhaus backed away from the ghastly mummy. He understood now what this place was – a tomb for the giant snakes the lizardmen kept in their temple. Reptiles sacred to their strange god, the great serpents were preserved in death as they were nurtured in life. Unfortunately, the lizardmen had preserved the monsters only too well.

The patroon stumbled as he retreated, falling over the pile of gold he had ripped from the floor. Desperate, he seized a brick in each hand. Turning back to the towering serpent, he held the plundered treasure out to it.

The giant serpent seemed to regard van Sommerhaus's offering for an instant. Then great leathery folds of skin snapped open to either side of its withered head. Decayed jaws fell open and the mummified cobra lunged downward.

Lukas van Sommerhaus shrieked as he vanished into the maw of the cobra, his dreams of wealth and power engulfed by the darkness of the serpent's belly.

CHAPTER THIRTEEN

The Prophet's Test

ADALWOLF FINISHED HIS inspection of the walls at the intersection, then waved his gruesome companions forwards with his torch. There was no mistaking the suspicion in Thanquol's face despite his bestial countenance. The mercenary felt a twinge of disgust when he saw the grey seer prod Boneripper ahead of him on the chance that Adalwolf was trying to betray him and hadn't reported one of the deadly snake-stones. It was an idea that seemed to occur to the ratman every hundred feet or so.

Because of Thanquol's paranoid precautions, whatever progress they were making in finding Hiltrude had slowed to a crawl. Adalwolf felt sorely tempted to abandon the skaven and find Hiltrude on his own, but he knew he couldn't. The crafty grey seer was right. He'd never be able to find her on his own. He had to rely on the ratman's sense of smell if he was going to rescue Hiltrude.

If it wasn't already too late.

Boneripper slipped into the intersection, moving with the eerie smoothness and silence that was so incongruous with his huge frame. The rat ogre's crimson eyes glared into the darkness, careful to avoid directly looking at Adalwolf and his torch lest the light spoil the monster's night-vision.

Thanquol waited several heartbeats, tapping out the time on the floor with his staff. When Boneripper failed to explode or crumble into powder, the grey seer came scurrying up to join him, clinging to his leg like a pilot fish to a shark's fin.

'Which way now?' Adalwolf asked the grey seer.

Thanquol gave him a curious stare, the kind of look someone might give a feeble-minded idiot. He tugged at his whiskers and his eyes narrowed into crafty little slits. Adalwolf fought the urge to feed the monster his fist.

'This way,' Thanquol told him, lifting his head and making a show of sniffing at the air. 'Yes-yes, breeder-thing smell strong this way,' he elaborated, pointing the metal head of his staff down the left-hand turn in the corridor.

'You're sure?' Adalwolf said. 'I'd hate for you to be wrong. I might miss some of those glyphs you're so worried about if Hiltrude isn't with me.'

Thanquol gnashed his teeth together. 'Yes-yes,' he said. 'Slave-meat wants to make whelps. I find-scent breeder-thing. Don't worry-fear!' He gestured at the passageway again with his staff. 'This way. Yes-yes.'

Adalwolf was about to warn Thanquol about what would happen if he tried any tricks when the passage behind them was suddenly filled with hissing, charging lizardmen. Instinctively, the mercenary dropped his torch and drew one of the pistols. He'd reloaded the weapons, a tortuous process with one of his arms broken, but he'd done so for very different reasons. Now, before he could even think about it, he was sighting down the barrel and sending a bullet smashing into the foremost of the scaly blue mass of reptiles. He heard the sharp bark of a skink as one of the smaller lizardmen was thrown back by the impact of the bullet.

Adalwolf started to draw the second pistol before he remembered that the lizardmen weren't the only things he had to worry about. Even if he had drawn the weapon, he would not have had time to fire. Roaring like a blood-mad bull, Boneripper charged into the reptiles. The rat ogre's huge claws ripped a gory swathe through the small skinks, tossing their mangled bodies before him like chaff before a sickle.

The skinks retreated before Boneripper's assault. For an instant Adalwolf thought the monster had routed them, but then he saw the real reason for their flight. The smaller lizardmen were clearing a path for two of their huge cousins. Boneripper growled a challenge to the two kroxigor and soon he was locked in mortal combat with the scaly brutes.

Adalwolf watched the battle for only a few seconds before furry hands were turning him around. Grey Seer Thanquol pressed the fallen torch into his hand and gestured frantically at the corridor ahead.

'Fast-quick! Run-flee!' Thanquol squeaked.

Adalwolf squirmed free of the ratman's filthy touch. He looked in shock at Thanquol. 'You're going to just leave him?' he asked, pointing back to where Boneripper struggled with the kroxigor.

'Yes-yes!' Thanquol snapped. 'Hurry-quick! Breeder-thing close-close!'

Shaking his head in disbelief at the callousness of the grey seer, Adalwolf sprinted down the corridor at what he hoped was a fast enough pace to keep him ahead of the lizardmen once they got past Boneripper. He could hear Thanquol's scurrying feet close behind him.

He didn't see the crafty gleam in the grey seer's eyes, or the way he ground his fangs together as though imagining them locked about a certain slave-thing's throat.

THE AIR WAS heavy with the hot, damp, rotten reek of the jungle as Hiltrude and Schachter were carried from the pyramid. Each of the humans was held by a hulking kroxigor, slung over the backs of the giant lizardmen like sacks of potatoes. The huge reptiles set them down roughly on a little flat ledge that circled the pyramid at its midsection. The captives blinked painfully at the blazing sun, blinding after the gloom of the tunnel-like halls within the temple.

Their captors did not allow them time to recover their sight. Almost as soon as the kroxigor set them down, skinks were scrambling over them. The smaller lizardmen slashed their bindings with little obsidian knives while at the same time retying their arms behind their backs. As soon as they were tied, the skinks forced them to their feet, prodding and pushing them to the long flight of stone steps set into the face of the pyramid.

Hiltrude stumbled as she tried to mount the stairway. The steps were shallow, the incline was nearly vertical and she couldn't balance herself properly with her arms folded against the small of her back. She had taken only a few steps before she fell, smashing painfully against the jagged stairs. Her body began to slide down the stairs. She could see the cracked paving stones of the plaza far below and a thrill of horror swept through her. Frantically, she braced her legs to catch her weight and arrest her fall. It was only when she stopped sliding that the skinks moved in, pulling her back onto her feet and pushing her ahead of them.

She could see the robed figure of Xiuhcoatl climbing the stairs, scrambling up them as effortlessly as a squirrel climbing a tree. Her blood turned cold when she saw the other skink priests waiting for him at the top of the pyramid. They were standing around the altar, the same altar they had seen the lizardmen making their gory sacrifices upon.

Hiltrude screamed then. She twisted her body around, trying to throw herself from the side of the pyramid. Better to be smashed against the plaza below than be butchered on Xiuhcoatl's altar. But this time the lizardmen were ready for her. Cold, scaly hands caught her before she could fall, pulling her back. Skinks surrounded her on every side, prodding and nudging her towards the waiting priests.

'Don't worry,' Schachter called to her from below. 'The bastards can only kill us once.'

As Hiltrude looked up and saw Xiuhcoatl gazing down at her, she wasn't sure if the captain was right. It wasn't anger she saw in the prophet's eyes, it was more emotionless than that. But there was judgement there, stern and without pity. He knew they were the ones who had broken the magic that kept the underfolk from violating his temple. The Temple of Sotek had been profaned and they were responsible.

She read that in Xiuhcoatl's staring eyes, and more. To purify the temple would take much blood and much pain.

Their blood.

Their pain.

THE STRANGE SNAKE-GLYPH shattered beneath the blow of the weird golden club Adalwolf had taken from the corpse of one of the skinks. He could almost imagine little wisps of energy rising from the stone as it crumbled away. There was no mistaking, however, the eager glint that filled Thanquol's beady eyes.

'Quick-quick!' Thanquol urged him, pointing down the corridor where another of the serpent glyphs could be seen jutting from the wall. 'Scaly-things close-close!'

Adalwolf didn't have to ask the ratman how he knew that. He could hear the skinks running up the hall behind them, their claws scratching against the stone floor. It could be only a matter of minutes before the reptiles caught them, and this time they didn't have Boneripper to hold the monsters back.

The mercenary ran past Thanquol, attacking the snake-stone with his club. The ophidian head cracked as he struck it. A second blow sent the glyphs crumbling to the floor. The hair on Adalwolf's arms stood on end as he felt the power within the ward escaping into the darkness. Thanquol chittered excitedly, racing past the man and gesturing impatiently at still another of the snake-stones.

Adalwolf glanced behind him. The lizardmen were much closer now. Perhaps the reptiles were using the stink of Thanquol's fur to guide them through the dark. The idea caused a troubling thought to occur to him. How was it that Thanquol hadn't smelled the lizardmen before? With his sharp nose he should have picked up their scent long before the skinks ambushed them? But why would Thanquol let them be ambushed? It had cost him his giant bodyguard to escape the attack.

'Fast-hurry, quick-quick!' Thanquol squealed at him, hopping on one foot in his frantic eagerness.

There was his answer, Adalwolf realised. The grey seer had allowed the lizardmen to find them and chase them so that he could force Adalwolf to hurry, to be driven like a hunted beast, to act without thinking about what he did.

The mercenary smiled coldly at Thanquol, glaring at him as he slowly marched towards the ratman. 'Just where is Hiltrude?'

Thanquol lashed his tail, then lifted his head and made a great show of sniffing the air. 'Breeder-thing near! Fast-quick!' He pointed a shaking claw at the snake-stone.

'You're lying,' Adalwolf told him. His fingers tightened about the grip of his club. He stared past Thanquol, noting the way the corridor seemed brighter ahead. Not the flicker of a torch, but something cleaner. Rage built up inside him as he realised he was looking at daylight.

Thanquol saw his anger. The grey seer dropped into a crouch, dragging his sword from its sheath. 'Fool-meat! Scaly-things catch-kill both of us!'

'I don't care about that,' Adalwolf snarled. 'You tricked me! You let me have hope!' He took a step towards the ratman, swinging the club before him.

'Wait-listen! Breeder-thing near-close!' Thanquol insisted, parrying the sweep of Adalwolf's club with his sword. Even with only one arm, the mercenary's greater strength sent the grey seer reeling. Thanquol shrieked in abject terror as he stumbled close to the snake-stone.

'It's me or the magic fire, monster!' Adalwolf shouted. He swung the club at Thanquol's head, the blow coming so close to striking home that it grated against one of his horns. 'Either way will suit me fine.'

'Listen-listen!' Thanquol pleaded, throwing himself low to avoid Adalwolf's club. The grey seer scrambled across the floor like a giant rat, cringing against the wall. 'I find-take breeder-thing! Smell-scent!' he whined, tapping his nose with the side of his sword.

Adalwolf didn't give any credit to the grey seer's begging. The monster had tricked him once, he wasn't going to let it happen again. He would not put it past Thanquol to simply be playing for time so that he could be captured by the lizardmen rather than killed by the enraged mercenary.

The golden club came smashing down, denting itself on the hard floor as Thanquol dived away from the crushing blow. He made a desperate slash of his sword, but the strike missed Adalwolf's leg by a good six inches. The mercenary spun on the cringing monster and brought the club swinging around in a savage arc that would spatter Thanquol's brains on the wall.

The grey seer threw himself flat, the club whistling over his head before smashing into the wall. Adalwolf felt the terrific impact throb through his bones, his hand going so numb that the club nearly fell from his fingers. His flesh crawled as he realised he'd not only missed his enemy but had left himself completely helpless.

Thanquol didn't spring at him with his rusty sword. Instead, the skaven leapt to his feet, chittering laughter rippling past his fangs. He turned tail and ran, not into the darkness where the sounds of the pursuing lizardmen were growing louder, but ahead, towards the daylight.

Raw horror raced down Adalwolf's spine when he understood the reason for Thanquol's laughter. The last blow he had aimed at the grey seer had missed him, striking the wall instead. But not just any part of the wall. Unintentionally he had shattered the last of the snake-stones! Whether Thanquol had goaded him into accidentally breaking the ward or if it was just another example of the devil's luck that seemed to surround the monster, Adalwolf did not know. All that he knew was his enemy was going to escape.

Already resigned to a lonely death, the mercenary was determined to see Thanquol precede him on the long road to hell.

Tossing aside the golden club in disgust, Adalwolf drew the duelling pistol from his belt and raced after the fleeing ratman. The greater speed of the skaven gave Adalwolf small hope of catching the monster, but he was determined to try. He called upon Myrmidia and Verena and all his gods and goddesses, begging them for this one small favour. Let him avenge himself on his enemy.

Thanquol vanished through the stone archway that formed the entrance to the corridor. The daylight was almost blinding as Adalwolf hurried after him. Such was his disorientation and the urgency that sped his legs that he nearly pitched headfirst down the side of the pyramid when he left the tunnel. Only the merest chance allowed him to shift his weight back in time, to fall back against the wall of the pyramid instead of crashing down to the plaza far below.

His vision was still mostly a stinging blur, all colours washed out into different vibrancies of white. Adalwolf cursed the biting light of the sun, cursed the valuable moments it gave Thanquol to escape him.

In the midst of his cursing, a snarling figure pounced into the edge of his vision. Thanquol's heavy staff cracked against his face, nearly breaking his jaw as it knocked him down. He screamed in pain as he fell, landing upon his broken arm. The pistol tumbled through his fingers, clattering along the narrow ledge.

More from instinct than conscious thought, Adalwolf rolled his painwracked body as soon as he landed. Instantly he heard the edge of Thanquol's sword scraping the stones he had been lying on. He kicked out with his boot towards the source of the sound and grinned savagely when he was rewarded by Thanquol's pained squeak.

'Dung-rutting slave-meat!' Thanquol snarled at him. 'I'll cut-gut your nethers and feed them to you!'

Thanquol's staff cracked against Adalwolf's side, sending slivers of pure agony rushing through him as his broken bones scraped against each other. But the mercenary did not let the pain overcome him. He seized the head of Thanquol's staff, using it as a lever against his enemy. However fast and sneaky the skaven was, Adalwolf was bigger and stronger. Before Thanquol was even aware of what was happening, Adalwolf swung the grey seer around, slamming him into the wall of the pyramid.

The grey seer was more distinct now, no longer a blur of brightness in Adalwolf's whitewashed eyes. He could see the grey fur standing up on the monster's neck, the ugly fangs gleaming in his mouth. Thanquol's claws tightened about his sword and he started to rush forwards to deliver a stabbing thrust to the man's belly.

Suddenly, Thanquol's eyes became wide with terror, an ugly musky smell rising from his body. The sword clattered from his fingers, bouncing down the narrow stone steps set into the face of the pyramid. Quivering, the skaven gave a short sharp squeak of fear, then ripped his staff free from Adalwolf's grasp. Frantically, Thanquol ran down the side of the pyramid, dropping to all fours as he raced for the ruins far below.

Adalwolf turned his head, wondering if Thanquol had seen the lizardmen emerge from the corridor. Instead he found himself staring at the desolate city beyond the pyramid and the jungle that surrounded it. There were things in the jungle now, a great multitude of reptiles of all sizes and description. He saw lumbering armoured behemoths, howdahs lashed across their scaly backs as though they were Arabyan war elephants. He saw great carnivorous brutes like the one they had seen on the trail, only these were saddled after the fashion of Bretonnian destriers. He saw a horde of tall, powerful lizardmen, warrior reptiles that were neither the hulking kroxigor of the spawning pools or the wiry skinks of the temple. The soldier lizards formed ranks and columns, marching to the sound of strange pipes and ominous drums.

There was an entire army mustering at the edge of the jungle, fanning out to form a ring around the ruined city. In the midst of the strange army, his eyes drawn to it like those of a fly to a spider, was a weird, bloated, toadlike creature hovering upon a great golden dais. Even Adalwolf could sense the power of the strange being. It was as though a piece of the sun had broken off and fallen into the jungle, such was its magnitude. The skink prophet that had so terrified

Thanquol was nothing beside the aura of ancient might that emanated from the toad-creature. No wonder the ratman had turned tail and run!

Thinking of Thanquol made Adalwolf glance back down the side of the pyramid. The fleeing skaven had covered almost half of the distance between himself and the plaza below. Adalwolf glanced about him for a loose brick, an old bone, anything he might hurl after Thanquol and perhaps make him fall. He smiled as something better rewarded his quick search. He had thought his pistol lost when Thanquol pounced on him, but the weapon had not rolled over the lip of the ledge.

Grinning, Adalwolf stood and coldly aimed the pistol at Thanquol's back.

Before he could fire, a sharp scream rose from somewhere behind and above him. Adalwolf spun around, certain it was Hiltrude's voice. He gazed up the face of the pyramid, staring at the flat summit where the altar stood. The skink priests were once more gathered there, the robes and feathers of Xiuhcoatl fluttering about him in the hot, damp wind. The skink prophet held a gleaming knife in his clawed hand as he leaned over the altar.

Upon the altar, stretched and tied as the ratmen had been, shrieking in terror, was Hiltrude!

Adalwolf gave no further thought to Thanquol. He sighted down the barrel of his pistol, aiming at the distant shape of Xiuhcoatl. There was little chance of the bullet striking the prophet at such a distance, but Adalwolf prayed that the noise of the discharge might frighten him off.

Taking careful aim and praying once more to his gods, Adalwolf slowly pulled the trigger.

LORD TLACO WATCHED the corrupted algorithm as it scurried down the face of the Temple of the Serpent. The slann shifted his attention away from the noxious disharmony and instead focused upon the low phase algorithm, the unknown quotient, standing upon the ledge above the fleeing xa'cota. He could see the warm-quick emotions as irrational sums warring for control of the unknown quotient's mental processes. At the top of the temple, Lord Tlaco could see Xiuhcoatl, the skink's presence as inscrutable as the other times the mage-priest had contemplated him.

Through the confusion of irrationalities that filled the mind of the unknown quotient, Lord Tlaco could see patterns. One set of patterns would spell destruction for the xa'cota. Another set brought challenge to the Prophet of Sotek. Which pattern would the unknown quotient add into itself? Which algorithm would it seek to negate?

The Old Ones had a purpose when they had added the low phase algorithms to the Great Math. It did not matter that none of the slann had ever truly decided upon the purpose of that addition, or even if the work the Old Ones had begun had been finished or left incomplete. Unlike the persistent fractals and the corrupted algorithms, the warm-quick had their place within the harmony. They had purpose.

Lord Tlaco had invested much attention to bringing the unknown quotient here to serve such a purpose. Which would it choose? Xiuhcoatl or the xa'cota? Which would its irrational sums tell it was the answer to the equation?

The slann's eyes narrowed as he saw the unknown quotient's thoughts become constant. It had made its choice. Lord Tlaco watched as the human pointed his weapon at Xiuhcoatl and fired.

That is the answer to the problem, Lord Tlaco decided, shifting one of its flabby fingers, using it to manipulate the patterns of the Great Math.

The equation is solved, the slann thought. The new unknown was why.

ADALWOLF WATCHED IN disbelief as his bullet exploded the top of Xiuhcoatl's skull. The skink prophet didn't even cry out as the impact of the shot lifted him off his feet. The body flew over the side of the pyramid, clattering down the shallow stairway in a tangle of feathered talismans and golden charms.

The other skink priests were as shocked by the sudden and violent death of Xiuhcoatl as Adalwolf. The lizardmen blinked about them in confusion, their mouths gaping in stunned silence.

He didn't know how long he could expect the lizardmen to be overcome by the death of their leader. Shifting his grip on the pistol so that he might use its heavy butt like a bludgeon, Adalwolf took to the stairs, rushing up them at a frenzied pace, heedless of the lethal fall waiting for him if he stumbled in his mad rush up the face of the pyramid. The danger that threatened him was little compared to the revenge the lizardmen were sure to take upon

Hiltrude when they recovered. The vision of her dripping heart being ripped from her body by the reptilian priests spurred him on. He ignored the flare of pain that shot through him with every step as the bones of his shattered arm ground against each other. He was oblivious to the hot, stinging breath that rasped through his lungs. All that mattered to him was reaching the girl in time.

Adalwolf cleared the last few steps in a bounding leap, landing upon the roof of the pyramid in a pantherish crouch. The skink priests blinked, their pupils widening in surprise as they found this wild man kneeling beside the altar. One of the priests started to lift his feathered staff. The mercenary sprang at him, smashing the pistol against the top of his skull. The skink staggered under the first blow, then slumped lifelessly against the altar as Adalwolf pressed his attack.

A sharp hiss warned Adalwolf that a second skink was rushing at him from behind. He spun, hurling the bloody pistol at the skink's face. Fangs cracked as the weapon smashed into the lizardman's mouth, causing him to veer away from the mercenary and clutch at his bleeding face.

There was no time to pursue the wounded priest, for already the third of its fellows was rushing at Adalwolf, the sharp tip of its staff aimed at him like a spear. He braced himself, waiting for the moment he wanted. As the skink rushed at him, he shifted and grabbed at the staff. Much as he had when fighting Thanquol, he caught the staff in a grip of iron and used his greater strength and size to swing his foe around. The lean skink was even less of a burden than the horned skaven and Adalwolf's spin flung the reptile far out over the side of the roof. The lizardman uttered a chirp of fright as it plummeted to the plaza below.

The last of the skink priests glared at Adalwolf with cold, unblinking eyes. Slithering noises whispered through its teeth and an awful light began to gather about its scaly claws. The mercenary understood the reason for the bold attacks of the other priests. They had been meant to distract him to give this last priest time to work its magic. Adalwolf threw the feathered staff he held at the skink, but the hurled weapon seemed to lose momentum before it even came near the skink, clattering harmlessly on the stones in front of the priest's feet.

Gleaming teeth shone in the skink's face as the priest raised one of his glowing claws. Adalwolf looked for someplace he might take cover. The only hiding place was the altar and to take advantage of it would be to expose Hiltrude to whatever magic the reptile was evoking.

Adalwolf stood where he was and glared defiantly at the lizardman. 'I hope you choke on those words,' he spat.

The skink abruptly stopped his incantation, the glow fading from his claws. It cocked his head to the side, staring at Adalwolf with a look of surprise and confusion that was even greater than his shock at Xiuhcoatl's death. Calmly, the priest set its staff down on the ground, then sat down beside it, folding his legs and tail beneath his body.

Adalwolf stared suspiciously at the skink, wondering what trick it was playing at. He watched the creature carefully, circling around it to reach the altar. The skink gave no further notice of the man, but kept its eyes staring at the palms of its own hands.

Hiltrude sobbed when she saw Adalwolf's face appear above her, tears of relief rolling down her cheeks. The mercenary gave her a reassuring smile, then fumbled at the thongs the lizardmen had used to bind her to the altar. Whatever knots the skinks had used, they were complex enough to baffle even a seafaring man. Adalwolf soon abandoned any hope of untying her and looked for something to cut her free instead.

The ceremonial knife Xiuhcoatl had thought to use on Hiltrude was resting on the ground beside the altar. Adalwolf leaned down and quickly grabbed it. As he did so, he saw the shivering mass lying sprawled at the foot of the altar. A grim smile appeared on his face as he saw Captain Schachter's situation.

The treacherous sea captain could wait. Adalwolf stood and returned his attention to Hiltrude. With a last look at the skink to make sure he was still behaving, the mercenary began sawing at the ties that bound Hiltrude's hands.

As soon as her arms were free, Hiltrude wrapped them around Adalwolf's neck in a crushing embrace. She pulled herself off the altar and crushed her soft lips against his. It took more effort than he would have believed possible to free himself from her arms.

'I have to free your legs,' Adalwolf told her, gently pushing her away. A sudden thought came to him.

He would need to turn his back on the skink. 'Keep your eyes on that monster. Warn me if he moves.'

'I prayed you would come,' Hiltrude told him as he sawed at the cords. 'I didn't dare to hope you'd come in time.'

Adalwolf slashed the last of the cords and helped Hiltrude lower herself from the altar. 'You can thank that slinking coward Thanquol I found you in time,' Adalwolf said. 'He promised he'd lead me to you if I helped him get out, though I'm sure he never intended to keep his word. Sometimes even liars get caught in their own lies.'

Hiltrude started to hug him again, then noticed the flare of pain that swept across his face when she touched his arm. A mixture of pity and concern filled her eyes as she noticed Adalwolf's injury. She studied the crude binding he had made for himself from one of his pant legs. Shaking her head in disapproval, she started to rip at the tatters of her own dress to make a more secure bandage.

'No time for that,' Adalwolf scolded her. 'There was an entire mob of reptiles chasing me when I escaped the pyramid and there's an entire army of them moving to surround the city! We have to get out of here! Now!'

The mercenary grabbed Hiltrude's hand and started to lead her towards the stairs when Schachter's voice cried out.

'For the love of Shallya and the grace of Manann, don't leave me!' the captain wailed.

Adalwolf stared coldly at the man, then his gaze shifted to the now empty altar. It was no better than the villain deserved. Hiltrude's soft hand pressed against his chest as he turned away.

'You can't leave him,' she said. 'Not like this. Not with them.'

A stab of guilt made Adalwolf frown. Whatever Schachter had done, he was still human. Hiltrude was right; no man of conscience could abandon another to the mercies of inhuman monsters. Except for her, though, he realised that was exactly what he would have done.

The mercenary leaned over Schachter, sawing through the cords with a deft motion of the knife. The sea captain rubbed his bruised wrists and grinned at Adalwolf. 'Don't get the idea I did this for you,' the mercenary warned him. 'I just don't want your sorry face haunting me at night is all.'

'I won't forget this,' Schachter assured him. 'By Handrich and old Jack o' the Sea, I won't!' The captain stood and rubbed his legs, working circulation back into them. 'What's the plan now? You mean to go back inside and look for van Sommerhaus?'

Adalwolf turned away as Hiltrude looked at him hopefully. After her own impossible rescue, she seemed to think he could do anything. In a way, he was almost sad he was too rational to think he could. If the patroon was still inside the pyramid, they'd never find him. He stared out across the ruins, watching as the army of lizardmen slowly surrounded it. Soon there would be no escape. But where would they escape to?

A smile spread across his face as he spotted a grey robed figure racing through the ruins. If anybody knew an escape route, it would be Thanquol!

The warrior pointed at the distant ratman. 'We have to follow Thanquol!' he said. 'He'll know a way out of here and I'm sure he can be convinced the only way to save his skin is to save ours too.'

Hiltrude gasped in horror at the idea. 'We escape the lizardmen only to run back into Thanquol's paws!'

Adalwolf shook his head. 'He's lost all of his followers. It's just him and us now.' He gazed out across the ruins, unpleasantly aware of the cordon the lizardmen were throwing around the city and the presence of the toad-creature at the edge of the jungle. 'We have to hurry before we lose him.'

'I'll be with you in a moment,' Schachter told the others. He picked up one of the feathered staves lying on the roof and strode towards the sitting skink.

'Schachter! Leave it alone!' Adalwolf cried, afraid the man would provoke the reptilian priest into unleashing whatever magic he had been conjuring.

The sea captain hesitated as he lifted the staff, but it wasn't because of Adalwolf's shout. Schachter studied the unmoving lizardman, staring at the curious white spots that were spreading across the skink's scaly hide. It was like watching mould growing on bread. He backed away from the reptile, suddenly losing his interest in bashing its head in.

'Plague!' Schachter gasped, making the sign of Shallya as he spoke the ghastly word.

Adalwolf started towards the sitting priest to see for himself, but Hiltrude held him back. 'You said we had to go. Let's go,' she said, her voice quivering with terror much as it had when the sailors had proposed using fire to burn away the man-eating plants.

The mercenary relented. The skink could keep the secret of whatever weird doom had claimed it. Carefully, he made his way to the stairs, grateful that he had Hiltrude beside him to keep his balance. Descending was going to be harder than his mad rush to the top. For one thing, there was no way to avoid noticing how far it was to the bottom.

Halfway down they found the entrance way Thanquol and Adalwolf had used to escape the pyramid. The opening was littered with the bodies of lizardmen now, all of them sporting the most hideous wounds. Adalwolf felt all the warmth drain out of him when he saw the bodies. He knew what kind of creature was capable of wreaking such havoc. He kept silent, though. It wouldn't do any good to tell the others that Thanquol might not be alone for long.

There were others though, lizardmen that hadn't quite been finished off in the fight. None of them were in any condition to cause trouble, simply lying strewn about the ledge, their lifeblood seeping out of their mangled frames. The mouths of the skinks gaped as they tried to suck air into their bodies and their eyes were swollen and crusted over. The same ghastly white fungus Schachter had described was quickly spreading across their scaly skin, visibly expanding even as they watched.

Schachter stooped over one of the mutilated skinks and removed the golden sword clutched in its dead claw. He tested the balance of the unwieldy blade. Grinning, he turned back towards Adalwolf.

'Damn sight better than a knife,' Schachter told the mercenary. Hiltrude could feel Adalwolf's body grow tense.

Schachter laughed and tossed the weapon to Adalwolf. 'This one's yours,' he said. 'I'll see about finding others for myself and the girl.'

'If we get back, these'll be worth a few guilders,' Adalwolf commented as he studied the strange double-headed sword.

'I was thinking the same thing,' Schachter answered, a gleam in his eye.

CHAPTER FOURTEEN

Hunters and Prey

WHEN HE HEARD the pistol shot, Thanquol's paws instantly flew to his chest. It took several minutes of poking and patting to assure himself that he hadn't been shot. He gritted his teeth in a feral scowl. He knew it had been a mistake to give that simpering human a weapon! The villainous, unthankful wretch had tried to put a bullet in his back!

Thanquol muttered a quiet prayer of gratitude to the Horned Rat for spoiling the man-thing's aim. However dire his circumstances, he should have known better than to arm an unpredictable animal. Humans couldn't be trusted with all their insane ideas and irrational attachments. Any thinking creature would have been content to be led out of the pyramid, but not a human! Oh no, the fool-meat had to demand to be led to his breeder first!

The grey seer looked back at the pyramid as he leaped to the cracked stones of the plaza. He wondered if he dared send a spell searing into the human. As afraid as he was of drawing Xiuhcoatl's attention, he was even more afraid that the great fat frog-thing he'd spotted in the jungle would notice. That creature had appeared to Thanquol's senses less as a thing of flesh and blood but more as a bloated sack of raw magical energy. He'd seen warpstone deposits that were puny beside the power he sensed in the fat frog-thing. Seeing the frog-mage up close had risen rather prominently to the top of Thanquol's phobias. Going back to Skavenblight and explaining his failure to the Nightlord wasn't such a poor prospect by comparison.

Thanquol lashed his tail in annoyance. He wouldn't get back to Skavenblight if the back-shooting man-thing put a bullet through his spine. Perhaps Xiuhcoatl and the frog-mage wouldn't notice a small spell; one only big enough to scorch the human's eyes out of his face.

His beady red eyes blinked in confusion as Thanquol stared up at the pyramid. The human wasn't even looking at him, he was dashing up the stairs as fast as he could, making for the roof of the dreadful temple. He was just thinking that terror of the grey seer's powers had sent the man-thing running when Thanquol noticed the greasy tang of reptile blood in the air. He shifted his gaze in the direction of the smell and was shocked to see a scaly blue body tumbling down the steps of the pyramid.

The faint smell of gunpowder rising from the lizardman told Thanquol how he had met his end. The white robe and feathered ornaments made him realise that the victim of Adalwolf's bullet had been Xiuhcoatl.

Thanquol clapped his paws together and leaped off the ground, squeaking in delight.

The clever, bold little slave-thing! He knew there was a reason he had conquered his own petty fears and doubts and given the human those pistols. Lesser skaven would have thought only of their own skins, unable to think past getting a bullet in their back. Not he! His was the sort of genius that might exhibit itself once in a generation. He had foreseen the possibilities of a human with a pistol. For the good of the quest, he had dismissed his own fears and put the man-thing in the position to kill Xiuhcoatl!

Actually, the more he thought about it, the story would probably sound even more heroic if he avoided any mention of the human at all. Thanquol wondered if he should say he'd shot the cursed Prophet of Sotek or if it would be even more awe-inspiring to say he'd slaughtered the lizardman with one of his spells.

The problem was still vexing the grey seer when he saw a pack of excited skinks erupt from the tunnel he and the human had escaped through. Thanquol glared at the lizardmen, thumbed a piece of warpstone from his pocket and started to imagine the spell he would evoke. Then he remembered the frog-mage out in the jungle.

Magic probably wasn't a good idea just now, Thanquol decided as he turned tail and scurried away from the Temple of the Serpent. The very last thing he wanted was to draw that thing's attention. It might even draw the awful conclusion that it had been he and not the human who had killed Xiuhcoatl.

Thanquol wasn't sure if frog-things could get angry, but he was sure he didn't want to find out.

ADALWOLF WINCED AS Hiltrude tightened the binding around his broken arm. Staring down at the mouldy corpses of the lizardmen, the mercenary was certain the maimed limb was infected with the same putrescence. He wondered how quickly the disease would overwhelm him and how much it would hurt. Somehow, he didn't take the skink priest's quiet acceptance of the sickness as a good example of how it felt to have white mould erupting from your skin.

He looked longingly down the side of the pyramid. A quick fall and it would be all over, Adalwolf thought. But that would leave Hiltrude alone with Schachter again. The mercenary shook his head. He couldn't abandon her to the villain. If it came to it, he cut Schachter's throat before his own.

The sea captain almost seemed to sense Adalwolf's thoughts. He backed away from the sprawled bodies of the lizardmen. Three gold swords and two clubs were stuffed beneath his belt and he had tied the arms of his coat together to make a bag to carry still more loot he'd pulled off the bodies. Schachter's face flushed with embarrassment when he saw Hiltrude and Adalwolf staring at him.

'If we get out of here, you'll be glad I brought this along,' Schachter told them, hefting the heavy sack onto his shoulder. 'There's enough here to set the three of us up pretty good if we get back.'

'You sure about that?' Hiltrude challenged. 'I mean, about splitting it?'

Schachter couldn't look in her eyes, instead staring at his feet. 'You want me to leave it then?'

'It might remove certain temptations,' the courtesan shot back.

Adalwolf shook his head. 'Bring the bag, Schachter,' he said. 'We've wasted enough time on it. Thanquol's probably out of the city by now.'

'Not the way he's leaking,' Schachter smiled, nodding his head at the trail of black blood staining the steps of the pyramid. 'You must have cut him pretty good in your scuffle.'

Adalwolf thought about that. Thanquol hadn't looked hurt when he scurried off. He glanced again at the mangled lizardmen and shuddered as he considered what the black blood was more likely to belong to. Still, even if he was wrong in his assumption, Schachter's advice was sound. If it was Boneripper's blood, then the rat ogre could only be following Thanquol's scent. That meant if they followed the blood, they would still find Thanquol.

He only hoped they did so before Boneripper. Adalwolf was certain the beast would rip the ratman apart when he caught up to him. He wasn't concerned about the ratman, of course, but they needed whatever escape route the slinking sorcerer had waiting to get him out of Lustria.

'We can't count on that,' Adalwolf objected. 'He's a magician, remember? Once he's far enough away from the pyramid, he'll whistle up some kind of spell to set him right. Then where will we be?' He didn't want to frighten the others with his suspicions that Thanquol was not alone, but neither did he want them to be caught off-guard. If Boneripper had rejoined his tyrannical master, they would need all their wits sharp, not lulled into a false confidence by the thought of trailing a lone wounded ratman.

The thought sobered Schachter. Straining under the weight of his coat, the seaman hurried down the narrow stairway, recklessly taking them three and four at a time.

'What are you standing around for!' Schachter shouted. 'We've got a rat to catch!'

THROUGHOUT THANQUOL'S LONG flight through the ruined streets of Quetza, he'd had the impression of being pursued. Sometimes he would hear the faint scuffle of feet against stone, or the clatter of rubble being disturbed, or the scrape of claws against the crumbling walls. He managed to keep one step ahead of his pursuers, however, constantly darting into the confusing maze of alleyways and collapsed buildings that formed much of the sprawling city.

All of his tricks, however, weren't enough to fool his hunters. They kept following him, always just out of sight, always just at the edge of his hearing. Thanquol tried to pick up their scent, but when he sniffed the air he found his nose filled with a foulness that caused it to run. An abominable taint was in the atmosphere, a sickly vapour that seemed to rise from the very stones of Quetza. Thanquol thought of the long war between Clan Pestilens and the lizardmen and wondered what manner of contagions the plague priests had brewed to conquer the city.

Whatever vile diseases the plague monks had created, they had lingered long after the serpent-devil Sotek drove them into the sea. The foul vapours had seeped into the very stones, lurking and waiting like some venomous spider. Thanquol wondered why he hadn't detected it before. The only answer was that somehow, in some feat of sorcery of such magnitude that it made the grey seer's fur crawl, Xiuhcoatl had suppressed the lingering plague vapours so that Quetza would be safe for the lizardmen to build their temple.

If true, it was another example of the potency of the scaly creatures and their magic. More than ever, Thanquol was determined to get his tail out of Lustria and back to civilised lands. The deranged maniacs of Clan Pestilens could keep the damn jungles! In fact, Thanquol would suggest to the Council of Thirteen that they ship all of the Under-Empire's malcontents and undesirables to Lustria as an efficient method of disposal.

The grey seer breathed a good deal easier once he was back under the shadowy overhang of the jungle. When he reached the edge of Quetza, he gave one last look back, trying to spot his pursuers. He was certain they hadn't given up. The ease with which they navigated the city made him certain they were Xiuhcoatl's followers. Strangely, the idea was more appealing than the alternative: scouts from the frog-mage's army. Thanquol quickly glanced from side to side and sniffed at the air, but there was no sign that the closing pincers of the lizardmen were near. He chittered in amusement as he considered the huge army of reptiles surrounding the city. They would be too late in their encirclement of Quetza – because he would already be long gone!

Still chittering with nervous humour, Thanquol darted down the jungle trails Tsang Kweek's gutter runners had chopped through the jungle. Already vines and creepers were starting to choke the path again, but it was clear enough for Thanquol to follow. There was even a strong smell of skaven clinging to the path, making it doubly easy for him to find his way. It was certainly a sign of the Horned One's favour that Thanquol had survived where so many of Clan Eshin's vaunted killers and murderers had died.

Thanquol smiled viciously as he remembered his fallen comrades. Shiwan Stalkscent, the arrogant little murder-master. Shen Tsinge, the treacherous little sorcerer. Tsang Kweek, the slinking little spy. Kong Krakback, the bullying little thug.

Blinking in bewilderment, Thanquol paused as he ran down the jungle trail. For a moment, he'd thought he'd heard Kong's voice. But that was, of course, impossible. Kong was dead, along with all of his warriors. They had sacrificed their lives so that the rest of the expedition could get inside the Temple of the Serpent. If he'd heard anything, it had been Kong's ghost, and since he didn't like that idea, he decided he hadn't heard anything at all.

The smell of skaven was much stronger now and Thanquol was certain he'd reached the clearing where they had made their camp. He'd need some of the supplies they'd left behind to provision himself on the trek back to the beach. With enough food buried around the campsite to feed a few hundred skaven, he was certain there would be enough to keep himself in good state for some time.

Grey Seer Thanquol emerged into the clearing and immediately his face twisted into a scowl. The ground was torn up in every direction, churned by the claws of animals. Some filthy jungle beast had been digging up Thanquol's supplies!

Then the grey seer's eyes noticed the carefully stacked piles of roots and tubers and withered sheets of salted meat. Animals wouldn't do that he realised, a chill sweeping down his spine. It could only mean that the lizardmen had already been here and found this place!

Spinning about to flee back into the jungle, Thanquol was thrown back into the clearing by a powerful blow. His mouth filled with blood as his fangs bit into his own tongue, his lungs gasping for air as the wind was knocked out of him by his violent fall. A savage tug ripped his staff from his hand while a clawed foot pressed down on his chest.

Thanquol sputtered and spat foul-tasting blood from his mouth. He tried to think what sort of appeal would ingratiate himself to the lizardmen.

Perhaps he could offer to show them where Clan Pestilens still had strongholds in the jungle? Surely the reptiles hadn't wiped out all of the plague monks and they'd probably be most eager to finish the job to avoid another of their cities ending up like Quetza!

His mind racing with thoughts of how to save his skin by betraying his race, Thanquol was slow to notice that his attackers weren't scaly. Big, black-furred skaven surrounded him, their armour caked in blood, their bodies striped with crusty wounds. He saw Kong Krakback's ugly sneer as the hulking skaven warrior glared at him from the edge of the clearing.

'Kong!' Thanquol coughed, finding the vocalisation difficult with the foot of a skaven warrior planted on his chest. 'I am happy-pleased to see-find you alive! We are victorious! Serpent-priest is dead-dead!'

The big skaven didn't seem to hear him, instead running his paw along the length of the notched sword he held in his other hand. The toothy smile on Kong's face was perfectly primal in its expression of murderous hate.

'They won't listen-hear your lies, grey traitor!' a shrill, snickering voice raked across Thanquol's ears. He had to twist his neck to an uncomfortable angle to stare at the speaker. What he saw was a black-cloaked assassin crouched upon the same fallen log Thanquol had used as his own perch after assuming control of the expedition. The assassin, like the skaven warriors, bore the marks of hard fighting on his body and his cloak was a mass of bloody rags. It wasn't the killer's new injuries that interested Thanquol, however, but the old one he saw through a rent in the ratman's hood, the scabby splotch against the side of his head where an ear had been cut off.

'You!' was all the grey seer could think to say.

Chang Fang grinned back at him and lashed his tail in amusement. 'So, Thanquol-meat, you remember me! You have betray-trick so many, I worry-fear you would not know me! I am Chang Fang,' the assassin declared, straightening himself into a proud pose. 'Chang Squik was my triad-kin. When you betrayed him, you betrayed me. For that, you die-suffer!'

Thanquol's body shivered in a spasm of pure fear. Chang Squik? But that bumbling killer had been dead for years! What kind of lunatic held a grudge for such a long time! It was madness! Besides, he wasn't the one who had caused Chang Squik's death, it had been that damnable dwarf and his pet human!

'You die slow,' Chang Fang hissed, hopping down from his perch and drawing one of his wicked knives. 'I make you suffer-scream much-much,' he added with an insane giggle.

'But we can go back!' Thanquol shouted. He could see it was useless trying to reason with the assassin, but surely Kong and his warriors weren't so far gone as to ignore him. 'Xiuhcoatl's dead! I killed him! We can go back and claim the Nightlord's reward!'

Thanquol's words only brought chittering laughter from the other skaven. The ratman pinning him to the ground lashed his scaly tail across the grey seer's face. The impact stung like that of a whip.

'No lie-words!' the warrior snarled, leaning his weight onto Thanquol, driving the breath from his lungs.

'Thanquol kill-slay scaly-meat?' laughed Kong Krakback. The big black skaven was fingering his sword in such a way now that the grey seer thought if Chang Fang didn't hurry the warrior was going to do the job first. 'How Thanquol-meat kill-slay snake-priest? Trip over snake-priest while running away?'

The grey seer gnashed his fangs at Kong's casual insult against his courage, then tried to think of a lie that would sound believable to the black skaven. They'd never believe he'd arranged for one of the humans to kill Xiuhcoatl, even if he couched the story in terms that made it sound like a happy accident rather than brilliant planning and careful strategy.

A cunning gleam came into his eye. 'Boneripper!' the grey seer squealed. 'I sent-told Boneripper to slay-kill!'

Chang Fang leaned over the prone Thanquol, a string of drool hanging from the assassin's eager fangs. 'Too bad you not keep-take rat ogre,' he giggled. 'Now you suffer-scream much-much. Then die-rot!'

The assassin raised his knife, the blade gleaming in the hot sunlight.

Thanquol screwed his eyes shut, his entire body flailing as he tried to escape the warrior pinning him to the ground. 'Xiuhcoatl dead-dead!' he yelled. 'Boneripper slay-kill! Boneripper! Boneripper!'

Lord Tlaco shifted upon his dais, allowing his attendant skinks to pour cool spring water over his mottled skin. The dark spots upon the slann's hide shifted position ever so slightly, setting the skink scribes surrounding it into a frenzy of activity as they recorded the new markings. The mage-priest paid them scant attention, allowing only the lower hemispheres of its brain to guide them in positioning the army around Quetza.

None of the servants of Sotek could be allowed to leave the city. Lord Tlaco had sent that message into the brains of the priests who had survived Xiuhcoatl. They understood the need for their own destruction. With Xiuhcoatl's death, the Prophet's magic had been broken. The powerful wards which restrained the sorcerous diseases infesting the very stones of Quetza had been broken. Every lizardman in the city was now a carrier of the plagues that had caused it to be abandoned many sun-cycles past. They could not be allowed to bring the contagion to other cities.

The priests Lord Tlaco had telepathically contacted had met the news with the fatalistic acceptance that denoted those who understood the Great Math and their own value within it. The slann did not have to worry about them irrationally behaving like low-phase algorithms desperate to delay their own negation. However, there were many others who served the Temple of the Serpent, minions less aware of the Great Math. These might try to escape and bear the contagion away with them.

The mage-priest flicked one of his webbed hands. A phalanx of saurus warriors bobbed their heads in unison, acknowledging the command. The dark-scaled soldier-lizards jogged off at a quick march, moving to encircle the northern perimeter of Quetza. They would reinforce the skink skirmishers already lurking at the jungle's edge, waiting with their bows to strike down any lizardmen trying to leave the city. They would maintain their positions for the next three lunar cycles. By then there would be nothing to fear from Quetza. Nothing would be left alive within the ruins to act as a courier for the plague.

Lord Tlaco's eyes widened as one of his army's scouts came scurrying towards the slann's dais. Instinctively, the mage-priest's armoured temple guard closed ranks around the levitating dais. A slight shifting of its skin spots had the skull-helmed lizardmen stepping aside for the scout.

In a rapid series of gestures and hisses, the chameleon skink explained that several low-phase algorithms – what the scout called 'soft-skins' – had emerged from the city and were fleeing into the jungle to the south. The skirmishers had watched them go, but had obeyed Lord Tlaco's command that the humans were not to be harmed.

It was a slight misinterpretation of its orders, but overall Lord Tlaco was pleased. The slann didn't need all of the low-phase algorithms. It only needed the one that had been used to resolve the thought problem that had vexed Lord Tlaco. The slann had its solution, Xiuhcoatl had been killed. But did the Prophet's death condemn his god or exonerate it? That was a problem that could only be resolved by studying the vector that had negated Xiuhcoatl's value. Did the low-phase algorithm possess a rational value or was it a decaying fractal, a corrupted algorithm like the xa'cota?

That was an answer that could only be determined by studying the human who had made the decision to shoot Xiuhcoatl instead of the xa'cota. Lord Tlaco wasn't certain simple dissection would allow him to understand why the low-phase algorithm made its choice. It was preferable to study its value before negation rather than after. Trying to impress that factor into every mind in his army as well as the thought-pictures that would ensure the lizardmen could differentiate Lord Tlaco's subject from the others demanded an uncomfortable amount of concentration on the slann's part. He would have to tap into those hemispheres of its brain that were already working upon other disharmonies in the Great Math to do so.

It had been easier just to order the army to allow anything that wasn't a lizardman to leave the city. Warm-bloods could not carry the plague the xa'cota had used to kill Quetza, so there was no danger in allowing them to pass.

Now that their escape had been reported, however, Lord Tlaco decided it was time to collect its subject. The slann's spots shifted into a determined pattern and the skink scribes set down their styluses and bowed their heads. Those elements of the army the slann had kept in reserve for just this purpose turned their heads so that, from the mightiest saurus warchief to the small-brained terradons and razordons, every eye was fixed upon Lord Tlaco. The mage-priest sent the necessary impressions and factors into the minds of this fragment of its army.

Like a single gigantic creature, the lizardmen hurried into the depths of the jungle, one purpose driving them all: to collect Lord Tlaco's specimen and return with it to the mage-priest.

CHANG FANG'S KNIFE hurtled downwards. The assassin held his weapon not in the stabbing thrust of an expert killer, but in the slashing stroke of a crazed butcher. He had decided he would start his revenge by cutting Thanquol's horns from his skull. Then he would move to lower and more tender bits of the grey seer's anatomy.

Before the assassin's knife could even nick the grey seer's horn, he found himself flying through the air. Chang Fang was so intent upon his vengeance that he didn't see the bloody mangled mass until it slammed into him, carrying him away with it across the clearing. The assassin twisted his body in mid-air so that it was the torn mass of the corpse that smacked into the bole of a mangrove instead of his own back. The assassin toppled back to earth along with what he now knew was the wreckage of one of Kong's clanrats. He tried to brace himself for the fall, but his best effort had gone into twisting the corpse about so it would absorb the collision with the tree. He struck the ground hard and it took several precious seconds to blink away the spots that danced before his eyes.

Across the clearing, Kong and his warriors were showing no less surprise than Chang Fang. They stared in gaping horror at the hulking shape that loomed out of the jungle towards them. There was no question who had killed the clanrat and then thrown the still twitching corpse across the clearing to knock down the assassin.

After killing the kroxigor, Boneripper had followed Thanquol's scent through the pyramid, mutilating any lizardmen that got in his way. When the grey seer made his retreat from Quetza, it was Boneripper who followed him through the ruins and later into the jungle. Perhaps some dim sense of betrayal and abandonment was working on the rat ogre's mind, confusing his feelings towards Thanquol. Perhaps he was simply too weary from his battles with the lizardmen to catch up to his fleeing master before. Whatever his reasons, Boneripper had been content to linger after Thanquol, making no effort to catch him.

At least until he heard Thanquol frantically crying his name. Any resentful thoughts vanished as the obedience that had been beaten into the rat ogre's brain took over. Moving with the speed and stealth of a jaguar, the huge monster rushed through the forest, a living engine of havoc.

Boneripper beat his huge claws upon his chest and roared at Thanquol's enemies. The ferocious display might have frightened Kong and his warriors more if the sudden movement hadn't opened some of the wounds Boneripper had suffered in his fight with the kroxigor. The sight and smell of blood excited the skaven at the most primitive level of their minds. The hulking rat ogre had gone from terrifying foe to wounded prey.

Two of Kong's warriors rushed at Boneripper from either side, while the leader himself and a third skaven charged at him from the fore. The rat ogre roared a second time, then brought both of his clawed hands slashing in an arc before his body. The clanrat charging at him from the right was eviscerated by the unexpected speed of the monster's attack. He collapsed in a squeaking mess, frenziedly pawing at the dirt in his death agonies.

The skaven to Boneripper's left came up short, recalling the horrific speed with which the monster could move. For a moment, however, his eyes were locked on the mangled shape of his comrade. It was a fragment of distraction that the ratman would never repeat. Boneripper sprang at him, smashing him flat with the palm of his paw and grinding his skull into the earth until it was jelly.

Kong Krakback slashed at Boneripper's flank, opening a great gash just above the monster's knee. Out of the corner of his eye, however, he could see the ratman who had joined his attack turning to flee. He turned his head to snap a wrathful order to the coward, but the words never left his throat.

Feeling the bite of Kong's sword, Boneripper spun, swinging the crushed body he had been pounding into the ground. The flailing legs of the corpse smashed into Kong's head, spilling him onto the ground and knocking the sword from his hand.

Boneripper dabbed a paw to the fresh wound in his leg. He sniffed at the dark blood that coated his fingers and glared at the black skaven trying to crawl away from him. Roaring like a gold-mad dragon, Boneripper descended upon the dazed Kong. The rat ogre's scythe-like claws closed around the squirming skaven's body and lifted him into the air. Kong shrieked as he was held dangling before Boneripper's hate-filled eyes.

Slowly and maliciously, the rat ogre tore Kong Krakback limb from limb.

WHILE BONERIPPER FINISHED with Kong and his clanrats, a desperate Thanquol struggled against the warrior still pinning him to the ground. A twist of his body had caught the ratman unawares, knocking him down. Unfortunately for Thanquol, the treacherous wretch had the temerity to fall across his own body, effectively trapping him even more completely than before.

Thanquol squirmed and struggled beneath the fallen warrior. The clanrat abused him mercilessly with fang and claw, just as desperate to keep Thanquol trapped as the grey seer was to be free. Fear of being withered by one of Thanquol's spells gave the clanrat a frantic tenacity. Thanquol gored the ratman's shoulder with one of his horns and still his enemy refused to release him. Even a lucky bite that severed a few furry fingers wasn't enough to make him let go.

A new menace reared up at the edge of Thanquol's vision. Actually it was an old menace, but the grey seer wasn't of a mind to quibble over semantics. One glance at the look in Chang Fang's eyes told him the assassin had abandoned his ideas about killing the grey seer slowly. He'd drawn a different knife, an ugly black thing from which corrosive green drops sizzled. A weeping blade! The deadliest of Clan Eshin's weapons! One nick, one drop of poison on his body and Thanquol would be as dead as the Grey Lords!

Desperately, Thanquol worked his legs beneath the body of the clanrat on top of him. He ignored the bites and scratches now, keeping his eyes locked on the approaching Chang Fang. He had to time things just right or what he had in mind wouldn't work. As the assassin glared down at him, as the weeping blade started its descent, Thanquol squealed a quick prayer to the Horned Rat and set every muscle in his body into motion.

Legs and arms pressed against the clanrat's body, lifting him up and pushing him forward. At the same time, Thanquol used his flanks and shoulders to slither completely under the skaven warrior. He could imagine the ratman's confusion, but he wouldn't be confused for long.

A sharp squeak told Thanquol that Chang Fang's blade had found a victim, the victim his own frantic efforts had presented it. Quickly Thanquol flung the now slack body of the clanrat forward, hurling it at the assassin. Chang Fang leapt nimbly away from the macabre missile, but in doing so he'd been forced to leave the weeping blade trapped in the body. Now he snarled at Thanquol from across the twitching corpse.

Thanquol scowled at the murderous traitor and raised one of his paws. Green light glowed in his eyes, energy crackled around his fingers. He saw the sudden terror that crept across Chang Fang. The assassin didn't know about the sliver of warpstone Thanquol had crushed between his fangs even before regaining his feet, not that the knowledge would have done him any good.

'Say hello to Chang Squik, fool-meat,' Thanquol snapped as he sent a blast of lightning crackling into Chang Fang's face.

The grey seer recoiled as a blinding flash of light exploded before him. When his vision cleared he could see Chang Fang tearing into the jungle, his tattered cloak smoking but otherwise unharmed. Thanquol had a moment of horror, wondering if he'd nibbled a bad piece of warpstone and his body had internalised too much of its energies. After a few heartbeats without bursting into a ball of fire, Thanquol decided his fear was unfounded. He stared and saw a molten blob of metal lying on the ground where Chang Fang had been standing when he unleashed his spell. Apparently the assassin had carried an amulet to protect him against the grey seer's magic. An intelligent precaution, Thanquol conceded. But it wasn't going to save Chang Fang now.

'Boneripper!' Thanquol shouted. He pointed a claw at the jungle into which the assassin had fled. The rat ogre stalked towards the trees, absently tossing aside the last shreds of what had been Kong Krakback. 'Fetch the traitor-meat!'

Boneripper growled an inarticulate acknowledgement and began to smash his way through the small trees that barred his path. Thanquol grinned as he watched the monster make short work of the trees. Without his weeping blade, Chang Fang was as good as dead when Boneripper caught up with him. And the rat ogre would. The skaven hadn't been weaned who could match the endurance of Clan Moulder's creations.

The grin faded on Thanquol's face as a troubling thought came to him. He'd used a spell just a moment ago. His glands clenched as he considered what he had done.

'Boneripper, you stupid dolt!' Thanquol raged, rushing up to the rat ogre and smacking him with his staff. 'You're supposed to protect me!'

The rat ogre blinked at him in confusion, then hung his head in guilt and moved away from the trees.

Thanquol tapped his claws against the head of his staff and lashed his tail nervously. Maybe the frog-mage hadn't noticed? That was certainly possible. Surely anything that powerful must have better things to think about. What kind of flies it was going to eat, for instance.

Then an uglier thought came to Thanquol. Chang Fang was getting away. He might be able to live with that fact, except for another fact that went with it. Chang Fang knew where their ship was! Denied any other chance to kill the grey seer, the assassin could still set sail and strand him in this green hell!

Panic in his eyes, Thanquol smacked Boneripper with his staff and turned the rat ogre back towards the jungle. 'Hurry-quick, whelp-licker! Fetch-find traitor-meat!'

Boneripper just stared at his master for a moment. Then, with what might almost have been a sigh, he began tearing his way through the thick growth of the jungle once more.

Thanquol watched the rat ogre make rapid progress. In no time at all, Boneripper was out of view. The grey seer stroked his whiskers, quite pleased with himself. His bodyguard would catch up with Chang Fang and once Boneripper was through with him, the only boat the assassin would need was a funeral barge.

The grey seer stopped stroking his whiskers as he glanced at the jungle around him, listening to all its strange sounds, breathing all of its strange smells. He thought about the frog-mage and its army.

Hiking up his robes so he wouldn't trip on them, Thanquol rushed down the trail Boneripper was making.

'Wait for me, you moron!'

'WAIT FOR US, you moron!'

Hiltrude's cry brought Schachter to a halt. The sea captain took the delay to set down his bag and wipe the sweat from his forehead. Though he wouldn't admit it, lugging the heavy sack of plunder was taking its toll on his strength. When they had first set out, trekking across the silent, crumbling streets of Quetza, there had been a real chance he might have left his companions behind in his eagerness to catch up to Thanquol. Now, after hours creeping first through the ruins and then into the humid hell of the jungle, Hiltrude's peevish scolding was more so she could vent her own frustration at their progress than any threat he would get too far ahead.

Adalwolf ground his teeth and cursed under his breath. Something was certainly wrong with his arm. He didn't dare to look at it, but he could feel it throbbing against his body. It felt cold, as if there wasn't a drop of blood in it. He had to keep from laughing at the irony of the sensation. Here they were sweating in the damp heat of the jungle and his arm felt as cold as a piece of Norsca. He knew if he started laughing, he might never stop.

Hiltrude stuck by him, letting her strength compensate for his. The mercenary considered the strange sort of courage she possessed. There were different kinds of bravery, he knew. His kind was the steel backbone of battle. Hers was the quiet tenderness that refused to abandon a friend in need. Stromfels's Teeth! She hadn't even been able to abandon Schachter when she had every reason to leave him to the lizardmen!

She used Schachter's delay to inspect Adalwolf's arm. She tried to hide it, but he saw the grim flicker that crossed her expression. That bad, he thought. If it wasn't for her, he'd just lie down and wait for Morr to open the gates for him.

But she was here. Just as she wouldn't abandon him, he couldn't abandon her. Not to Schachter, not to the jungle. Not to Thanquol, if they ever found that slinking rat.

The blood trail was still easy enough to follow. Adalwolf was certain now it was coming from Bone-ripper. There was no way Thanquol could have leaked so much and kept going. He didn't like the idea of running into the monster again. At every turn in the trail he kept hoping to see the rat ogre's huge body lying on the ground. It would be one less thing to trouble his mind.

Myrmidia knew there were enough of those to occupy his thoughts. When they'd managed to escape into the jungle, he thought they'd been quick enough to make it before the army of lizardmen completed their ring around the ruins. Now he wasn't so sure. There was something sinister about the frequent rustling they heard rising from the jungle around them. He almost wished he was one of the underfolk when a faint, musky reptile smell wafted its way out of the jungle. The ratmen would know if the smell belonged to simple beasts or something more sinister.

His thoughts drifted to his glimpse of the toad-creature and the aura of awesome power he had sensed surrounding it. Somehow, he could not overcome the idea that the terrible creature had been aware of him as much as he had been aware of it. Adalwolf didn't know what interest such a being could have in a mere man. He thought about an alchemist he had once had dealings with, back when his wife was with their first child. The alchemist had a grisly hobby. He would collect molluscs and pull them apart in a desire to understand how they could function without any bones to support them.

Adalwolf felt an icy chill run through his body, a chill that had nothing to do with his broken arm. He didn't like the idea that the toad-creature thought of him like the alchemist had thought of his snails and slugs.

'Break time's over,' Hiltrude declared, not quite keeping a slight groan out of her voice. Adalwolf stared at her in confusion, unable to remember when she had set him down at the side of the trail. He did his best to help as she lifted him back to his feet.

'I didn't fancy this spot anyway,' Schachter said, grunting as he slung his bag over his shoulder. 'In fact, I'm not even going to put it in my memoirs.'

The poor joke brought smiles to the faces of his companions. Adalwolf's expression darkened an instant later. Schachter's friendly humour was meant to get them off their guard. He'd already seen the captain's true colours. Nothing was going to make him forget the kind of man he really was.

Nothing except maybe fever from an infected arm.

Schachter had only taken a few steps when he held up his hand in warning. The captain turned his eyes to either side of the trail. An instant later he dropped his bag to the ground and drew two of the swords thrust beneath his belt.

Before Adalwolf had a chance to think Schachter was himself developing a fever, the bushes seemed to burst apart as two scaly blue bodies leapt onto the trail.

These weren't the scrawny skinks they had fought in the temple. They were the big warrior-lizards

Adalwolf had seen from the top of the pyramid. Each of the reptiles was taller than a man, though much more lean. Powerful talons tipped their muscular legs and their thick tails looked strong enough to break a man's bones. The lizardmen wore chequered loinclouts and necklaces of animal fangs looped through gold wire. Each of the monsters held a saw-edged golden sword that made the weapons Schachter brandished look like paring knives.

The saurus warriors stared at the humans, their thick tongues flitting between jaws filled with long fangs. For the space of a heartbeat, the lizardmen didn't move, they simply stared, almost as though they were studying the strange intruders.

Then both of the reptiles bobbed their heads in a weird, somehow threatening gesture. Adalwolf could actually see their scaly hands tightening around their weapons as the lizardmen came stalking towards them.

CHAPTER FIFTEEN

Rat Hunt

ADALWOLF DREW THE ungainly sword from his belt and shuffled in front of Hiltrude, trying to place himself between the courtesan and the advancing lizardmen. His arm trembled as the weight of the blade taxed his weakened muscles and a sheen of sweat began to rise on his forehead.

'Get her out of here,' he told Schachter. The mercenary took another staggering step towards the reptiles. A cry of alarm rose from behind him and his advance was broken. Hiltrude's arms wrapped about his waist, pulling at him, trying to drag him back.

'They'll kill you!' she yelled at him, her voice cracking with emotion.

Adalwolf tried to twist out of her grasp. 'I can still buy time for you to get away,' he growled at her as he struggled to get free.

'Take your own advice, sell-sword,' Schachter's grim voice declared. The sea captain gave Adalwolf and Hiltrude a hard stare. 'I'll hold them as long as I can.' He didn't wait for any argument. With a last wistful look at the bag of loot he'd left on the ground, Schachter charged the saurus warriors.

The reptiles weren't alarmed by the charging human and the shrill battle cry that rose from his lips. They didn't so much as blink as the desperate, ragged figure stormed down the trail at them. Waiting with eerie, emotionless patience, the saurus warriors met Schachter's attack.

Schachter chopped at the first of the unmoving lizardmen with an overhand swing of one of his swords that should have opened it from belly to groin. Even as his sword-arm was lashing out, however, the saurus snapped from its seemingly imbecilic lethargy. The reptile twisted its body in a writhing, undulating spasm that should have snapped the spine of a human. Schachter's golden sword slashed through only emptiness as it made its butchering sweep. The saurus continued the sinuous motion of its scaly frame, rolling along the back of Schachter's arm as the sea captain's momentum caused him to overextend himself. The lizardman raised its own sword, bringing it crunching down into Schachter's body.

Screaming in agony, Schachter crumpled to the earth, his sword-arm cut through nearly to the bone. Doubled over in pain, he cringed away from the lizardman as the reptile hacked at him again. The slashing blow missed him by a hair's-breadth.

Desperately, he thrust the sword clutched in his good arm at the saurus, forgetting in his fright that the blades of the lizardmen were made for cutting rather than stabbing. The blunt head of the sword smacked ineffectually against the thick scales of the reptile's body. An instant later, the saurus pivoted and brought its powerful tail cracking around. The blow crashed into Schachter's legs, spilling him onto the ground.

The other saurus left Schachter to his comrade and continued its menacing advance. Adalwolf locked eyes with the reptile, trying to find anything he recognised as thought or intention in the slitted inhuman orbs. The lizardman paused only a few feet from him, crooking its head in a gesture of curiosity, studying him with keen interest.

Without warning, the reptile suddenly sprang. Adalwolf raised his weapon to parry the sweep of the lizardman's sword. The two blades clanged sharply as they crashed against each other. Adalwolf was thrown back as the momentum of the saurus nearly threw him off his feet. The reptile's scaly muzzle hissed at him, inches from his own face, the monster's eyes fixed on him with a weird, almost fascinated intensity.

The lizardman pressed in close, using its greater strength to push Adalwolf back. The saurus knew its strange foe was weak, could feel the vigour in the mercenary's good arm faltering with each backward step. It would be easy for it to finish the fight quickly, but killing the warm-blood was not an option. Lord Tlaco needed the strange creature alive and alive was how he would be brought to the slann. Using its entire body as a bludgeon, the lizardman surged against Adalwolf, forcing him back several steps. The human's sword grated along the edge of the lizardman's blade as his arm shivered with the strain of holding the reptile back.

Hiltrude's wailing cry split the air and the saurus shuddered as its hip was gouged. Like an Arabyan harridan, the woman had come from behind Adalwolf and charged at the reptile. Concentrating on the mercenary, the lizardman was too slow to react. Hiltrude swung the golden blade Schachter had given her in a clumsy, overhanded fashion, but with enough momentum to drive the edge deep into the scaly hip of the monster.

Hissing in challenge, the saurus rounded on its attacker. The woman retreated before the violent savagery of the reptile, the bloody sword falling through her slackened fingers. The lizardman shoved Adalwolf, sending the mercenary staggering away. Bobbing its head in a threat display, the reptile turned towards Hiltrude. It took only one stalking step, then nearly fell as the deep wound in its hip caused its leg to buckle. The pain of its injury was something it would take a few minutes for his primitive nervous system to transmit to its brain, but the saurus could not ignore the damage that had been done. It stared at the bleeding gash, clapped a clawed hand to the injury to keep the bone from poking through the skin, then coldly returned it attention to Hiltrude.

The courtesan tried to retreat before the lizardman, watching in horror as the reptile stalked after her, dragging its injured leg behind him and balancing himself with frequent slaps of its tail against the ground. She looked with despair at the sword she had let fall from her hand, knowing that her fear and inexperience had left her defenceless before this monster. It had been a reckless impulse that had made Hiltrude rush to aid Adalwolf despite the warrior's constant pleas for her to run. She had hoped she could take the reptile by surprise, but had been unready for the drag of the heavy sword in her hands or the terror of actually striking such a formidable creature. She didn't have a warrior's knowledge of what constituted a killing wound, lashing out almost blindly against the lizardman.

Now she was appreciating the magnitude of her mistake. There was no pity, no compassion in the lizardman's cold eyes as the creature limped after her. Even hate might have comforted her, at least it would have given the reptile a hint of humanity about it. Instead she saw only a merciless determination, as passionless as the hunger of a shark or the predation of a spider.

With her eyes on the saurus, Hiltrude was unaware when her slow retreat brought her to the edge of the trail. Her feet slid out from under her as she encountered a pile of leaves slimy with rot and decay. She landed on her back, groaning in pain as a rock bit into her soft flesh. The saurus quickened its pace, primal hunting instincts exciting it at the prospect of helpless prey. The lizardman loped forwards, its head still undulating in its threatening fashion.

Hiltrude screamed as the lizardman loomed over her, its sword raised for the killing blow. She kicked out at it, her legs locking around its injured one. She rolled her body, using all the leverage she could to twist the lizardman's wounded leg. The tactic worked. The saurus uttered a frightened chirp then crashed loudly as its leg was pulled out from under it.

Raking pain seared up Hiltrude's body as the lizardman's scrabbling claws gouged her legs. The reptile hissed at her as it struggled to rise, its mouth gaping in a monstrous fashion that displayed each of its long fangs and the powerful jaws in which they were set. Until now, Hiltrude hadn't thought it was possible to make the lizardmen mad. Now she wished they were as devoid of emotion as she had imagined. The sword, she was sure, would have been much quicker than the reptile's claws and fangs.

Pulling itself along her body, its claws digging into her soft flesh, the saurus propelled itself towards Hiltrude's throat. The woman beat her tiny fists on its head, but the blows couldn't do much more than annoy it and make it blink its eyes. Once it snapped at one of the dainty fists, its fangs scraping along the knuckles and drawing a welter of blood from her torn skin. The taste of blood in its mouth only goaded the lizardman further and it dug its claws even deeper into the woman's body as it stretched its head towards the pulsing veins in her neck.

The saurus recoiled, a gasping croak bubbling up its throat. It tried to reach behind itself, but its hands couldn't find the blade that had crunched through its spine. Adalwolf had already ripped the ungainly sword free. Now he drove it down again, cleaving through the top of the lizardman's skull. The reptile's entire body shivered, its tail lashing furiously in the mud and leaves. The mercenary grunted, struggling to pull the sword free, but it had bitten too deeply. At last, he simply kicked the twitching body onto its side and helped Hiltrude slide out from under it.

The mercenary stared pityingly at Hiltrude, sorry for the cuts and bruises she had suffered, embarrassed because he hadn't been able to protect her. She seemed to read his thoughts, giving him a look of sympathy. She started to open her mouth to speak, but suddenly her eyes went wide with renewed fear.

Adalwolf spun around and found himself staring into the countenance of the other saurus warrior. The reptile's fangs were bared, its head undulating in what the mercenary now understood was a kind of silent battle cry to these creatures. The sword in the lizardman's hand was slick with Schachter's blood. The mercenary clenched his own empty fist and stared at the blade buried in the dead reptile's skull. Like Hiltrude, he cursed himself for allowing his sword to leave his hand.

The saurus hissed angrily as it came creeping forwards, its eyes darting from Adalwolf to Hiltrude and back. At the first sign of trouble from its comrade, the lizardman had broken off its fight with Schachter to aid the other saurus. Too late to help, the reptile looked quite ready to avenge.

Adalwolf tried to push Hiltrude into the jungle. With luck, she could get a few minutes to escape before the lizardman finished with him. The courtesan resisted, however, instead closing her hand around his own. Her lip trembled with fear, but she stared defiantly at the reptile, offering the saurus her own silent challenge.

The lizardman cocked its head to one side, puzzled by the curious behaviour of the humans. For a moment, it was still, even its head unmoving. Before it could move back to the attack, however, the lizardman was thrown forwards as a shrieking body crashed into him from behind.

Schachter was a bloody mess, his shoulder laid open to the bone, his side gashed so deeply that ribs poked through his flesh every time he took a breath. His scalp had been torn, painting his face crimson. But he still had his sword and he still knew how to use it. Pure adrenaline powered the sea captain's frenzied assault on the lizardman. After pitching the reptile forward, Schachter's sword crunched into the creature's arm, all but severing it at the elbow.

The stunned reptile spun about to confront the raging human, its muscular tail sweeping about like the whip of a coachman. Schachter leapt over the bludgeoning tail, coming in close to the lizardman. His sword smashed into the reptile's throat, causing it to gag noisily and stagger. He pressed the attack, kicking the saurus in its knee, dropping it to the ground. Burying the edge of his sword in the lizardman's side, Schachter screamed as the reptile's jaws locked around his other hand. He let the sword drop from his grasp and tried to gouge the lizardman's eyes in an effort to make the reptile release him. His efforts only made the monster bite down harder.

Blood streamed from the socket of the lizardman's mutilated eye. The creature's entire body twitched and writhed as its lungs started to fill with blood from its throat wound. A muscular spasm brought the lizardman's jaws snapping together with a bone-crushing pop.

Schachter fell away from the dying lizardman, blood fountaining from his severed wrist. He tried to staunch the spurting blood, but dropped to his knees instead. A moment later he was sprawled on his back, colour draining out of him.

Adalwolf and Hiltrude rushed beside the dying sea captain. The mercenary could tell it was much too late to help him. Even without blood loss, the wound in his side was a mortal one. The two survivors could only look on in helplessness.

Schachter saw the look of wonder in their faces and a bitter laugh tortured his ravaged body. 'Couldn't… run out… on… you,' he gasped. 'Not… after… you saved…'

The captain's eyes became glassy, his breath fell silent. Adalwolf could only shake his head. A rough kind of honour had ruled the man after all, something deeper than the lust for wealth. Adalwolf knew that he owed his life to the unexpected gratitude of the man he would have left behind.

There was no time to spare to bury Schachter, even if Hiltrude or Adalwolf had felt up to the task. Instead, the two dragged the bag of gold across the trail and set it beside the dead sea captain.

Somehow, they felt he would understand the gesture.

THE SHRIEK OF parrots, the stench of rotting jungle growth, and the damp, smothering grip of air that felt like it had been soaked in boiled urine – these were Thanquol's complaints of the day. He tried to keep in Boneripper's monstrous shadow as much as was possible, though even that effort did little to ease the fury of the sun burning down from the Lustrian sky. The grey seer was sorely tempted to call off their pursuit of Chang Fang until nightfall. The hideous thought of being stranded by the assassin made him reluctantly set aside such pleasant ideas. The slinking Eshin traitor would have much to answer for when Thanquol caught him! He wondered if he would stake Chang Fang out for the ants or just feed him piece by piece to the sharks. Perhaps he could devise a way to do both…

A groaning rumble shuddered through the jungle, frightening Thanquol from his schemes of vengeance. He leaped off the ground, landing on all four paws, his breath coming in wheezing gasps. He looked about, trying to find the source of the terrible sound. His eyes narrowed spitefully and he bruxed his fangs when he saw Boneripper uprooting another tree that stood in the path with much the same clamour.

'Mouse-brained oaf!' Thanquol cursed the rat ogre, smacking his flank with the head of his staff. Boneripper turned around, staring at him stupidly with his dull eyes. Thanquol winced when he saw the tangle of leeches fastened to Boneripper's arms, their bodies bloated with the rat ogre's blood. He quickly scratched at his own arms to make sure he hadn't acquired a similar mantle of parasites.

'Find Chang Fang!' he snapped. 'Quick-quick!'

Boneripper didn't move, instead continuing to stare at his master. The longer the big brute continued to stand there looking at him, the more Thanquol started to appreciate the immense muscles beneath his leech-draped arms, the sword-like claws that tipped his fingers, the necklace of skulls that hung about his neck. Maybe he'd been just a little hasty reprimanding his dutiful bodyguard.

'Good-nice Boneripper,' Thanquol said, taking a tenuous step back. He fingered a little nugget of warpstone, wondering if he was far enough away from the frog-thing to dare use his magic.

Before the grey seer could act, the huge rat ogre was charging towards him, the ground shaking from his thunderous footfalls. Thanquol squeaked in fright, leaping out of the crazed rat ogre's way, hugging his staff across his body and frantically thrusting the warpstone into his mouth. He crashed into a thicket, feeling the thorns dig into his fur and snag in his robes. He thrashed about in the ugly plants trying to pull himself free enough that he might weave the aethyr into a spell that would settle the problem of Boneripper's rebellion.

Just as he pulled himself free, Thanquol noticed that Boneripper wasn't interested in him. The rat ogre was storming back down the path, beating his chest in challenge with his clawed hands. The grey seer was starting to think the jungle heat had deranged his bodyguard when a patch of trees suddenly burst apart and an enormous reptile lumbered onto the trail.

The sour stink of musk dripping down his leg barely registered as Thanquol stared in horror at the gigantic beast. It was like some great scaly bird crossed with a crocodile, lumbering about on two immense, tree-like legs while scrawny useless-looking arms dangled from its chest. Its head looked like nothing so much as a dwarf steam-shovel he'd once helped some Clan Skryre warlock-engineers steal, its fangs impossibly large even for so massive a head. A long tail smashed the trees behind it, splintering them like old mouse bones.

More frightening to Thanquol than the beast itself was the monster who rode it. A snakeskin saddle adorned with talismans of gold was lashed about the big reptile and from this seat reared a massively built saurus warrior, its powerful body pitted and slashed with old scars from countless battles. The lizardman wore armour fashioned from bones and many of its scales had been painted with strange glyphs that hurt the ratman's eyes to look upon. The head of the saurus chief was locked within a helm fashioned from the skull of a horned reptile and in its claws it carried a murderous lance with a golden blade.

The lizardman roared something in its own language of hisses and then began to undulate its head in rapid – and threatening – fashion. The carnosaur it rode lowered its huge head and lunged forwards. The saurus chief urged his mount towards Thanquol, its yellow eyes locked upon the terrified grey seer. Opening its maw to utter its own deafening roar, the carnosaur charged, swatting Boneripper aside with a sidewise sweep of its head.

Seeing twenty tons of reptilian death barrelling down at him made Thanquol remember the nugget of warpstone he'd popped into his mouth. Fat frog-things were forgotten as he bit down on the rock, grinding it into powder with his fangs. Frantically, Thanquol swallowed each portion as it slid onto his tongue.

Invigorating power swelled within him, quickening his pulse, making his limbs feel as though steel had been poured onto his bones. Thanquol straightened out of his cringing posture, glaring defiance at the onrushing saurus chief. What was such a crude creature beside the godlike power that now coursed through his veins? Nothing! Less than nothing! With a single flick of his claw he would hurl the lizardman and its slavering mount across the jungle and back to Quetza! He'd smash their scaly carcasses into paste and then grind that paste into powder so fine even an ant couldn't make a meal of it! Then he'd find that impertinent frog-thing and pop every wart on his slimy body before burning out his eyes and...

Intoxicating visions of what he would do to his enemies with the power searing through his body almost made Thanquol forget about the reptiles thundering down the trail towards him. Something like panic made him flinch when he realised they were only a few dozen yards away. Then he remembered who he was and the powers at his command.

Calmly, Grey Seer Thanquol pointed his staff at the carnosaur and its rider. A few sharp curses, a few focused thoughts, and he sent a storm of warp-lightning crashing into the reptiles. He grinned in savage triumph. Then his eyes widened in appreciative horror as he saw the warp-lightning being funnelled into the golden amulets riveted into the saurus chief's scales. Beast and master came roaring through the magical onslaught as unfazed as a fish in a flood!

Whining in sheer terror, Thanquol dived back into the thicket. The chief's lance came so close to him that it tore a great flap in the back of his robe. But the momentum of the carnosaur could not be stopped. The immense monster kept thundering down the trail. It was several dozen yards before the lizardman could turn it back around.

By that time, Thanquol was back on the trail, conjuring another spell to destroy his enemy. Still invigorated by the warpstone, he held his staff on high, muttering invocations to the Horned Rat. As the carnosaur turned to charge him again, he brought the staff smashing down against the ground. The earth trembled and shuddered as the focused malignancy of his magic coursed through it. Trees cracked and toppled, stones were sent bouncing into the jungle. A jagged fissure opened, snaking straight down the trail towards the onrushing carnosaur.

Just as the sorcerous fissure should reach the reptile's feet, it stopped. Even more incredible, as the monster lumbered forwards, the ground closed up before it. Thanquol could see the charms nailed into the saurus chief's hide blazing with magical energies. Those ancient amulets were doing more than simply warding off his sorcery, they were actively undoing it!

Thanquol felt his gorge rise and his nethers shrink as the carnosaur charged at him for the second time. He could not tear his eyes from the cold orbs of the saurus chief. He could sense the primordial, passionless hate in the lizardman's mind and knew that here was an old enemy to all his kind. There would be no treating with this beast, no bribe he could offer the lizardman to spare his life. Helpless to turn away, Thanquol could only watch as the chief's golden lance came stabbing towards him.

Before the lance could be driven home, the carnosaur reared back, almost throwing its rider. Interposing itself between the reptiles and Thanquol was a big black shape. Boneripper snarled up at the saurus, then dived straight at the carnosaur.

Thanquol blinked in amazement as he watched Boneripper's claws tear through the carnosaur's thick scales, opening a great gash in its chest where those tiny arms dangled uselessly. The carnosaur swatted at him with those arms, but Boneripper seized one in his jaws and with a sidewise twist of his head popped it from its socket.

Maddened with pain, the carnosaur jerked away from Boneripper. The saurus chief made the mistake of trying to restrain its retreat. Twisting about, the giant reptile arched its back and neck, writhing and turning, trying to unseat the lizardman upon its back, its tiny brain shifting blame for its pain onto its rider now that he had drawn its attention.

Quickly, Thanquol raised his staff, hoping that what he had in mind would work. Potent wards of protection such as the lizardman wore often required at least some concentration on the part of their wearers. At the moment, the saurus chief was fully occupied just staying in his saddle.

Green lightning burst from Thanquol's staff, searing across the trail and smashing full into the saurus chief. Unlike the first time, the amulets riveted into its scales didn't absorb the energies. This time the deadly burst of magical energy swirled and crackled around it, blackening its scales and melting the golden trinkets embedded in its skin. The straps holding it into the saddle snapped as the lightning seared it and it was pitched from the back of the furious carnosaur, then smashed beneath its pounding feet.

The carnosaur continued its mindless madness, snapping at its back where Thanquol's fire had burned it. The great brute was oblivious to the rat ogre who circled it. Boneripper watched and waited, choosing the moment when the reptile's weight was shifted to one side to pounce. The rat ogre crashed into the side of the unbalanced carnosaur, using its own weight to throw it across the trail. A stand of bamboo splintered as the beast smashed into it, the jagged shafts punching through its scaly body as it impaled itself upon them with its own momentum.

Boneripper raked his claws across the belly of the pinned carnosaur, the sword-like talons shredding the soft scales of its underside. The reptile struggled to pull itself off the bamboo stakes, trying to snap at

Boneripper with its jaws. One of its legs had been broken in the fall, but the other proved a greater menace to the rat ogre, slashing his shoulder open. He staggered away from the attack, glaring at the flailing reptile.

Ignoring Thanquol's demands to leave the dying beast alone, Boneripper leapt on top of the reptile's body, scrambling around so that he could grab the monster's leg at the hip, well away from the flashing claws. Grunting with effort, the rat ogre locked both of his arms around the offending limb and began to pull.

Thanquol stopped calling on his bodyguard to leave the carnosaur alone. Instead he watched the gory spectacle play itself out, earnestly hoping all the while that Boneripper would be a lot calmer when he was finished.

In fact, the grey seer was thinking it might be a good idea to start being nicer to Boneripper. It would be somewhat safer that way.

THEY COULD FEEL the jungle watching them. At first Adalwolf laid the sensation down to his own fearful imagination, but as he and Hiltrude penetrated deeper into the forest, he knew it was something more. Every hair on his body was crawling with apprehension. It was more than simple imagination. He could see that Hiltrude felt it too, but decided not to add to her fear by voicing his own concerns.

The fight with the soldier-lizards had made a sinister impression. Wounded and alone in a strange land, even the smaller lizardmen that had served in the Temple of the Serpent would have been enough of a challenge for them. Adalwolf knew they had been lucky to survive one encounter with the saurus warriors. If they would live, they would need to keep their wits about them, try to avoid drawing the attention of the reptiles.

Even before the strange sensation of being watched, the mercenary didn't find that a likely prospect. The image of the toad-creature's army surrounding the ruins of Quetza was too fresh in his mind. A legion of the powerful soldier-lizards had emerged from the jungle to encircle the city. There could be hundreds, even thousands of the monsters prowling the jungle looking for them, every one far more at home in the savage rainforests than the humans. It was only a matter of time before the lizardmen found them.

Their one hope was the black drops of blood they followed. Adalwolf was certain now that the trail could only belong to Boneripper. Anything else would have died from such blood loss but the rat ogre was too stupid and too stubborn to realise the fact. Perhaps whatever sorcerous arts had allowed the underfolk to breed such a beast had also endowed it with a super-normal vitality. Adalwolf didn't know, he only knew that the beast lived and while it lived it gave them hope: a trail to follow that would lead them to Thanquol's escape route out of this green hell.

It was a horrible thought to understand that their only prayer of salvation lay in the treacherous paws of Thanquol. Adalwolf would have rather entrusted his life to one of the merwyrms that guarded the shores of Ulthuan, but there was no other choice. They could follow Thanquol and hope to either steal or share his way out of Lustria or they could simply sit down and wait for the lizardmen to catch them.

At least there was no sign that Thanquol had any help other than Boneripper. When they had followed the trail back to the skaven encampment, Adalwolf had feared the worst. The air had been so thick with the smell of ratmen, he'd expected an entire swarm of the fiends to be waiting for them. Instead they had found a half-dozen ratkin ripped apart in a variety of ghastly ways he was certain only Boneripper could manage. It seemed Thanquol had had a very final falling out with those minions who had escaped from Quetza.

The two humans had lingered in the ghoulish clearing only long enough to scavenge supplies from the underfolk's stores. Hiltrude had become sick at the very idea of carrying the ratmen's provisions, much less the thought of eating them. The most appealing things appeared to be the pulpy innards of enormous beetles. The menu only got worse from there. It had taken all of Adalwolf's skills of persuasion to induce the courtesan to pick up the ghastly fodder, assuring her they would only eat the filth as a last resort.

Even worse than the food was the water. The ratmen had used an assortment of increasingly foul-smelling bladders to carry their water. Adalwolf tried to convince himself the abominable-looking things hadn't been stitched together from the kidneys of dead skaven. The bladders gave the water inside them a pungent reek and an even more loathsome taste, but the mercenary knew from experience that a few hours under the Lustrian sun would make them drink even this filth and praise the gods for providing it.

From the encampment, they followed Boneripper's trail deeper into the jungle. It was impossible to be certain after the peculiarities of the path they had followed from the beach, but Adalwolf had the impression they were travelling in a largely southward direction. He was thankful for the rat ogre's savage facility at tearing apart the foliage, making their own progress much easier. Even so, he was careful to set a pace that both he and Hiltrude would be able to maintain. Exhausting themselves wouldn't let them catch Thanquol.

Several times the trail made by Boneripper would cross over into a larger trail. Adalwolf could tell from the smell that the wider trail had been cut by a great number of ratmen. Perhaps it marked the way Thanquol's expedition had journeyed to Quetza. But if so, why didn't the grey seer stick to it? If he feared pursuit, clearly he would have compelled Boneripper to be more careful about hacking a trail through the jungle.

The only answer Adalwolf could come up with was that Thanquol was looking for something, something important enough that he wouldn't leave Lustria without it. The infrequent returns to the old path his ratmen had made were perhaps done so that he could regain his bearings. The mercenary was thankful for whatever delay made the grey seer shun a straight run to wherever he was going. Anything that slowed him down was to the advantage of the desperate humans who followed him.

Days passed before they saw a more tangible sign of their quarry beyond the occasional footprint or some trinket Thanquol had decided was too heavy to continue carrying. It was also a grim reminder that even as they hunted the ratman, other things hunted them in turn.

The carcass of the giant reptile was strewn across the trail, impaled upon the bamboo trees that flanked the left side of the path. Adalwolf shuddered to see the thing, reminded of the great carnosaur they had encountered so long ago. There was no question as to the thing's death – one of its hind legs had been torn from its socket. Even the robust vigour of a carnosaur wasn't able to overcome that sort of mutilation.

Adalwolf was surprised to find a saddle strapped to the reptile's back. He smiled bitterly as he noted the gold adornments dangling from the snakeskin harness. There was wealth enough in this hideous place to choke every king in the Old World and every bit of it was as useless to them as a volume of Tarradash was to an orc.

Some little way from the dead carnosaur, they found the corpse of a lizardman, one of the hulking warrior breed. Its body was strangely burnt and there was a sulphurous reek rising from it.

'Looks like Thanquol's not so timid about using his magic now,' Adalwolf said.

Hiltrude shuddered and turned away from the grisly corpse. She covered her face in her hands. 'It's hopeless!' she sobbed. 'Those things are going to catch us!'

Adalwolf reached his arm around her, trying to soothe her despair. He winced as she pressed against him, her shoulder brushing the broken limb tied against his chest. 'Maybe they like the taste of rat better than us,' he said. 'We haven't seen any of them in days. Maybe that's because they have been bothering Thanquol instead.'

'But if they do catch him!' Hiltrude cried. 'He's the only one that might know how to get out of here!'

Adalwolf stroked her tangled hair. 'One worry at a time,' he told her. His eyes hardened as he looked over her shoulder. Gently, he nudged her away from the side of the trail, turning her around so that she wouldn't see what he had seen.

The mercenary repressed a shiver as they limped back down the trail. It hadn't been the sight of the little cannibal lizards that had so upset him, though he had seen their hideous capabilities firsthand. No, it had been the way they stared back at him, dozens of sets of unblinking eyes watching him with an air of rapt attention. It was more than the way an animal watched prey. There had been a chilling sense of purpose, of intelligence in that stare.

Once again, Adalwolf thought of the tremendous power he had felt rising from the toad-creature. He wondered what it was doing and if it had used some of its magic to make the vermin of the jungle its spies.

* * *

Lord Tlaco sat upon his dais, unheeding of the swaying rhythm of his strange chariot. Dispensing with the ancient magics that kept the golden dais in defiance of gravity, the slann allowed his temple guard to conduct it through the jungle. The brawny saurus warriors bent their backs beneath the long bronze rods upon which the dais rested. They moved in eerie unison, each saurus mirroring his opposite as they marched through the primordial forest.

The slann devoted a fraction of its awareness upon his surroundings, using a portion of its knowledge of the Great Math to bend trees away from the path of its minions, to drain ponds and fill gullies that might otherwise interfere with the march. Beasts of the jungle recoiled from the mental call of the mage-priest, or else came in their crawling, slithering, hopping multitudes to obey the slann's command. A numberless legion spread through the jungle, peering under every bush, listening at every thicket, tasting the air of every path with forked tongues. All were looking for the fragile warm-blood Lord Tlaco sought, the unknown quotient that must be quantified to explain the equation.

Many were the eyes of Lord Tlaco, but there was a limit to what the tiny minds of tree frogs and mud snakes could accomplish, whatever their numbers. The swarming reptiles of the jungle could be trusted to find the decaying algorithm, but they could not be depended upon to contain it.

The blemishes on the slann's skin shifted and expanded. The pale skink attendant crouching beside Lord Tlaco stood in response, the fold of skin at the top of its head fluttering like the signal flag of a warship. The skink gestured and hissed at the slann's retinue, imparting to them the commands it had read in the mage-priest's shifting hue.

Lizardmen hissed in reply, a rolling susurrus that crawled through the jungle like a primal force. Birds fled from the trees as the sound of the reptiles washed over them, monkeys scrambled to the forest floor, panthers retreated still deeper into their shadowy lairs. The simple beasts of the jungle knew that sound. The lords of Lustria were on the hunt.

Like waves breaking upon a rocky shore, Lord Tlaco's retinue evaporated into the jungle, spreading out to scour the forest for the specimen their master required. Soon, only the slann, his temple guard and a few skink attendants remained.

The mage-priest made a slight motion of his hand and his small company began to march once more. There was neither chance or coincidence to one who truly understood the Great Math, only a question of probabilities, greater and lesser. For the unknown quotient to escape the slann's hunters was a lesser probability. However, it was one that Lord Tlaco was not going to ignore.

Anything with purpose could be predicted according to the Laws of the Old Ones. A decaying algorithm was still a fragment of harmony, a value within the Great Math. Lord Tlaco knew where the specimen was going. He knew why and how.

The slann also knew the warm-blood would never get there.

Even the least probabilities were against him.

* * *

SOPPING WET, CHANG Fang dropped onto the deck of the *Black Mary* and began to wring out the dripping tatters of his cloak. The assassin bruxed his fangs in annoyance. He had Grey Seer Thanquol to thank for all of his misfortunes. Thanquol and that stupidly loyal rat ogre of his! If he'd known what trouble that brute was going to cause, he would have slit its throat on the voyage over! That worthless conjure-rat Shen Tsinge too!

Chang Fang tried to calm himself. He'd reached the ship well ahead of Thanquol. That was all that mattered. It would take only a few hours to get the vessel ready and then he'd be able to leave Lustria behind. With a little luck, the currents might take the ship someplace connected to the Under-Empire. Still, even if he never saw another skaven again, he could at least comfort himself with the image of Thanquol rotting away in the jungle.

Maybe the grey seer would even get as far as the beach. Chang Fang almost squealed in delight imagining the look on Thanquol's face when he saw his only hope of escape sailing off over the horizon – without him!

The assassin clapped his paws together and looked about him, wondering where he should start to get the ship ready to sail. He twitched his whiskers in confusion when he noticed that the mainsail was already raised. Suddenly an annoyance he hadn't really thought about in his frantic swim to reach the ship before Thanquol occurred to him.

Who had moved the boats from the beach? And who had fastened them into their places against the ship's hull?

Chang Fang drew the knives from the folds of his cloak and stared suspiciously at his suddenly sinister surroundings. He heard a plank creak somewhere beneath him, then another and another. Every hair on his body shivered as a decayed, putrid stench rose from the *Black Mary's* hold.

There was something uncomfortably familiar about that smell.

CHAPTER SIXTEEN

Escape from Lustria

HILTRUDE COULD FEEL her heart pounding against her ribs, feeling as though it were trying to hammer its way out of her body. Her lungs felt like they were on fire and her legs felt like lead. She was certain that every step she took would be her last, but somehow her fear made her go on.

Any hope that the lizardmen would ignore them in favour of tracking down Thanquol had vanished. For hours they had heard the reptiles scrambling through the undergrowth, following them just out of eyesight. Sometimes a strange chirp or bark would sound from the trees, rising with a sinister sense of purpose that made Hiltrude's skin crawl. She knew the sounds weren't the idle chatter of monkeys or the cries of birds, but the calls of skink hunters shadowing their prey.

Sometimes they would catch a fleeting glimpse of blue-scaled stalkers moving through the trees. Such instances seemed deliberate to Hiltrude, as though the lurking lizardmen were revealing themselves in order to frighten the two humans away from a particular path. In their sorry condition, wracked with fever, tired from days of trudging through the sweltering heat, sickened by the abominable rations of the ratmen, the two fugitives didn't answer whatever challenge the skinks offered. Instead they turned, trying to find a different way through the jungle.

Whatever hope they had of keeping to Thanquol's trail was lost now. Forced from the grey seer's path by the encroaching lizardmen, they now made their way almost at random through the rainforest. Hiltrude couldn't escape the idea that the lizardmen were guiding them somewhere, herding them like cattle towards some definite end. It was a thought that made her gag in horror, memories of Xiuhcoatl and the altar atop the pyramid rising in her mind.

Adalwolf's fever was worse, his movements reduced to a pained stumble. More and more he was forced to lean upon Hiltrude for support. The courtesan didn't begrudge his weakness, she only hoped that she would be able to find the strength within her to bring them both through their ordeal safely. That cold, practical side of her that had so dominated her life was only a tiny voice now, chiding her for not leaving the sick man and taking her chances on her own. She didn't listen to that ugly part of her soul. Adalwolf hadn't left her behind. Even if she felt nothing for him, that alone would be reason enough to stay by his side.

The chirps and barks of the skinks rose from the bushes around them once more. There could not be many of the reptiles, Hiltrude thought, otherwise the creatures would have already overwhelmed them. Why they did not attack with poisoned arrows and javelins as they had the ratmen, she did not know. That there was some sinister meaning in their reluctance to attack she was certain. The lizardmen were leading them somewhere. But where?

They soon had their answer. Driven onwards by the chirps of the skinks, the two fugitives jogged down the game trail they had been following, mustering such speed as was still left in their bodies. Beyond the limit of her endurance, Hiltrude collapsed when the trail suddenly opened into a grassy clearing. Some giant of the forest had once stood here until the elements had finally brought it crashing down. Rotten piles of wood showed where the carcass of the tree had collapsed long ago. Now, at the centre of the clearing, a green-leafed successor grew.

Adalwolf crashed to the ground beside Hiltrude. He landed on his broken arm, a pained scream scraping through his clenched teeth. Hiltrude rolled him onto his back, trying to ease his suffering.

A louder shriek boomed across the clearing, a sound at once magnificent and terrible. It was like the roar of steel in a furnace and the groan of a warship upon a troubled sea. The sound pulsed through the ears of the two humans, throbbing through their bodies with a sting like electricity. They lifted their heads, Adalwolf's broken arm forgotten as they focused upon the source of the awful scream.

Within the branches of the lonely tree, something moved. They had not noticed the reptile before, so still had it been, its green scales blending into the leaves around it. Now, however, the beast had been aroused. It crept along the thick branch upon which it stood with great crawling hops of its body. Two short, clawed legs let the reptile grip the tree, the rest of its body rising in a lurching, hunchbacked fashion. When the creature reached the edge of the branch, it sat for a moment, studying the two humans with a glazed, hungry cast in its dull yellow eyes.

The reptile crouched upon the branch for a time, looming over them like some scaly vulture. Then the folds of its wrinkled body opened wide, snapping into great leathery pinions. The winged reptile threw back its beaked head, its warbling shriek again pulsing through the jungle. Swiftly the reptile launched itself from the branch, soaring down from the tree, its eyes fixed upon the prey the skinks had driven to it.

As the terradon took wing, Hiltrude noticed the patch of scaly blue skin clinging to its back. Only when the blue scales started to move on their own did she realise that there was a skink clutching the winged monster's back, riding the flying reptile as a man might ride a horse! The skink bore a long stabbing spear in its claws and with a deft motion of the weapon, it brought the terradon hurtling even faster upon the two fugitives.

Hiltrude cast about her for the golden sword Schachter had given her. She rose to her knees, huddling close to Adalwolf, flailing the sword in a desperate arc before them, trying to place a barrier of biting metal between them and the flying reptile.

The woman's frantic efforts caused the terradon to shriek in surprise and rear back from the flashing blade. Its skink rider, however, had more intelligence than the beast. A single expert jab with its spear and the lizardman tore the sword from Hiltrude's fingers, sending it flying across the clearing.

Hiltrude's first impulse was to run after the sword, but Adalwolf grabbed her ankle before she could move, pulling her down before the skink could run her through with his spear. The mercenary rose to his feet, shouting and leaping, waving his hand over his head in an effort to grab the attention of their attackers. Seeing the terradon fix its eyes on him, he ran across the clearing, intent on drawing the reptiles away from Hiltrude.

The terradon shrieked and dived after the mercenary. Hiltrude could see the skink on its back pull on the bony headcrest that jutted from the back of the reptile's head, causing it to veer away from Adalwolf before it could sink its talons into him. The terradon croaked and snarled in frustration, but the skink did not release its headcrest until it was sure it was back under control.

By that time Adalwolf had drawn his own sword and was bracing himself for the terradon's second attack. Hiltrude watched the man trembling with the effort, his arm shaking as though with an ague. The terradon hovered above him, making its grisly croaking sounds, snapping at the skink on its back with its fanged beak.

Finally the terradon was allowed to dive at the man once more. The skink's spear lashed out again, tearing the sword from Adalwolf's fingers with the same precise, expert twisting motion that had disarmed Hiltrude so effectively. The courtesan cried out, expecting to see the skink impale Adalwolf with a second thrust of his spear, as he had nearly done to her. Instead the crest on the skink's neck fluttered open and it shifted its grip on the spear, driving at Adalwolf with the blunt end of the weapon rather than the jagged tip.

Cold horror rushed through Hiltrude's body as she understood the skink's intention. The lizardman wanted to take Adalwolf alive, to use the flying steed to carry him back to the Temple of the Serpent and its waiting altar!

Hiltrude's cry didn't faze the skink as it struck out at Adalwolf with its spear, but the sound was enough to distract the hovering terradon that it shifted its position and foiled the lizardman's aim. The jabbing thrust of the spear's blunt end, instead of crashing into Adalwolf's head and stunning him instead passed harmlessly over his shoulder.

Martial instincts honed in hundreds of battles made Adalwolf grab the end of the spear without thinking. Savagely he pulled at the weapon, ripping it from the hands of the skink and nearly causing the lizardman to lose its grip on the terradon's back.

Confused and enraged by the conflict around it, the terradon dived back at Adalwolf, its talons spread for slaughter. The mercenary awkwardly fumbled with the skink's spear, trying to turn it around so that he might stab at the reptile with the weapon's edge. The one-armed man looked up, his eyes wide with horror as he saw the reptile nearly upon him.

Hiltrude screamed again, hoping to draw the terradon back away from the helpless Adalwolf. The sound wasn't effective as it had been before. Quickly she unslung the pack of skaven provisions she carried. Gripping the rotten bag by its straps, she spun her body around and flung the pack at the winged reptile.

The provisions splattered across the terradon's back, covering it in unspeakable bits of wormy meat and rancid fruit. The reptile shrieked in alarm, rising high into the air. Its eyes shifted angrily, studying the clearing and narrowing when they focused upon Hiltrude. Screaming its warbling cry, the terradon dived towards Hiltrude.

Again, the skink rider pulled at the crest of its almost brainless mount. The terradon hissed in protest, snapping at its master. The skink had nearly turned the beast about when suddenly its body was pierced from behind. The barbed head of its own spear erupted from its chest. The skink released the terradon and pawed futilely at its mortal wound.

The weight of the skink on the end of the spear pulled the weapon from Adalwolf's hands. The terradon rose into the air again, the lifeless skink tumbling off its back and crashing to earth. Adalwolf rushed to recover the spear before the winged monster could turn on him again. He did not count upon the single-mindedness of the beast, however. Instead of turning upon him, the terradon dived straight at Hiltrude.

This time there was no guiding intelligence to curb the terradon's predatory instincts. The reptile came hurtling at Hiltrude like a leathery thunderbolt. Its talons slashed through her soft skin, sinking deep into her flesh. Fluttering its wings, its warbling cry all but drowning out Hiltrude's screams, the terradon lifted its prey into the sky.

Adalwolf rushed after the fleeing monster, shouting and waving his arm, trying anything to get it to take interest in him again. But the terradon could not be tricked into releasing its catch. The mercenary could only watch helplessly from the ground as the terradon settled into the branches of the tallest tree bordering the clearing. He made a desperate cast of the spear at the reptile as it landed, but the shaft fell well short of its target. He looked desperately at the tree, but knew he could never climb it with a broken arm.

By then, it was too late. The screams had stopped.

Desolate, Adalwolf stumbled away from the clearing. He no longer cared where his steps took him, only that they took him away from the grotesque slobbering sounds descending from the terradon's perch as it feasted on its prey.

Grey Seer Thanquol peered through the branches of the mangroves, studying the swamp. He wrinkled his face as the stagnant, sour reek of the place smashed against his senses. His first instinct was to avoid this place, to detour however many leagues were necessary to avoid setting one paw on its slimy ground. That was a luxury he couldn't afford. Chang Fang had come this way, Boneripper's insistence that the assassin's trail led here was proof of that. The rat ogre couldn't communicate how long ago Thanquol's enemy had been here, but it didn't really matter. He was still ahead of the grey seer, still well on his way to getting to the ship before Thanquol.

Sidestepping the swamp wasn't an option. There wasn't the time to go around. Thanquol's second instinct was to tuck his tail between his legs and scurry across the bog as fast as his feet would carry him. This too he dismissed with an effort of self-control. There was no way to tell where the decayed zombies might be lurking, waiting for fresh meat to rend with their rotten claws. The undead might be lying in wait under the mud or hidden beneath the scummy water. There was no telling and no way to pick their scent out from the rancid stink of the swamp itself.

Thanquol squinted as he stared at the crumbling fort the human pirates had built long ago. There was no sign of activity there, but last time there hadn't been any sign either. Not until festering corpses had lurched out of the ruins to attack the skaven.

The grey seer bruxed his fangs and tugged at his whiskers. Caution was a good thing, but it wouldn't help him if Chang Fang sailed away in the ship.

Screwing up his courage, Thanquol dropped down from his perch in the branches of a mangrove tree. He scurried over to Boneripper, swatting the rat ogre's flank with his staff and pointing a claw at the swamp. 'Go-quick!' he snarled. 'First-lead, I will follow!'

The rat ogre wrinkled his face in distaste as he turned and drew a lungful of stagnant swamp smell into his lungs. For an ugly moment, Thanquol thought Boneripper was going to defy his commands. Then the hulking beast's body rumbled as a sigh shook through him. With an air of resignation, Boneripper loped off into the mud.

Thanquol waited a few moments to see if anything rose up out of the slime to attack his bodyguard, then quickly scurried after Boneripper. He glanced at the scummy water to either side of the sand bank, unsettled to see the cold eyes of crocodiles watching him with a predatory regard. Fumbling at the clasp, Thanquol thumbed open the little ratskull box that held his snuff. He inhaled a noseful of the warpstone powder, feeling a thrill of warmth and vigour rush through him. The snuff didn't make him like the crocodiles any better, but at least his mind found it harder to focus on them as a tide of contrasting emotions flittered through his brain.

Of course, even the warpstone snuff wasn't enough to make Thanquol forget about the zombies. Every step closer to the tower he expected to see the undead rear up out of the muck. His first encounter with the things had been bad enough.

Then again, he didn't have Chang Fang around trying to feed him to the things either. Thanquol could be happy about that. Or at least he would be if the assassin's absence didn't mean he was probably on the ship getting it ready to sail away and maroon the grey seer in this lost world of lizards and snakes!

'Fast-quick!' Thanquol growled, striking Boneripper's back to encourage the brute to greater speed.

THE CHIRPS AND barks of the lizardmen sounded around him once more after Adalwolf fled the clearing. There was a frantic quality to the sounds now. Perhaps the lizardmen were asking each other what they should do now that he'd killed their chief and their flying monster was only interested in filling its gullet.

The mercenary thought about just sitting down and waiting for the skinks to come for him, but he didn't think they would. They were watchers, sent to monitor him, to herd him to their masters. Even if the reptiles stood and fought, they would soon overcome him. His thoughts weren't about escape now. That idea had died with Hiltrude. Now the only thing that goaded him on was the hope of revenge. He would make the lizardmen suffer. Killing the lower creatures wouldn't hurt the reptiles greatly, but if he could find the toad-creature...

Adalwolf ignored the common sense that told him it was madness to think he could kill the toad-creature. If even a man who knew less about wizardry than a street sweeper could sense the aura of magic surrounding the amphibian, then surely it was more than capable of using that magic to protect itself. But he was far beyond reason now. It was something to keep him going.

He didn't think finding the toad-creature would be a problem. Adalwolf had noticed the way the lizardmen seemed hesitant to kill him. Even the skink chief on the terradon had made every effort to keep his beast from hurting the mercenary. The reptiles wanted him alive, to bring him somewhere. He was certain that wherever that was, the toad-creature would be there.

It would do no good to fall into the claws of the lizardmen though. He had to keep out of their clutches, to force the toad-creature to come to him, to meet him on his own terms and on ground of his own choosing. That was his only hope now. His only hope for revenge.

Thrashing sounds in the brush ahead announced a new effort by the skinks to capture him. Adalwolf sprang behind the cover of a fallen log just as an armoured reptile the size of a lion thrust itself from where it had buried itself in the ground. The burrowing monster was a dull brown in colour, its body heavy with big thorn-like spikes that covered it from the tip of its snout to the end of its club-like tail. The reptile hissed menacingly at him as it shook the earth from its back.

Before the razordon could lunge at the man, however, a skink came scrambling around its flank, jabbing it with a short spear. The bigger reptile's fury ebbed and it just stared at Adalwolf, content now to simply block his way.

The ground behind the mercenary now rose up and a second razordon emerged, blocking the way back. Like the first reptile, this one too had its entourage of skink tenders. Goading the armoured reptile with their spears, the skinks moved their monster towards Adalwolf, trying to trap the man between the beasts.

Crying out in challenge, Adalwolf threw the bladder of foul water into the face of the beast behind him. The creature was blinded for an instant, its horned body heaving as it sent spikes shooting out of its skin in every direction. Skinks dropped flat to the earth to avoid the deadly missiles.

Already turned to face the first razordon, Adalwolf did not see the unexpected reaction the one behind him had when the black water splashed in its eyes. Unfamiliar with the creatures of Lustria, his first awareness of the razordon's ability to throw its spines was when six of them came stabbing into his back.

Screaming in pain, it took every last piece of willpower for Adalwolf to stay on his feet. He reached behind his back, frantically trying to pull the spines from his flesh. His skin throbbed where the spines had hurt him, a stinging burn as though he had backed against a hot stove.

A skink rushed at him with a club, but Adalwolf drove his boot into the lizardman's belly, pitching him onto the ground. The mercenary could see more of the wiry lizardmen emerging from the jungle, surrounding him on each side. One of the razordon tenders encouraged the beast to shoot a volley of spines into the ground near Adalwolf. The meaning was clear. He was to stay where he stood.

Adalwolf glared at the skink and spat on the little line of spines. Gritting his teeth, he threw himself off the trail, crashing into the undergrowth. Vines slashed his face, thorns cut his skin, but he would not relent. If the lizardmen wanted him, they were going to have to work for their prize.

SCRAMBLING OVER THE side of the *Black Mary*, Grey Seer Thanquol flopped to the deck. His heart was pounding like a drum, electrified by the terror that had gripped him during his frantic swim from the beach. With every stroke he'd relived the awful horror of the landing in Lustria, smelling again the tang of skaven blood in the water as the sharks feasted, knowing that at any moment he might be the next to fill their jaws.

Thanquol cursed Chang Fang as he shook the sea from his dripping fur. It was just like the slinking murderer to take all of the boats back to the ship, forcing Thanquol and Boneripper to make the dangerous swim if they would gain the *Black Mary* in time. Every instant the grey seer had expected a shark to drag him under, for all of his magnificent ambitions and schemes to end in the belly of a hungry fish.

But the favour of the Horned Rat was still upon him. His god would not suffer the most brilliant genius in all skavendom to die in such a senseless way! Thanquol had not seen a single shark, not even a suggestion of a dorsal fin splitting the waves. Even Boneripper, with his torn body still dripping blood, had been able to make the swim safely. The grey seer had watched most carefully for the slightest sniff of a shark when he had sent the rat ogre to test the waters.

Perhaps the sharks were all asleep, digesting the feast of skaven flesh they'd enjoyed when the *Black*

Mary landed. It was just like Thanquol's return to the swamp. There hadn't even been a whiff of any zombies about. Surely the Horned Rat was bestowing his protection upon the grey seer, striking fear into the craven hearts of his enemies and making them cower in their holes until he had passed!

Thanquol pinched the folds of his robe, wringing a stream of water from the soaked garment. He hated the salty stink of the sea, but at least it was better than the humid clinging heat of the jungle. And it was a smell he knew meant he was going home, so he couldn't completely despise it. Soon he would be sailing back to civilization, to stalk once more through the streets of Skavenblight. He would return in triumph, victoriously presenting himself before the Nightlord and humbly relating the magnificent destruction he had brought upon Xiuhcoatl and the Temple of the Serpent! Clan Eshin would be indebted to him, and Thanquol would use their favours well! He would send their spies and killers to look after his many enemies. Those he could not threaten into submission would die, and their deaths would make all skavendom tremble. Tisqueek and the other seerlords would learn their place and then it would be time for him to turn his attentions to that incompetent fool Seerlord Kritislik. With the strength of Clan Eshin his to command, Thanquol would arrange an accident for the decrepit Seerlord and then there would be a new scent in the Shattered Tower – the scent of Seerlord Thanquol!

Vengeful thoughts reminded Thanquol of something he'd left unfinished. He clapped his paws together and rubbed them eagerly. It was so kind of Chang Fang to take so much time getting all the boats back to the ship. Without that delay, the idiot might have succeeded in his plan to strand Thanquol in Lustria. But, of course, the fool had pitted himself against a force of destiny when he set his puny brain against the genius of Thanquol!

'Chang Fang!' Thanquol cried out. 'You can come out now, you turd-sniffing dung-licker! I won't hurt-hurt you!' As he spoke, Thanquol tucked a small piece of warpstone into his cheek pouch. He thought he'd start by burning off one of the assassin's legs with a bolt of warp-lightning. Then he'd see where the mood took him from there.

Only the sound of the ship's creaking hull and the waves rolling against the shore answered Thanquol's call. The grey seer lashed his tail in annoyance. He didn't like the idea of setting sail with an assassin hidden somewhere aboard. He almost wished that Shiwan Stalkscent had left guards behind to keep cowards like Chang Fang from sneaking back onboard. Then again, he had to grudgingly concede that Shiwan had a point when he decided any skaven he left with the ship would be tempted to head back to the Under-Empire as soon as their leaders were out of sight.

'Chang Fang, you cringing whelp-chewer! Your mother was a he-mouse and your sire was an asthmatic bat!' Thanquol snarled, shouting so that his voice would carry to the quarterdeck and the cabins below. He glared angrily at the ship around him, trying not to jump every time the shadow of a sail moved. The assassin might be anywhere, waiting to sink a knife in his ribs!

Baring his fangs, Thanquol rounded on Boneripper, striking the rat ogre with his staff. 'Idiot-meat!' he hissed at his bodyguard. 'Find-fetch Chang Fang!'

Boneripper stared stupidly at Thanquol. The rat ogre didn't budge. Instead he just turned his head and looked straight up into the rigging of the ship.

Thanquol cringed, expecting a ferocious assassin to drop down on him, eyes agleam with murder, daggers dripping with poison. He scurried around to take shelter behind Boneripper, hoping Chang Fang might be too busy tackling the rat ogre to kill the grey seer.

When he took a few breaths without a knife stabbing into his flesh, Thanquol became curious. Cautiously he peered around Boneripper's bulk. Carefully he followed the rat ogre's gaze upwards.

Fluttering from the mainmast was something that hadn't been there before. It was a square of black cloth broken by the ghoulish image of a skull hovering over crossed blades. It took a moment for Thanquol to remember the flag the pirates they had taken the ship from had flown. This was similar to the banner the skaven had cut down and thrown into the sea, but the longer Thanquol stared at it, the more he began to notice disturbing differences from the flag he remembered. The black field wasn't smooth cloth, it was furry, fashioned from the uncured hide of some animal. The blades weren't colourful patches stitched into the flag, but were real knives tied against their furry setting. And the skull wasn't sewn, it was a real skull set into the middle of the flag. And it wasn't a human skull: it was the long, lean skull of a skaven!

Boneripper had found Chang Fang.

Thanquol stared at the gruesome Jolly Roger for a long time, a mixture of elation and horror pulsing through him. The assassin was dead, there was no need to fear him sneaking around the black guts of the ship waiting for his chance to murder Thanquol. That was a cause for celebration. Unfortunately, it left the disturbing question of what had killed Chang Fang.

The grey seer's nose twitched as a rotten smell rose from the hold of the ship. His keen ears could hear a clumsy sort of shuffling beneath his feet. A cold chill ran down Thanquol's legs as he vented the musk of fear. He knew that smell and he could guess what kind of feet made those stumbling sounds.

Turning, the grey seer saw a skeletal shape lumber out from the dark doorway set into the face of the quarterdeck. It grinned at him with a fleshless smile, a rusty cutlass clenched in its bony fist. The zombie pirate's eye shone with an empty hunger, the same pitiless hatred of all things living it had shown when it had emerged from the fort in the swamp.

Thanquol understood now why he hadn't been attacked in the swamp. After the skaven fled, the zombies had followed their trail back to the beach. In life they had been pirates, in death they had been abandoned to the stinking jungles of Lustria. At least until the skaven had brought a new ship to them.

* * *

ADALWOLF STOOD ATOP a little grassy mound. It was an effort just to stand now, further flight from the lizardmen was something that almost brought tears of laughter to him as he thought about it. His back was swollen where the razordon spines had struck him, the venom in the wounds drawing every insect in the jungle to him. His broken arm was completely numb by contrast, a dead icy weight against his chest. More than the physical pain, it was the fatigue of his soul that crippled him. He had no purpose now. There would be no reckoning with the toad-creature, no revenge for Hiltrude.

Skinks surrounded him on every side now. Wherever he turned he could see their scaly blue bodies, little arrows nocked in the strings of their short bows, their unblinking eyes staring back at him. Even if he had the strength to go on, there was no escape from this place.

At first he thought it was the fever playing tricks on his mind when he saw the trees start to change. It was as though some omnipotent force was folding the jungle, parting it like a gambler shuffling cards. The jungle swirled around him, churning and undulating like an angry sea. The skinks vanished, the trees vanished, the thickets and saw grass. In the twinkling of an eye, everything around him changed, only the grassy mound beneath his feet had stayed the same. It was an anchor of reality that secured his reeling mind as he tried to cope with the impossible thing he had experienced.

Diethelm had expounded upon the weird qualities of the path they had followed through the jungle.

Now Adalwolf knew the priest had been right. He felt very small when he considered the kind of power it must take for even the mightiest wizard to bend space and time in such a fashion.

His new surroundings were a sandy strip along the shore of the sea. The smell of brine overwhelmed the stink of the jungle and even the harsh light of the sun seemed somehow cleaner without the leaves of the jungle filtering it.

A bitter joy flashed through Adalwolf's heart when he saw a distant speck bobbing at anchor far down the beach. It was a ship, he couldn't be mistaken. He almost cried to see the sight, the hope that he had longed to find. But it was too late for that now. He would never leave this place. His bones would lie in the jungle with those of Hiltrude, forgotten by the world.

Adalwolf turned to face the green wall of the jungle and for the first time he was aware that he was not alone. A phalanx of saurus warriors, even bigger than the ones they had fought in the jungle, stood watching him with the same passionless interest as the skinks he had left behind.

But he only gave scant notice to the fearsome lizardmen. Adalwolf's interest was almost instantly captivated by the bloated frog-like thing that squatted upon a golden dais in the midst of the saurus warriors. The slann's eyes were limpid pools of amber as they studied the mercenary.

Adalwolf relaxed his hold on the sword. This close to the mage-priest, even his mad lust for revenge couldn't make him ignore the amphibian's aura of power. A mouse would have better chances against a dragon than he would fighting such a being.

The slann's eyes narrowed with interest as Adalwolf lowered his weapon. A voice, neither harsh nor soothing, echoed through his brain. It promised succour. His wounds would be tended, his hurts healed, the fever driven from his body, the venom drained from his veins. All he had to do was submit, to accept his part in the Great Math. There was no need for his sum to be negated prematurely.

Adalwolf shook his head, trying to drive the voice out of his head. He glared at the bloated slann. It was offering him life, but that wasn't something he wanted anymore.

LORD TLACO STARED back at the unknown quotient. The warm-blood had a kind of intelligence, but it had no concept of the Great Math. What it wanted and what it didn't want had nothing to do with the harmonies of the Old Ones. The mage-priest shifted the spots on his skin. The skink perched on the dais beside the slann quickly interpreted the changes in his skin. Lifting its head, the skink chirruped and hissed to Lord Tlaco's temple guard.

Almost as a single entity, the temple guard dropped their swords and pulled heavy clubs from their snakeskin belts. They stalked away from Lord Tlaco's dais and marched towards the grassy mound and the sickly creature standing on it.

ADALWOLF'S FIST TIGHTENED about the sword in his hand as he saw the lizardmen marching towards him. He knew he couldn't hope to fight them any more than he could hope to fight their master. They would beat him into submission, drag him off for whatever purpose the slann needed him for. There was no hope of victory here.

But there was still a way to cheat his enemies and deny them their triumph.

Lord Tlaco actually leaned forwards in his seat, his skin spots opening wide as something like amazement flushed through the slann's body. Before his ordered mind could come to grips with the absolute madness of the warm-blood it was already too late to stop it. Adalwolf brought the serrated edge of his sword against his neck and with one savage pull cut open his carotid artery.

The dying human toppled from the mound, rolling against the feet of the temple guard. The lizardmen knelt beside the body, staring back at Lord Tlaco, looking to the slann for guidance. The mage-priest slumped back into his seat. He knew far too little about the anatomy of decaying algorithms to repair the damage Adalwolf had done. Given a little time, Lord Tlaco would be able to telepathically confer with another slann who had contemplated the biology of lower phase organisms. By that time, however, the human would be long dead.

Unable to understand the self-negation of its unknown quotient, Lord Tlaco ordered his temple guard to gather the body. Dissection was unlikely to yield the results the slann required to explain the decision Adalwolf had made, the choice to kill

Xiuhcoatl instead of Thanquol. Still, the mage-priest would be thorough in his experiment. The condemnation or vindication of the cult of Sotek might yet be found within Lord Tlaco's results.

GREY SEER THANQUOL scurried up into the *Black Mary*'s rigging, terror throbbing through his brain. The pirate captain stared at him with its decayed face, worms dripping from the corners of its mouth and poking from the gashes in its forehead. The zombie pointed a fleshless talon at the grey seer and its undead crew began to shuffle out from the shadow of the quarterdeck.

'Boneripper!' Thanquol shrieked down to his bodyguard. 'Kill-slay! Kill-slay!'

The rat ogre lumbered into the advancing pack of zombies, growling at the undead pirates. He brought one of his massive claws sweeping around, tearing apart a zombie at its waist and hurling the thing's torso against the rail of the ship. A second flash of his claws opened another zombie from groin to chin, decayed innards tumbling from the ghastly wound to slop across the deck. The rat ogre tore at a third pirate, wrenching both its arms clean from their sockets and knocking the creature from off its feet.

An eager gleam crept into Thanquol's eyes as he clung to the rigging. These things were no match for Boneripper! The rat ogre would quickly slaughter the decayed humans and this time the damned pirates would stay dead! There was no way a pack of stumbling corpses could match the strength and swiftness of a rat ogre trained by the master killers of Clan Eshin!

Even as his spirits started to rise, Thanquol's tail twitched in fear. The zombies Boneripper had attacked were still moving! The legless torso was crawling along the deck towards the rat ogre, the second zombie staggered onwards with its guts dragging behind it, the armless husk flopped and slithered like some hideous worm. More zombies shambled out from the ship's cabin, silently obeying the pointing talon of their captain. The deck itself creaked and groaned as zombies down in the hold pounded against the planks, clawing their way up from the darkness to join the attack.

Boneripper roared and waded into the ever increasing horde. Heads were smashed into paste by his fists, bodies were ripped asunder by his claws, bones snapped between his fangs and still the zombies came, relentless and remorseless. They slashed at the rat ogre with corroded swords, hacked at him with decayed axes and stabbed at him with rusty spears. Boneripper could easily dodge the clumsy attacks, but he couldn't avoid them all. Bit by bit, the pirates were overwhelming the giant brute.

The splintering of wood announced the success of the zombies down in the hold tearing their way up through the deck. Stiffly the creatures pulled themselves up through the ragged holes they had torn, heedless of the slivers of wood that stabbed into their flesh as they emerged. For all their ungainly motion, Thanquol was impressed at how quickly a sizable mob of zombies rose from the hold to surround his bodyguard.

The grey seer bruxed his fangs. He'd hoped to let Boneripper settle with the undead, just in case any of the things decided to come back and haunt their destroyer. The example of Vorghun of Praag was a little too fresh in Thanquol's mind to make him especially eager to test his luck against the living dead. One reanimated liche hungry for his soul was enough to give him nightmares.

Now, however, he saw that he had no choice. He could either help Boneripper fight the zombies, or he could let the pirates overcome his bodyguard. Once that happened, he knew their next target would be himself. Briefly the idea of swimming back to shore came to Thanquol, but he quickly dismissed it with a shudder. He'd take his chances with ghosts and wraiths.

Flicking the bit of warpstone from his cheek pouch with his tongue, Grey Seer Thanquol bit down on the little rock, feeling its magical energies course through his veins. A green light blazed from his eyes as the intoxicating flush of power roared through his brain. He snickered at his own fears of only a moment before. What did he have to fear from ghosts! If any of these things dared try to haunt him he'd blast their souls back to Nagash the Foul and grind their bones into dust!

Thanquol glared down at the pirate captain. Clinging to the rigging with one paw, he extended the other and pointed at the zombie. A shrill, snarling incantation scraped the air. There was a burst of light about Thanquol's hand, then the pirate captain was enveloped in flame! Thanquol chittered evilly as he watched the zombie stumble about, a walking torch. The cutlass fell to the deck as the arm holding it was burned from the captain's body, the rest of the zombie's remains slumping to the deck soon after.

Cackling with glee, Thanquol turned his attention to the twice-dead captain's crew. Pointing his claw at another zombie, the grey seer caused it to also be engulfed in green fire. The creature bumbled into one of its fellows, the flames from its body scorching the other zombie as well. His brain roaring with the intoxicating rush of power, Thanquol started hurling spells down into the undead.

With their ranks being depleted by Thanquol's magic, the zombies lost their numerical advantage against Boneripper. The rat ogre rallied, leaping back into the combat with renewed vigour. Once again, the torn and mangled debris of the undead were hurled across the deck. Whole or dismembered, Boneripper attacked the monsters with equal ferocity, even clawing at the burning zombies when they staggered blindly towards him.

Thanquol grinned, baring his fangs in a wicked smile. The undead pirates were no menace now. Soon the ship would be his. He would sail back to the Under-Empire in triumph and never again smell the jungle stink of Lustria!

The grey seer relented in his sorcerous assault on the zombies, content now to simply watch Boneripper finish the job. Even with the slight assistance provided by warpstone, Thanquol didn't like to over exert his powers. It was an unseemly abuse of the gifts the Horned Rat had bestowed upon him.

Thanquol laughed as he watched some of the zombies he'd set on fire staggering across the deck. The blind stupid things didn't even notice Boneripper until the rat ogre tore them apart! Other zombies stumbled into each other or cracked their heads against the mast. One of the burning pirates even fell into one of the holes the zombies had torn in the deck, pitching headfirst into the hold below.

A thrill of horror banished the last invigorating effects of the warpstone from Thanquol's brain. A sudden nagging memory rose in his mind, a memory of the long voyage across the sea and how Thanquol had paced the ship from top to bottom during that time. Sheer boredom had made him learn every nook and cranny on the vessel. Now that knowledge screamed at him, screamed at him with such panic that he vented his glands.

The hole the burning zombie fell down was right above the *Black Mary's* powder magazine!

Squealing in fright, Thanquol scrambled as high as he could in the rigging, then dived into the sea. He plunged deep into the warm waters, so deep it was a fight for him to claw his way back to the surface. When his head was again above water and he'd gulped enough air to satisfy his starved lungs, Thanquol glanced back at the ship.

The *Black Mary* was still there, bobbing upon the waves. Thanquol was just starting to curse himself for allowing a mistaken memory to throw him into a panic when the ship suddenly exploded in a violent fireball.

EPILOGUE

Grey Seer Thanquol sputtered and coughed as he pulled his soggy mass over the side of the rowboat. He shook his entire body, trying to fling the worst of the sea water from his fur, then slumped wearily against the gunwales. A cunning grin spread across his face. For all of his ordeals, the Horned One had not abandoned him. How else to explain the providential appearance of this boat – hurled intact from the fiery death of the *Black Mary*? Thanquol had spotted it almost as soon as he'd fought his way back to the surface after his daring dive into the sea. Like a drowned whelp bobbing about in a water trough the boat had drifted away from the burning debris of the pirate ship.

It had taken him only a few terrified minutes to claw his way through the waves to reach the little boat. At any instant he expected to feel the sharp jaws of a shark tugging at his leg, but if any of the predators were about they didn't notice the lone ratman swimming above them and he reached the boat safe if a bit soaked.

Thinking of sharks made Thanquol snap out of his fatigue. In a panic he yanked his dangling tail out of the water, stroking the naked, scaly extremity to ensure himself that nothing had nibbled at it. Breathing a gasp of relief, he slumped back into the bottom of the boat. He was safe for the moment. Chang Fang was dead. The zombies were dead – well, more dead than they had been. Xiuhcoatl was dead. All of his enemies were gone to their most deserved rewards. Once more, Grey Seer Thanquol had emerged triumphant, his genius carrying him to glories no other ratman would dare dream of!

Although, Thanquol thought as he forgot his enemies and considered his own situation, there wasn't much glory around. He was wet and alone in a little boat bobbing about in a shark-infested sea thousands of food-stops from even the most remote outpost of skavendom. The closest land was a reptile-ridden hell of biting insects, tropical diseases and withering heat. As he took stock of the situation, he mumbled a curse too low for the Horned Rat to hear. There was a skin of water stuffed under the benches in the boat but not even a sniff of food. Thanquol's belly growled at him as he made the observation and he could feel his mouth watering at the very thought of food. There hadn't been any time to really stop and eat during the mad race to reach the ship before

Chang Fang. Thanquol had never been much for privation, even when necessity called for it.

Suddenly the boat gave an alarming lurch to the side. For an instant, Thanquol thought one of the sharks had risen up to chew its way through the boat to get him. As the little vessel continued to tilt lower into the sea, water streaming over the gunwales, the grey seer's terror mounted. It only lessened slightly when he saw a huge black arm reach over the side and pull a gigantic furry body into the boat. Even when the creature settled down, sagging wearily into the stern, the rowboat sat alarmingly low in the water.

Thanquol's nose wrinkled at the unpleasant smell of burned fur rising from Boneripper's scorched body. Wooden splinters jutted from the rat ogre's hide where shrapnel from the exploding ship had driven them home. The brute was cut in dozens of places, his thick black blood oozing slowly from the wounds to mix with the water sloshing about Thanquol's ankles.

There couldn't be much strength left in the rat ogre. One sniff told Thanquol as much. Just like the witless slob to get himself crippled right when the grey seer needed him the most! Who was going to row the little boat someplace safe? Certainly it was unfair of Boneripper to expect his master to do such a thing! The stupid lummox should have stayed in the water and fed the sharks...

Thanquol pulled at his whiskers and a sinister gleam crept into his eyes. What did Boneripper weigh? Maybe eight hundred pounds? Certainly not less than five hundred.

The grey seer's belly growled as he quietly thanked the Horned Rat for his bounty.

UPON THE SHORE, Lord Tlaco watched as Grey Seer Thanquol began to row away from the burning wreck of the pirate ship. The slann considered this cruel little creature, plucking his thoughts from the matrix of the Great Math. How unlike the unknown quotient, that curious warm-blood that had taken his own life when rescue was offered to him. This corrupted algorithm was utterly selfish, fully aware of his own decay and decline towards negation and reaching out with every essence of his being to stave off that inevitable eventuality.

It was a contrast to be certain. The xa'cota might have made an interesting specimen to compare with the human had the warm-blood allowed himself to be captured. Now, however, Lord Tlaco doubted if there was any especial value in acquiring the ratman. The xa'cota carried diseases that could harm the skinks and other minion breeds and through their sickness even a slann might fall ill and die. That would not aid its study of the Great Math if the mage-priest were to perish in a plague.

No, there was something more to the corrupted algorithm than even the threat of disease. Lord Tlaco could sense a connection between the ratman and one of those dread persistent fractals that had cast their shadow upon the harmonious equations of the Old Ones. To invite such a being into his laboratories would be to endanger all of the slann's other researches. The mere presence of an algorithm connected to the persistent fractals invited corruption.

The slann's spots shifted. A dozen of its temple guard started to wade into the waves, their axes clenched tightly in their jaws. They would overturn the boat and butcher the noxious creature and end its menace to the Great Math.

Abruptly, Lord Tlaco's eyes dilated and a low croak rumbled from his wide mouth, arresting the advance of the lizardmen. The little skink minion perched upon the slann's dais chirped and hissed, calling the warriors back.

Casting his thoughts through the potentialities of the Great Math, Lord Tlaco tried to see the possibilities of this corrupted algorithm that had drawn his attention. The mage-priest was pleased by the way the xa'cota's value ingratiated itself into other equations. If the slann had been capable, he would have found the degeneration of those problems highly amusing.

The xa'cota was a greater menace to his own kind than he was to the Great Math. Through him, much could be done to undermine the rest of his kind. The corrupted algorithm's selfishness, greed and ambition would lead him into conflict with others of his kind, conflict that could greatly weaken the xu'cota as a species.

Yes, the potentialities of probability made it desirable that the xa'cota should return to his own kind. Focusing its consciousness upon the matrix of reality, Lord Tlaco excited the currents of the sea, creating a new undersea stream that would speed the corrupted algorithm back across the World Pond. The slann would uncreate the environmental change his magic had caused once it had served its purpose. A shift of his skin-spots told the skink attendant to remind the mage-priest to do so before the next lunar cycle.

Lord Tlaco remained with his retinue on the beach, watching the tiny dot of Thanquol's boat dwindling on the horizon. Only when the grey seer was completely lost to sight did the slann give the command to return into the jungle. He expended some of his magic to weave a corridor through the trees, a pathway that would bring them quickly back to the pyramids of Xlanhuapec, the City of Mists.

Now that the experiment was at an end, the mage-priest was keen to study what results he had acquired.

Their influence on the Great Math would be a thing worth contemplating over the next century.

ABOUT THE AUTHOR

C. L. Werner was a diseased servant of the Horned Rat long before his first story in *Inferno!* magazine. His Black Library credits include the Chaos Wastes books *Palace of the Plague Lord* and *Blood for the Blood God, Mathias Thulmann: Witch Hunter, Runefang* and the *Brunner the Bounty Hunter* trilogy. Currently living in the American south-west, he continues to write stories of mayhem and madness set in the Warhammer World.

Visit the author's website at www.clwerner.wordpress.com

ULRIKA THE VAMPIRE

WARHAMMER

BLOODBORN

NATHAN LONG

UK ISBN 978-1-84416-824-8 US ISBN 978-1-84416-825-5

UK ISBN 978-1-844970-013-9 US ISBN 978-1-84970-014-6

WARHAMMER

MATHIAS THULMANN
WITCH HUNTER

WITCH HUNTER · WITCH FINDER · WITCH KILLER

Buy these omnibuses or read free extracts at *www.blacklibrary.com*

C·L·WERNER

UK ISBN 978-1-84416-669-5 US ISBN 978-1-84416-554-4

WARHAMMER

C · L · WERNER

BRUNNER THE BOUNTY HUNTER

BLOOD & STEEL · BLOOD MONEY · BLOOD OF THE DRAGON

UK ISBN 978-1-84416-866-8 US ISBN 978-1-84416-867-5